HOMEBOUND

Falkirk Council Library Services

This book is due for return on or before the last date indicated on the
label. Renewals may be obtained on application.

Bo'ness	01506 778520	Falkirk	503605	Grangemouth	504690
Bonnybridge	503295	Mobile	506800	Larbert	503590
Denny	504242			Slamannan	851373

11 SEP 2018

18 OCT 2012

-- NOV 2012

0/ SEP 2013

21/7/15.

6 - MAR 2017

THE WITNESS

THE WITNESS

Nora Roberts

**WINDSOR
PARAGON**

First published 2012
by Piatkus
This Large Print edition published 2012
by AudioGO Ltd
by arrangement with
Little, Brown Book Group

Hardcover   ISBN: 978 1 4713 0110 0
Softcover   ISBN: 978 1 4713 0111 7

British Library Cataloguing in Publication Data available

Printed and bound in Great Britain by
MPG Books Group Limited

For Laura Reeth

Master of details

Elizabeth

The barb in the arrow of childhood suffering is
    this:
its intense loneliness; its intense ignorance.

OLIVE SCHREINER

1

Elizabeth Fitch's short-lived teenage rebellion began with L'Oréal Pure Black, a pair of scissors and a fake ID. It ended in blood.

For nearly the whole of her sixteen years, eight months and twenty-one days she'd dutifully followed her mother's directives. Dr. Susan L. Fitch issued *directives,* not orders. Elizabeth had adhered to the schedules her mother created, ate the meals designed by her mother's nutritionist and prepared by her mother's cook, wore the clothes selected by her mother's personal shopper.

Dr. Susan L. Fitch dressed conservatively, as suited—in her opinion—her position as chief of surgery of Chicago's Silva Memorial Hospital. She expected, and directed, her daughter to do the same.

Elizabeth studied diligently, accepting and excelling in the academic programs her mother outlined. In the fall, she'd return to Harvard in pursuit of her medical degree. So she could become a doctor, like her mother—a surgeon, like her mother.

Elizabeth—never Liz or Lizzie or Beth—spoke fluent Spanish, French, Italian, passable Russian and rudimentary Japanese. She played both piano and violin. She'd traveled to Europe, to Africa. She could name all the bones, nerves and muscles in the human body and play Chopin's Piano Concerto—both Nos. 1 and 2, by rote.

3

She'd never been on a date or kissed a boy. She'd never roamed the mall with a pack of girls, attended a slumber party or giggled with friends over pizza or hot fudge sundaes.

She was, at sixteen years, eight months and twenty-one days, a product of her mother's meticulous and detailed agenda.

That was about to change.

She watched her mother pack. Susan, her rich brown hair already coiled in her signature French twist, neatly hung another suit in the organized garment bag, then checked off the printout with each day of the week's medical conference broken into subgroups. The printout included a spreadsheet listing every event, appointment, meeting and meal, scheduled with the selected outfit, with shoes, bag and accessories.

Designer suits; Italian shoes, of course, Elizabeth thought. One must wear good cuts, good cloth. But not one rich or bright color among the blacks, grays, taupes. She wondered how her mother could be so beautiful and deliberately wear the dull.

After two accelerated semesters of college, Elizabeth thought she'd begun—maybe—to develop her own fashion sense. She had, in fact, bought jeans *and* a hoodie *and* some chunky-heeled boots in Cambridge.

With cash, so the receipt wouldn't show up on her credit card bill, in case her mother or their accountant checked and questioned the items, which were currently hidden in her room.

She'd felt like a different person wearing them, so different she'd walked straight into a McDonald's and ordered her first Big Mac with large fries and a chocolate shake.

The pleasure had been so huge, she'd had to go into the bathroom, close herself in a stall and cry a little.

The seeds of the rebellion had been planted that day, she supposed, or maybe they'd always been there, dormant, and the fat and salt had awakened them.

But she could feel them, actually feel them, sprouting in her belly now.

'Your plans changed, Mother. It doesn't follow that mine have to change with them.'

Susan took a moment to precisely place a shoe bag in the Pullman, tucking it just so with her beautiful and clever surgeon's hands, the nails perfectly manicured. A French manicure, as always—no color there, either.

'Elizabeth.' Her voice was as polished and calm as her wardrobe. 'It took considerable effort to reschedule and have you admitted to the summer program this term. You'll complete the requirements for your admission into Harvard Medical School a full semester ahead of schedule.'

Even the thought made Elizabeth's stomach hurt. 'I was promised a three-week break, including this next week in New York.'

'And sometimes promises must be broken. If I hadn't had this coming week off, I couldn't fill in for Dr. Dusecki at the conference.'

'You could have said no.'

'That would have been selfish and shortsighted.' Susan brushed at the jacket she'd hung, stepped back to check her list. 'You're certainly mature enough to understand the demands of work overtake pleasure and leisure.'

'If I'm mature enough to understand that, why

5

aren't I mature enough to make my own decisions? I want this break. I need it.'

Susan barely spared her daughter a glance. 'A girl of your age, physical condition and mental acumen hardly *needs* a break from her studies and activities. In addition, Mrs. Laine has already left for her two-week cruise, and I could hardly ask her to postpone her vacation. There's no one to fix your meals or tend to the house.'

'I can fix my own meals and tend the house.'

'Elizabeth.' The tone managed to merge clipped with long-suffering. 'It's settled.'

'And I have no say in it? What about developing my independence, being responsible?'

'Independence comes in degrees, as does responsibility and freedom of choice. You still require guidance and direction. Now, I've e-mailed you an updated schedule for the coming week, and your packet with all the information on the program is on your desk. Be sure to thank Dr. Frisco personally for making room for you in the summer term.'

As she spoke, Susan closed the garment bag, then her small Pullman. She stepped to her bureau to check her hair, her lipstick.

'You don't listen to anything I say.'

In the mirror, Susan's gaze shifted to her daughter. The first time, Elizabeth thought, her mother had bothered to actually look at her since she'd come into the bedroom. 'Of course I do. I heard everything you said, very clearly.'

'Listening's different than hearing.'

'That may be true, Elizabeth, but we've already had this discussion.'

'It's not a discussion, it's a decree.'

6

Susan's mouth tightened briefly, the only sign of annoyance. When she turned, her eyes were coolly, calmly blue. 'I'm sorry you feel that way. As your mother, I must do what I believe best for you.'

'What's best for me, in your opinion, is for me to do, be, say, think, act, want, become exactly what you decided for me before you inseminated yourself with precisely selected sperm.'

She heard the rise of her own voice but couldn't control it, felt the hot sting of tears in her eyes but couldn't stop them. 'I'm tired of being your experiment. I'm tired of having every minute of every day organized, orchestrated and choreographed to meet your expectations. I want to make my own choices, buy my own clothes, read books *I* want to read. I want to live my own life instead of yours.'

Susan's eyebrows lifted in an expression of mild interest. 'Well. Your attitude isn't surprising, given your age, but you've picked a very inconvenient time to be defiant and argumentative.'

'Sorry. It wasn't on the schedule.'

'Sarcasm's also typical, but it's unbecoming.' Susan opened her briefcase, checked the contents. 'We'll talk about all this when I get back. I'll make an appointment with Dr. Bristoe.'

'I don't need therapy! I need a mother who *listens,* who gives a shit about how I feel.'

'That kind of language only shows a lack of maturity and intellect.'

Enraged, Elizabeth threw up her hands, spun in circles. If she couldn't be calm and rational like her mother, she'd be *wild.* 'Shit! Shit! Shit!'

'And repetition hardly enhances. You have the rest of the weekend to consider your behavior.

7

Your meals are in the refrigerator or freezer, and labeled. Your pack list is on your desk. Report to Ms. Vee at the university at eight on Monday morning. Your participation in this program will ensure your place in HMS next fall. Now, take my garment bag downstairs, please. My car will be here any minute.'

Oh, those seeds were sprouting, cracking that fallow ground and pushing painfully through. For the first time in her life, Elizabeth looked straight into her mother's eyes and said, 'No.'

She spun around, stomped away and slammed the door of her bedroom. She threw herself down on the bed, stared at the ceiling with tear-blurred eyes. And waited.

Any second, any second, she told herself. Her mother would come in, demand an apology, demand obedience. And Elizabeth wouldn't give one, either.

They'd have a fight, an actual fight, with threats of punishment and consequences. Maybe they'd yell at each other. Maybe if they yelled, her mother would finally hear her.

And maybe, if they yelled, she could say all the things that had crept up inside her this past year. Things she thought now had been inside her forever.

She didn't want to be a doctor. She didn't want to spend every waking hour on a schedule or hide a stupid pair of jeans because they didn't fit her mother's dress code.

She wanted to have friends, not approved socialization appointments. She wanted to listen to the music girls her age listened to. She wanted to know what they whispered about and laughed

8

about and talked about while she was shut out.

She didn't want to be a genius or a prodigy.

She wanted to be normal. She just wanted to be like everyone else.

She swiped at the tears, curled up, stared at the door.

Any second, she thought again. Any second now. Her mother had to be angry. She had to come in and assert authority. Had to.

'Please,' Elizabeth murmured as seconds ticked into minutes. 'Don't make me give in again. Please, please, don't make me give up.'

Love me enough. Just this once.

But as the minutes dragged on, Elizabeth pushed herself off the bed. Patience, she knew, was her mother's greatest weapon. That, and the unyielding sense of being right, crushed all foes. And certainly her daughter was no match for it.

Defeated, she walked out of her room, toward her mother's.

The garment bag, the briefcase, the small, wheeled Pullman were gone. Even as she walked downstairs, she knew her mother had gone, too.

'She left me. She just left.'

Alone, she looked around the pretty, tidy living room. Everything perfect—the fabrics, the colors, the art, the arrangement. The antiques passed down through generations of Fitches—all quiet elegance.

Empty.

Nothing had changed, she realized. And nothing would.

'So I will.'

She didn't allow herself to think, to question or second-guess. Instead, she marched back up, snagged scissors from her study area.

In her bathroom, she studied her face in the mirror—coloring she'd gotten through paternity—auburn hair, thick like her mother's but without the soft, pretty wave. Her mother's high, sharp cheekbones, her biological father's—whoever he was—deep-set green eyes, pale skin, wide mouth.

Physically attractive, she thought, because that was DNA and her mother would tolerate no less. But not beautiful, not striking like Susan, no. And that, she supposed, had been a disappointment even her mother couldn't fix.

'Freak.' Elizabeth pressed a hand to the mirror, hating what she saw in the glass. 'You're a freak. But as of now, you're not a coward.'

Taking a big breath, she yanked up a hunk of her shoulder-length hair and whacked it off.

With every snap of the scissors she felt empowered. *Her* hair, *her* choice. She let the shorn hanks fall on the floor. As she snipped and hacked, an image formed in her mind. Eyes narrowed, head angled, she slowed the clipping. It was just geometry, really, she decided—and physics. Action and reaction.

The weight—physical and metaphorical, she thought—just fell away. And the girl in the glass looked lighter. Her eyes seemed bigger, her face not so thin, not so drawn.

She looked . . . new, Elizabeth decided.

Carefully, she set the scissors down, and, realizing her breath was heaving in and out, made a conscious effort to slow it.

So short. Testing, she lifted a hand to her exposed neck, ears, then brushed them over the bangs she'd cut. Too even, she decided. She hunted

10

up manicure scissors, tried her hand at styling.

Not bad. Not really good, she admitted, but different. That was the whole point. She looked, and felt, different.

But not finished.

Leaving the hair where it lay on the floor, she went into her bedroom, changed into her secret cache of clothes. She needed product—that's what the girls called it. Hair product. And makeup. And more clothes.

She needed the mall.

Riding on the thrill, she went into her mother's home office, took the spare car keys. And her heart hammered with excitement as she hurried to the garage. She got behind the wheel, shut her eyes a moment.

'Here we go,' she said quietly, then hit the garage-door opener and backed out.

*   *   *

She got her ears pierced. It seemed a bold if mildly painful move, and suited the hair dye she'd taken from the shelf after a long, careful study and debate. She bought hair wax, as she'd seen one of the girls at college use it and thought she could duplicate the look. More or less.

She bought two hundred dollars' worth of makeup because she wasn't sure what was right.

Then she had to sit down because her knees shook. But she wasn't done, Elizabeth reminded herself, as she watched the packs of teenagers, groups of women, teams of families, wander by. She just needed to regroup.

She needed clothes, but she didn't have a plan,

a list, an agenda. Impulse buying was exhilarating, and exhausting. The temper that had driven her this far left her with a dull headache, and her earlobes throbbed a little.

The logical, sensible thing to do was go home, lie down for a while. Then plan, make that list of items to be purchased.

But that was the old Elizabeth. This one was just going to catch her breath.

The problem facing her now was that she wasn't precisely sure which store or stores she should go to. There were so many of them, and all the windows full of *things.* So she'd wander, watch for girls her age. She'd go where they went.

She gathered her bags, pushed to her feet—and bumped into someone.

'Excuse me,' she began, then recognized the girl. 'Oh. Julie.'

'Yeah.' The blonde with the sleek, perfect hair and melted-chocolate eyes gave Elizabeth a puzzled look. 'Do I know you?'

'Probably not. We went to school together. I was student teacher in your Spanish class. Elizabeth Fitch.'

'Elizabeth, sure. The brain trust.' Julie narrowed her sulky eyes. 'You look different.'

'Oh. I . . .' Embarrassed now, Elizabeth lifted a hand to her hair. 'I cut my hair.'

'Cool. I thought you moved away or something.'

'I went to college. I'm home for the summer.'

'Oh, yeah, you graduated early. Weird.'

'I suppose it is. Will you go to college this fall?'

'I'm supposed to go to Brown.'

'That's a wonderful school.'

'Okay. Well . . .'

'Are you shopping?'

'Broke.' Julie shrugged—and Elizabeth took a survey of her outfit—the snug jeans, riding very low on the hipbones, the skinny, midriff-baring shirt, the oversized shoulder bag and wedge sandals. 'I just came to the mall to see my boyfriend—my *ex*-boyfriend, since I broke up with him.'

'I'm sorry.'

'Screw him. He works at the Gap. We were supposed to go out tonight, and now he says he has to work till ten, then wants to hang out with his bros after. I've had it, so I dumped him.'

Elizabeth started to point out that he shouldn't be penalized for honoring his obligations, but Julie kept talking—and it occurred to Elizabeth that the other girl hadn't spoken more than a dozen words to her since they'd known each other.

'So I'm going over to Tiffany's, see if she wants to hang, because now I've got no boyfriend for the summer. It sucks. I guess you hang out with college guys.' Julie gave her a considering look. 'Go to frat parties, keggers, all that.'

'I . . . There are a lot of men at Harvard.'

'Harvard.' Julie rolled her eyes. 'Any of them in Chicago for the summer?'

'I couldn't say.'

'A college guy, that's what I need. Who wants some loser who works at the mall? I need somebody who knows how to have fun, who can take me places, buy alcohol. Good luck with that, unless you can get into the clubs. That's where they hang out. Just need to score some fake ID.'

'I can do that.' The instant the words were out, Elizabeth wondered where they'd come from. But Julie gripped her arm, smiled at her as if they were

13

friends.

'No bull?'

'No. That is, it's not very difficult to create false identification with the right tools. A template, photo, laminate, a computer with Photoshop.'

'Brain trust. What'll it take for you to make me a driver's license that'll get me into a club?'

'As I said, a template—'

'No, Jesus. What do you want for it?'

'I . . .' Bargaining, Elizabeth realized. A barter. 'I need to buy some clothes, but I don't know what I should buy. I need someone to help me.'

'A shopping buddy?'

'Yes. Someone who knows. You know.'

Eyes no longer sulky, voice no longer bored, Julie simply beamed. 'That's *my* brain trust. And if I help you pick out some outfits, you'll make me up the ID?'

'Yes. And I'd also want to go with you to the club. So I'd need the right clothes for that, too.'

'You? Clubbing? More than your hair's changed, Liz.'

Liz. She was Liz. 'I'd need a photo, and it will take a little while to construct the IDs. I could have them done tomorrow. What club would we go to?'

'Might as well go for the hottest club in town. Warehouse 12. Brad Pitt went there when he was in town.'

'Do you know him?'

'I wish. Okay, let's go shopping.'

It made her dizzy, not just the way Julie piloted her into a store, snatched up clothes with only the most cursory study. But the *idea* of it all. A shopping buddy. Not someone who preselected what was deemed appropriate and expected her

14

to assent. Someone who grabbed at random and talked about looking hot, or cool, even sexy.

No one had ever suggested to Elizabeth that she might look sexy.

She closed herself in the dressing room with the forest of color, the sparkle of spangles, the glint of metallic, and had to put her head between her knees.

It was all happening so fast. It was like being caught in a tsunami. The surge just swept her away.

Her fingers trembled as she undressed, as she carefully folded her clothes, then stared at all the pieces hanging in the tiny room.

What did she put on? What went with what? How did she know?

'I found the most awesome dress!' Without even a knock, Julie barged right in. Instinctively, Elizabeth crossed an arm over her breasts.

'Haven't you tried anything on yet?'

'I wasn't sure where to start.'

'Start with awesome.' Julie shoved the dress at her.

But really, at its length it was more of a tunic, Elizabeth thought, and in a screaming red, ruched along the sides. Its razor-thin straps sparkling with silver.

'What do you wear with it?'

'Killer shoes. No, lose the bra first. You can't wear a bra with that dress. You've got a really good body,' Julie observed.

'I'm genetically predisposed, and maintain fitness and health through regular daily exercise.'

'Get you.'

And the naked—or nearly—human body was natural, Elizabeth reminded herself. Just skin,

15

muscle, bone, nerve.

She laid her bra on her folded clothes, then shimmied into the dress.

'It's very short,' she began.

'You're going to want to ditch those Mom panties and buy a thong. *That* is definitely club-worthy.'

Elizabeth took a breath, turned to the triple mirror. 'Oh.'

Who was that? Who was that girl in the short red dress?

'I look . . .'

'Awesome,' Julie declared, and Elizabeth watched a smile bloom on her own face.

'Awesome.'

She bought the dress, and two others. And skirts. She bought tops that rode above her waist, pants that rode below it. She bought thongs. And she rode that tsunami to shoes with silver heels she'd have to practice walking in.

And she laughed, like any ordinary girl shopping with a friend at the mall.

She bought a digital camera, then watched Julie make up her face in the bathroom. She took Julie's picture, and several backups against the pale gray of the stall door.

'That's going to work?'

'Yes, I can make it work. How old should you be? I think it's best if we stay as close as possible to the legal age. I can use everything from your valid driver's license and just change the year.'

'Have you done this before?'

'I've experimented. I've read and studied identity fraud, cyber crimes. It's interesting. I'd like to . . .'

'Like to what?'

'I'd like to study computer crimes and prevention, investigation, more seriously. I'd like to join the FBI.'

'No bull? Like Dana Scully.'

'I don't know her.'

'*X-Files*, Liz. Don't you watch TV?'

'My viewing of popular and commercial television is limited to an hour a week.'

Julie rolled her big, chocolate eyes. 'What are you, six? Jesus Christ.'

'My mother has very definite opinions.'

'You're in college, for God's sake. Watch what you want. Anyway, I'll come to your place tomorrow night. Say nine? We'll take a cab from there. But I want you to call me when you finish the ID, okay?'

'Yes.'

'I tell you what, breaking up with Darryl was the best thing I ever did. Otherwise, I'd've missed all this. We're going to party, Liz.' Laughing, Julie did a quick, hip-swiveling dance right there in the ladies' room. 'Big time. I've gotta go. Nine o'clock. Don't let me down.'

'No. I won't.'

Flushed from the day, Elizabeth hauled all the bags to her car. She knew what girls in the mall talked about now.

Boys. Doing it. Julie and Darryl had done it. Clothes. Music. She had a mental list of artists she needed to research. Television and movie actors. Other girls. What other girls wore. Who other girls had done it with. And back to boys.

She understood the discussions and topics were a societal and generational trope. But it was one she'd been shut out of until today.

And she thought Julie liked her, at least a little. Maybe they'd start to hang out. Maybe she'd hang out with Julie's friend Tiffany, too—who'd done it with Mike Dauber when he'd come home on spring break.

She knew Mike Dauber, or she'd had a class with him. And he'd passed her a note once. Or he'd passed her a note to pass to someone else, but that was something. It was contact.

*   *   *

At home, she laid all the bags on her bed.

She'd put everything away in plain sight this time. And she'd remove everything she didn't like—which was nearly all she owned—and box it up for charity. And she'd watch *The X-Files* if she wanted to, and listen to Christina Aguilera and 'N Sync and Destiny's Child.

And she'd change her major.

The thought of it had her heart spearing up to her throat. She'd study what she wanted to study. And when she had her degrees in criminology, in computer science, she'd apply to the FBI.

Everything had changed. Today.

Determined, she dug out the hair color. In the bathroom, she arranged everything, performed the recommended spot test. While she waited, she cleaned up the shorn hair, then purged her closet, her dresser, neatly hung or folded her new clothes.

Hungry, she went down to the kitchen, heated one of the prelabeled meals and ate while studying an article on falsifying IDs on her laptop.

After she'd done the dishes, she went back upstairs. With a mix of trepidation and excitement

18

she followed the directions for the hair color, set the timer. While it set, she arranged everything she needed for the identification. She opened the Britney Spears CD Julie had recommended, slid it into her laptop's CD player.

She turned up the volume so she could hear as she got in the shower to wash the color out of her hair.

It ran so black!

She rinsed and rinsed and rinsed, finally bracing her hands on the shower wall as her stomach began to churn in anticipation and not a little dread. When the water ran clear, she toweled off, wrapped a second towel around her hair.

Women had altered their hair color for centuries, Elizabeth reminded herself. Using berries, herbs, roots. It was a . . . rite of passage, she decided.

It was a personal choice.

In her robe, she faced the mirror.

'My choice,' she said, and pulled the towel off her hair.

She stared at the girl with pale skin and wide green eyes, the girl with short, spiky raven-black hair that framed her narrow, sharp-boned face. Lifting a hand, she scratched her fingers through it, feeling the texture, watching it move.

Then she stood straighter, and she smiled.

'Hi. I'm Liz.'

2

Considering all the help Julie had provided, it seemed only fair to Elizabeth to work on Julie's driver's license first. Creating the template was simple enough. Everything she'd researched claimed the quality of the identification depended largely on the quality of the paper and laminate.

That presented no problem, as her mother didn't believe in cutting corners on supplies.

With scanner and computer she produced a decent enough replica, and through Photoshop she added the digital photo, tweaked it.

The result was good but not good enough.

It took several hours and three attempts before she felt she'd created something that would pass the check-in at a nightclub. Actually, she thought it might very well pass a more rigorous police check. But she hoped it wouldn't come to that.

She set Julie's aside.

It was too late to call Julie, Elizabeth noted when she checked the time and found it was nearly one in the morning.

In the morning, then, she thought, and started on her own identification.

Photo first, she decided, and spent the best part of an hour with her new makeup, carefully copying the steps she'd watched Julie take at the mall. Darkening the eyes, brightening the lips, adding color to the cheeks.

She hadn't known it would be so much fun—and considerable work—to play with all the colors and brushes and pencils.

Liz looks older, she thought, studying the results. Liz looks pretty and confident—and normal.

Flushed with success, she opened the hair products.

Trickier, she discovered, but she believed—with practice—she'd learn. But she liked the careless, somewhat messy spikes. So different from her reddish brown, long and straight and uninspired hair, this short, spiky, glossy black.

Liz was new. Liz could and would do things Elizabeth hadn't even imagined. Liz listened to Britney Spears and wore jeans that showed her navel. Liz went to clubs on Saturday night with a girlfriend, and danced and laughed and . . . flirted with boys.

'And boys flirt back with Liz,' she murmured. 'Because Liz is pretty, and she's fun, and she's not afraid of anything.'

After calculating and setting the angles, the background, she used her new camera on a timer for several shots.

She worked till after three, finding the process simpler with the second document. It was nearly four by the time she put away all the tools and equipment, dutifully removed her makeup. She was certain she'd never sleep—her mind was so full, so busy.

She went under the moment she shut her eyes.

And for the first time in her life, barring illness, she slept soundly until noon. Her first act was to rush to the mirror to make certain she hadn't dreamed it all.

Her second was to call Julie.

'Are we set?' Julie asked, after she'd answered on half a ring.

'Yes. I have everything.'

'And it's totally good, right? It'll do the job?'

'They're excellent counterfeits. I don't foresee any problem.'

'Awesome! Nine o'clock. I'll get the cab, have it wait—so be ready. And make sure you look the part, Liz.'

'I tried the makeup last night. I'm going to practice with it, and my hair, this afternoon. And practice walking in the heels.'

'You do that. I'll see you later. Party time!'

'Yes, I'll—' But Julie had already hung up.

She spent all day on what she now thought of as Project Liz. She dressed in new cropped pants and top, made up her face, worked with her hair. She walked in the new shoes, and when she felt she had that process down, danced.

She practiced in front of the mirror, after finding a pop-music station on the radio. She'd danced before like this—alone in front of the mirror—teaching herself the moves she'd observed at dances in high school. When she'd been miserably on the sidelines, too young and too plain for any boy to notice.

The heels made the moves, the turns somewhat problematic, but she liked the way they kept her just a little off balance, forced her to loosen her knees, her hips.

At six, she took out her labeled meal, ate it while checking her e-mail. But there was nothing, nothing at all from her mother. She'd been sure there would be—some lecture, something.

But Susan's patience was endless, and her use of silence masterful.

It wouldn't work this time, Elizabeth determined.

This time Susan was in for a shock. She'd walked out on Elizabeth, but she'd come home to Liz. And Liz wouldn't be taking that summer program at the university. Liz would be amending her schedule and classes for the coming term.

Liz wasn't going to be a surgeon. Liz was going to work with the FBI, in cyber crimes.

She gave herself thirty minutes to research universities with the highest-rated programs in her new field of study. She may have to transfer, and that might pose a problem. Though her college fund was tied to her trust—and came through her grandparents—they might cut her off. They'd listen to their daughter, follow her lead.

If so, she'd apply for scholarships. Her academic record would hold her there. She'd lose a semester, but she'd get a job. She'd go to work. She'd earn her way to her own destination.

She shut everything down, reminding herself tonight was for fun, for discovery. Not for worries or plans.

She went upstairs to dress for her first night out. Her first night of real freedom.

*   *   *

Because she'd dressed so early, Elizabeth had too much time to think, to question, to doubt. She was overdressed, under-made-up and her hair was wrong. No one would ask her to dance, because no one ever did.

Julie was eighteen, older and experienced, and knew how to dress, how to behave in social situations, how to talk to boys. She herself was bound to do or say something inappropriate. She'd

23

embarrass Julie, then Julie would never speak to her again. That tenuous bond of friendship would be broken forever.

She worked herself up into such a state of panicked excitement she felt feverish, queasy. Twice she sat down, head between her knees, to fight off anxiety attacks, and still she answered the door at Julie's buzz with sweaty palms and a thundering heart.

'Holy shit!'

'It's wrong. I'm wrong.' All the doubts and fears peaked into self-disgust and mortification as Julie stared at her. 'I'm sorry. You can just take the ID.'

'Your hair.'

'I don't know what I was thinking. I only wanted to try—'

'It's *awesome*! You look totally awesome. I wouldn't've recognized you. Oh my God, Liz, you completely look twenty-one, and really sexy.'

'I do?'

Julie cocked a hip, fisted a hand on it. 'You've been holding out.'

The pulse in her throat throbbed like a wound. 'Then it's all right? I look right?'

'You look so way right.' Julie circled a finger in the air, got a blank look. 'Do the turn, Liz. Let's see the whole package.'

Flushed, nearly teary, Elizabeth turned in a circle.

'Oh, yeah. We're going to slay tonight.'

'You look awesome, too. You always do.'

'That's really sweet.'

'I like your dress.'

'It's my sister's.' Julie did a turn and posed in the halter-neck black mini. 'She'll kill me if she finds

24

out I borrowed it.'

'Is it nice? Having a sister?'

'It doesn't suck to have an older one who wears the same size I do, even if she is a bitch half the time. Let me see the ID. Meter's running, Liz.'

'Oh. Yes.' Liz opened the evening bag she'd chosen from her mother's collection, took out Julie's fake license.

'It looks real,' Julie said after a frowning study, then stared up at Elizabeth with wide, dark, eyes. 'I mean, you know, *real* real.'

'They came out very well. I could do better, I think, with more sophisticated equipment, but for tonight, they should do.'

'It even feels real,' Julie murmured. 'You've got skills, girl. You could make a serious fortune. I know kids who'd pay big-time for docs like this.'

Panic flooded back. 'You can't tell anyone. It's just for tonight. It's illegal, and if anyone finds out—'

Julie swiped a finger over her heart, then her lips. 'They won't find out from me.' Well, except Tiffany and Amber, she thought. She shot Elizabeth a smile, certain she could convince her new BFF to make up a couple more just for close friends.

'Let's get this party started.'

After Elizabeth shut and dead-bolted the door, Julie took her hand and pulled her along in a run for the waiting cab. She slid in, gave the driver the name of the club, then swiveled in her seat.

'Okay, plan of action. First thing is to be chilly.'

'Should I have brought a sweater?'

Julie laughed, then blinked when she realized Elizabeth was serious. 'No, I mean we have to be cool, act like we go to clubs all the time. Like this is

25

no big deal for us. Just another Saturday night.'

'You mean we stay calm and blend in.'

'That's what I said. Once we're in, we grab a table and order Cosmos.'

'What are they?'

'You know, like the *Sex and the City* girls?'

'I don't know who they are.'

'Never mind. It's fashionable. We're twenty-one, Liz; we're in a hot club. We order fashionable drinks.'

'Oh.' Elizabeth slid closer, lowered her voice. 'Won't your parents know if you've been drinking?'

'They split last winter.'

'Oh. I'm sorry.'

Julie shrugged, looked away out the window for a moment. 'It happens. Anyway, I don't see my dad until Wednesday, and my mom's away for the weekend on some retreat with her boring friends. Emma's out on a date, plus she doesn't care, anyway. I can do what I want.'

Elizabeth nodded. They were both the same. No one at home to care. 'We'll have Cosmos.'

'Now you're talking. And we scope. That's why we'll dance with each other at first—it gives us time to check out the guys—and let them check us out.'

'Is that why girls dance together? I wondered.'

'Plus, it's fun—and a lot of boys won't dance. You got your cell phone?'

'Yes.'

'If we get separated, we call. If a guy asks for your number, don't give him your home number. The cell's okay, unless your mother monitors your calls.'

'No. No one calls me.'

'The way you look, that's going to change

tonight. If you don't want him to have your number, give him a fake one. Next. You're in college, anyway, so you're cool there. We'll say we're roommates. I'm a liberal arts major. What are you majoring in again?'

'I'm supposed to go to medical school, but—'

'Better stick with that. Truth when possible. You don't get as mixed up.'

'I'll be in medical school, then, starting an internship.' Even the thought of it depressed her. 'But I don't want to talk about school unless I have to.'

'Boys only want to talk about themselves, anyway. Oh, God, we're like almost there.' Julie opened her purse, checked her face in a little mirror, freshened her lip gloss, so Elizabeth did the same. 'Can you get the cab? I got a hundred out of my mother's cash stash, but otherwise I'm tapped out.'

'Of course.'

'I can pay you back. My dad's an easy touch.'

'I don't mind paying.' Elizabeth took out the cab fare, calculated the tip.

'Oh, man, I've got goose bumps. I can't believe I'm going to Warehouse 12! It's totally the bomb!'

'What do we do now?' Elizabeth asked as they climbed out of the cab.

'We get in line. They don't let everybody in, you know, even with ID.'

'Why?'

'Because it's a hot club, so they turn off the dorks and dogs. But they always let in the hot chicks. And we are so the hot chicks.'

It was a long line, and a warm night. Traffic grumbled by, rumbling over the conversations of

others who waited. Elizabeth took in the moment—
the sounds, the smells, the sights. Saturday night,
she thought, and she was queuing up at a hot club
with beautiful people. She was wearing a new
dress—a *red* dress—and high, high heels that made
her feel tall and powerful.

No one looked at her as if she didn't belong.

The man checking IDs at the door wore a suit
and shoes with a high shine. His dark hair, slicked
back in a ponytail, left his face unframed. A scar
rode his left cheekbone. A stud glinted in his right
earlobe.

'He's a bouncer,' Elizabeth whispered to Julie. 'I
did some research. He removes people who cause
trouble. He looks very strong.'

'All we have to do is get by him and get in.'

'The club's owned by Five Star Entertainment.
That's headed by Mikhail and Sergei Volkov. It's
believed they have ties to the Russian Mafia.'

Julie did her eye roll. 'The Mafia's Italian. You
know, *The Sopranos*?'

Elizabeth didn't know what singing had to do
with the Mafia. 'Since the fall of Communism in the
Soviet Union, organized crime in Russia has been
on the rise. Actually, it was already very organized,
and headed by the SS, but—'

'Liz. Save the history lesson.'

'Yes. Sorry.'

'Just pass him your ID, and keep talking to me.'
Julie pitched her voice up again as they wound their
way to the door. 'Dumping that loser was the best
thing I've done in months. Did I tell you he called
me three times today? God, as if.'

A quick smile for the bouncer, and Julie held
out her ID as she continued her conversation with

Elizabeth. 'I told him forget it. He can't make time for me, somebody else will.'

'It's best not to commit to one person, certainly not at this stage.'

'You got that.' Julie held out her hand for the club stamp. 'And I'm ready to check out the rest of the field. First round's on me.'

She stepped around the bouncer while he performed the same check and stamp on Elizabeth, and her grin was so huge Elizabeth wondered it didn't swallow the man whole.

'Thank you,' she said, when he stamped the back of her hand.

'You ladies have fun.'

'We are the fun,' Julie told him, then grabbed Elizabeth's hand and pulled her into the wall of sound.

'Oh my God, we're in!' Julie let out a squeal, mostly drowned out by the music, then bounced on her heels as she gave Elizabeth a hug.

Stunned by the embrace, Elizabeth jerked stiff, but Julie only bounced again. 'You're a genius.'

'Yes.'

Julie laughed, eyes a little wild. 'Okay, table, Cosmos, dance and scope.'

Elizabeth hoped the music covered the pounding of her heart as it had Julie's squeal. So many people. She wasn't used to being with so many people in one place. Everyone moving or talking while the music pumped, pumped, pumped, a flood saturating every breath of air. People jammed the dance floor, shaking, spinning, sweating. They crowded into booths, around tables, at the long curve of the stainless-steel bar.

She was determined to be 'chilly,' but a

29

sweater wouldn't be necessary. Body heat pulsed everywhere.

Getting through the crowd—dodging, weaving, bumping bodies—kicked Elizabeth's heart rate to a gallop. Anxiety clutched at her throat, pressed on her chest. Julie's death grip on her hand was the only thing that kept her from bolting.

Julie finally beelined for a table the size of a dinner plate.

'Score! Oh my God, it's like *everybody*'s here. We've gotta keep scoping a table closer to the dance floor. This is so completely awesome. The DJ is slamming it.' She finally focused on Elizabeth's face. 'Hey, are you okay?'

'It's very crowded and warm.'

'Well, yeah. Who wants to go to an empty, cold club? Listen, we need drinks and now, so I'm going to go to the bar. I'll buy, since you paid for the cab. That'll give me time to start scoping. You do the same from here. Two Cosmos, coming up!'

Without Julie's hand to anchor her, Elizabeth gripped hers together. She recognized the signs—anxiety, claustrophobia—and deliberately focused on steadying her breathing. Liz didn't panic just because she'd been swallowed up in a crowd. She ordered herself to relax, starting with her toes and working her way up.

By the time she reached her belly, she'd calmed enough to take on the role of observer. The owners—and their architect—had made good use of the warehouse space, utilizing an urban industrial motif with the exposed ductwork and pipes, the old brick walls. The stainless steel—bar, tables, chairs, stools—reflected back the flashing color of the lights—another pulse, she thought, timed to the music.

Open iron stairs on either side led up to a second level, open as well. People crowded the rails there, or squeezed around more tables. There was likely a second bar on that level, she thought. Drinks were profit.

Down here, on a wide raised platform, under those flashing lights, the DJ worked. Another observer, Elizabeth decided. Raised in a position of authority and honor where he could see the crowd. His long, dark hair flew as he worked. He wore a graphic T-shirt. She couldn't make out the art with the distance, but it was virulent orange against the black cloth.

Just beneath his perch, several women moved sinuously, rocking their hips in an invitation to mate.

Calm again, she tuned in to the music. She liked it—the hard, repetitive beat; the pounding of drums; the rough, metallic scream of guitar. And she liked the way different dancers chose to move to it. Arms in the air, arms cocked like a boxer's with hands fisted, elbows jabbing, feet planted, feet lifting.

'Wow. Just wow.' Julie set martini glasses filled with pink liquid on the table before she sat. 'I nearly spilled these coming back, which would have bummed. They're eight dollars each.'

'Alcoholic beverages make up the biggest profit margin in clubs and bars.'

'I guess. But they're good. I drank a little of mine, and it's like *pow*!' She laughed, leaned in. 'We should make them last until we find some guys to buy us drinks.'

'Why would they buy us drinks?'

31

'Duh. We're hot, we're available. Drink some, Liz, and let's get out there and show our stuff.'

Obediently, Elizabeth sipped. 'It's good.' Testing, she took another sip. 'And it's very pretty.'

'I want to get lit and loose! Hey, I love this song. Time to shake it.'

Once again, Julie grabbed Elizabeth's hand.

When the crowd closed in around her, Elizabeth shut her eyes. Just the music, she thought. Just the music.

'Hey, nice moves.'

Cautiously, Elizabeth opened her eyes again, concentrated on Julie. 'What?'

'I was afraid you'd be dorky, you know. But you've got moves. You can dance,' Julie elaborated.

'Oh. The music's tribal and designed to stimulate. It's simply a matter of coordinating legs and hips. And mimicry. I've watched others dance a lot.'

'Whatever you say, Liz.'

Elizabeth liked moving her hips. Like the heels, it made her feel powerful, and the way the dress rubbed her skin added a sexual element. The lights made everything surreal, and the music itself seemed to swallow all.

Her discomfort with the crowd eased, so when Julie bumped hips with her, she laughed and meant it.

They danced, and danced more. Back at their tiny table, they drank Cosmos, and when a waitress came by, Elizabeth carelessly ordered more.

'The dancing makes me thirsty,' she said to Julie.

'I've got a nice buzz going already. And that guy over there is totally checking us out. No, don't look!'

32

'How can I see him if I don't look?'

'Take my word, he's totally cute. I'm going to give him the eye and the hair toss in a second, then you, like sort of really casual, turn in your chair. He's got blond hair, kind of curly. He's wearing a tight white T-shirt and a black jacket with jeans.'

'Oh, yes, I saw him before, over by the bar. He was talking to a woman. She had long, blond hair and wore a bright pink dress that showed a lot of cleavage. He has a gold hoop earring in his left ear, and a gold ring on the middle finger of his right hand.'

'Jesus, do you actually have eyes in the back of your head like my mom used to say she did? How do you know when you haven't looked?'

'I saw him, over by the bar,' Elizabeth repeated. 'I noticed him because the blond woman seemed very angry with him. And I remember because I have an eidetic memory.'

'Is it fatal?'

'No, it's not a disease or condition. Oh.' Flushing a little, Elizabeth hunched her shoulders. 'You were joking. It's commonly called a photographic memory, but that's not accurate, as it's more than visual.'

'Whatever. Get ready.'

But Elizabeth was more interested in Julie—the eye, which included a tipped head, slow, secretive smile and a shift of the eyes from under the lashes. This was followed by a quick shake and toss of the head that lifted Julie's hair and had it drifting down again.

Was it innate? Was it learned behavior? Some combination of both? In any case, Elizabeth thought she could emulate it, though she no longer

33

had hair to toss.

'Message received. Oh, he's got such an adorable smile. Oh my God, he's coming over. He's like actually coming over.'

'But you wanted him to. That's why you . . . sent the message.'

'Yeah, but—I bet he's at least twenty-four. I bet. Follow my lead.'

'Excuse me?'

Elizabeth looked up as Julie did but didn't risk the smile. She'd need to practice first.

'I wonder if you can help me with something.'

Julie executed a modified hair toss. 'Maybe.'

'I'm worried my memory is failing because I never forget a beautiful woman, but I can't recall either of you. Tell me you haven't been here before.'

'First time.'

'Ah, that explains it.'

'I guess you're here a lot.'

'Every night. It's my club—that is,' he said with a dazzling smile, 'I have an interest in it.'

'You're one of the Volkovs?' Elizabeth spoke without thinking, then felt the heat rise as he turned sizzling blue eyes on her.

'Alex Gurevich. A cousin.'

'Julie Masters.' Julie offered a hand, which Alex took, kissed stylishly on the knuckles. 'And my friend Liz.'

'Welcome to Warehouse 12. You're enjoying yourselves?'

'The music's great.'

When the waitress came with the drinks, Alex plucked the tab off the tray. 'Beautiful women who come to my club for the first time aren't allowed to buy their own drinks.'

Under the table, Julie nudged Elizabeth's foot while she beamed at Alex. 'Then you'll have to join us.'

'I'd love to.' He murmured something to the waitress. 'Are you visiting Chicago?'

'Born and bred,' Julie told him, taking a long swallow of her drink. 'Both of us. We're home for the summer. We're at Harvard.'

'Harvard?' His head cocked; his eyes dazzled. 'Beautiful and smart. I'm half in love already. If you can dance, I'm lost.'

Julie took another drink. 'You're going to need a map.'

He laughed, held out his hands. Julie took one, rose.

'Come on, Liz. Let's show him how a couple of Harvard girls get down.'

'Oh, but he wants to dance with you.'

'Both.' Alex kept his extended hand out. 'Which makes me the luckiest man in the room.'

She started to decline, but Julie gave her another version of the eye behind Alex's back, which involved a lot of rolling, eyebrow wiggling, grimacing. So she took his hand.

He wasn't actually asking her to dance, but Elizabeth gave him credit for manners when he could have left her sitting alone at the table. She did her best to join in without getting in the way. It didn't matter, she loved dancing. She loved the music. She loved the noise rising around her, the movements, the smells.

When she smiled it wasn't practiced, just a natural curve of her lips. Alex sent her a wink and a grin as he laid his hands on Julie's hips.

35

Then he lifted his chin in a signal to someone behind her.

Even as she turned to look, someone took her hand, gave her a quick spin that nearly toppled her on her heels.

'As always, my cousin is greedy. He takes two while I have none.' Russia flowed exotically through the voice. 'Unless you take pity and dance with me.'

'I—'

'Don't say no, pretty lady.' He drew her close for a sway. 'Just a dance.'

She could only stare up at him. He was tall, his body hard and firm against her. Where Alex was bright, he was dark—the long wave of his hair, eyes that snapped nearly black against tawny skin. As he smiled at her, dimples shimmered in his cheeks. Her heart rolled over in her chest and trembled.

'I like your dress,' he said.

'Thank you. It's new.'

His smile widened. 'And my favorite color. I'm Ilya.'

'I'm . . . Liz. I'm Liz. Um. *Priyatno poznakomit'sya.*'

'It's nice to meet you, too. You speak Russian.'

'Yes. Well, a little. Um.'

'A beautiful girl wearing my favorite color who speaks Russian. It's my lucky night.'

No, Liz thought, as, still holding her close, he lifted her hand to his lips. Oh, no. It was her lucky night.

It was the best night of her life.

3

They moved to a booth. It all happened so smoothly, so seamlessly, it seemed like magic. As magical as the pretty pink drink that appeared in front of her.

She was Cinderella at the ball, and midnight was a lifetime away.

When they sat he stayed close, kept his eyes on her face, his body angled toward hers as if the crowds and the music didn't exist. He touched her as he spoke, and every brush of his fingers over the back of her hand, her arm or shoulder was a terrible thrill.

'So, what is it you study at Harvard?'

'I'm in medical school.' It wouldn't be true, she promised herself, but it was true enough now.

'A doctor. This takes many years, yes? What kind of doctor will you be?'

'My mother wants me to follow her into neurosurgery.'

'This is a brain surgeon? This is big, important doctor who cuts into brains.' He skimmed a fingertip down her temple. 'You must be very smart for this.'

'I am. Very smart.'

He laughed as if she'd said something charming. 'It's good to know yourself. You say this is what your mother wants. Is it what you want?'

She took a sip of her drink, and thought he was very smart, too—or at least astute. 'No, not really.'

'Then what kind of doctor do you want to be?'

'I don't want to be a doctor at all.'

'No? What, then?'

37

'I want to work in cyber crimes for the FBI.'

'FBI?' His dark eyes widened.

'Yes. I want to investigate high-tech crimes, computer fraud—terrorism, sexual exploitation. It's an important field that changes every day as technology advances. The more people use and depend on computers and electronics, the more the criminal element will exploit that dependence. Thieves, scam artists, pedophiles, even terrorists.'

'This is your passion.'

'I . . . I guess.'

'Then you must follow. We must always follow our passions, yes?' When his hand brushed over her knee, a slow, liquid warmth spread in her belly.

'I never have.' Was this passion? she wondered. This slow, liquid warmth? 'But I want to start.'

'You must respect your mother, but she must also respect you. A woman grown. And a mother wants her child to be happy.'

'She doesn't want me to waste my intellect.'

'But the intellect is yours.'

'I'm starting to believe that. Are you in college?'

'I am finished with this. Now I work in the family business. This makes me happy.' He signaled the waitress for another round before Elizabeth realized her glass was nearly empty.

'Because it's your passion.'

'This is so. I follow my passions—like this.'

He was going to kiss her. She might not have been kissed before, but she'd imagined it often enough. She discovered imagination wasn't her strong suit.

She knew kissing imparted biological information through pheromones, that the act stimulated all the nerve endings packed in the lips,

38

in the tongue. It triggered a chemical reaction—a pleasurable one that explained why, with few exceptions, kissing was part of human culture.

But to *be* kissed, she realized, was an entirely different matter than theorizing about it.

His lips were soft and smooth, and rubbed gently over hers, with the pressure slowly, gradually increasing as his hand slid up from her hip to her rib cage. Her heart tripped above the span of his hand as his tongue slipped through her lips, lazily glided over hers.

Her breath caught, then released with an involuntary sound, almost of pain—and the world revolved.

'Sweet,' he murmured, and the vibration of the words against her lips, the warmth of his breath inside her mouth, triggered a shiver down her spine.

'Very sweet.' His teeth grazed over her bottom lip as he eased back, studied her. 'I like you.'

'I like you, too. I liked kissing you.'

'Then we must do it again, while we dance.' He brought her to her feet, brushed his lips to hers again. 'You aren't—the word, the word . . . jaded. This is the word. Not like so many women who come in to dance and drink and flirt with men.'

'I don't have a lot of experience with any of that.'

Those black eyes sparkled in the pulsing lights. 'Then the other men aren't so lucky as me.'

Elizabeth glanced back toward Julie as Ilya drew her to the dance floor and saw that her friend was also being kissed. Not gently, not slowly, but Julie seemed to like it—in fact, was fully participating, so—

Then Ilya drew her into his arms, swaying with

her unlike all the others who rushed and shook and spun. Just swaying while his mouth came to hers again.

She stopped thinking about chemical reactions and nerve endings. Instead, she did her best to participate fully. Instinct brought her arms up to lock around his neck. When she felt the change in him, the hardening pressing against her, she knew it was a normal, even involuntary, physical reaction.

But she knew the wonder of it all the same. She'd caused the reaction. He wanted her, when no one ever had.

'What you do to me,' he whispered in her ear. 'Your taste, your scent.'

'It's pheromones.'

He looked down at her, brow knitted. 'Is what?'

'Nothing.' She pressed her face to his shoulder.

She knew the alcohol impaired her judgment, but she didn't care. Even knowing the reason she didn't care was because of the impairment, she lifted her face again. This time she initiated the kiss.

'We should sit,' he said after a long moment. 'You make my knees weak.'

He held her hand as they walked back to the table. Julie, eyes overbright, face flushed, popped to her feet. She teetered a minute, laughed, grabbed her purse.

'We'll be right back. Come on, Liz.'

'Where?'

'Where else? The ladies'.'

'Oh. Excuse me.'

Julie hooked arms with her as much for balance as solidarity. 'Oh my God. Can you believe it? We like got the hottest guys in the club. Jesus, they're so sexy. And yours has that accent. I wish mine

40

had the accent, but he kisses so much better than Darryl. He practically owns the club, you know, and like has this house on the lake. We're all going to get out of here and go there.'

'To his house? Do you think we should?'

'Oh, we should.' Julie shoved open the bathroom door, took a look at the line for the stalls. 'Typical, and I really have to pee! I've got such a buzz! How's your guy—does he kiss good? What's his name again?'

'Ilya. Yes, he's very good. I like him, very much, but I'm not sure we should go with them to Alex's house.'

'Oh, loosen up, Liz. You can't let me down now. I'm totally going to do it with Alex, and I can't go over there with him alone—not on the first date. You don't have to do it with Ilya if you're all virginal.'

'Sex is a natural and necessary act, not only for procreation but, certainly in humans, for pleasure and the release of stress.'

'Get you.' Julie elbowed her. 'So you don't like think I'm a slut for doing it with Alex?'

'It's an unfortunate by-product of a patriarchal society that women are deemed sluttish or cheap for engaging in sex for pleasure while men are considered vital. Virginity shouldn't be a prize to be won, or withheld. The hymen has no rewarding properties, grants no powers. Women should—no, must—be allowed to pursue their own sexual gratification, whether or not procreation is the goal or the relationship a monogamous one, just as a man is free to do so.'

A lanky redhead fluffed her hair, then gave Elizabeth a dazzling smile as she walked by. 'Sing it,

41

sister.'

Elizabeth leaned close to Julie as the woman continued out. 'Why would I sing?' she whispered.

'It's just an expression. You know, Liz, I figured you for a cross your legs, no touching below the waist and only over the clothes sort.'

'A lack of experience doesn't make me a prude.'

'Got it. You know I sort of thought I'd ditch you once we were in and I hooked up, but you're fun—even if you talk like a teacher half the time. So, you know, sorry for sort of thinking it.'

'It's all right. You didn't. And I know I'm not like your friends.'

'Hey.' Julie wrapped an arm around Elizabeth's shoulders for a squeeze. 'You are my friend now, right?'

'I hope so. I've never—'

'Oh, thank God.' On that fervent call, Julie made a staggering dash as a stall opened. 'So we're going to Alex's, right?'

Elizabeth looked around the crowded restroom. All the women freshening makeup and hair, waiting in line, laughing, talking. She was probably the only virgin in the room.

Virginity wasn't a prize, she reminded herself. So it wasn't a burden, either. It was hers to keep or lose. Her choice. Her life.

'Liz?'

'Yes.' On a steadying breath, Liz walked toward the next open stall. 'Yes,' she said again. Closing the door, and her eyes. 'We'll go. Together.'

*   *   *

At the table, Ilya lifted his beer. 'If these girls are

42

twenty-one, I'm sixty.'

Alex only laughed, shrugged. 'They're close enough. And mine's in heat, believe me.'

'She's drunk, Alexi.'

'So what? I didn't pour the drinks down her throat. I'm up for some fresh meat, and I'm fucking getting laid tonight. Don't tell me you're not planning to nail down the hot brunette, bro.'

'She's sweet.' A smile tugged at Ilya's mouth. 'And just a little underripe. She's not so drunk as yours. If she's willing, I'll take her to bed. I like her mind.'

Alex's lips twisted. 'Give me a fucking break.'

'No, I do. It adds something.' He glanced around. Too much the same, he thought of the women who passed by, too much predictable. 'Refreshing—this is the word.'

'The blonde's setting it up so we'll go to my place. All of us. She said she won't go unless her friend goes. You can have the spare room.'

'I prefer my own place.'

'Look, it's both of them or neither. I didn't put in over two hours getting her primed to have her walk her fine ass out of here because you can't close the deal with the friend.'

Ilya's eyes went hard over his beer. 'I can close the deal, *dvojurodny brat*.'

'And which do you think will close it tight, *cousin*? The crap apartment you're still living in, or my house on the lake?'

Ilya jerked a shoulder. 'I prefer my simpler place, but all right. We'll go to yours. No drugs, Alexi.'

'Oh, for Christ's sake.'

'No drugs.' Ilya leaned forward, stabbed a finger on the table. 'You keep it legal. We don't know

43

them, but mine, I think, would not approve. She says she wants to be FBI.'

'You're shitting me.'

'No. No drugs, Alexi, or I don't go—and you don't get laid.'

'Fine. Here they come.'

'Stand up.' Ilya kicked Alex under the table. 'Pretend you're a gentleman.'

He rose, held out a hand to Liz.

'We'd love to get out of here,' Julie announced, wrapping herself around Alex. 'We'd love to see your house.'

'Then that's what we'll do. Nothing beats a private party.'

'This is okay with you?' Ilya murmured as they started out.

'Yes. Julie really wants to, and we're together, so—'

'No, I don't ask what Julie wants. I ask if you want.'

She looked at him, felt a sigh and a tingle. It mattered to him, what she wanted. 'Yes. I want to go with you.'

'This is good.' He took her hand, pressed it to his heart as they wove through the crowd. 'I want to be with you. And you can tell me more about Liz. I want to know everything about you.'

'Julie said boys—men—only want to talk about themselves.'

He laughed, tucked his arm around her waist. 'Then how do they learn about fascinating women?'

As they got to the door, a man in a suit came up, tapped Ilya on the shoulder.

'One moment,' Ilya said to Liz as he stepped aside.

44

She couldn't hear much, and that was in Russian. But she could see by her glimpse of Ilya's profile that he wasn't pleased with what he heard.

But she was reasonably sure his snarled *chyort voz'mi* was a curse. He signaled the man to wait, then guided Liz outside, where Alex and Julie waited.

'There's something I must take care of. I'm sorry.'

'It's all right. I understand.'

'Bullshit, Ilya, let somebody else handle it.'

'It's work,' Ilya said shortly. 'It shouldn't take long—no more than an hour. You go, with Alexi and your friend. I'll come as soon as I finish.'

'Oh, but—'

'Come on, Liz, it'll be all right. You can wait for Ilya at Alex's. He's got all kinds of music—and a flat-screen TV.'

'You wait.' Ilya leaned down, kissed Elizabeth long and deep. 'I'll come soon. Drive carefully, Alexi. You have precious cargo.'

'So now I have two beautiful women.' Unwilling to lose the momentum, Alex took both girls by the arms. 'Ilya takes everything seriously. I like to party. We're too young to be serious.'

A dark SUV glided up to the curb. Alex signaled, then caught the keys the valet tossed him. He opened the door. Trapped by manners and obligation, Liz climbed in the back. She stared at the door of the club, craning her neck to keep it in view even when Alex drove away, with Julie singing along to the stereo.

*   *   *

It didn't feel right. Without Ilya, the rush of excitement, anticipation, faded away, left everything flat and dull. Combined with the alcohol, riding in the backseat triggered a bout of motion sickness. Queasy, and suddenly brutally tired, she rested her head against the side window.

They didn't need her, Elizabeth thought. Both Julie and Alex sang and laughed. He drove entirely too fast, taking corners in a way that made her stomach pitch. She would not be sick. Even as the heat flashed through her, she willed herself to breathe, slow and even. She would not humiliate herself by being sick in the backseat of Alex's SUV.

She lowered her window a few inches, let the air blow over her face. She wanted to lie down, wanted to sleep. She'd had too much to drink, and this was yet another chemical reaction.

And not nearly as pleasant as a kiss.

She concentrated on her breathing, on the air across her face, on the houses, cars, streets. Anything but on her churning stomach and head.

As he wound along Lake Shore Drive, she thought how close they were, relatively, to her home in Lincoln Park. If she could just go home, she could lie down in the quiet, sleep off the nausea and spinning head. But when Alex pulled up at a pretty old two-story traditional, she thought at least she could get out of the car, stand on solid ground.

'Got some great views,' Alex was saying as he and Julie got out. 'I thought about buying a condo, but I like my privacy. Plenty of room to party here, and nobody bitches the music's too loud.'

Julie staggered, laughed a little wildly when Alex caught her and squeezed his hand on her ass.

Elizabeth trailed behind, a miserably queasy fifth

46

wheel.

'You live here by yourself,' she managed.

'Plenty of room for company.' He unlocked the front door, gestured. 'Ladies first.'

And he gave Elizabeth's ass a teasing pat as she walked in.

She wanted to tell him he had a beautiful home, but the fact was everything was too bright, too new, too modern. All hard edges, shiny surfaces and glossy leather. A bright red bar, a huge black leather sofa and an enormous wall-screen TV dominated the living room, when the wide glass doors and windows leading to a terrace should have been the key point.

'Oh my God, I love this.' Julie immediately flopped onto the sofa, stretched out. 'It's like decadent.'

'That's the idea, baby.' He picked up a remote, clicked, and pounding music filled the room. 'I'll fix you a drink.'

'Can you make Cosmos?' Julie asked him. 'I just love Cosmos.'

'I'll hook you up.'

'Maybe I could have some water?' Elizabeth asked.

'Oh, Liz, don't be such a buzzkill.'

'I'm a little dehydrated.' And God, God, she needed more air. 'Is it all right if I look outside?' She walked toward the terrace doors.

'Sure. *Mi casa es su casa.*'

'I want to dance!'

As Julie lurched up, began to bump and grind, Elizabeth pulled open the doors and escaped. She imagined the view was wonderful, but everything blurred as she hobbled to the rail, leaned on it.

47

What were they doing? What were they thinking? This was a mistake. A stupid, reckless mistake. They had to go. She had to convince Julie to leave.

But even over the music, she could hear Julie's Cosmo-slurred laughter.

Maybe if she sat down out here for a few minutes, cleared her head, waited for her stomach to settle. She could claim her mother had called. What was one more lie in an entire night of them? She'd make up some excuse—a good, logical excuse to leave. Once her head cleared.

'There you are.'

She turned as Alex stepped out.

'One of each.' Gilded in the low light, he carried a glass of water and ice in one hand, and a martini glass of that pretty pink—that now made her stomach turn.

'Thank you. But just the water, I think.'

'Gotta feed that high, baby.' But he set the drink aside. 'You don't have to be out here all alone.' He shifted, pressed her back against the rail. 'The three of us can party. I can take care of both of you.'

'I don't think—'

'Who knows if Ilya's coming? Work, work, work, that's what he does. You caught his eye, though. Mine, too. Come back inside. We'll have a good time.'

'I think . . . I'll wait for Ilya. I need to use your bathroom.'

'Your loss, baby.' Though he only shrugged, she thought she caught something mean flicker in his eyes. 'Go left. It's off the kitchen.'

'Thank you.'

'If you change your mind,' he called off as she

48

ran to the door.

'Julie.' She grabbed Julie by the arm as Julie tried to execute an unsteady dance-floor spin.

'I'm having such a good time. This is the best night ever.'

'Julie, you've had too much to drink.'

After a *pffht* sound, Julie shook Elizabeth off. 'Not possible.'

'We have to go.'

'We have to stay and *partay*!'

'Alex said both of us should go to bed with him.'

'Eeuw.' Snorting with laughter, Julie spun again. 'He's just messing around, Liz. Don't get all brainiac nerd on me. Your guy'll be here in a few minutes. Just have another drink, chill.'

'I don't want any more to drink. I feel sick. I want to go home.'

'Not going home. Nobody gives a shit there. Come on, Lizzy! Dance with me.'

'I can't.' Liz pressed a hand to her stomach as her skin went clammy. 'I need to—' Unable to fight it, she made the dash to the left, caught a glimpse of Alex leaning on the terrace doors, grinning at her.

On a half-sob, she stumbled through the kitchen and nearly fell on the tiles as she bolted for the bathroom door.

She risked the half-second it took to lock the door behind her, then fell to her knees in front of the toilet. She vomited sick, slimy pink, and barely managed a breath before she vomited again. Tears streamed out of her eyes as she pulled herself up, using the sink as a lever. Half blind, she ran the water cold, scooped some into her mouth, splashed more on her face.

Shuddering, she lifted her head, saw herself in the mirror—white as wax, with the mascara and eyeliner smudged under her eyes like livid bruises. More of it tracked down her cheeks like black tears.

Shame washed through her even as the next bout of sickness had her dropping to her knees again.

Exhausted, the room spinning around her, she curled on the tiles and wept. She didn't want anyone to see her like this.

She wanted to go home.

She wanted to die.

She lay shivering, her cheek pressed to the cool tiles until she thought she could risk sitting up. The room stank of sickness and sweat, but she couldn't go out until she'd cleaned herself up.

She did her best with soap and water, rubbing her face until her skin was raw, pausing every minute or so to lean over, fight off another wave of nausea.

Now she looked pale *and* splotchy, her eyes glassy and rimmed with red. But her hands trembled, so her attempt to repair her makeup was almost worse than nothing at all.

She'd have to swallow the humiliation. She'd go out on the terrace, in the fresh air, and wait until Ilya came. She'd ask him to take her home, and hoped he'd understand.

He'd never want to see her again. He'd never kiss her again.

Cause and effect, she reminded herself. She'd lied, and lied and lied, and the result was this new mortification, and worse, this glimpse of what might be, only to have it all taken away.

Lowering the lid of the toilet, she sat, clutching her purse, bracing herself for the next step. Wearily, she took off her shoes. What did it matter? Her feet hurt, and Cinderella's midnight had come.

She walked with as much dignity as she could muster through the kitchen with its big black appliances and blinding white counters. But when she started to make the turn into the living room, she saw Alex and Julie, both naked, having sex on the leather sofa.

Stunned, fascinated, she stood frozen for a moment, watching the tattoos on Alex's back and shoulders ripple as his hips thrust. Under him, Julie made guttural groaning sounds.

Ashamed of watching, Elizabeth backed up quietly and used the door off the kitchen to access the terrace.

She'd sit in the dark, in the air, until they were finished. She wasn't a prude. It was just sex, after all. But she wished, very strongly, they'd had that sex behind a closed bedroom door.

Then she wished she had more water for her abused throat, and a blanket because she felt cold—cold and empty and very, very frail.

Then she dozed off, huddled in the chair in a dark corner of the terrace.

She didn't know what woke her—voices, a clatter—but she came awake, stiff and chilled in the chair. She saw by her watch she'd slept for only about fifteen minutes, but she felt even worse than she had before.

She needed to go home. Cautious, she crept over to the doors to see if Julie and Alex had finished.

She didn't see Julie at all, but Alex—wearing only black boxers—and two fully dressed men.

Biting her lip, she crept a little closer. Maybe they'd come to tell Alex that Ilya had been delayed.

51

Oh, God, she wished he'd come, take her home.

Remembering what she looked like, she kept to the shadows as she eased toward the door Alex had left open.

'For fuck's sake, speak English. I was born in Chicago.' Obviously annoyed, Alex stalked over to the bar, poured vodka into a glass. 'What do you want, Korotkii, that can't wait till tomorrow?'

'Why put off till tomorrow? Is that American enough for you?'

The man who spoke had a compact, athletic body. The short sleeves of his black T-shirt strained against his biceps. Tattoos covered his arms. Like Alex, he was blond and handsome. A relation? Elizabeth wondered. The resemblance was subtle but there.

The man with him was bigger, older and stood like a soldier.

'Yeah, you're a fucking Yankee-Doodle.' Alex tossed back the vodka. 'Office hours are closed.'

'And you work so hard.' Korotkii's smooth voice glided over the words. But under the smooth, the intriguing accent, rough, jagged rock scraped. 'It takes hard work, this stealing from your uncle.'

Alex paused in the act of pouring white powder from a clear bag onto a small square mirror on the bar. 'What're you talking about? I don't steal from Sergei.'

'You steal from the clubs, from the restaurant; you take off the top from the Internet scams, from the whore profits. From all you can reach. You think this isn't stealing from your uncle? You think he is a fool?'

Sneering, Alexi picked up a thin metal tool and began to tap it against the powder.

Cocaine, Elizabeth realized. Oh, God, what had she done coming here?

'Sergei has my loyalty,' Alexi said as he cut the powder, 'and I'll speak to him about this *bullshit* tomorrow.'

'You think he doesn't know how you pay for the Rolex, the Armani, Versace, this house, all your other toys—and your drugs, Alexi? You think he doesn't know you made a deal with the cops?'

The little tool rattled when Alex dropped it. 'I don't deal with cops.'

He's lying, Elizabeth thought. She could see it in his eyes, hear it in his voice.

'They picked you up two days ago, for possession.' Korotkii's gesture toward the cocaine was pure disgust. 'And you dealt with them, *mudak.* Betray your family for your freedom, for your fine life. Do you know what happens to thieves and traitors, Alexi?'

'I'll talk to Sergei. I'll explain. I had to give them something, but it was bullshit. Just bullshit. I played them.'

'No, Alexi, they played you. And you lost.'

'I'll talk to Sergei.' When he backed up, the second man moved—fast for his girth—trapped Alexi's arms behind his back.

Fear lived on his face, and in fear he spoke in Russian. 'Don't do this. Yakov, we're cousins. Our mothers are sisters. We share blood.'

'You're a disgrace to your mother, to your blood. On your knees.'

'No. Don't.'

The second man shoved Alexi to the ground.

'Don't. Please. We're blood. Give me a chance.'

'Yes, beg. Beg for your worthless life. I would let

53

Yegor break you to pieces, but your uncle said to show mercy, for his sister's sake.'

'Please. Have mercy.'

'This is your mercy.' Korotkii drew a gun from the small of his back, pressed the barrel to Alexi's forehead and fired.

Elizabeth's legs gave way. She fell to her knees, her hand clamped over her mouth to trap the scream.

Korotkii spoke softly as he put the gun to Alexi's temple, fired twice more.

His expression never changed, held like a mask as he murdered. Then it sharpened as he looked up and toward the kitchen.

'I don't feel good, Alex. I need to lie down, or maybe we should— Who are you?'

'Ah, fuck your mother,' he muttered, and shot Julie twice, where she stood. 'Why didn't we know he had his whore with him?'

The second man walked over to Julie, shook his head. 'This is a new one. Very young.'

'She won't be older.'

Elizabeth's vision grayed. It was a dream. A nightmare. Because of the drinking and being sick. She'd wake up any second. Huddled in the dark, she stared at Alex. There was hardly any blood, she noted. If it was real, wouldn't there be more blood?

Wake up, wake up, wake up.

But the terror only spiked when she saw Ilya come in.

They'd kill him, too. The man would shoot him. She had to help. She had to—

'God damn it, what have you done?'

'What I was ordered to do.'

'Your orders were to break his arms and to do it

54

tomorrow night.'

'The orders changed. Our informant got us word. Alexi went to bed with the cops.'

'Christ. Motherfucker.'

Elizabeth watched in horror as Ilya kicked the dead Alex, once, twice, three times.

One of them, she thought. He was one of them.

Ilya stopped, pushed at his hair, then saw Julie's body. 'Ah, fuck. Was that necessary?'

'She saw us. We were told his whore left with another man.'

'It was this one's bad luck he was looking for fresh meat. Where's the other one?'

'Other?'

The beautiful dark eyes went to ice. 'There were two. This one and another—short, black hair, red dress.'

'Yegor.'

With a nod, the big man drew a knife and started up the stairs. Ilya gestured, and, following orders, Korotkii moved toward the kitchen while Ilya walked to the terrace doors.

'Liz,' he murmured. 'It's all right, Liz. I'll take care of you.'

He slid a knife out of his boot, held it behind his back, flipped on the outside lights.

He saw her shoes, scanned the terrace, rushed to the rail.

'There's no one here,' Korotkii told him from the doorway.

'There was. Find her.'

4

She ran blindly, eyes wide and glazed, breath ripping out of her lungs in sobs and gasps. She couldn't release the scream clawing at her throat. They might hear. If they heard, if they caught her, they'd kill her.

Like Julie.

She fought her instinct to run for the street. There could be more of them, more like Ilya. How could she know the car she flagged down wasn't one of them? How could she know if she beat her fists on the door of a house, one of them wouldn't answer?

She had to run, get away as far and as fast as she could. She had to hide.

If there was a fence, she climbed it. If there was a hedge, she pushed and fought her way through. When the ground scraped and tore at her bare feet, she choked back the cries of pain. She hid from the moonlight, scrabbling like a mole for the dark places.

A dog barked madly as she raced across someone's yard.

Don't let them hear, don't let them come.

Don't look back.

Something tore into her side. For a terrifying moment as she pitched forward, she thought she'd been shot. But she lay on the ground, drawing her knees in, the harsh whoops of her breath scoring her throat.

A cramp, just a cramp. But with it came a powerful surge of nausea. Pushing to her hands and knees, she gagged, wept, gagged, racked by dry heaves.

Shock, she told herself as her teeth chattered. Sweating and shivering at the same time, dizzy, nauseated, rapid pulse. She was in shock, and she needed to *think*.

To warm herself, she rubbed her hands rapidly over her arms as she struggled to slow her breathing. She crawled over to retrieve the purse that had flown out of her hand when she'd fallen. She'd managed to hold on to it during the flight, so she comforted herself that she *had* been thinking on some level.

She needed to call the police; she needed help.

'Take out the phone,' she whispered, coaching herself. 'Push memory one. Tell them . . . tell them . . .'

'Nine-one-one, what is your emergency?'

'Help me. Can you help me?'

'What is the nature of your emergency?'

'He shot them.' Tears flooded her eyes, all but drowned her voice. 'He shot them, and I ran.'

'Ma'am, are you reporting a shooting?'

'He killed them. He killed Julie. I ran away.'

'I'm going to send help. Give me your location.'

'I don't know where I am.' She covered her mouth with her hand, struggled not to break down. 'I ran. I just ran. I think I'm near Lake Shore Drive. Wait. Will you wait? Don't go.'

'I'm right here. What's your name?'

'I'm Elizabeth. I'm Elizabeth Fitch.'

'Elizabeth, do you recognize anything? A landmark, an address?'

'I'm going to find one. I'm behind a house. A gray stone house with turrets.' She limped toward the house, shaking violently when she stepped into the glow of security lights. 'It has—it has a paved driveway, and a big garage. Decks, and—and gardens.'

'Can you walk to the street?'

'I am. I can see it. There are streetlights. If I go where it's light and they come, they'll see me.'

'Just keep talking. Keep your phone on, Elizabeth. We're using your signal to find you.'

'I see an address. I see the numbers.' She read them off.

'The police are on their way. Help is coming, Elizabeth. Are you hurt?'

'No. No, I ran. I was outside when they came in. I was on the terrace. They didn't know. They didn't see me. He shot them. He shot them. He killed Julie.'

'I'm sorry. Where did this happen?'

'I don't know. I didn't get the address. It was on Lake Shore Drive. We shouldn't have gone there. We shouldn't have gone to that house. Julie's dead.'

'Who is Julie, Elizabeth?'

'Ju— Julie Masters. My friend Julie. A car's coming. I have to hide.'

'It's the patrol car. It's help.'

'Are you sure?' Panic crushed her chest, shut off her air. 'Are you sure?'

'They're on the radio right now, approaching the address. I'm going to tell them to turn on the bubble light. You'll see it.'

'Yes. Yes. Oh, God. I see it.' She stumbled forward, into the light. 'Thank you.'

'You're safe now, Elizabeth.'

They wanted to take her to the hospital, but when she grew only more anxious, they took her

58

to the station. She huddled under the blanket one of the officers wrapped around her shoulders, and continued to shiver in the back of the patrol car.

They took her to a room with a table and chairs. One of the officers stayed with her while the other went to get her coffee.

'Tell me what happened.'

He'd given her his name, she remembered. Officer Blakley. He had a stern face and tired eyes, but he'd given her a blanket.

'We went to the club. Julie and I, we went to the club.'

'Julie Masters.'

'Yes.'

'What club?'

'Warehouse 12. I . . .' She had to tell the truth. No more lies. 'I made fake IDs for us.'

His face barely registered surprise as he wrote in his little book. 'How old are you?'

'Sixteen. I'll be seventeen in September.'

'Sixteen,' he repeated, studying her, voice and eyes flat. 'Where are your parents?'

'It's just my mother. She's out of town at a medical convention.'

'She'll need to be notified.'

Elizabeth only shut her eyes. 'Yes. She's Dr. Susan L. Fitch. She's registered at the Westin Peachtree Plaza hotel, in Atlanta.'

'All right. And you forged identification to gain entrance to Warehouse 12.'

'Yes, I'm sorry. You can arrest me, but you have to find the men who killed Julie.'

'You said you were in a house, not a club.'

'We met Alex at the club. We went to his house. We shouldn't have. We'd been drinking.

59

We shouldn't have. I got sick, then I went outside because . . .' Tears slid down her cheeks again. 'I went outside, and two men came in. They shot Alex, then when Julie came into the room, they shot her. I ran.'

'You don't know where this house is?'

'I could find it. I could take you, or draw you a map. But I didn't look at the address. It was stupid. I was stupid. Please, we can't just leave her there.'

'Do you have this Alex's full name?'

'I . . . Yes!' Thank God. 'Alex, but the man who killed him called him Alexi. Alexi Gurevich.'

Blakley went very still, and his eyes sharpened. 'You're telling me that you were in Alexi Gurevich's house, and witnessed a double murder?'

'Yes. Yes. Yes. Please.'

'Just a minute.' He rose as the second officer came in with the coffee. Blakley murmured to him. Whatever he said had his partner shooting Elizabeth a quick look before he hurried out of the room.

'Given your age,' Blakley told her, 'we're notifying Child Services. A detective will be in to speak with you.'

'But Julie. Can I take you to the house first? I left her. I just left her there.'

'We know where Gurevich lives.'

He left her alone, but within fifteen minutes someone came in and gave her a vending machine cup of chicken soup. She hadn't thought she could eat, but at the first sip her abused stomach begged for more.

Despite the food and the coffee, reaction set in with dragging fatigue. Surrendering, Elizabeth laid her head on the table, closed her eyes.

60

Outside the room, Detective Sean Riley stepped up to the two-way glass beside his partner. 'So that's our wit.'

'Elizabeth Fitch, age sixteen, daughter of Dr. Susan L. Fitch, chief of surgery, Silva Memorial.' Brenda Griffith took a long drink of her Starbucks coffee. She'd been a cop for fifteen years, so calls in the middle of the night were routine. But coffee helped ease the blow. 'CPS is coming in.'

'Have we verified?'

'Gurevich took one to the forehead, two behind the ear. Low-caliber, close-range. Female vic— her ID says Julie Masters—age twenty-one, but according to the wit, the age is bogus. Officers on scene report she took two head shots.'

'Fucking sixteen.' Riley, a twenty-year vet with chronic back pain and thinning brown hair, shook his head. 'She's lucky to be alive.'

'Since she is, let's find out what she knows.' Brenda stepped out. 'Let me take the lead; go soft. If half of what she said in her statement's true, she's had a hell of a night. Here comes CPS.'

'I'll get the kid a Coke or something,' Riley said. 'We'll both start soft.'

Elizabeth woke with a jolt of terror, stared at the woman with the pretty face and black hair hauled back in an explosive ponytail.

'Sorry. I didn't mean to startle you. I'm Detective Griffith. This is Ms. Petrie from Child Services. My partner will be right in. He thought you might want a pop.'

'I fell asleep. How long . . .' She looked at her watch. 'Oh, God. It's nearly morning. Julie—'

'I'm very sorry about your friend.'

'It's my fault. We shouldn't have gone. I knew

61

it was wrong. I just wanted to . . . I forged driver's licenses.'

'So I hear. Can I see yours?'

'All right.' Elizabeth took the license out of her purse.

Griffith studied it, turned it over, lifted her eyebrows, glanced at Elizabeth. 'You're telling me you made this yourself?'

'Yes. I'd been experimenting on how it's done. And Julie wanted to go to Warehouse 12, so I made them. I know it's illegal. There's no excuse. Am I under arrest?'

Griffith glanced at Petrie, then back to Elizabeth. 'I think we'll hold off on that. Were you acquainted with Alexi Gurevich prior to last night?'

'No. He came over to our table. We had Cosmos.' She pressed her hands to her face. 'God, did it really happen? I looked the club up on the Internet before we went. I'd never been to a nightclub. I read some articles that said it was suspected that the owners were part of the Russian Mafia. But I never thought—when he came over, then Ilya—'

'Ilya? Is that Ilya Volkov?'

'Yes. We danced with them, and sat in a booth, and he kissed me. Nobody ever kissed me before. I wanted to know what it was like. He was so nice to me, and then—'

She broke off, that glint of fear back in her eyes when the door opened.

'Elizabeth, this is my partner, Detective Riley.'

'Got you a Coke. My daughter can't live without a Coke in the mornings.'

'Thank you. I'm not supposed to drink . . .' Elizabeth let out a half-laugh. 'That's stupid, isn't it? I drank alcohol until I was sick. I watched two people be murdered. And I don't want to disobey my mother's directive about soft drinks.'

She opened it, poured it into the plastic cup. 'Thank you,' she said again.

'Elizabeth.' Griffith waited until she had Elizabeth's attention again. 'Did you, Julie, Gurevich and Ilya Volkov leave Warehouse 12 and go to Gurevich's residence?'

'No. Just the three of us. Ilya had to take care of something at the club. He was going to come—and he did, but later. After.'

'Did Ilya Volkov murder Gurevich and Julie?'

'No. It was a man named Yakov Korotkii. I can describe him, or do a sketch, or work with a police artist. I remember his face. I remember it very well. I have an eidetic memory. I don't forget. I don't forget,' she repeated, with her voice rising, body shaking.

'Detectives,' Ms. Petrie began. 'Elizabeth has been through a severe trauma. She's had enough for the night.'

'No. No. I need to help. I need to do something.'

'We have her mother's permission to question her,' Griffith stated.

'My mother?'

'She's been notified. She'll fly back in the morning.'

Elizabeth closed her eyes. 'All right.'

'Elizabeth. This is important. How do you know the man who killed Gurevich and Julie was Yakov Korotkii?'

'Alex called him by his last name when they talked. Julie . . . she must have been in the bathroom. I fell asleep for a little while, out on the

63

terrace. Their voices—Alex's and the two men's—woke me.'

'Two men.'

'The other was bigger, burlier. Korotkii called him Yegor. Korotkii said Alex had stolen from his uncle. Alex called him—the uncle—Sergei. He denied it, but he was lying. I could see he was lying. Korotkii, he was . . . Have you seen a cobra kill a mouse? How it watches, so patient. How it seems to enjoy those moments before the strikes as much as the strike itself? It was like that. Alex was dismissive, as if he were in charge. But he wasn't in charge. Korotkii was in charge. And Alex became afraid when Korotkii said they knew he was cooperating with the police. That Sergei knew. He begged. Do you need to know what they said to each other?'

'We'll get back to that.'

'The burly man pushed Alex to his knees. And then Korotkii took a gun from behind his back. He must have had a holster. I didn't see. He shot him here.'

Elizabeth touched her fingers to her forehead.

'He put the gun against his forehead, and he shot him. It wasn't loud at all. Then he shot him twice more. Here.

'I almost screamed. I had to put my hand over my mouth so I wouldn't scream. Korotkii called Alex a . . . It's a very strong Russian oath.'

'You speak Russian.'

'Not fluently. I'd never heard the expression before, but it was . . . self-explanatory. I only mention it because that was how quick it all happened. He called Alex, even though he was dead, a name. Then Julie came in, from the kitchen direction. There's a powder room off the kitchen. She said, "Alex, I don't feel good. We should—" That's all she said. Korotkii turned, and he shot her. She fell. I could see she was dead, but he shot again. And he cursed in Russian. I couldn't hear for a minute. There were screams in my head. I couldn't hear. Then I heard Ilya. I thought they would kill him, too. I wanted to warn him, to help him. And then . . .'

'Take a minute.' Riley spoke gently in what Griffith knew wasn't his going-in-soft voice but sincere concern. 'Take your time.'

'They spoke in Russian, but I could understand all—or nearly all—of it. Ilya was angry, but not so much that Alex was dead.'

She closed her eyes, took a breath, and relayed the conversation she'd heard word for word.

'That's pretty exact,' Riley commented.

'I have an eidetic memory. I ran, because Ilya knew I'd come to the house. I knew he'd ask about me. I knew they'd kill me, too. So I ran. I didn't pay attention to where I ran—I just ran. I left my shoes. I couldn't run in the shoes, the heels, so I left them on the terrace. I didn't think. I just reacted. If I'd thought, I would've taken them with me. They must have found the shoes. So they know I saw. They know I heard.'

'We're going to protect you, Elizabeth. I promise you.' Griffith reached out, laid her hand over Elizabeth's. 'We're going to keep you safe.'

Griffith stepped out of the room with Riley, clamped her hands on her head. 'Jesus Christ, Riley, Jesus Christ on a pogo stick. Do you know what we've got?'

'We've got an eye witness with a memory like

65

a computer, who speaks Russian. We've got motherfucking Korotkii, that slick bastard Ilya Volkov. And if God's good, we'll get Sergei. If she holds up, she'll break the back of the Volkov crew.'

'She'll hold up.' Eyes hard and bright, Griffith glanced toward the door. 'We've got to call in the brass, Riley, get her into a safe house. We're going to need the U.S. Marshals Service.'

'Screw that.'

'We ask, or they take. We ask, we stay in.'

'God damn it, I hate when you make sense. Let's get it started. You know what else I noticed about the witness?'

'What's that?'

'She looked nearly as sick about her mother coming in as she did about the rest of it.'

'I think getting grounded's the least of her worries.'

*   *   *

Elizabeth let it blur. It didn't matter where they took her. She wanted only to sleep. So she slept in the car with the two detectives and Ms. Petrie. When the car stopped, she got out without complaint, all but sleepwalking into a small, clapboard house. She accepted the T-shirt and cotton pants Detective Griffith gave her, even managed to change into them in the small bedroom with the narrow twin bed. She feared her dreams but was powerless against the exhaustion.

She lay on top of the bed, used the cop blanket to cover herself. She felt the tears slide through her lashes as she closed her eyes.

Then she felt nothing.

She woke midday, dry and hollow.

She didn't know what would happen next. All of her life she'd known exactly what was expected of her, when it was expected. But there was no list, no schedule, to lean on now.

It shamed her to be hungry, to wish for coffee, a shower, a toothbrush. Everyday things, ordinary things. Julie would never be hungry again, or do ordinary things.

But she got up, wincing a little as her sore feet hit the floor. She hurt, she realized, all over. She should hurt, she determined. She should be in misery.

Then she remembered her mother. Her mother was coming back, might already be back. That, she decided, would be more punishment than pain and hunger.

Wanting the punishment, she cracked the door open. Listened.

She heard voices—just the rumble of them—smelled coffee. Smelled, she realized with another wince, herself. She wanted the punishment but hoped she could take a shower before it was delivered.

She stepped out, walked toward the sound of the voices.

And froze.

A stranger stood in the small white-and-yellow kitchen. A tall man, almost gangly, he poured coffee from a carafe into a thick white mug. He paused in the act of it, smiled at her.

He wore jeans, a white shirt—and a shoulder holster.

'Good morning. Or afternoon. I'm Deputy U.S. Marshal John Barrow. It's all right, Elizabeth.

We're here to keep you safe.'

'You're a U.S. Marshal.'

'That's right. Later today, we're going to take you to another safe house.'

'Is Detective Griffith here?'

'She'll be here later. She got you some clothes, some things.' He paused for another moment when Elizabeth only stared at him. 'You gave her your key, told her it was all right if she went to your house, got you some clothes, your toothbrush, that sort of thing.'

'Yes. I remember.'

'I bet you could use some coffee, some aspirin.'

'I . . . I'd like to take a shower, if that's all right.'

'Sure.' He smiled again, set the carafe and mug down. He had blue eyes but not like her mother's. His were a deeper tone, and warm.

'I'll get your bag. I'm here with Deputy Marshal Theresa Norton. I want you to feel secure, Elizabeth—do they call you Liz?'

Tears stung the back of her eyes. 'Julie called me Liz. Julie did.'

'I'm sorry about your friend. You've had a rough time of it, Liz. Theresa and I are going to look out for you.'

'They'll kill me if they find me. I know that.'

Those warm blue eyes looked straight into hers. 'They won't find you. And I won't let them hurt you.'

She wanted to believe him. He had a good face. Thin, like the rest of him, almost scholarly. 'How long do I have to hide?'

'Let's take it a day at a time for now. I'll get your stuff.'

She stood exactly where she was until he came

back, carrying her travel Pullman.

'Why don't I fix up some food while you're cleaning up,' he suggested. 'I'm a better cook than Terry. That's not saying much, but I won't poison you.'

'Thank you. If it's no trouble.'

'It's not.'

'I'm sorry. I don't know where the shower is.'

'That way.' He pointed. 'Then hang a right.'

He watched her go, then picked up his coffee, stared into it. He set it down again when his partner walked in from the outside.

'She's up,' he said. 'Jesus, Terry, she looked closer to twelve than twenty-one. She should never have gotten in that club.'

'You saw the ID she forged. She could make a living.' Small, tough, pretty as a daisy, Terry hit the coffeepot. 'How's she holding up?'

'By one rough strand of grit, if you ask me. Polite as your great-aunt Martha.'

'If I had a great-aunt Martha, she'd be a bitch on wheels.'

'She never asked about her mother. About Griffith, but not her own mother. That tells you something. I'm going to fix her some bacon and eggs.'

He pulled open the refrigerator, got out what he needed.

'Do you want me to contact the prosecutor? You know he wants to talk to her asap.'

'Let's give her time to get some food in her belly. But, yeah, better if he meets with her here before we move her. And better if she has a little time before she realizes she could be living in a safe house for months.'

'Maybe years. How could somebody smart enough to be going to Harvard—at sixteen, no less—get herself mixed up with the Volkovs?'

'Sometimes being sixteen's enough.' John laid bacon in the skillet, set it sizzling.

'I'll make the call. Tell them two hours—give her time to get dressed, eat, settle.'

'Check on the mother's ETA while you're at it.'

'Will do.'

5

By the time Elizabeth came back in, wearing jeans and a blue tank with a thin froth of lace at the edges, he'd piled a plate with bacon, eggs, toast.

'Did Detective Griffith pack everything you needed?'

'Yes. I wasn't sure what to do with the suitcase. You said we weren't staying here.'

'Don't worry about it. Eat while it's hot.'

She stared at the plate. 'That's a lot of food.' Bacon? Her nutritionist would have a heart attack.

The idea of the reaction made her smile.

'You look hungry.'

'I am.' The smile stayed in place when she looked up at him. 'I'm not supposed to eat bacon.'

'Why?'

'Processed meat, sodium, animal fat. It's not on my approved list. My mother and my nutritionist have devised a very specific meal plan.'

'Is that so? Well, it's a shame to let it go to waste.'

'It would be.' The scent drew her to the table.

'And you went to the trouble to cook it for me.' She sat, picked up a slice of bacon, took a bite. Closed her eyes. 'It's good.'

'Everything's better with bacon.' He set a tall glass of juice and three Tylenol beside her plate. 'Take those, drink that. I can see the hangover.'

Now the smile fell away. 'We shouldn't have been drinking.'

'No, you shouldn't have. Do you always do what you should do?'

'Yes. I mean, before yesterday. And if I'd done what I should have yesterday, Julie would be alive.'

'Liz, Julie's dead because Yakov Korotkii is a murderer, because the Volkovs are very bad people. You and Julie did something stupid. She didn't deserve to die for it. And you're not responsible. Take the Tylenol, drink the juice. Eat.'

She obeyed more out of the habit of obedience than desire now. But, oh, the food was so good, so comforting.

'Will you tell me what happens now? I don't know what happens now, and it's easier to know what I'm expected to do.'

He brought his coffee to the table, sat down with her. 'A lot of what happens next depends on you.'

'Because my testimony as to what happened, what I saw, what I heard, will be necessary to convict Yakov Korotkii on the murder charges, and the other man as his accomplice. And Ilya as an accessory after the fact. Also, it could implicate Sergei Volkov, though that may be hearsay, I'm not clear on that. He would be the most desired target, as it appears he's the head, or one of the heads, of the organization.'

John leaned back in his chair. 'You seem to have

71

a solid grasp on the situation, as it stands.'

'I've been monitoring some criminal justice courses, and doing a lot of reading.'

'Since yesterday?'

'No.' She nearly laughed, but it caught in her throat. 'Since I started college. I'm interested.'

'But you're studying to be a doctor.'

She looked down at her plate, carefully scooped up a bite of scrambled egg. 'Yes.'

He got up, opened the fridge again, took out a Coke for himself, then a second. He cocked a brow in question.

'I'm not supposed to— Yes, please. I'd like a Coke.'

He opened both, then sat as a compact woman with blond hair in a sleek ponytail stepped in. 'Liz, this is Deputy Marshal Norton. Terry, Liz.'

'How're you doing today, Liz?'

'Better, thank you.'

'Liz was just asking about the process, though she seems to have a handle on it. Terry's contacted the U.S. Attorney's Office. You'll have a representative from Child Services present while they talk to you, if your mother hasn't arrived by that time. Your cooperation is voluntary, Liz, but—'

'I could be held as a material witness. It won't be necessary. I have to cooperate, I have to testify. Will you tell me if the Volkovs are Russian Mafia?'

'What we believe and what we can prove—'

'I want to know what you believe,' Elizabeth interrupted. 'I think I should know my situation. I may be a minor, legally, but I'm not a child. I have an IQ of two hundred and ten, and excellent comprehension skills. I know I behaved foolishly, but I'm not foolish. I understand if I witnessed

72

murders carried out on orders of what would be the *pakhan*—the boss—I'm a target. If I testify, Korotkii or one like him will do whatever can be done to stop me. Even after I testify, and particularly if my testimony leads to convictions, I'll be a target. In retribution.'

She paused, took a sip of Coke right from the can. Amazing.

'I was impaired last night—this morning, more accurately. From drinking, being sick, then from shock. I didn't fully assess the situation. But I have now. If the Volkovs are simply very bad men, a loosely formed gang of thugs and criminals, it's a difficult situation. If they are organized crime, if they are Red Mafia, it's much more. I want to know.'

She watched the two deputies exchange a look.

'Once I'm able to access a computer,' Elizabeth added, 'I'll be able to research and find the answer for myself.'

'I bet you could,' John murmured. 'We believe— hell, we know—the Volkovs are organized crime. We know they're heavily involved in weapons and human trafficking, in computer fraud—a specialty—in protection, theft, drugs. They're a wide-reaching organization, with considerable legitimate—or legitimate enough—interests, such as nightclubs, restaurants, strip joints and real estate. Law enforcement's been able to peck away a bit, but the hierarchy hasn't been touched. We know Korotkii is Sergei Volkov's mechanic—his hit man. But we've never been able to pin him.'

'He liked killing Alex. He felt great contempt for Alex. With Julie . . . killing Julie annoyed him. Nothing more, nothing less. I'm sorry, I can't finish

73

the food.'

'It's okay.'

She looked down at her hands for a moment, then back up into John's eyes. 'I won't be able to go back to Harvard. I won't be able to go home again. If I testify, I'll have to go into the Witness Protection Program. Isn't that what will happen?'

'You're getting a little ahead of yourself,' Terry told her.

'I always think ahead. I didn't last night, and there was a terrible price. Would I be able to go to another university, under another name?'

'We could make that work,' John said. 'We take good care of our witnesses, Liz. You can look that up on the computer, too.'

'I will. They don't know who I am. I mean to say I only told Ilya my first name. He only knew Liz— and really it's always been Elizabeth. And I . . . before we went to the club, I cut and dyed my hair. I don't look like this.'

'Like the hair,' Terry said. 'It's a good look for you.'

'I look very different. Last night with makeup, and the dress, the hair, I looked very different than I did. Maybe there's a way to give testimony without them finding out who I am. I know it's a slim chance, but I'd like to try to believe that. For now, anyway.'

Terry shifted as her cell phone beeped. She pulled it from the case on her belt. 'Norton. Yeah. Copy that.'

She replaced the phone. 'They're bringing your mom in.'

'All right.' Rising, Elizabeth took her plate to the sink. 'I'll do the dishes.'

'I'll give you a hand,' John said.

'No. If you don't mind, I'd like a little time alone before my mother gets here.'

'Sure.' He laid a hand on her shoulder. 'It'll be all right, Liz.'

She only nodded and kept her hands busy, out of sight. So no one could see them tremble.

By the time the plainclothes officers brought her mother to the door, she felt she had herself under control. In the sparsely furnished living room, Elizabeth got to her feet as Susan came in. One look told her the apology she'd practiced would be far from adequate.

'For God's sake, Elizabeth, what have you done to your hair?'

'I . . .' Thrown off balance, Elizabeth lifted a hand to her hair. 'I'm sorry.'

'I'm sure you are.'

'Dr. Fitch, I'm Deputy Marshal Barrow, and this is Deputy Marshal Norton. We understand this is a very difficult situation. If we could sit down, we'll explain exactly what precautions we're taking to protect your daughter.'

'That won't be necessary. I've already been briefed. If you'll excuse us, I'd like to speak to my daughter alone.'

'I'm sorry, Dr. Fitch, for her protection, it's necessary for at least one of us to remain with Elizabeth at all times.'

Elizabeth glanced his way, wondered why he'd left her alone in the kitchen.

'Very well. Sit down, Elizabeth.' Susan remained standing. 'There are no acceptable explanations, no rational reasoning, for your behavior. If the facts have been related to me accurately, you broke the law by forging documents you used to gain entrance to a nightclub with another minor. Where you consumed alcohol. Are these facts accurate?'

'Yes. Yes, they're accurate.'

'You compounded this by showing yet more poor judgment by accompanying a man you'd just met to his home. Did you engage in sexual relations with this man?'

'No.'

'It's imperative you answer truthfully, as you may have contracted an STD or become pregnant.'

'I didn't have sex with anyone.'

Susan eyed her as coldly as she might a specimen under a microscope. 'I'm unable to trust your word. You'll submit to an examination as soon as possible. Actions have consequences, Elizabeth, as you know very well.'

'I didn't have sex with anyone,' Elizabeth said flatly. 'Julie had sex with Alex, and now she's dead. It seems the consequence is too harsh for the action.'

'By your actions you put yourself and this other girl in serious jeopardy.'

The words were like stones, hurled at her limbs, cracking bone.

'I know. I have no excuse.'

'Because there is none. Now a girl is dead, and you're under police protection. You may also face criminal charges—'

'Dr. Fitch,' John interrupted. 'Let me assure you and Elizabeth. There will be no charges.'

'Is that for you to decide?' she snapped, then turned straight back to Elizabeth. 'I'm aware that girls of your age often show poor judgment, often defy authority. I made allowances for that in our

76

conversation before I left for Atlanta. But I expect better than this debacle from someone with your intellect, your resources, your upbringing. It's only through the whims of providence you weren't killed.'

'I ran away.'

'At last showing common sense. Now, get your things. I'll arrange for one of the gynecologists on staff to examine you before we go home.'

'But . . . I can't go home.'

'This is a poor time to exhibit misplaced independence.'

'Elizabeth is under the protection of the U.S. Marshals Service,' John began. 'She's the only witness to a double homicide. The man who committed those homicides is suspected of being an assassin in the Volkov *bratva*. That's Russian Mafia, Dr. Fitch, if those facts weren't related to you.'

'I'm aware of what Elizabeth reported to the police.'

Elizabeth knew that tone—the chief-of-surgery tone that demanded no nonsense, brooked no argument, accepted no discussion.

'I'm also told she wasn't seen by this man, and her name is unknown to him and his associates. I intend to take my daughter home, where she will be properly disciplined for her unfortunate behavior.'

'You can intend anything you want, Dr. Fitch, but Liz is under the protection of the U.S. Marshals Service.'

John spoke so calmly, so matter-of-factly, Elizabeth could only stare at him.

'She'll be moved from this location tonight, to one we feel is more secure. Your residence is not a secure location, and her safety is our priority. As I

77

assume it would be yours.'

'I have the resources to hire private security, if necessary. I've contacted my lawyer. Elizabeth can't be forced to testify on this matter.'

'They're not forcing me. I've agreed to testify.'

'Your judgment continues to be poor. This is my decision.'

He'd called her Liz, Elizabeth thought. He'd called her Liz and defied Dr. Susan L. Fitch's directive—to her face. So she would *be* Liz. She wouldn't crumble like Elizabeth.

'No, it's not.' The world did not end when she spoke the words. 'I have to testify. I can't go home.'

A flash of shock overlaid the brutally cold anger on Susan's face. 'Do you have any concept of the consequences of *this*? You won't be able to participate in the summer program, or study at Harvard in the fall. You'll both delay and impair your education, and you'll put your life, your *life*, Elizabeth, into the hands of people whose true agenda is to convict this man, at whatever cost to you.'

'Julie's dead.'

'Nothing can change that, but this decision could ruin your life, your plans, your future.'

'How can I just go home as if none of this happened? Go back to my life? And your plans, because they've never been mine. If their agenda is to convict the murderers, I accept that. Yours is for me to do nothing, to obey, to live the life you've designed for me. I can't. I can't do that anymore. I have to try to do what's right. That's the consequence, Mother. And I have to accept the consequence.'

'You'll only compound your mistake.'

'Dr. Fitch,' John began. 'The federal prosecutor is coming here to talk with Liz—'

'Elizabeth.'

'You'll hear what he has to say. What steps will be taken. You can take a little time. I understand this is a shock. We'll move you and your daughter to the new location, where you can take a few days to consider, to talk.'

'I have no intention of going anywhere with you, and am under no obligation to go anywhere with you. I expect you'll come to your senses in a day or two,' she said to Elizabeth. 'Once you realize the limits of your current circumstances, and the true scope of those consequences. I'll tell Dr. Frisco you're ill, and will catch up on the work. Think carefully, Elizabeth. There are steps taken that can never be undone.'

She waited, her mouth flattening when Elizabeth failed to respond.

'Contact me when you're ready to come home. Deputies,' she said, and walked to the door.

John beat her to it. 'One moment, Doctor.' He picked up his radio. 'Barrow. Dr. Fitch is coming out. She'll need to be escorted to her residence.'

'Copy that. We're clear out here.'

'You don't approve of my decision in this situation,' Susan said.

'You don't need or want my approval, but no. Not by a long shot.'

'You're right. I neither need nor want your approval.' She walked out without a backward glance.

When he stepped back, he saw Terry sitting on the arm of Elizabeth's chair, a hand lightly laid on the girl's shoulder.

'People react to fear and worry in different ways,' he began.

'She wasn't afraid or worried, or not primarily. Primarily, she's angry and inconvenienced. I understand that.'

'She was wrong,' Terry told her. 'I know she's your mom, but she was way off base.'

'She's never wrong, and she's never been a mom. Is it all right if I go to my room for a while?'

'Sure. But, Liz,' John added when she got up, 'nobody's never wrong.'

'Bitch,' Terry said under her breath when Elizabeth left the room. 'Coldhearted bitch, coming in here, not one fucking hair out of place, kicking that girl at a time like this.'

'She never touched her,' John murmured. 'She never put her arms around that kid, never asked how she was, never said she was glad she wasn't hurt. Jesus Christ, if that girl's life's been like that, witness protection might be an upgrade.'

*   *   *

Elizabeth spent two hours with Mr. Pomeroy from the U.S. Attorney's Office. She had to go through it all again, every step of the night, this time with interruptions that demanded clarifications, made her backtrack, jump forward, go back again. With him were three others, all in dark suits. One of them took notes, even though they recorded the interview.

Detectives Riley and Griffith had come, too, so the house felt very small, very crowded.

At one point, Pomeroy eased back in his chair, frowned.

'Now, Elizabeth, you admit you'd had several alcoholic drinks. How many? Three, four? More?'

'A little more than four. I couldn't finish the last. When we got to Alex's, I had some water. He made me another drink, but I didn't want it. I didn't feel well.'

'And in fact got sick. After you were sick, you fell asleep out on the terrace. How often do you drink?'

'I don't. I mean to say I've had small amounts of wine, as my mother believes I should develop a sophisticated palate, but I'd never had a mixed drink before.'

'So it was your first experience with that kind of alcohol, and you consumed nearly five glasses throughout the evening, became ill, slept—or passed out—outside. Yet you claim you can identify the individuals who entered the home and shot Alexi Gurevich and Julie Masters? And at what distance?'

'About ten feet. But I can be sure. I saw them very clearly. They were in the light.'

'Wouldn't you have been impaired after knocking back all that alcohol, after partying yourself sick?'

Shamed, she stared down at the hands she had clutched in her lap. 'I'm sure my reaction time was impaired, and surely my judgment. But not my eyesight or hearing.'

Pomeroy nodded at one of the men with him. The man stepped forward, laid several photographs on the table.

'Do you recognize any of these men?' he asked her.

'Yes.' She pointed to one at the right corner of the layout. 'That's Yakov Korotkii. That's the man

81

who shot Alex, then Julie. His hair's longer in the photograph.'

'Do you know this man?' Pomeroy asked her. 'Had you met him before?'

'I never met him. I only saw him, and only last night, when he shot Alex and Julie.'

'All right.' Pomeroy picked up that set of photos, and the man set down another pile. 'Do you recognize anyone here?'

'This man. They called him Yegor. I don't know the rest of his name. He was with Korotkii. He restrained Alex, then pushed him down to his knees.'

'And once more.' Again, the photos were removed, others laid out.

'That's Ilya.' Because her lips trembled, she pressed them tight. 'Ilya Volkov. He came in after . . . after Julie and Alex were dead. Only a few minutes after. He was angry. He spoke in Russian.'

'How do you know he was angry?'

'I speak Russian, not very well. They said . . . this is translated. Is that all right?'

'Yes.'

She took a breath, relayed the conversation.

'Then I ran. I knew they'd start looking for me, and if they found me, they'd kill me because I'd seen. When I stopped running, I called nine-one-one.'

'That's good. You did very well, Elizabeth. We're going to arrest these men. It may be necessary for you to identify them again, in a lineup. They won't be able to see you.'

'Yes, I know.'

'Your testimony will help put very dangerous men behind bars. The U.S. Attorney's Office is very grateful.'

'You're welcome.'

He smiled at that. 'We'll talk again. We'll be seeing a lot of each other over the next weeks. If you need anything, Elizabeth, anything at all, one of the marshals will get it for you, or you can contact me. We want you to be as comfortable as possible.'

'Thank you.'

Tension she hadn't been aware of melted away when he left.

As Terry had earlier, Griffith sat on the arm of her chair. 'He was tough on you because it's going to be hard. What you're doing, what the defense team will do to discredit your testimony. It's not going to be an easy road.'

'I know. Are you still part of the investigation?'

'It's a joint investigation, because Riley and me pushed for it. It's the feds' ball, but we're still on the court. How are you holding up?'

'I'm all right. Everyone's been very considerate. Thank you for getting my things.'

'No problem. Do you need anything else?'

'I'd like my laptop. I should have asked you before, but I wasn't thinking clearly.'

'You're not going to be able to e-mail anyone, go into chat rooms, post on boards.'

'It's not for that. I want to study, and research. If I could have my computer, some of my books . . .'

'I'll check it out.'

That had to be good enough.

When night fell, they put her in a car with John and Terry. Griffith and Riley drove behind; more marshals took the lead.

As they sped along the expressway, it occurred to her that only twenty-four hours ago she'd put on her new red dress, her high, sparkling shoes.

And Julie, eyes bright, voice giddy, had sat beside her in a cab. Alive.

Everything had been so different.

Now everything was different again.

They pulled directly into the garage of a simple two-story house with a wide, deep yard. But for the car, the garage stood empty—no tools, no boxes, no debris.

The door leading to the interior boasted a deadlock.

The man who opened the door had some gray threaded through his dark brown hair. Though nearly as tall as John, he was more filled out—muscular in jeans and a polo shirt, his weapon holstered at his side.

He stepped back so they could enter the kitchen—bigger than the one they'd just left. The appliances more modern, the floor a buff-colored tile.

'Liz, this is Deputy Marshal Cosgrove.'

'Bill.' He extended a hand and an encouraging smile to Elizabeth. 'Welcome home. Deputy Peski—that's Lynda—is doing a perimeter check. We'll be keeping you safe tonight.'

'Oh . . . But—'

'We'll be back in the morning,' John told her. 'But we'll get you settled in before we go.'

'Why don't I take you up, show you your room,' Terry suggested, and before Elizabeth could agree or protest, Terry had picked up her suitcase and started out.

'She looks younger than I figured,' Bill commented.

'She's worn out, still a little glazed over. But the

84

kid's solid. She held up to two hours with Pomeroy without one fumble. A jury's going to love her.'

'A teenage girl taking down the Volkovs.' Bill shook his head. 'Go figure.'

*   *   *

Sergei Volkov was in his prime, a wealthy man who'd come from wretched poverty. By the age of ten he'd been an accomplished thief who'd known every corner, every rat hole, in his miserable ghetto in Moscow. He'd killed his first man at thirteen, gutting him with an American-made combat knife he'd stolen from a rival. He'd broken the arm of the rival, a wily boy of sixteen.

He still had the knife.

He'd risen through the ranks of the Moscow *bratva,* becoming a brigadier before his eighteenth birthday.

Ambition had driven him higher until, with his brother Mikhail, he'd taken over the *bratva* in a merciless, bloody coup even as the Soviet Union crumbled. It was, in Sergei's mind, a moment of opportunity and change.

He married a woman with a lovely face and a taste for finer things. She'd given him two daughters, and he'd been amazed at how deeply he'd loved them from their first breath. He'd wept when he'd held each child for the first time, overcome with joy and wonder and pride.

But when, at last, he'd held his son, there were no tears. That joy, that wonder and pride, were too deep for tears.

His children, his love and ambition for them, pushed him to emigrate to America. There he could present them with opportunities, with a richer life.

And he'd deemed it time to expand.

He'd seen his oldest child married to a lawyer, and had held his first grandchild. And wept. He'd set up his younger daughter—his artist, his dreamer—in her own gallery.

But his son, ah, his son, his businessman with a degree from the University of Chicago, there was his legacy. His boy was smart, strong, clearheaded, cool-blooded.

All the hopes and hungers of the young boy in the Moscow ghetto had been realized in the son.

He worked now in his shade garden of his Gold Coast estate, waiting for Ilya to arrive. Sergei was a hard and handsome man with shocks of white waving through his dark hair, thick black brows over onyx eyes. He kept himself rigorously fit and satisfied his wife, his mistress and the occasional whore.

His gardens were another source of pride. He had landscapers and groundskeepers, of course, but spent hours a week when he could puttering, digging in the dirt, planting some new specimen with his own hands.

If he hadn't become a *pakhan*, Sergei believed he might have lived a happy, very simple life as a gardener.

In his baggy shorts, the star tattoos on his knees grubby with earth and mulch, he continued to dig as he heard his son approach.

'Chicken shit,' Sergei said. 'It's cheap, easy to come by, and it makes the plants very happy.'

Confounded, as always, by his father's love of dirt, Ilya shook his head. 'And smells like chicken shit.'

'A small price to pay. My hostas enjoy, and see there? The lungwort will bloom soon. So many secrets in the shade and shadows.'

Sergei looked up then, squinting a bit. 'So. Have you found her?'

'Not yet. We will. I have a man checking at Harvard. We'll have her name soon, and from there, we'll have her.'

'Women lie, Ilya.'

'I don't think she lied about this. She studies medicine there, and is unhappy. Her mother, a surgeon, here in Chicago. I believe this is also true. We're looking for the mother.'

Ilya crouched down. 'I won't go to prison.'

'No, you won't go to prison. Nor will Yakov. I work on other avenues as well. But I'm not pleased one of my most valued brigadiers sits now in a cell.'

'He won't talk.'

'This doesn't worry me. He will say nothing, as Yegor will say nothing. The American police? *Musor.*' He dismissed them as garbage with a flick of the wrist. 'They will never break such as these. Nor would they break you if we were not able to convince the judge on the bail. But this girl, she worries me. It worries me, Ilya, that she was there and lives. It worries me that Yakov had no knowledge she and the other were there.'

'If I hadn't been delayed, I would have been there, and would have stopped it. Then there would be no witness.'

'Communication, this was a problem. And is also been dealt with.'

'You said to keep an eye on him, Papa, to stay close to him until he could be disciplined for stealing.'

Ilya shoved up, yanked off his sunglasses. 'I would have cut off his hand myself for stealing from the family. You gave him everything, but all he thinks of is more. More money, more drugs, more women, more show. My cousin. *Suki.*' He snarled the word for traitor. 'He spits in our faces, again and again. You were good to him, Papa.'

'The son of your mother's cousin. How could I not do my best? Still, I had hopes.'

'You took him in, him and Yakov.'

'And Yakov has proven himself worthy of that gift time and again. Alexi?' Sergei shrugged. 'Chicken shit,' he said with half a smile. 'Now he'll be fertilizer. The drugs. He was weak for them. This is why I was strict with you and your sisters. Drugs are business only. For drugs—that is the root—he steals from us, betrays us and his own blood.'

'If I'd known, I'd have been there, to watch him beg like a woman. To watch him die.'

'The information on his arrest, on the deal the bastard made with the cops, only came to us that night. He had to be dealt with quickly. I sent Yakov and Yegor to check his house, to see if he was there. So perhaps he was dealt with too quickly. Mistakes were made, as the Americans say. You've not been one to whore with Alexi in the past. His taste was always less refined than yours.'

'I was to stay close,' Ilya repeated. 'And the girl, she was intriguing. Fresh, unspoiled. Sad. A little sad. I liked her.'

'There are plenty of others. She's already dead. Now you'll stay for supper. It will please your mother, and me.'

'Of course.'

6

Two weeks passed, then the start of another. Elizabeth could count on one hand the number of times she'd been allowed to leave the house. And never alone.

She was never alone.

She, who'd once longed for companionship, now found the lack of solitude more confining than the four walls of her room.

She had her laptop. They'd blocked her access to e-mail and chat boards. Out of boredom and curiosity, she hacked through the blocks. Not that she planned to contact anyone, but it gave her a sense of accomplishment.

She kept that small triumph to herself.

She had nightmares, and kept them to herself as well.

They brought her books, and music CDs. She only had to ask. Devouring the popular fiction and music her mother so strongly disapproved of should have given her a sense of freedom. Instead, it only served to highlight how much she'd missed, and how little she knew of the real world.

Her mother never came.

Every morning John and Terry relieved the night shift, and every evening Bill and Lynda relieved them. Sometimes they made food; breakfast seemed to be John's specialty. For the most part, they brought it in. Pizza or burgers, chicken or Chinese. Out of guilt—and partially out of defense—Elizabeth began to experiment in the kitchen. Recipes were just formulas, as far as she could see. The kitchen a kind of laboratory.

And in experimenting, she found an affinity. She liked the chopping and stirring, the scents, the textures.

'What's on the menu?'

From her seat at the table, Elizabeth glanced up as John walked in. 'I thought I might try this stir-fry chicken.'

'Sounds good.' He got himself coffee. 'My wife does stir-fry to trick the kids into eating vegetables.'

She knew he and his wife, Maddie, had two children. A seven-year-old boy, Maxfield, named for the painter Maxfield Parrish, and Emily—for Emily Brontë—age five.

He'd shown her pictures, the ones from his wallet, and told her funny little stories about them.

To personalize himself; she understood that. And it had, but it also forced her to realize there were no funny little stories about her as a child.

'Do they worry about you? Being in law enforcement?'

'Max and Em? They're too young to worry. They know I chase bad guys, and that's about as far as it goes right now. Maddie?' He sat with his coffee. 'Yeah, some. It's part of the package. And it can be tough on her, the long hours, the time away from home.'

'You said she was a court reporter.'

'Yeah, until Max came along. Best day of my life, that day in court. Even though I could barely remember my own name with her sitting there. Most beautiful woman I'd ever seen. I don't know how I got lucky enough to talk her into going out with me, much less marrying me.'

'You're a very solid man,' Elizabeth began.

90

'Physically attractive. You're kind and have a broad worldview, varied interests. And the fact that you're in a position of authority, carry a weapon, can be attractive to a woman on a visceral level.'

His eyes laughed at her over his coffee. 'You're like nobody else, Liz.'

'I wish I were.'

'Don't. You're a stand-up girl, scary smart, brave, compassionate—and you have varied interests as well. I can't keep up with the variety. Science, law enforcement, health and nutrition, music, books, now cooking. Who knows what's next?'

'Will you teach me to handle a gun?'

He lowered his coffee. 'Where did that come from?'

'It could be one of my varied interests.'

'Liz.'

'I'm having nightmares.'

'Oh, honey.' He laid a hand over hers. 'Talk to me.'

'I dream about that night. I know it's a normal reaction, an expected one.'

'That doesn't make it easier.'

'It doesn't.' She stared down at the cookbook, wondered if her world would ever be as simple as ingredients and measurements again.

'And I dream about going in, to do the lineup. Only he sees me, Korotkii. I know he sees me, because he smiles. And he reaches behind his back, like he did that night. And everything slows down when he takes out the gun. Nobody reacts. He shoots me through the glass.'

'He didn't see you, Liz.'

'I know. That's rational and logical. But this is about fear and emotion—subconscious fears and

91

emotions. I try not to dwell on it, try to keep busy and occupied.'

'Why don't I contact your mother?'

'Why?'

The genuine puzzlement had him biting back an oath. 'You know we have a psychologist available for you. You said you didn't want to talk to one before, but—'

'I still don't. What's the point? I understand what's happening, and why. I know it's a process my mind has to go through. But he kills me, you see. Either at the house because in the dreams he finds me, or at the lineup because he sees right through the glass. I'm afraid he'll find me, he'll see me, he'll kill me. And I feel helpless. I have no power, no weapon. I can't defend myself. I want to be able to defend myself. I don't want to be helpless.'

'And you think learning to shoot will help you feel more in control, less vulnerable?'

'I think it's one answer.'

'Then I'll teach you.' He took out his weapon, pulled out the magazine, and set it aside. 'This is a Glock 19. It's standard-issue. It holds fifteen rounds in this magazine.'

Elizabeth took it when he offered. 'It's polymer. I looked it up.'

'Of course you did.'

'It's not as heavy as I thought it would be. But it's not loaded, so that accounts for some of the weight.'

'We'll keep it unloaded for now. Let's talk about safety.'

She looked up, into his eyes. 'All right.'

After some basics, he had her stand, showed her how to sight, how to grip. And Terry walked in.

'Jesus Christ, John.'

'It's not loaded,' Elizabeth said quickly.

'I repeat, Jesus Christ.'

'Give us a minute, Liz.'

'Oh. All right.' More reluctant than she'd imagined, she gave the gun back to John. 'I'll be in my room.'

'What the hell are you thinking?' Terry demanded the minute Elizabeth left the room.

'She wants to learn how to handle a gun.'

'Well, I want George Clooney naked in my bed, but I haven't attempted kidnapping. Yet.'

'She's having nightmares, Terry.'

'Crap.' Terry wrenched open the refrigerator, got out a Coke. 'I'm sorry, John, this all seriously sucks for that kid. But letting her handle your service weapon isn't an answer.'

'She thinks it is. She doesn't want to feel defenseless. Who can blame her? We can tell her all day long she's safe, we'll protect her, but she's still powerless. It's not just about what we tell her, but what she feels.'

'I know that, John, I know. I understand she's scared, and she's got to be bored out of her mind. We can't change that, not really.'

'Her life's never going to be the same, Terry, and we can't forget that, either. We can't forget she's not just the witness, she's a teenage girl. If learning proper gun safety and operation helps her, then I'm going to see she gets taught. Because the least she deserves is a decent night's sleep.'

'Crap,' Terry repeated. 'Okay, I get it. I do. But . . .'

'But?'

'I'm thinking.'

'Good, keep doing that. I'm going to try out the line that worked on you on the boss. I want to get clearance to take her into the range.'

'Rub a lamp while you're at it. That may help.'

John just smiled and, taking out his phone, walked into the next room.

Terry huffed out a breath. After a moment's consideration, she got out a second Coke, then walked upstairs to Elizabeth's bedroom. She knocked.

'Come in.'

'Playing with guns always makes me thirsty.' Terry walked over to the bed where Elizabeth sat, handed her the Coke.

'I hope you're not angry with John. It was my fault.'

'I'm not mad.' Terry sat beside her. 'It caught me off guard, that's all. John told me you're having nightmares. You're scared. I can tell you not to be, but the truth is, in your place I'd be scared, too.'

'I couldn't do anything. In the nightmares, I can't do anything, either, so he kills me, too. I want to learn how to take care of myself. You won't always be there. You and John or Bill and Lynda. Or whoever they send. One day, you won't be there, and I have to know I can take care of myself. My mother won't go.'

'You don't know—'

'I do know.' She said it calmly, without emotion, surprised she felt calm and emotionless. 'When it comes time for you to relocate me, give me a new identity, she won't go with me. Her life's here, her career. I'll be seventeen soon. I can file for emancipation if I need to. I would get it. When I turn eighteen, I'll have some money from my trust fund. And more when I'm twenty-one. I can study, and I can work. I can cook a little now. But I can't defend myself if something happens.'

'You're smart enough to have done some research on the program. We haven't lost a witness who's followed our security guidelines.'

'I've followed someone else's guidelines my entire life, so I'm used to that.'

'Oh, Liz. Hell.'

'That was passive-aggressive,' Elizabeth said with a sigh. 'I'm sorry. But the point is, they'll never stop looking for me. They believe in revenge and restitution. I know you'll do everything you can to keep them from finding me, but I need to know, if the worst happened, if they did find me, I could fight back.'

'There are more ways to fight back than with a gun.'

'And yet you carry one.'

'Two.' Terry tapped her ankle. 'Approved backup weapon. If you want to learn how to shoot, John's your man. But there are more ways. I could teach you some self-defense. Hand to hand.'

Intrigued, Elizabeth sat back. 'Actual fighting?'

'I was thinking more defensive moves, but, yeah, fighting back.'

'I'd like to learn. I'm a good student.'

'We'll see about that.'

John came to the open door. 'Five a.m. Be ready. We've got permission to use the range.'

'Thank you. So much.'

'Terry?'

'Five. In the morning. Hell. I'm in.'

*　　　*　　　*

95

Three times a week before the sun rose, John took her to the basement range. She grew accustomed to the feel of the gun in her hands, the shape, the weight, the recoil. He taught her to aim for body mass, to group her shots, to reload.

When she learned the trial had been delayed, she vented her frustration on the range.

On alternate days, Terry instructed her in self-defense. She learned how to use her opponent's weight and balance to her advantage, how to break a hold, how to punch from the shoulder.

The nightmares still came, but not every night. And sometimes, in them, she won.

As the first month passed, her old life seemed less hers. She lived in the spare, two-story house with the high security fence, and slept each night with federal marshals on guard.

Lynda lent Elizabeth romance novels, mysteries, horror fiction out of her own collection. While summer burned through to August, Lynda cut Elizabeth's hair again—with considerable more skill—and showed her how to retouch the roots. On long, quiet evenings, Bill taught her to play poker.

And the time dragged like eternity.

'I'd like to have some money,' she told John.

'You need a loan, kid?'

'No, but thank you. I'd like my own money. I have a savings account, and I want to withdraw some.'

'Taking you to the bank would involve unnecessary risk. If you need something, we'll get it for you.'

'My mother could withdraw it. It's like the gun. It's for security.' She'd thought it through. She had

96

time to think everything through. 'When I finally testify, and I'm relocated, I think it'll happen quickly. I'd like to have money—my own money—when it happens. I want to know I can buy what I need and not feel obligated to ask.'

'How much did you have in mind?'

'Five thousand.'

'That's a lot of money, Liz.'

'Not really. I'm going to need a new computer, and other supplies. I want to think about tomorrow instead of today. Today just keeps being today.'

'It's frustrating, I know, having to wait.'

'They'll delay as long as they can, hoping to find me. Or hoping I'll lose courage. But they can't delay forever. I have to think about the rest of my life. Wherever that is, whoever I'll be. I want to go back to school. I have a college fund that would have to be transferred. But there are other expenses.'

'Let me see what I can do.'

She smiled. 'I like when you say that. With my mother, it's always yes or no. She rarely, if ever, says maybe, because maybe is indecisive. You say you'll see what you can do, which isn't maybe, isn't indecisive. It means you'll take some action. You'll try. It's much better than no, and almost as good as yes.'

'All that.' He hesitated a moment. 'You never mention your father. I know he's not in the picture, but under the circumstances—'

'I don't know who he is. He was a donor.'

'A donor?'

'Yes. When my mother decided to have a child, to have that experience, she screened numerous donors, weighing their qualifications. Physical attributes, medical history, family history, intellect

97

and so on. She selected the best candidate and arranged to be inseminated.'

She paused, looked down at her hands. 'I know how it sounds.'

'Do you?' he murmured.

'I exceeded her expectations, intellectually. My health's always been excellent. I'm physically strong and sound. But she wasn't able to bond with me. That part of the process failed. She's always provided me with the best care, nutrition, shelter, education possible. But she couldn't love me.'

It made him sick in the gut, in the heart. 'The lack's in her.'

'Yes, it is. And knowing her part of the process failed makes it very difficult for her to feel or show any affection. I thought, for a long time, I was to blame. But I know that's not true. I knew when she left me. She left me because she could, because I made a choice that allowed her to walk away. I could make her proud of me, proud of what she'd accomplished in me, but I could never make her love me.'

He couldn't help himself. He drew her against him, stroked her hair until she let out a long breath, leaned on him. 'You'll be all right, Liz.'

'I want to be.'

He met Terry's eyes over her head, saw the sheen of tears and pity in them. It was good she'd heard, John thought. Because the kid had two people who cared about her, and would do whatever it took to make sure she was all right.

*   *   *

Sergei met with his brother and nephew, as well as

98

Ilya and one of his most trusted brigadiers. Children splashed in the pool under the watchful eyes of the women while others sat at long picnic tables already spread with a bounty of food. Cold drinks nestled in wide, stainless-steel tubs of ice. On the lawn some of the older children played boccie or volleyball while their music banged out an incessant beat.

Little pleased Sergei more than a loud, crowded party with family and friends. He captained the enormous grill his oldest daughter and son-in-law had given him for his birthday, appreciating this American tradition. His gold Rolex and the crucifix hanging around his neck gleamed in the brutal summer sun, while over his cotton shirt and pants he wore a bright red bib apron that invited everyone to kiss the cook.

As the grill smoked, he turned fat burgers, all-meat franks and long skewers of vegetables brushed with his secret marinade.

'The mother goes to the hospital,' Sergei's nephew Misha said. 'She is there many hours every day, often through the night. She has dinner maybe once a week with the man she sleeps with. Four times each week, she goes to the fancy gym where she has a trainer. She goes to the beauty parlor for her hair, her fingernails. She lives her life like she has no daughter.'

Sergei merely nodded as he transferred the vegetables to a platter.

'I went through her house,' the brigadier told him. 'I checked her phone. Calls to the hospital, to her boyfriend, to another doctor, to the salon for her hair. There are none to the police, to the marshals, to the FBI.'

'She must see the girl,' Mikhail insisted. He was

more rounded than his brother, and his hair was going white in wide streaks. 'She is the mother.' He looked over to the pool, where his own wife sat laughing with their daughter while their grandchildren played in the pool.

'I think they aren't close.' Ilya sipped at his beer.

'A mother is a mother,' Mikhail insisted. 'She would know where her daughter is.'

'We can take her,' Misha suggested. 'On her way to the hospital. We can . . . persuade her to tell us where the girl is.'

'If the mother is a mother, she will not tell.' Sergei began arranging burgers on another platter. 'She will die before. If she is not such a mother, and my information is she is not, she may not know. We take her, they move the girl, add more guards. So, we watch the mother who is not such a mother.'

'In the house,' the brigadier said, 'there's nothing of the daughter's outside the bedroom. And there's not much there. What is, is boxed. Like storage.'

'So you see.' Sergei nodded. 'I have a different way, one that ends this and leaves nothing of us behind. Tell Yakov to be patient a little longer, Misha. The next time we have a party, it will be to celebrate his return. But now'—he lifted the platter, stacked with burgers and dogs—'we eat.'

*   *   *

When the summer dragged on, Elizabeth reminded herself that if she were home, she would have given in—most likely—and would be enduring the summer program at the hospital. Otherwise, she wouldn't have done anything all that different from what she did now.

100

Study, read. Except now she listened to music, watched movies on DVD or television. Through summer reruns of *Buffy the Vampire Slayer*, she believed she'd begun to learn contemporary slang.

When she was able to go back to college, she might know more of the language, might fit in better.

To continue her quest for security, she went to the practice range. She'd learned self-defense and poker.

Nothing could bring Julie back, and playing what-if was a useless process. It made more sense to look at the advantages of her summer confinement.

She would never be a surgeon.

At some point, she'd take on a new identity, a new life, and find some way to make the best of it. She could study whatever she wanted. She had a feeling joining the FBI was no longer an option, but she didn't ask. It might have been foolish, but not knowing a definitive answer left a sliver of hope.

She embraced the routine, grew comfortable with it.

Her birthday didn't change routine. It just meant that today she was seventeen. She didn't feel any different, or look any different. This year there would be no birthday dinner—prime rib with roasted vegetables followed by carrot cake—or any possibility of the car her mother had promised. Contingent on her academic achievements and deportment, of course.

It was just another day, one day closer to her court appearance and what she thought of as freedom.

As neither Terry nor John mentioned her birthday, she assumed they'd forgotten. After all, why should they remember? She gave herself the gift of a day off from studying, and decided she'd make a special dinner—*not* prime rib—as a personal celebration.

It rained, drenching and thunderous. She told herself it made the kitchen only homier. She considered baking a cake, but that seemed self-serving. And she hadn't yet tried her hand at real baking. Preparing spaghetti and meatballs from scratch seemed challenging enough.

'God, that smells fabulous.' Terry paused in the center of the kitchen, inhaled deeply. 'You almost make me think about learning how to make something besides mac and cheese.'

'I like doing it, especially when it's something new. I've never made meatballs. They were fun.'

'We all have our own fun.'

'I can put some of the sauce and meatballs in a container for you to take home. You'd just have to add the pasta. I made a lot.'

'Well, Lynda called in sick, so you'll have Bill and Steve Keegan. I bet they can pack it away.'

'Oh. I'm sorry Lynda's not well.' Routine, Elizabeth thought. It always gave her a jolt when it changed on her. 'Do you know Marshal Keegan?'

'Not really. John knows him a little. He's got five years in, Liz. Don't worry.'

'No, I won't. It just takes me a little time to get used to new people, I guess. It doesn't matter. I'm going to read after dinner, and probably go to bed early.'

'On your birthday?'

'Oh.' Elizabeth flushed a little. 'I wasn't sure you knew.'

'You have no secrets here.' On a laugh, Terry

moved over to take another sniff of the sauce. 'I get you like to read, but can't you come up with anything more fun on your birthday?'

'Not really.'

'Then you need some help.' She gave Elizabeth a pat on the shoulder before she walked out.

Reading was fun, Elizabeth reminded herself. She checked the time, noting that the change of shift was coming up soon. The sauce could simmer until Bill and this new deputy wanted to eat, but she really had made a lot, so she'd put some in containers for John and Terry.

Like a reverse birthday gift, she decided.

'Help's arrived.'

Elizabeth turned from reaching high into a cupboard for lidded containers.

Terry stood grinning with a box wrapped in shiny pink paper with a big white bow trailing ribbons. Beside her, John held a small gift bag and a white bakery box.

'You . . . you got me gifts.'

'Of course we got you gifts. It's your birthday. And we got cake.'

'Cake.'

John set the box down on the table, flipped up the lid. 'Double-chocolate fudge with buttercream icing.'

'My pick,' Terry informed her. 'Happy birthday, Liz.'

'Thank you.' The cake said the same, in fancy pink piping. It had rosebuds and pale green leaves.

'It's not carrot cake,' she murmured.

'I have a religious objection to any pastry made from a vegetable,' Terry told her.

'It's very good, really. But this looks much

better. This looks . . . like a real birthday cake. It's beautiful.'

'We'll have to save room for it *and* the ice cream,' John said. 'After the birthday dinner. We were going to get pizza, but you started those meatballs, so we adjusted.'

Everything went bright, as if the sun burst through the pounding rain. 'You're going to stay.'

'I repeat, it's your birthday. No way I'm missing out on ice cream and cake. We'll wait for the others for eats, but I think you should open your gifts now.'

'Really? It's all right?'

'Obviously, the genius doesn't comprehend the power of birthday. Here.' Terry pushed the box into Elizabeth's hands. 'Open mine. I'm dying to see if you like it.'

'I like it already.' And she began to carefully slit the tape.

'I knew it. She's one of those. One of those,' Terry explained, 'who takes ten minutes to open a gift instead of ripping away.'

'The paper's so pretty. I didn't expect anything.'

'You should,' John told her. 'You should start expecting.'

'It's the best surprise.' After folding the paper, Elizabeth lifted the lid. She lifted out the thin cardigan with ruffles flowing down the front and tiny violets scattered over the material.

'It's beautiful. Oh, there's a camisole with it.'

'That's not your mother's twin set,' Terry declared. 'You can wear it with jeans, or dress it up with a skirt. It looked like you.'

No one had ever told her she looked like ruffles and violets. 'I love it. I really love it. Thank you so much.'

'My turn. I had a little help picking these out. So if you don't like them, blame my wife.'

'She helped you? That was so nice of her. You have to thank her for me.'

'Maybe you should see what it is first.'

Flustered, thrilled, Elizabeth dug into the tissue paper for the little box. The earrings were a trio of thin silver drops joined together by a tiny pearl.

'Oh, they're wonderful. They're beautiful.'

'I know you always wear those gold studs, but Maddie thought you might like these.'

'I do. I love them. I don't have anything but the studs. I got my ears pierced the day before . . . the day before. These are my first real earrings.'

'Happy seventeen, Liz.'

'Go, try it all on,' Terry ordered. 'You know you're dying to.'

'I really am. It's all right?'

'Birthday power. Go.'

'Thank you.' Riding on the thrill, she wrapped Terry in a hug. 'So much. Thank you.' Then John. 'I am happy. I'm happy seventeen.' She clutched her gifts and raced for the stairs.

'It's a hit.' Terry let out a long sigh. 'She hugged. She never hugs.'

'Never got them. I gave her mother the secure-line number—again. Told her we were going to get Liz a cake for her birthday, and we'd make arrangements to bring her in for it. She declined. Politely.'

'A polite bitch is still a bitch. I'll be glad when this is over for her, you know? And for us. But I'm going to miss that kid.'

'So am I. I'm going to call Maddie, let her know

Liz liked the earrings.' He glanced at the time. 'I'll call in, check on Cosgrove's and Keegan's ETA. I expected to hear they were en route by now.'

'I'll set the table, see if I can fancy it up a bit, make it celebrational.'

She got out plates and flatware, and thought of flowers. 'Hey, John?' On impulse, she moved toward the living room. 'See if Cosgrove can make a stop, pick up some flowers. Let's do it up right.'

He gave a nod of assent, continued to talk to his wife. 'Yeah, she loved them. She's upstairs putting them on. Hey, put the kids on. I probably won't be home till they're in bed.'

Terry walked back into the kitchen, thinking she should sample a little of that red sauce, just to make sure it passed muster. Even as she reached for a spoon, John called out.

'They're rolling in now.'

'Copy that.' One hand on her weapon out of habit, Terry went to the garage door, waited for the signal. Three quick knocks, three slow.

'You guys are in for a treat. We've got—'

Bill came in fast. 'We may have some trouble. Where's John?'

'In the living room. What—'

'Bill thinks he spotted a tail,' Keegan said. 'Where's the witness?'

'She's . . .' Something wrong. Something off. 'Did you call it in?' she began, and pulled out her phone.

She nearly dodged the first blow, so it skated down her temple. Blood slid into her eye as she went for her weapon, shouted to John.

'Breech!'

The butt of Keegan's gun smashed viciously across the back of her head. She went down,

106

overturning a chair with a crash in the fall to the tiles.

Weapon drawn, John flattened against the wall in the living room. He needed to make the stairs, get to Liz.

'Don't shoot him,' Keegan said quietly as he holstered his own gun and took Terry's. 'Remember, we don't want any holes in him.'

Bill nodded. 'I got him, John. I got the bastard. Terry's down! She's down! Keegan's calling it in. Secure the wit.'

John heard Keegan's voice over the drum of rain, rapidly relaying the situation.

And he heard the creak of a floorboard.

He came out, weapon up. He saw Bill moving on him, saw his eyes. 'Drop your weapon. Drop it!'

'Terry's down! They're going to try for the front.'

'Lower your weapon, now!'

John saw Bill glance to the left, pivoted, elbowed back before Keegan could land a blow. As John dived to the right, Cosgrove fired. The bullet caught his side, burned like a brand. Thinking of Elizabeth, he returned fire as he raced for the stairs. Another bullet hit his leg, but he didn't slow. He caught a glimpse of Keegan moving into position, fired on the run.

And took a third bullet in the belly.

His vision grayed, but somehow he kept moving. He caught sight of Elizabeth running out of the bedroom.

'Get inside. Get back inside!'

He lurched forward, shoving her in, locking the door before he fell to his knees.

'Oh my God.' She grabbed the shirt she'd just taken off, used it to apply pressure to his abdomen.

'It's Cosgrove and Keegan.'

'They're marshals.'

'Somebody got to them.' Teeth gritted, he risked a look at his belly wound, felt himself slipping. 'Oh, Jesus. Maybe they've been dirty all along. Terry. She's down. Maybe dead.'

'No.'

'They know I'm in here with you, that I'll fire on anyone who tries coming in the door.' As long as he could hold a weapon. 'But they know I'm hit.' He gripped her wrist with his left hand. 'It's bad, Liz.'

'You'll be all right.' But she couldn't stop the blood. Already her shirt was soaked through, and it just kept pouring out of him, flooding like the rain. 'We'll call for help.'

'Lost the phone. Keegan, he's got connections— in the service, he's connected. He's moved up fast. Don't know who else might be in it. Can't know. Not safe, kid. Not safe.'

'You have to lie still. I have to stop the bleeding.' Pressure, she told herself. More pressure.

'They should have rushed me. Planning something else. Not safe. Listen. Listen.' His fingers dug into her wrist. 'Gotta get out. Out the window. Climb down, jump down. But get out. You run. You hide.'

'I'm not leaving you.'

'You're going. Get your money. Can't trust the cops, not now. More in it. Have to be. Get your money, what you need. Fast. God damn it. Move!'

She did it to keep him calm. But she wouldn't leave him.

She stuffed the money in a bag, a few items of clothing at random, her laptop.

'There. Don't worry,' she said. 'Someone will

108

come.'

'No, they won't. I'm gut shot, Liz, lost too much blood. I'm not going to make it. I can't protect you. You have to run. Get my secondary weapon—ankle holster. Take it. If one of them sees you, comes after you, use it.'

'Don't ask me to leave you. Please, please.' She pressed her face to his. He was so cold. Too cold.

'Not asking. Telling. My job. Don't make me a failure. Go. Go now.'

'I'll get help.'

'Run. Don't stop. Don't look back. Out the window. Now.'

He waited for her to reach it. 'Count to three,' he ordered as he crawled for the door. 'Then go. I'll keep them off you.'

'John.'

'Make me proud, Liz. Count.'

She counted, slid out. She gripped the gutter as rain lashed against her face. She didn't know if it would hold her, didn't think it mattered. Then she heard the volley of gunfire, and shimmied down like a monkey.

Get help, she told herself, and began to run.

She was less than fifty yards away when the house exploded behind her.

Brooks

This above all—to thine own self be true.
And it must follow, as the night the day.
Thou canst not then be false to any man.

WILLIAM SHAKESPEARE

7

Arkansas, 2012

Sometimes being the chief of police in a little town tucked into the Ozarks like a sleepy cat in the crook of an elbow just sucked right out loud.

As a for instance, arresting a guy you played ball with in high school because he grew up to be an asshole. Though Brooks considered being an asshole a God-given right rather than a criminal offense, Tybal Crew was currently sleeping off several more than one too many shots of Rebel Yell.

Brooks considered overindulging in whiskey, on occasion, another God-given right. But when that indulgence invariably caused a man to stumble home and give his wife a couple of good, solid pops in the face, it crossed the line to criminal offense.

And it sucked. Out loud.

And it sucked louder yet as sure as daisies bloomed in the spring, Missy Crew—former co-captain of the Bickford Senior High School cheerleading squad—would rush into the station before noon, claiming Ty hadn't clocked her, oh no. She'd run into a door, a wall, tripped on the stairs.

No amount of talk, sympathy, annoyance, charm, threats would persuade her—or him—they needed some help. They'd kiss and make up as if Ty had been off to war for a year, likely go home and fuck like rabid minks.

In a week or two, Ty would get his hands on another bottle of Rebel Yell, and they'd all go

113

around again.

Brooks sat in his preferred booth at Lindy's Café and Emporium, stewing over the situation as he ate breakfast.

Nobody fried up eggs and bacon and home fries like Lindy, but the fat and grease and crunch just didn't cheer Brooks up.

He'd come back to Bickford six months before to take on the job as chief after his father's heart attack. Loren Gleason—who'd tried to teach Ty Crew and just about every other high-schooler the mysteries of algebra—bounced back. And with the nutrition and exercise regimen Brooks's mother had put the poor guy on, he was healthier than he'd likely been in his life.

But still, the incident had left Brooks shaken, and needing home. So after a decade in Little Rock, a decade on the Little Rock PD, the last five as a detective, he'd turned in his papers and scooped up the recently open position of chief.

Mostly, it was good to be home. He hadn't known how much he'd missed it until he'd moved back full-time. It occurred to him that he'd probably say the same about Little Rock, should he ever go back, but for now, Bickford suited him just fine. Just dandy.

Even when the job sucked.

He liked having breakfast once or twice a week at Lindy's, liked the view of the hills outside his office window and the steadiness of the job. He liked the town, the artists, the potters, weavers, musicians—the yogis, the psychics, and all the shops and restaurants and inns that drew the tourists in to sample the wares.

The hippies had come and settled in the sixties—

114

God knew why his mother, who'd changed her name from Mary Ellen to Sunshine and still went by Sunny, wandered down from Pennsylvania about a decade later. And so Sunshine had charmed or corrupted—depending on who was telling the story—a young, first-year math teacher.

They'd exchanged personal vows on the banks of the river, and set up house. A few years and two babies later, Sunny had bowed to the gentle, consistent pressure only his father could exert, and had made it legal.

Brooks liked to taunt his sisters that he was the only Gleason actually born in wedlock. They rebutted that he was also the only Gleason who had to pack heat to do his job.

He settled back with his coffee, easing himself into the day by watching the goings-on outside the window.

While it was too early for most of the shops to open, The Vegetable Garden had its sign out. He tried to spread his patronage around, so he stopped in for soup now and again, but he was an unapologetic carnivore, and just couldn't see the purpose in something like tofu disguised as meat.

The bakery—now, they were doing some business. And Cup O' Joe likely had its counter full. February had barely turned the corner into March, but the tourists from up north often moseyed down early in the year to get out of the worst bite of winter. The Bradford pears hinted at blossoms. In a week they'd put on their show. Daffodils crowded together in sidewalk tubs, yellow as sticks of butter.

Sid Firehawk's truck farted explosively as it drove by. On a sigh, Brooks made a mental note to give Sid one more warning to get his goddamn muffler replaced.

Drunken wife smackers and noise polluters, Brooks thought. A hell of a long way from Robbery-Homicide. But mostly it suited him. Even when it sucked.

And when it didn't, he thought, straightening in his seat for a better view.

He could admit to himself he'd planted himself in that seat early, on the off chance she'd come to town.

Abigail Lowery of the warm brown hair, exceptional ass and air of mystery. Pretty cat-green eyes, he thought, though she mostly kept them behind sunglasses.

She had a way of walking, Abigail Lowery did, with a purpose. She never moseyed or strolled or meandered. She only came into town every couple of weeks, shopped for groceries. Always early in the day but never on the same day. On rarer occasions, she went into one of the other shops, did her business briskly.

He liked that about her. The purpose, the briskness. He thought he might like more about her, but she kept to herself in a way that made your average hermit look like a social butterfly.

She drove a big, burly, black SUV, not that she did a lot of driving around that he'd noticed.

As far as he could tell, she stayed on her own spread of land, pretty as a picture and neat as a pin, according to the FedEx and UPS guys he'd subtly pumped for information.

He knew she planted both a vegetable garden and a flower garden in the spring, had her own greenhouse and a massive bullmastiff with a brindle coat she called Bert.

She was single—at least she had no one but Bert living with her, and wore no ring. The delivery guys termed her polite and generous, with a tip on Christmas, but standoffish.

Most of the townspeople termed her odd.

'Top that off for you?' Kim, his waitress, held out the pot of coffee.

'Wouldn't mind, thanks.'

'Must be working. You looked cross as a bear when you walked in; now you're all smiles.' She gave him a pat on the cheek.

She had a motherly way, which made him only smile wider, as she was barely five years his senior. 'It's getting the motor running.'

'I'd say *she* got it running.' Kim lifted her chin toward Abigail as she walked into the market on the near corner. 'Got looks, anybody can see that, but she's a strange one. She's lived here almost a year, and not once has she stepped foot in here, or any of the other restaurants. She's barely gone into any of the shops or businesses, either. Orders mostly everything online.'

'So I hear.'

'Nothing against Internet shopping. I do a bit of it myself. But we've got plenty to offer right here in town. And she barely has a word to say. Always polite when she does, but barely a word. Spends nearly every minute of every day up there on her place. All alone.'

'Quiet, mannerly, keeps to herself. She must be a serial killer.'

'Brooks.' Kim let out a snort and walked over to her next table, shaking her head.

He added a little sugar to his coffee, stirred it lazily with his eyes on the market. No reason, he decided, he couldn't go on over. He knew how to mosey. Maybe pick up some Cokes for the station or . . . he'd think of something.

Brooks lifted a hip for his wallet, peeled out some bills, then slid out of the booth.

'Thanks, Kim. See you, Lindy.'

The beanpole with the gray braid down to his ass let out a grunt, waved his spatula.

He strolled out. He had his father's height, and given Loren's post–heart attack regimen, they shared the same lanky build. His mother claimed he got his ink-black hair from the Algonquin brave who'd captured his great-great—and possibly one more great—grandmother and made her his wife.

Then again, his mother was often full of shit, and often on purpose. His changeable hazel eyes could shift from greenish to amber or show hints of blue. His nose listed slightly to the left, the result of a grounder to third, a bad hop and missed timing. Sometimes he told a woman, if she should ask, that he'd gotten it in a fistfight.

Sometimes he was full of shit, like his mother.

The high-end market carried fancy foods at fancy prices. He liked the smell of the fresh herbs, the rich colors of the produce, the gleam of bottles filled with specialty oils, even the glint of kitchen tools he'd have no earthly idea how to use.

To his mind, a man could get along just fine with a couple of good knives, a spatula and a slotted spoon. Anything else was just showing off.

In any case, when he needed to shop for groceries—a chore he hated like rat poison—he frequented the Piggly Wiggly.

She was easy to spot as she selected a bottle of the pricy oil, then one of those strange vinegars.

And though it wasn't as easy to spot, he registered the fact she had a sidearm under her hooded jacket.

He continued down the short aisle, considering.

'Ms. Lowery.'

She turned her head, and he had a good full-on look at her eyes for the first time. Wide and green, like moss in the shadows of a forest.

'Yes.'

'I'm Brooks Gleason. I'm chief of police.'

'Yes, I know.'

'Why don't you let me carry that basket for you? It must be heavy.'

'No, thank you. It's fine.'

'I can never figure out what people do with stuff like that. Raspberry vinegar,' he added, tapping the bottle in her basket. 'It just doesn't seem like a workable marriage.'

At her blank stare, he tried one of his best smiles. 'Raspberries, vinegar. They don't go together in my mind. Who thinks of things like that?'

'People who cook. If you'll excuse me, I—'

'Me, I'm a throw-a-steak-on-the-grill kind of guy.'

'Then you shouldn't have any need for raspberry vinegar. Excuse me. I have to pay for my groceries.'

Though in his experience the smile generally turned the tide with a woman, he refused to be discouraged. He just walked with her to the counter. 'How are you doing out at the old Skeeter place?'

'I do very well, thank you.' She took a slim wallet out of a zippered compartment in her bag.

Angling it, he noted, so he couldn't get a peek inside.

119

'I grew up here, moved to Little Rock for a spell. I moved back about six months after you got here. What brought you to Bickford?'

'My car,' she said, and had the clerk smothering a laugh.

A hard shell, he decided, but he'd cracked tougher nuts. 'Nice car, too. I meant what drew you to this part of the Ozarks?'

She took out cash, handed it to the clerk when he rang up her total. 'I like the topography. I like the quiet.'

'You don't get lonely out there?'

'I like the quiet,' she repeated, and took her change.

Brooks leaned on the counter. She was nervous, he noted. It didn't show, not on her face, her eyes, her body language. But he could feel it. 'What do you do out there?'

'Live. Thank you,' she said to the clerk when he'd loaded the market bag she'd brought with her.

'You're welcome, Ms. Lowery. See you next time.'

She shouldered the market bag, slipped her sunglasses back on, and walked out without another word.

'Not much for conversation, is she?' Brooks commented.

'Nope. Always real polite, but she doesn't say much.'

'Does she always pay in cash?'

'Ah . . . I guess so, now that you mention it.'

'Well. You take care now.'

Brooks chewed it over as he walked to his car. Lack of conversational skills or inclination was one thing. But the sidearm added an element.

Plenty of people he knew had guns, but there weren't many of them who hid them under a hoodie to go out to buy raspberry vinegar.

It seemed like he finally had an excuse to take a drive out to her place.

He stopped in at the station first. He commanded three full-time deputies on revolving shifts, two part-time, a full-time and a part-time dispatcher. Come summer, when the heat moved in like hell's breath, he'd put the part-timers on full-time to help handle the tempers, the vandalism that came with boredom, and the tourists who paid more attention to the views than the road.

'Ty's being a pain in the ass.' Ash Hyderman, his youngest deputy, sulked at his desk. Over the winter he'd tried growing a goatee without much luck, but hadn't quite given it up.

He looked like he'd smudged his top lip and chin with butterscotch frosting.

'I got him breakfast like you said to do. He stinks like a cheap whore.'

'How do you know how a cheap whore smells, Ash?'

'I got imagination. I'm going home, okay, Brooks? I pulled the night shift since we had that stinking Ty back in the pen. And that damn cot about breaks your back.'

'I need to take a run. Boyd's due in about now. He can take over. Alma's due in, too. We're covered as soon as they get here.'

'Where you going? You need backup?'

Brooks thought Ash would like nothing better than if they'd had some gang of desperados scream into town, blasting at everything. Just so he could be backup.

'I just want to check something out. Won't be long. I'm on the radio if anything comes in. Tell Boyd to try to talk some sense into Missy when she comes crying how Ty never touched her. It won't work, but he should try.'

'The thing is, Brooks, I think she must like it.'

'Nobody likes a fist in the face, Ash. But it can get to be a habit. On both sides. I'm on the radio,' he repeated, and left.

*   *   *

Abigail struggled with nerves, with temper, with the sheer irritation at having a task she particularly enjoyed spoiled by a nosy police chief with nothing better to do than harass her.

She'd moved to this pretty corner of the Ozarks precisely because she wanted no neighbors, no people, no interruptions to whatever routine she set for herself.

She drove down the winding up-and-down private road to her house in the woods. It had taken weeks to devise a blueprint for sensors, ones that wouldn't go off if some rabbit or squirrel approached the house. More time to install them and the cameras, to test them.

But it had been worth it. She loved this house of rough-hewn logs and covered porches. The first time she'd seen it she thought of it as both fairy tale and home.

A mistake, she knew. She'd weaned herself off attachments, but she'd fallen for this spot. So wonderfully quiet she could hear the creek bubble and sing. So private and secluded, with its deep woods. And secure.

She'd seen to the security herself, and she trusted no one else.

Well, she thought, as she stopped the car. Except Bert.

The big dog sat on the covered front porch of the two-story cabin. Body alert, eyes bright. When she got out of the car, she signaled release. He bounded to her, all hundred and thirty pounds of him wriggling in joy.

'There's my good boy. Best dog in the world. So smart. Just so smart.' She gave him a brisk rub before retrieving her market bag. 'You wouldn't believe the morning I had.'

She took out her keys as they walked to the house together on the narrow stone path. 'Minding my own business, buying supplies, and the chief of police comes into the market to interrogate me. What do you think of that?'

She unlocked the two dead bolts, the police lock, then stepped inside to deactivate the alarm with a code she changed every three to five days.

'That's what I thought, too.' She locked the door, secured the riot bar. 'He was rude.'

She crossed the living room she'd set up for relaxation. She loved curling up there, a fire crackling, Bert at her feet. Reading or watching a DVD. And she had only to toggle over to have the view of her security cameras come on the large flat screen.

She moved back to the kitchen, with its secondary office area she'd set up in lieu of a dining room.

Out of habit, she checked the locks on the rear door, the tells she left on the windows. But she wasn't afraid here. She believed, at last, she'd found

123

a place where she wasn't afraid. Still, vigilance was never wasted. She turned on the kitchen TV screen so it synched with the security cameras. She could put her groceries away—what she'd managed to buy before being interrupted—and do a perimeter check.

She gave Bert one of the gourmet dog treats she kept in a tin. She'd convinced herself he could tell the difference between them and lesser dog biscuits.

As her bodyguard, he deserved the best.

'I've got some work to do after this. I have to earn my fee on the Bosto account. Then we'll go out, get some exercise. Give me an hour, then—'

She broke off, and Bert came to full alert as the drive alarm beeped.

'We're not expecting any deliveries today.' She laid her hand on the gun holstered at her side. 'It's probably just someone who made a wrong turn. I should put up a gate, but we get so many deliveries.' She frowned as she watched the car approach, then moved to the computer, zoomed in.

'Oh, for God's sake. What does he want now?'

Her tone had Bert growling low in his throat. 'Pillow.' Her code word for stand down had the dog relaxing again but watching her for any distress. 'Pillow,' she repeated, then signaled for him to come with her.

Bert had a very successful way of discouraging visitors.

She deactivated the alarm, unlocked the front door and stepped out on the porch as the chief of police pulled up behind her SUV.

It made her itchy. He hadn't blocked her in, or not altogether. She could get around him if she needed to. But the intent was there, and she didn't like it.

'Ms. Lowery.'

'Chief Gleason. Is there a problem?'

'Well, funny you should ask, because that was going to be my question. Before I do, let me just say that's a really big dog.'

'Yes, he is.'

Hip cocked, thumbs in front pockets, his body language read relaxed and casual. But his eyes, Abigail noted, were sharp, observant. Were authority.

'Is he going to rip my throat out if I walk over there?'

'Not unless I tell him to.'

'I'd appreciate if you'd not. Why don't we go inside?'

'Why would we?'

'It's friendlier. But we're fine out here. The place looks good. Better than I remember.' He nodded to a patch of ground she'd marked off and covered with black plastic. 'Going for flowers or vegetables?'

'Flowers. If you came all the way out here to ask if there's a problem, I'll just tell you no. There's no problem here.'

'Then I've got a follow-up. Why are you carrying a gun?'

She knew the instant of surprise must have shown, and wished for her sunglasses. 'I live alone. I don't know you, and you came uninvited, so I have a gun and the dog for protection. I have a license.'

'It's good you do. The thing is, you were wearing that gun when you went in to buy fancy vinegar. I don't think you needed protection in the gourmet

125

market.'

Sharp and observant, she thought again, and berated herself for not taking a smaller weapon. 'I have a concealed-carry license. I'm within my rights.'

'I'm going to ask to see your license, if you don't mind.'

'I do mind. Why do people say that when they know very well the person they say it to minds?'

'Empty manners, I guess.' He spoke pleasantly, patiently—she thought of the ability as a talent, and a weapon.

'I do want to see the license, just to cover things—Abigail, isn't it?'

She turned without a word, took out her keys. She felt him follow her onto the porch. 'I'll bring it out.'

'You know, you're making me wonder why you're so hell-bent on keeping me out of the house. You running a meth lab, a bordello, running guns, making explosives?'

'I'm doing nothing of the sort.' Her hair, a blunt, shoulder-skimming drape of golden brown, swung out as she turned. 'I don't *know* you.'

'Brooks Gleason, chief of police.'

Yes, she decided, anyone who could deliver sarcasm with such a pleasant drawl, such an easygoing smile, had skills.

'Your name and occupation don't change the fact I don't know you.'

'Point taken. But you've got a big-ass dog there who's giving me the stink eye because he knows you're upset and I'm the reason. He must go a hundred and twenty pounds.'

'One thirty-three.'

Brooks gave Bert a long study. 'I've got about thirty pounds on him, but he's got sharper teeth and you've got a sidearm.'

'So do you.' She shoved the door open, and when Brooks stepped inside, she held up a hand. 'I want you to wait here. I'm going to put him on guard. He'll restrain you if you don't stay here. You have no right to wander around my house.'

'All right.'

'Bert. Hold.' She turned to the stairs, started up.

'Define "restrain."?'

Nearly out of patience—the police chief appeared to have more than his share—she paused, snapped, 'Stay where you are and you won't have to find out.'

'Okay, then.' He let out a breath as she disappeared up the stairs. He and the dog eyed each other. 'So, Bert, what do you do around here for fun? Not talking, huh? Nice place.' Cautious, Brooks stood very still, turned only his head. 'No muss, no fuss.'

And triple locks, a riot bar, secured windows, top-grade alarm system.

Who the hell was Abigail Lowery, and what—or whom—was she afraid of?

She came back down, a document in hand, gave it to him.

'A Glock 19? That's a serious gun.'

'All guns are serious.'

'You're not wrong.' He handed the license back to her, looked into her eyes. 'And you're not wrong that you don't know me. I can give you the name of my former captain in Little Rock. I was on the police force there for ten years before I moved back home. I'm a good cop, Abigail. If you tell me what kind of trouble you're in, I'll try to help you.'

Chief Gleason wasn't the only one with skills, she reminded herself. Her gaze and her voice remained absolutely steady and level. 'I'm not in trouble. I'm just living my life. I have work to do, and I'm sure you have work to do. I'd like you to leave now.'

'All right. If you change your mind.' He took out a card, set it on a table by the front door. 'My cell number's on it, too. If you want help, you just call.'

'I don't need help.'

'You've got a riot bar and three top-grade locks on your front door, security bars on your windows, and a better alarm system than my bank. I don't think all that's to keep the dog from getting out.'

He opened the front door, turned back to look at her. 'Do you like puzzles?'

'Yes, but I don't see how that's relevant.'

'I like them, too. See you around, Bert.' He shut the door.

Abigail stepped over, locked it, then, closing her eyes, knelt on the floor and pressed her face to the dog's strong neck.

8

Boyd Fitzwater, grizzle-haired and paunchy, manned the desk. He stopped chicken-pecking at the computer keyboard when Brooks walked by.

'Missy Crew came around. Like you'd expect, last night's black eye was an accident. She got creative this time. Said she tripped on the rug and Ty tried to catch her.'

'She fell into his fist?'

'That's just what she said. And him being a little drunk, he miscalculated when he tried to catch her.'

'And the neighbor calling us in because she ran out of the house half-naked and screaming?'

'That?' With a tight smile, Boyd shook his head. 'She saw a mouse, and not the one on her eye. Overreacted, and the neighbor shouldn't have bothered us. And before you ask, the reason she said Ty socked her last night is she was all confused. Because technically he did, but only trying to save her from a fall.'

'You let him go?'

'Couldn't much do otherwise.'

'No, but this crap is going to stop. The next call we get on them, I want whoever's on duty to call me. I want to handle it.'

'You're welcome to it. I tried, Brooks. Even had Alma talk to her, figuring she might listen to another woman.'

'Well, she didn't.' Alma Slope walked in from the break room. Her fingernails were painted electric blue today and matched the chunky beads around her neck. Her frizzy mop of guinea-gold hair had been clamped back with a blue silk flower.

She took a swig of the coffee in her hand, left a clear imprint of bold red lipstick on the rim. Pale green eyes, the only thing pale about Alma, peered out behind glasses with cat's-eye frames studded with rhinestones.

Her face, with its network of fine lines, registered annoyance as she fisted a hand on the hip of her faded Levis.

Alma admitted to sixty, but as she'd admitted to sixty before Brooks had left for Little Rock, he couldn't begin to guess the real age of his

129

dispatcher.

He wasn't sure Alma knew anymore.

'I took her in the break room, sat her down and talked to her like a Dutch uncle, whatever the hell that means. She started crying, so I thought I was getting somewhere. But she said how she loved Tybal, and he only gets mean when he's drinking. And here's the kicker. How it's all going to be all right if she can just get pregnant.'

'Jesus Christ.'

'She says she's trying real hard. Once they have a baby, Ty's going to settle right down.'

'I want the call when it comes,' Brooks repeated. 'Thanks for trying, Alma. You can take the patrol, Boyd. I've got some paperwork to see to.'

'I'll get on it.'

'You want some coffee, Chief?' Alma asked him.

'Wouldn't mind it.'

'I'll get it for you. Nothing much to do. It's quiet today.'

'May it continue.'

He went into his office, booted up his computer, picked up the ancient Slinky on his desk. Walking to the window, he moved his hands up and down to set the coils whispering. He liked the sound of it, found it soothing, like an old blanket or bare feet in warm grass.

He considered himself—and was considered by those who knew him—to be an even-tempered sort of man. Some would say a little on the low side of temper. So it surprised him just how much the incident with Abigail Lowery had pissed him off.

Take the dog. A beautiful son of a bitch, but there'd been no doubt if he'd made the wrong move, or she'd just had a fucking whim, that

130

beautiful son of a bitch would have sunk his teeth into him.

Brooks didn't mind unsettled situations, because he liked to settle them, find the answer or solution. Do the job, make the peace. But he damn well didn't like being at such a slippery disadvantage against an armed woman and her big-ass guard dog.

No laws broken, he thought. Not one. And yet.

Some people were unfriendly by nature. He'd never understood the type, but he knew them, had dealt with them. It was more than that with this woman. A whole basketful of more.

He'd found her a strange and interesting mix of nerves and confidence, straightforward and secretive. Northern accent, he considered. Still shy of thirty, if he was any judge, and—barring Alma— he generally was.

On the slim side, but there was a coiled spring in there. Pretty, though she'd worn no makeup, and her clothes had been simple. Good boots, well broken in. No jewelry, no nail polish, no bright colors.

Don't look at me—that's what she was saying, in his opinion. Don't notice me.

'What's got you worked up?' Alma stepped in, set his coffee on his desk. 'You've got your toy going,' she added when he turned.

'Just thinking.'

'Anything to do with the woman who bought the old Skeeter place?'

'Are you doing psychic readings these days?'

'I leave that to my girl.'

'How's Caliope doing?' Alma's daughter read tarot, palms and auras—and was one of his mother's tight circle of friends.

131

'She worked an engagement party the other night. Picked up three more bookings out of it.'

'Good for her.'

'It's a living. I heard you had what passes for a conversation with the Lowery girl over at the gourmet place.'

'She ain't no chatterbox.' He sat, picked up his coffee, put his boots on the desk. An invitation for Alma to sit. 'What do you know?'

'Not much, which bugs the hell out of me. What I got out of Dean McQueen, as he handled the property sale, is she contacted him by e-mail. Saw the sale online, asked some questions, thanked him politely. Few days later, she e-mailed again with an offer. Wasn't the asking price, but Dean told me it was a little above what he hoped he'd get, and she offered a cash deal.'

'Cash.'

'That's right. On the barrelhead. The Skeeters jumped on it. Well, you know Dean, he's a salesman, and he likes to talk it up. He says he couldn't get much more out of her than yes and no. She wired the earnest money from a bank in Kansas City. Drove in with that dog of hers for the settlement, pulling a U-Haul trailer. Signed the papers, handed over the cashier's check, from a bank in Fairbanks, Alaska, this time. Dean wants to take her to lunch to celebrate, but she shuts that down. Wants to take her to the property, walk her through and shut down again. She takes the papers, the keys, thanks everyone and that's that.'

'It's a puzzle,' Brooks murmured.

'People who say live and let live? They're not doing a lot of living, as far as I'm concerned.' She got up as the radio in the dispatch area squawked.

'It'd be interesting to find out what her deal is.'

'It would,' Brooks agreed. As Alma went out to answer the radio, his phone rang. 'Bickford Police Department, Chief Gleason.' For now, he put Abigail Lowery on his back burner.

He handled the paperwork, the phone calls, took a turn at foot patrol, where he listened to the owner of a pottery shop complain about the owner of the neighboring candle shop once again blocking his delivery entrance with his car.

And once again talked to the offender.

He picked up a ham-and-cheese panini, and while taking a late lunch at his desk, started puzzle solving.

He ran her tags, crunched into the chips he'd gotten with the sandwich. He read her date of birth, noted that she was twenty-eight, so he'd been on the mark there. Her license carried no restrictions. She was an organ donor with a clean driving record.

He accessed the database and ran her criminal.

No criminal record.

That should be enough, he told himself. She was, according to the data, a law-abiding citizen without so much as a single speeding ticket.

But . . .

Out of curiosity, he Googled her. He got several hits on the name, but none of them were his Abigail Lowery.

Caught up now, he continued to dig. He had her name, address, tag number, driver's license data. Since he knew she had a license to carry, he started with gun registration.

As the data came up, he sat back.

'Now, that's an arsenal,' he murmured.

In addition to the Glock 19, she had licenses for

133

a Glock 36, one for a Glock 26, a nine-millimeter Beretta, a long-range Sig, a nine-millimeter Colt Defender and a Smith & Wesson 1911, and a pair of Walther P22s.

Just what did the woman need with that many handguns? He was a cop, for God's sake, and other than his service weapon, he had only two others.

'Who the hell are you?'

'Hey, Brooks.'

The bombshell blonde stood kind of posed in his doorway. Sylbie's hair fell in gleaming waves over the shoulders of a white lace shirt loosely belted over jeans that were a thin coat of paint over long legs. She had eyes that reminded him of a tiger, tawny and just a little feral.

In high school he'd wanted her more than his next breath. And when he'd had her, his life had been a seesaw of bliss and misery.

Automatically, he toggled over to screen saver. 'How you doing, Sylbie?'

'Oh, I'm just fine. I've been working since dawn, so I'm giving myself a little break.' She glided into the room on those long legs, perched on the corner of his desk in a provocative cloud of fragrance. 'I thought I'd just drop in and see you, and see if you wanted to get together tonight.'

'I've got a lot going on here.'

'If the chief of police can't take the night off, who can?'

'The law's ever vigilant.'

She laughed, tossed that glorious mane of hair. 'Come on, Brooks. I thought I'd pick up a nice bottle of wine.' She leaned in. 'And you can take advantage of me.'

It didn't make him feel manly, but he had to

admit the few times they'd gotten together since he'd come home, he'd felt like the one being taken advantage of.

Not that he'd minded at the time. But afterward . . .

'That's a nice invitation, Sylbie, but I've got to work tonight.'

'Come on by after.'

'I don't think so.'

'You're hurting my feelings.'

'I don't want to do that.' But neither did he want to get caught up again. They'd come a long way since high school, when she'd captured his heart, then demolished it—and were a lot closer to her two divorces.

'If you want to play hard to get,' she began, sliding off the desk.

'I'm not playing.' She would have slithered right into his lap if he hadn't pushed to his feet. 'Look, Sylbie.'

As he was facing the door, he saw Abigail step into the opening, saw her immediate jolt of embarrassment.

'Ms. Lowery,' he said, before she could back away.

'I'm sorry to interrupt. I'll come back.'

'No, that's fine. I'll talk to you later, Sylbie.'

'I'm buying that wine,' she murmured, shot him her slow smile. She turned, angled her head as she studied Abigail.

'You're that woman who lives out at the Skeeter place.'

'Yes.'

'Everybody wonders what in the world you do out there all by yourself.'

135

'They shouldn't.'

'People have a curiosity. That's a natural thing. I'm Sylbie MacKenna.'

'One of the local potters. You do very good work. I bought one of your bowls.' Abigail looked at Brooks again. 'I can speak to you later, Chief Gleason.'

'You're here now. Sylbie's got to get on.'

'So official. He didn't used to be.' She gave Abigail a knowing smile. 'I'll see you later, Brooks.'

'She's very attractive,' Abigail commented.

'Always has been.'

'I'm sorry I interrupted. The woman, your . . .'

'Dispatcher?'

'Yes. She said I should just come back.'

'That's fine. Have a seat.'

'May I close the door?'

'Sure.'

After she'd done so, and taken a seat in his visitor's chair, silence ran for several beats.

'Something on your mind?' he asked her.

'Yes. I realize I mishandled our . . . business this morning. In the market, and when you came to my house. I wasn't prepared.'

'Do you have to prepare to have a conversation?'

'I'm not a social person, so I don't have many conversations, particularly with people I don't know. In the market, I felt uncomfortable with your interest in what I was buying.'

'My interest in what you were buying was a ploy for conversation.'

'Yes.'

Everything about her was cool, he thought, and still. He considered how she served as polar opposite to Sylbie, who always ran hot, always seemed to be moving.

'We're a small town, Abigail. A small resort town, full of New Agers and old hippies, second-generation hippies, artists. We're friendly.'

'I'm not. I'm sorry if that's rude, but it's fact. I'm not a friendly person, and I moved here for the quiet, the solitude. When you came to the house so soon after the market, it made me nervous, and angry. I have my reasons for carrying the pistol. I'm not obligated to share those reasons. I haven't done anything wrong.'

'That's good to know.'

'I like my property, and the land around it. I like this town. I feel comfortable here. I just want to be left alone.'

'What Sylbie said about curiosity's true. It's a natural thing. The more mysterious you are, the more people wonder.'

'I'm not mysterious.'

'You're a walking mystery.' He rose, came around the desk. As he did, he saw her brace, stay on alert, even when he leaned back against the front of the desk.

He wanted to ask her who'd hurt her, who she was afraid of. But he'd lose her if he did.

'You're a really attractive woman who lives alone—with a big, muscular dog—outside of the town proper. Nobody knows for sure where you came from, why you came here, what you do for a living. And since this is the South, nobody knows who your people are. You're a Yankee, so people will give you a certain latitude. We like eccentrics around here, it fits right in with the community. If people decide you're eccentric, they'll stop wondering.'

137

'By certain standards I am eccentric. I can be more so if that would satisfy everyone.'

He grinned at her, just couldn't help it. 'You're definitely different. What do you do for a living, Abigail? If it's not a mystery, or a matter of national security, you should be able to tell me. And that would be a simple conversation.'

'I'm a freelance computer programmer and software designer. I also design security systems, and improve or redesign existing systems, primarily for corporations.'

'Interesting. And not so hard to talk about.'

'Much of my work is highly sensitive. All of it is confidential.'

'Understood. You must be pretty smart.'

'I'm very smart.'

'Where'd you study?'

She stared at him, cool, calm, contained. 'You see, when you ask all these questions, it doesn't feel like conversation. It feels like interrogation.'

'Fair enough. Ask me a question.'

She frowned at him, eyes level. 'I don't have a question.'

'If you're so smart, you can think of one.' He pushed off the desk, went to a dorm-sized refrigerator and took out two Cokes. He handed her one, popped the top on the second. 'Something wrong?' he asked, when she just stared at the can in her hand.

'No. No. All right, a question. Why did you go into law enforcement?'

'See, that's a good one.' He pointed at her in approval, then leaned against the desk again, the hills at his back in view out the window. 'I like to solve problems. I believe in a lot of things. Don't believe in a lot, too, but one of the things I believe in is there's right and there's wrong. Now, not everybody figures right and wrong exactly the same. It can be a subjective sort of thing. When you're a cop, sometimes it is black and white, and sometimes you have to decide—in this situation, with these people, is it wrong, or just something that needs handling?'

'That seems very confusing.'

'Not really. It's solving problems, and the only real way to solve them is to use your head. And your gut.'

'The intellect is a more accurate gauge than emotion. The intellect deals with facts. Emotions are variable and unreliable.'

'And human. What good are laws if they're not human?'

He set his Coke down to take hers. He opened it for her, handed it back. 'You need a glass?'

'Oh. No. Thank you.' She took a small sip. 'Chief Gleason.'

'Brooks. Aren't you going to ask me how I got a name like Brooks?'

'I assume it's a family name.'

He pointed at her again. 'You'd assume wrong. Now, aren't you curious?'

'I . . . Yes, a little.'

'Brooks Robinson.'

'I'm sorry?'

'I was afraid of that. Baseball, Abigail. Brooks was one of the best third basemen to ever guard the hot corner. My mother came from Baltimore, where he played. My mama, she's a fiend for baseball. Even when she drifted here, back toward the tail end of the seventies, she followed baseball, and worshipped the Baltimore Orioles. According to her, when she watched Brooks win MVP in the 1970 World Series against the Cincinnati Reds, she vowed when she had a son, she'd name him Brooks.'

'She must be very serious about baseball.'

'Oh, she is. Where'd Abigail come from?'

'It's just a name.'

'I like Abigail. Old-fashioned class.'

'Thank you.' She rose. 'I need to go. I still have work to finish today. I apologize if I seemed rude this morning, and I hope I've cleared things up.'

'I appreciate you coming in. What I said this morning stands. If you need anything, call.'

'I won't, but thank you for the Coke and the conversation.' She handed the can back to him. 'Good-bye.'

When she left, he studied the can. What did it say about him, he wondered, that he was actively thinking of sending it off for DNA and prints?

Didn't seem right, on several levels, he decided. But he took the can to the restroom, poured the contents down the sink. Back in his office, he slipped the empty can into an evidence bag, and stored it in his bottom drawer.

Just in case.

The entire day left Brooks feeling restless, and it wasn't his usual state of mind. He didn't want his own company, and since he'd told Sylbie he had to work instead of just saying no, thanks, he couldn't justify dropping by McGrew's Pub for a beer, a game of pool, some conversation.

Instead of heading home, he drove to the end of Shop Street, hung a left and pulled into the rambling, never-quite-finished house behind his mother's Prius.

Scaffolding clung to the side, where he could follow the progress on her current mural. Sexy fairies, he noted, with flowing hair, delicate wings. Under the roofline on the front, burnished-skinned, leanly muscled men and women rode dragons with iridescent scales of ruby or emerald or sapphire.

It was impressive work, he thought. Maybe a little strange for house and home, but no one could miss the O'Hara-Gleason place.

He stepped onto the cherry-red porch to the door flanked by pointy-eared elves.

And stepped inside music and scent and color. Clutter and comfort reigned, dominated by his mother's art, cheered by the flowers his father brought home at least twice a week.

Tulips to celebrate the coming spring, Brooks decided. Every color of the rainbow and tucked into vases, bowls, pots scattered around the room. The black cat his father named Chuck curled on the sofa and barely slitted his eyes open to acknowledge Brooks.

'No, don't get up,' Brooks said under the blast of Fergie filling the house.

He wandered back, past his father's office, the tiny, crowded library, and into the hub—the kitchen.

The biggest room in the house, it mixed the thoroughly modern in sleek appliances—the cooktop with indoor grill, the glass-fronted wine cabinet—with the charm of lush pots of herbs, a thriving Meyer lemon tree blooming away. Crystal drops in varying shapes winked in the windows, catching the sun. More sun poured through the skylight in the lofted ceiling, over the bounty of

141

flowers and vines and fruit his mother had painted over the soft yellow.

He could smell fresh bread, and the allure of whatever she stirred on the stove while she sang along with Fergie. She gave Fergie a run for her money, Brooks thought.

As far as he was concerned, his mother could do damn near anything, and everything.

She had her hair, a gold-streaked brown, braided down her back, with silver beads dangling from her ears. Her bare feet tapped to the beat.

A peace symbol tattoo on her right ankle announced her sixties sensibilities.

'Hello, gorgeous.'

She gasped, then turned around with a laugh, eyes warm and brown. 'Hi, handsome. I didn't hear you come in.'

'You can't hear anything. How many times do I have to tell you kids to keep the music down?'

'It helps the creative process.' But she picked up a remote and muffled Fergie. 'What's up with you?'

'This and that. Where's Dad?'

'He had a meeting with parents. He'll be home soon. Stay for dinner?'

'Whatcha got?'

'Minestrone, rosemary bread and a field-greens salad.'

'I'm in.' He opened the fridge, got out a beer, waggled it.

'Well, if you insist.'

'I do.' He got out a second beer, opened them both.

'Now.' She gave him a little poke in the belly. 'What's up? I know your face.'

'You gave it to me.'

'And a fine job I did. You got troubles, sweetie?'

'Not really. Sylbie came by the station this afternoon.'

She took a swallow of beer. 'Mmmm.'

'And I know your mmmms. She wanted to hook up tonight.'

'Yet here you are in your mother's kitchen, opting for minestrone over sex.'

'You make really good minestrone. I lied to her.'

'And you are that rare creature, an honest cop.'

Now he poked her. 'You're just holding on to your flower child's disdain for authority. Anyway, it's one thing to lie to a suspect, that's the job. It's another just to lie. I don't like it.'

'I know. Why did you?'

'To avoid a scene, I guess, which is just stupid, as it's just postponing it. I don't want to go back to high school. Been there, done that, got the letter jacket. And she doesn't want me; she wants somebody. The sex is really good, but nothing else is.'

'So you're looking for more than sex.' Sunny wiped an imaginary tear away. 'My boy's growing up.'

'Maybe. I don't know. But I do know I don't want it with Sylbie. I'm hoping for the easy way. Somebody else catches her eye and she loses interest.'

'I thought you didn't want to go back to high school.'

'Yeah. I know I've got to fix it, and I should have when she came in today. Pisses me off that I didn't. So I will.'

'Good. She's not a happy woman, Brooks. She equates her worth with her looks and sexuality,

143

and she won't be happy until she doesn't. I think she could be happy, and make someone happy, once she realizes she has more to offer. You just remember you can fix the problem, but you can't fix her.'

'You're right. I'll work on it.'

'Now, what else. Something else in there.' She tapped his temple.

'I met, officially, Abigail Lowery today.'

'Oh, now, this is good. This is sit-down-and-relate-every-detail good.' She settled down at the breakfast counter, patted the next stool. 'I've been dying to pin that one down. What's she like?'

'At first I'd've said rude, abrupt and downright unfriendly, but with a little more exposure, I have to put it down to socially awkward.'

'Poor thing.'

'The poor thing carries a Glock on her hip to the fancy market.'

'A gun? When are people going to realize that going around armed is just asking for—'

She broke off when he tapped a finger to her lips.

'I know how you feel about guns, gun control and what you see as a perversion of the Second Amendment, Sunshine.'

She huffed, shrugged. 'It can never be too often repeated. But go on.'

He told her about the market, going out to her place, the dog, the locks. By the time he got to his digging into her licenses, and the number of registered handguns she owned, Sunny decided the story called for a second beer.

'What's she afraid of?'

'See that? Exactly. That's what I want to know.

144

And as chief of police around these parts, that's what I need to know. But to finish up, then Sylbie came in.'

Once he'd told her the rest, her outrage over the guns had subsided, and her focus shifted. 'That just breaks my heart.'

'What?'

'Honey, she's so alone. Of course she's socially awkward when she's got herself barricaded up by herself, and against God knows what. She's not sounding like one of those survivalists or those crazies thinking they've gotta load up on the guns and locks for the revolution or the Rapture. You said she does programming, and security business. Maybe she found something or invented something. Now the government's after her.'

'Why is it always the government, Ma?'

'Because I find it often is, that's why. She could've been a cyber spy or something like that.'

'I love you.'

She slitted her eyes, kicked him lightly in the shin. 'Now you're using those fine words to be amused and patronizing.'

He couldn't quite disguise the smirk. 'Let's just say she didn't strike me as the espionage type.'

'Well, they're not supposed to, are they? They're supposed to blend.'

'In that case, she's a crappy spy, because she doesn't blend.'

'All right, maybe she's on the run from an abusive boyfriend.'

'I didn't find anything in her record about filing charges.'

'Some women don't go to the police. Some just run.'

145

He thought of Missy and her latest black eye. 'And some stay. One thing I know, the way she's loaded up and barricaded, whatever she's hiding from—if that is the case—it's bad. And if the bad finds her, it finds her here. I'm responsible for here, and whether she likes it or not, for her.'

'I love you.'

'Was that amusement and patronizing?'

'No.' She cupped his face. 'That's just fact.'

9

As Sunny wound down the road toward Abigail Lowery's cabin, she doubted her son would approve. But she had a habit of doing as she pleased, as long as it didn't hurt anyone—unless they deserved it. In any case, her son's visit there the day before gave her the perfect excuse to drop by.

She parked, mentally clucked her tongue at the gas-guzzling SUV.

Still, she approved of the house, the way it nestled right into the landscape. She could see beds were being prepped for spring planting. And the glimpse of a corner of a greenhouse caught her eye and her envy.

It was a fine morning for a visit, she determined, with spring whispering on the air, the leaves a pretty haze of green on the trees, and the hint of wild dogwoods scattered around.

As insurance, she'd baked a huckleberry pie that morning. No one resisted her huckleberry pie.

She got out of her car, went up and knocked on the door.

When it opened a few cautious inches, she beamed out a smile.

'Hi, there. I'm Sunny O'Hara, Brooks's mama.'

'Yes.'

'I know Brooks came out to see you yesterday, and it made me think I should do the same. I thought, why, that girl's been here for nearly a year now, and I haven't paid her a call.'

'Thank you, Ms. O'Hara, but—'

'Sunny. I baked you a huckleberry pie.'

'Oh.'

In her life, Sunny had never seen anyone more baffled by a pie.

'Thank you. That's very nice of you. I'm afraid I have work, so—'

'Everybody can take a few minutes for pie. Do they call you Abby?'

'No, no, they don't.'

'Well, Abigail's a sweet, old-fashioned name. Abigail, I ought to tell you straight off I'm a woman who tends to get her way. You're going to find it's easier to just invite me in for a few minutes rather than deal with me coming around until you do. Now, I expect you've got a gun on you or nearby. I don't approve of guns, but I won't lecture you about it. Yet.'

She shot out another smile, bright as her name. 'I don't have one, or anything else dangerous on me. Except the pie. It's got a hell of a lot of calories in it, but you're slim as a willow stem, you can handle some calories.'

'I don't want to be rude, but—'

'Oh, I imagine you do,' Sunny interrupted, with considerable cheer. 'Who could blame you? I'll make you a deal. You ask me in, have a piece of pie. Then you can be rude, and I won't take offense.'

Trapped and annoyed, Abigail removed her hand from the gun fixed to the underside of the table by the door.

She didn't doubt the woman was Brooks Gleason's mother. She had the same pushy nature disguised as friendliness, the same bone structure.

Saying nothing, Abigail opened the door wider, stepped back.

'There, now, that wasn't so—oh, what a *gorgeous* dog.' Without a hint of fear, Sunny pushed the pie dish into Abigail's hands and crouched down. 'Oh, hello, big boy.' She looked up. 'Can I pet him? We lost our Thor about six weeks ago. Seventeen when we had to let him go, and blind as a bat.'

'I'm very sorry.'

'Oh, me, too. I cried my heart out. We still have old Chuck. That's our cat, but it's not the same. We're going to get another dog, but I'm just not ready to love like that again. It hurts so when you have to say good-bye.'

Helpless, Abigail clutched the pie. '*Ami,*' she said to the dog. '*Ami,* Bert. You can pet him now.'

Bert submitted to the strokes, even hummed a little at the pleasure. '*Ami?* That's French. Are you French?'

'No. I speak French.'

'How about that. Bert, you speak French, too? You're so handsome. He has hazel eyes, a little like Brooks's. What a good dog you are.'

Her eyes filled, and she sniffled back the tears as she straightened. 'Sorry. I'm just not over the loss.'

'Death is difficult.'

'It certainly is.' Sunny flipped back her braid, let

148

out a breath as she glanced around. 'You're very tidy, aren't you?'

'I . . . I suppose, yes. I prefer things in order.'

'I guess I like chaos, mostly. Anyway, I can never keep anything tidy for long. I have a painting that would work very well in your living room. It's what I do. I'm an artist.'

'I see.'

'I paint mainly mythical and mythological studies. Fairies, mermaids, gods and goddesses, dragons, centaurs—that sort of thing.'

'Mythology is fertile ground for artists and storytellers. Ah . . . did you paint the murals on the house off Shop Street?'

'Yes. That's our house.'

'It's very interesting. The work is very good.'

'Thanks. I enjoy it. How about some coffee to go with that pie?'

Abigail stared down at the pie. 'Ms. O'Hara.'

'Sunny.'

'Sunny. I'm not good company.'

'Oh, honey, that's okay. I am.'

However awkward and unsettling it might be, it had to be easier—and more efficient—to simply let the woman have her few minutes. And that would be that.

'I'll make the coffee.'

She started back toward the kitchen, thinking for the second time in two days she had someone in her house. Still, the woman meant no harm. Unless . . .

'Did your son ask you to come here?'

'No. In fact, he's not going to be pleased with me for intruding on you when he finds out. But I—oh! Oh! I love your kitchen. Look at all your counter space. I have this same cooktop—an older model.

And you grow your own herbs. So do I. Look at that, we've already found something in common. I love to cook. It's like painting, only you're mixing herbs and spices and mixing up sauces instead of paints.'

'I think of it as a science. There's a formula. If you diverge from the formula, you may create something new or slightly different.'

Sunny only smiled. 'However you look at it, you wouldn't have a kitchen like this unless you liked to cook, and were good at it.'

She walked over to look out the window. 'I'm envious of your greenhouse. I have a tiny one Loren and I built. We don't have room for a larger one. Got your lettuce in, I see. Looks like a nice-sized vegetable garden.'

'I grow most of my own vegetables and herbs.'

'So do we. I came here in the seventies with a group of other free spirits. We formed a kind of commune, an artist community, you could say—and grew our own food, wove our own cloths—sold our wares. A lot of us are still here. Old hippies.'

'You were part of the counterculture.'

'I like to think I still am.'

As Abigail brewed the coffee, got out cups and plates, Sunny glanced over to the office area. And raised her eyebrows at the views of the drive, the back area, sides, on the computer screen.

'Isn't that something? Nobody's going to sneak up on you, are they? You work on security systems, isn't that right?'

'I do.'

'There was a time nobody even locked a door at night around here, and if you had a shop and needed to run out, why you'd just leave a note.

People could come on in, and just leave the money on the counter if they wanted to buy something before you got back. Sometimes progress and change is a good thing; sometimes it isn't.'

'It's better to be secure.'

Socially awkward, Brooks had said. Yet the girl set out nice plates, put milk in a little pitcher, set out sugar, cloth napkins. She knew how to entertain company, even if the company was unexpected and not particularly welcome.

Sunny took a seat at the counter. She imagined Abigail had two stools only because they'd come as a set. Sunny added milk and considerable sugar to her coffee, then patted the second stool.

'Come on and sit. Tell me about Abigail.'

'There isn't anything to tell.'

'There's always something. What do you like to do?'

'I like my work.' Obviously reluctant, Abigail sat.

'I feel for people who don't. Besides your work?'

'I work quite a lot.' When Sunny just cocked her eyebrows, Abigail struggled to find more. 'Bert requires exercise, so we walk or hike. It was part of the appeal of this property, that there was enough land. I work in the greenhouse or the garden. It's satisfying. I like to read. I like television.'

'So do I, more than they say you should. But what do they know? And you like solitude.'

'I do.'

'When I was raising three kids, I used to think I'd pay any price for a few hours of alone.'

'I didn't realize your son had siblings.'

'Two older sisters.'

'You're very young to have children that age, in their thirties, I assume.'

151

'I was nineteen when I came to Bickford. I'd been rambling around for about two years.'

'You . . . you left home at seventeen?'

'The day after I graduated high school. I'd put too much time into that to walk away from it. But once that was done, I was gone.' Sunny snapped her fingers. 'I didn't get along with my parents, which is no surprise, as we saw everything, I mean everything, from opposite sides. We still do, mostly, but we've made amends. When I came here, I met a young schoolteacher. He was shy and sweet and smart, and had beautiful hazel eyes. I seduced him.'

'I see.'

'That part was easy, I was quite beguiling,' she said with a laugh. 'What wasn't easy was coming to realize I was making love with someone I'd fallen in love with. I was so sure I didn't want that kind of life. The man, the home, the roots, the family. But he was irresistible. He wanted to marry me. I said no, none of that for me.'

'Marriage as an institution is part of our culture's fabric, but it remains only a kind of contract, and unnecessary, as it's easily broken.'

'You might be speaking my own words from that time. When I learned I was carrying Mya, I agreed to a kind of handfasting. I was dabbling in Wicca back then. We had a lovely ceremony by the river, and moved into a tiny cabin, oh, not half the size of this. No indoor plumbing, either, and I was fine with that.'

She sighed into her coffee at the memory. 'I had two babies there. And it wasn't quite so fine. My man wanted a real marriage, a real home. He'd let me have my way for nearly three years. I realized it was time to let him have his. So we loaded up

152

the babies, went to the justice of the peace, made that legal contract. And with the money I'd made from my art—I got a greeting-card contract, and that was reasonably lucrative. And the money he'd saved from teaching, we bought that ramshackle of a house off Shop Street. We started fixing it up, and Brooks came along. I never regretted a moment. Not one.'

Abigail wasn't sure it was conversation when a virtual stranger imparted a synopsis of her life story. But it was fascinating.

'You're very fortunate.'

'Oh, I am. How's that pie?'

Abigail blinked, glanced down. She'd eaten nearly half, as she'd been caught up in Sunny's story. 'It's wonderful.'

'I'll give you the recipe.'

'I've never made a pie. It's just me. A pie doesn't seem practical.'

'There's nothing practical about a pie. We'll trade. I'll give you the recipe for one of yours.'

'I don't know what you'd like.'

'Surprise me.'

After an internal debate, Abigail walked over to her laptop, called up her recipe file. She printed out her recipe for chicken paprika. 'You can adjust the spices to taste.'

'This looks great. I think I'll stop at the market on the way home, pick up what I don't have, and try this tonight. Here, let me write out the recipe for the pie.' She pulled a notebook and pen out of her purse.

'You have it memorized?'

'I've been making this pie for too many years to count. It's Loren's favorite.'

153

'You smile when you say his name.'

'Do I? We've been married—I count from the handfasting—for thirty-six years. He still makes me happy.'

That, Abigail thought when she was alone again, was the most vital and compelling statement on a relationship. That happiness could last.

She studied the recipe in her hand. She'd transcribe it onto the computer later. Dutifully, she gathered up the plates and cups, and with some surprise noticed the time.

Somehow she'd just spent more than thirty minutes in her kitchen, having pie and coffee and fascinating conversation with a stranger.

'I suppose that means she's not a stranger now.'

She couldn't decide how it made her feel, couldn't decipher it. She looked at her work, looked at her dog.

'Hell. Let's go for a walk.'

*   *   *

'You did what?' Brooks gaped at his mother.

'You heard me very well. I took a pie over to Abigail's. We had a nice chat over pie and coffee. I like her.'

'Ma—'

'I think socially awkward's a good term for it. She's not shy, just rusty when it comes to interaction. Once we got going, we did just fine. We exchanged recipes.'

'You . . .' At his desk, Brooks dropped his head in his hands. 'Did you hear me last night?'

'Of course I did.'

'It may be she's on the run. It may be she's

in trouble. It may be, if that trouble finds her, dangerous. And you just breeze on over with pie?'

'Huckleberry. I had to make two so your father wouldn't get his feelings hurt. She's got a wonderful kitchen. And looking at the recipe she gave me, I'm betting she's quite a cook. She also has cameras or some such thing set up all over the property. I saw on her computer screen. She has views of the drive, and the back and so on.'

'Christ.'

'She spoke French to the dog.'

That had him lifting his head again. 'What?'

'I just wonder why somebody would teach their dog French, is all. She has very nice manners. She listens to you with her whole body. Something about her just pulled at me. I swear, I wanted to pet her like I did the dog.'

'You . . . you petted that big-ass monster dog?'

'She told it in French it was all right. He was very sweet. He's devoted to her, I could see that. Never strayed more than two feet away. He's a very good dog, and I'm sure a fine companion. But that girl needs a friend. Now, I've got to run by the store and pick up some things. I want to try this recipe she gave me.'

'Ma, I don't want you going over there until I know more.'

'Brooks.'

He was thirty-two years old, and that tone, that look, could still make his balls shrink to marbles.

'You're a grown man, but it still hasn't come to the point where you tell me what to do. If you want to find out more about her, why don't you go out there and be friendly, like I did?'

'And take her pie?'

'You might try a bottle of wine.'

*   *   *

He went with a nice, mid-range pinot grigio. It seemed reasonable, friendly without too many overtones. It also seemed like it was overthinking the whole thing, so he stopped thinking and just drove out there.

The rain that had blown in the night before teased out a little more green. Now, early-evening sun shimmered through those greening branches, splashed on the road, flickered on the busy water of the little stream that wound through.

He bumped his way up her drive, caught a glimpse of the smoke curling out of her chimney.

Then he saw her.

She stood, the big dog at the heel of her knee-high black boots. She wore jeans, a black leather jacket, and a gun on her hip.

He decided not to overthink the fact that everything about her at that precise moment struck him as grab-your-balls sexy.

It just was—right down to the edgy annoyance on her face.

He snagged the wine, slid out of the car.

'Evening.' He strolled toward her as if she wasn't packing a Glock, didn't have a dog who could probably sink its teeth into the jugular before he cleared his own weapon from its holster.

She eyed the bottle he carried. 'What's that?'

'It's a couple of things, actually. One, it's a pretty nice wine. Second, it's an apology.'

'For what?'

'My mother. I was over there for dinner the

156

other night, and mentioned I'd been out here. She hopped right on that. So . . . sorry for the intrusion.'

'So you're intruding to apologize for an intrusion.'

'Technically. But it's a pretty nice wine. So, been out for a walk?'

'Why?'

'You got some mud on your boots. Some rain last night. It gets things greening up, but it brings the mud, too. Do you always carry a gun when you walk your dog?'

She always carried a gun, period, but that wasn't any of his business. 'I was target shooting. The wine isn't necessary.'

'Wine's not necessary, but it's one of those enjoyable perks that comes along.' He turned it so the pretty straw-colored wine caught the light. 'Where are you set up, for target practice?'

'Why do you ask so many questions? Why do you keep coming here, with your wine and your pie? What is *wrong* with you people? What are you grinning at?'

'Which question do you want me to answer first?' When she merely gave him a stony stare, he shrugged. 'In order, then. I'm a naturally curious sort of man, plus cop. So questions are part of it. It's likely I got some of that curious from my mother, who came out here, with pie, because she was. And because she's a friendly sort of woman. I already explained about the wine. From my point of view, nothing's wrong with us. We just are what we are. Your point of view might come in different. I was grinning because I'd wondered if there was any temper in there. It lights you up. It's nice to see the light. Did I cover it?'

157

His eyes were amber in the late-afternoon sun, and his smile appealing. She thought he owned that easy, conversational style the way other men owned socks. 'You think you're charming.'

'Yeah. That's probably a flaw, but who wants perfect? I answered your questions, but you didn't answer mine. Where are you set up?'

'Why do you want to know?'

'A couple of reasons. One, that curiosity again. Second, as a cop, knowing I've got a woman who carries habitually? I'd like to know if she can handle what she carries.'

'I'm an excellent shot.'

'So you say. I could tell you I can tango like an Argentinean, but unless I demonstrate, I might be lying—or exaggerating.'

'It's doubtful every Argentinean can tango.'

'Like one who can, then.'

'If I demonstrate my shooting skills, will you leave me alone?'

'Well, now, Abigail, I can't make a deal like that. I may have to come back. What if a gang of extremists tried to abduct you? Or aliens. We've got any number of people around here who'll swear about those aliens—the E.T. kind, I mean. In fact, Beau Mugsley claims he gets abducted twice a year like clockwork.'

'That's absurd.'

'Not according to Beau Mugsley. Don't get him started on anal probes. And putting that aside, you're an intriguing woman.'

'I don't want to be intriguing.'

'And see that? Now you're just more intriguing.'

'And if there's intelligent life on other planets, I hardly think they'd spend their time attempting

158

an abduction on someone who's minding her own business.'

'You never know, do you?'

She simply didn't know how to argue with someone like him, someone who made no *sense?* and was so damn affable about it. Add in the tenacity and the cop curiosity, she determined she was stuck.

'I'll satisfy your misplaced concern about my target-shooting skills. Then you can go.'

'That's a good place to start.' He noted that she laid a hand on the dog's head before she turned. 'Ma tells me your dog speaks French,' Brooks said as he fell into step beside her. 'I took two years in high school, mostly—okay, completely—because the French teacher was hot. Smoking. Not a lot stuck with me, but I had two years of gazing at the hotness of Ms. Gardner.'

'Studies show adolescent males often make decisions based on sex. Many fail to grow out of it.'

'Can't really blame us for genetic makeup. That's an impressive setup.' He paused to study her target area.

Where he'd expected a couple of circle targets, she had a trio of police-style silhouettes on draw pulleys backed by thickly padded boards. Ear and eye protection sat on a wooden bench along with spare clips. By his gauge, she had them set at a good fifty feet.

'I don't have a second pair of ear protectors or glasses,' she said as she put them on.

'No problem.'

He stepped back, pressed his hands to his ears as she took position.

Cop stance, he noted, and she took it in a

159

smooth, practiced motion. She fired six rounds without a flinch, then holstered her weapon before pulling the target in.

'Nice grouping,' he commented. All six center mass, in a tight, damn-near-perfect pattern.

'As you can see, I'm an excellent shot. I'm capable.'

'No question of that,' he said as she picked up her brass, dropped them in a bucket. 'Mind if I try it out?'

She didn't answer, but took off the ear protectors and glasses, passed them to him.

She looked back to where the dog sat, patiently waiting. 'Pillow.'

'What?'

'I was speaking to my dog. Otherwise, he'd . . . object when you draw your weapon.'

'Wouldn't want that.' Brooks passed Abigail the wine, put on the glasses and the ear protectors.

'You use a Glock 22,' she noted. 'It's a good weapon.'

'Gets the job done.' Now he took his stance, loosened his shoulders, fired six rounds.

He glanced back at the dog as he holstered the weapon. Bert hadn't moved.

Abigail drew in the target, stood a moment, studying the grouping that was a near twin of hers.

'You're also an excellent shot.'

'I always figure if you carry, you'd better hit what you aim at. I got a good hand with a long gun. My mother's got a flower child's objection to guns, could be why I honed a skill with them. Standard rebellion, I suppose.'

'Yes.' She looked up at him. 'Have you shot anyone?'

'Not so far. I'd like to go on saying that. I had to draw my weapon a few times, but it never came to firing it.'

'Could you?'

'Yes.'

'How do you know if you never have?'

'Protect and serve.' He looked at her, those changeable eyes sober now. 'Protect comes first. I've got no business having a badge if I can't protect. But I'd be happy if it never came to putting a bullet into anyone.' He, too, picked up his brass. 'Have you?'

'Shot anyone? No. But then, I'd say that even if I had, to say I had would only lead to more questions.'

'You're not wrong. Could you?'

'Yes. I could.' She waited a moment. 'You don't ask how I know.'

'I don't have to. Have you got any of that pie left? And before you ask why, I'll tell you. Now that we've shown each other what good shots we are, I thought we could crack that bottle open, have a glass of wine and a piece of pie.'

'The wine was a ploy.'

'In part, but it's still a pretty good wine.'

He had his mother's charm, she decided, and very likely the same skill in getting his way. There was no point denying she found him physically attractive. Her hormonal reaction to his looks, his build, his demeanor, even his voice? Completely natural.

'I can't eat all the pie. It's too much for one person.'

'Shame to waste it, too.'

She stowed the protective gear in the seat of

161

the bench. 'All right. You can have the pie and the wine. But I won't have sex with you.'

'Now you hurt my feelings.'

'No, I haven't.' Deciding to make her position clear, she started for the house. 'I like sex.'

'See there, we just keep finding common ground. If this keeps up, we'll be best friends inside a week.'

'If I wanted friends, I'd join a book club.'

Loosening up, he thought, delighted with the sarcasm. 'I like to read, which is another check mark on common ground. But we were talking about sex.'

'The act of sex is a normal physical function, and a pleasant experience.'

'So far, we're on the same page.'

She took out her keys, unlocked the door. Once inside, she reset the alarm. 'It may be you find me physically attractive on some level.'

'All of them, actually.'

'And that may be the reason you came here, with wine. I'll have a glass of wine with you, but I won't have sex with you.'

'Okay.' Absolutely delighted with her, he followed her to the kitchen. 'Any particular reason why not, other than the fact we haven't even shared huckleberry pie yet?'

'You ask too many questions. Answering them is annoying and tiresome.'

'Damn that curiosity. Jesus, Abigail, did you smile?'

'It was probably a grimace.'

'Now you made a joke. Any minute you're going to put on a party hat and dance on the table.'

'You're funny. I'm not, so I can appreciate someone with natural humor.' She took off the jacket, opened a door to what he assumed was a small utility room and hung it on a peg. 'And you're physically attractive and fit. I prefer having sex with someone who keeps physically fit.'

She got out a corkscrew, and though he would have taken it, opened the wine for her, she set about doing so briskly and efficiently.

What the hell, he thought, and sat. 'So far the only strike against me is curiosity?'

'There are others. Proximity, for one, which would make it awkward and problematic when I no longer want to have sex with you.'

'What makes you think you're going to want to stop having sex with me?'

She got out two glasses, two small plates, two forks. 'The law of averages.'

'Oh, that. I defy the law of averages.'

'A lot of people believe they do. They don't.' She poured the wine, studying him as she offered a glass. 'I like your nose.'

'Abigail, you fucking fascinate me. Why do you like my nose?'

'It's been broken at some point. The lack of symmetry adds character and interest to your face. I like character.'

'And still, no sex for me.'

She smiled again, fully this time. 'I'm sure you have other options.'

'That's true. I make them take numbers, like at a deli.' He waited until she got out the pie, uncovered it. 'Do you want to know why I'm not going to have sex with you?'

He'd surprised her, he noted. Stirred her curiosity. 'Yes, I would.'

'You're attractive, and you look pretty . . .

163

physically fit to me. You've got a way of looking at me that feels like you're looking right through to the back of my brain. I don't know why that's sexy, but it is. You need help.'

'I don't want any help.'

'I didn't say anything about want. You need help, and I've got a weakness for people who need help. I like your dog even though I figure he's as dangerous, or damn near, as that Glock on your hip. I like the way you talk, like you're just a little rusty at it. I'd like to feel the shape of your mouth under mine. I'd like that more than I'd considered. But.'

On an exaggerated sigh, he lifted his hands, let them fall. 'I'm always going to have questions. So that's a problem. And while I'm a man, so I'm fairly up for sex if a woman sneezes in my direction, I generally like to get to know her first. Dinner, conversation, that sort of thing.'

'A date. I don't go on dates.'

'You know, hearing you say that doesn't surprise me. Now, we've shared an activity, shooting at targets. We've shared conversations and viewpoints. Now we're sharing wine and pie. If I stretch that, I could ease it over the line into a date.'

The look she gave him was the definition of flustered. 'It's not a date.'

'By your gauge.' He gestured at her with a forkful of huckleberry pie. 'I've got my own. That means the only thing stopping me from having sex with you is my naturally curious nature. I can work around that. I can decide it's not a problem for me; then the only thing stopping me from having sex with you is you being willing.'

'I'm not, so if we're going to talk, it should be

164

about something else. That wasn't a challenge,' she added, when it occurred to her. 'I didn't mean to pose a sexual challenge.'

'No, I got you didn't mean to, but it sure has that flavor. And it's tasty. Like the pie.'

He scooped up a bite. 'Did you design the security system here?'

She looked wary again. 'Yes.'

'Cameras, too?'

'Yes. Obviously, I don't actually manufacture the hardware.'

'Obviously.' He angled to study her computer station. 'It's quite a setup.'

'It's my work.'

'I'm okay on a computer. I can get done what I need to get done, usually find what I need to find. My father, now, he's amazing. I get a glitch, he's my man. It must be the math nerd in him. Were you a math nerd?'

At one time, she remembered, she was an everything nerd. Perhaps she still was. 'I enjoy math. Its logic.'

'I coulda figured.' He angled back to her, drank some wine. 'I like your place. My mother wants your kitchen.'

'You should get her a dog.'

'What?'

'She says she isn't ready, but it was clear by the way she behaved and reacted to Bert she is. She misses having a dog in her life. She—I'm sorry.' Color rose up to her cheeks. 'It's not my place.'

'We don't stand on place so much around here. She loved that dog. We all did. It just about flattened us when we had to have him put down.'

He looked down at Bert, resisted—because he

165

liked having his hand—reaching out to pet the dog.
'You really think she's ready to start with another?'

'I shouldn't have brought it up.'

'You did. I'm asking your opinion.'

'Then yes. It seemed to me she felt it would be disloyal if she herself got another dog. But a gift, from one of her children. That's different, isn't it?'

'It is. Thanks. She liked you, my mother.'

'I liked her. You should take the rest of the pie, and her dish.' Abigail rose to cover the remaining pie.

'Here's your hat; what's your hurry?'

'You weren't wearing a hat.'

'It's an expression. Like, say, don't let the door hit you in the ass on your way out.'

'Oh. Then yes, you have to go. I need to feed my dog, and I have work waiting. Please tell your mother I enjoyed the pie.'

'I will.' He rose, picked up the dish.

'And thank you for the wine. I'll let you out.'

At the front door he waited for her to unlock, turn off the alarm. Then he set the pie on the little table.

'Tell your dog to relax.'

'Why?'

'Because I want to put my hands on you, and I'm going to need them to drive after I do. I don't want him biting one off at the wrist.'

'I don't like to be touched.'

'You like sex. A kiss is somewhere between being touched and having sex. Aren't you curious, Abigail?'

'A little.' She studied his face in that X-ray manner, then looked to the dog. *'Ami,'* she said, laying a hand lightly on Brooks's arm. *'Ami,* Bert.'

Still, she stiffened when Brooks took her hand—her gun hand.

'*Ami,*' he murmured. 'That one stuck with me. So let's be friendly.'

He laid his other hand on her cheek, eased his way in. And she watched him. That ready, steady look in her eye just hit some chord in him. He kept it light, maybe a little over the friendly line, but light and soft. Lips meeting, eyes locked.

He pressed, just a bit more, body to body, until her hand came to his shoulder. Until it slid around to the back of his neck, up into his hair. Until her tongue teased his, and those watchful eyes went a deeper green.

As he stepped back, he released her hand. With a shake of his head, he picked up the pie. 'You know I'm going to have to come back.'

'It's a mistake.'

'For who?'

'For both of us.'

'Different points of view, remember.' He leaned in, quick—and this time friendly—touched his lips to hers. 'I'll be coming back. See you, Bert,' he added as he walked out and to his car.

Abigail closed the door, locked it before she heard his engine turn over. She let out a huff of breath, looked down at the dog.

'It's a mistake,' she repeated.

10

Brooks spent most of his day putting righteous fear in a trio of preadolescent shoplifters, dealing

167

with a traffic accident—which primarily involved preventing the two drivers from coming to blows—handling the resulting paperwork, and listening to Sid Firehawk whine when Brooks finally cited him for the blown-out muffler.

To reward himself, he opted to make a quick run to the bakery for some fancy coffee and a snickerdoodle, but Alma stuck her head in his office. Rainbow peace signs the size of babies' fists dangled from her ears.

'Grover called in. There's a dispute over at Ozark Art.'

'What kind of dispute?'

'He just said things were getting a little hot, and asked for you to go by.'

'All right. I'll walk over. I could stop at the bakery on the way back if you want anything.'

'Get away from me, Satan.'

'Just saying.' Brooks got up from his desk, grabbed his jacket.

'If a chocolate macadamia cookie and a skinny latte found their way onto my desk, it wouldn't be my fault.'

'No one could blame you.' As Brooks headed out, he wondered why she'd put the skinny in a latte when she was having a cookie. But that was one of the female mysteries he didn't worry himself into a headache over.

He glanced at the sky as he walked. The temperatures refused to settle, shooting up, diving down and clashing in the middle as a welcome mat for tornados. But the sky held to a harmless faded denim.

He crossed over to Shop Street, pleased to see the Saturday-afternoon bustle of locals and tourists.

He passed the gourmet market, thought of Abigail, and walked down another block to Ozark Art.

He didn't see any signs of a dispute through the display window. In fact, he didn't see Grover or a customer or anyone else. The little bell jingled as he stepped in, scanned the main showroom and its walls of paintings, the stands displaying sculptures, shelves of handblown glass and local pottery.

The air carried the fragrance of a spring woodland from one of those reed diffusers. Grover's work, he thought absently. The guy looked like a storybook gnome, and was a wizard with scents.

He started back toward the storeroom and office, saw no one at the checkout counter.

And heard the click of heels on wood.

Sylbie, hair tumbled, eyes slumberous, slipped out of the back room.

'Well, there you are . . . Chief.'

'What's the problem, Sylbie?'

'I'll tell you.' She crooked a finger, tossed her hair and her own personal scent as she opened the back-room door. 'In here.'

'Where's Grover?'

'He'll be back in a few minutes. Somebody has to watch the shop.'

Brooks felt the trapdoor creak under his feet. 'Sylbie, Grover called the station, said there was a dispute that needed police involvement.'

'There is a dispute, but there doesn't have to be. Come on into the back, and we'll settle it.'

'We'll settle it here.'

'All right, then.' She wore a dress swirled with black and white. And then she didn't.

'Jesus Christ, Sylbie.'

169

She laughed, again tossing her hair and perfume before she leaned against the doorjamb, naked but for a pair of high red heels that showed a peek of toenails painted the same shade.

'You didn't come see me the other night, Brooks. I had to drink that wine all by myself.'

'I told you I was busy. Put your clothes back on.'

'Now, that's something I don't recall you saying in the past.'

He kept his eyes on hers, surprised and a little disconcerted that it took little effort to keep them from roaming down. 'I'm saying it now. Put your dress on, Sylbie.'

'Come on over here and make me.'

'What's wrong with you?' he demanded. 'You talk Grover into calling the station, requesting an officer.'

'Not just any officer, honey.' She pursed her lips in a kiss. 'I wanted you.'

'Shut up.' Temper he rarely lost strained against the leash. 'If you're not back in that dress inside ten seconds, I'm arresting you.'

'Oh . . . you want to play that way.'

'Look at me, God damn it. Am I playing?'

His tone, his face, finally got through. Temper lit her eyes in turn as she bent down, pulled the dress back up.

'Don't you think for one minute you can speak to me that way.'

'I'll do more than speak to you if you pull something like this again. I'm the fucking chief of police, Sylbie. I'm on duty.'

She fit the dress straps in place with two defiant snaps. 'Like anything ever happens around here.'

'I'll tell you something that's going to happen.

I'm going to find Grover, and I'm going to fine him for calling in a false report.'

'You will not.'

'Believe it.'

She took a quick step forward. 'Don't do that, Brooks. Don't. He only did it because I asked him.'

'Then he'll know better next time. And so will you.'

'Why do you act this way?' Tears sizzled through the temper. 'You make it so I have to throw myself at you, and all you do is get mad. Back in high school, you couldn't keep your hands off me.'

'This isn't high school. I don't want high school.'

'You don't want me.'

He knew those tears. He'd swam through rivers of them before, and they were sincere enough. 'Sylbie, you're beautiful, probably the most beautiful woman I've ever laid eyes on. You're talented, and when you make an effort, you're an interesting companion. But I don't want you the way I did back then. I don't want what we had back then.'

'You didn't say that a couple weeks back when you were on top of me in my bed.'

'No, I didn't, and I'm sorry, Sylbie.' Plenty of sorry to go around, as far as he could see. 'The sex was always good with you and me, but we never did have much else going on.'

'What do you care, as long as you get off?'

'Honey, you ought to think better of yourself. I do.'

'Something's wrong with you.' Anger and embarrassment ran color hot in her face. 'You ought to want me when I'm offering.'

'If that's all you want, you know there are plenty

171

who'll be willing.'

'But not you.'

'No, not me.' They'd come to the end of that road, he realized, and felt little more than relief. 'Not anymore. Maybe we'll like each other better without the sex. One thing I can promise you, and you better hear me. If you ever pull a stunt like this again, you're going to see the inside of our cells down at the station.'

Her color stayed high, but her face went stony and cold. 'You've changed, Brooks.'

'God, I hope so. You'd best watch the shop until Grover gets back.' He started out, glanced back. 'That's a nice dress, Sylbie. Keep it on.'

When he stepped out, he spotted Grover—round-bodied, stoop-shouldered and balding—puffing on a Marlboro as he sat on the bench between his shop and the next.

'Oh, hey, there, Chief.'

'Hey, there, Grover. Come with me.'

'Ah . . .'

'There's a fine for calling in a false report, and you're paying it.'

'But I—'

'Next time a pretty woman asks you to do something stupid, think first.'

'But she said—'

'You take what she said up with Sylbie. I'm saying you don't call for help unless you need help. You don't waste my time, or the Bickford Police Department's time. I could put you in jail for what you did.'

Grover's face went splotchy, pink blooming over sick white as the man got shakily to his feet. 'Jail? Holy God. I just . . .'

172

'Don't just ever again. Fine's two thousand dollars.'

He was prepared to catch Grover, should he faint, and considered it a near thing. 'I-I-I—'

'I'm cutting it down to twenty-five dollars, giving you a stupidity discount. You come in by the end of the day and pay it, or it's back up to the two thousand. Clear?'

'Yes, sir. I'm sorry. I just thought—'

'No, you didn't think. Next time you will.'

'I'll pay it, Grover.' Sylbie stepped out. 'It's my fault. I'll pay the fine.'

'I don't care where it comes from, just pay it by five.'

'You didn't have to scare him so bad.' Sylbie sat on the bench, drew Grover down beside her and put her arm around his stooped shoulders. 'It was my fault.'

'No argument. Pay the fine, slate's clean.'

Though he'd lost his appetite for cookies, he crossed to the bakery, picked up Alma's order. He left it on her desk, went into his office and filled out the citation.

He puzzled over the charge, then opted for 'crying wolf.' It seemed to fit, and wouldn't embarrass anyone.

He took it out, set it beside Alma's latte. 'Either Grover or Sylbie's coming down to pay this citation. Don't ask.'

'Whenever somebody hears "Don't ask," they're duty-bound to.'

'Not when somebody else just bought them a latte and a chocolate macadamia cookie.'

Alma tapped her blue-tipped nails on the go-cup. 'So this is a bribe.'

'It could be so construed. Don't ask, Alma.' He glanced up as Ash walked in.

'I had to run some skateboarders off the parking lot down at the bank. Again. And I pulled Doyle Parsins over for speeding. Again. Some people never learn. You got cookies?'

'Cookie,' Alma said. 'Singular. Mine.'

'I swung by the Little League park. Saw that little Draper kid hit a solid three-bagger. And I got me a steamer. A cookie sure would top that off.'

Alma smiled as she took a deliberate bite, rolled her eyes in pleasure. 'Mmm-mmm!'

'That's just mean.'

Leaving them to it, Brooks went back in his office, shut his door. He spent some time poking at Abigail Lowery—who, he discovered, had a master's degree in computer science, and another in security engineering, both from MIT. Pretty impressive.

It took him a while, but he learned she worked on a freelance basis for a company called Global Network.

He switched his focus, poked at the company.

Privately owned, he discovered. Founded by one Cora Fiense, age thirty-three. No photo on file, not that he could find. But he scanned a couple of articles describing the small, exclusive company launched by a media-shy agoraphobic.

The website offered no real information on the owner or the employees, but simply stated that Global offered security system analysis and design.

He sat back, asked himself why he persisted. She hadn't done anything, as far as he could tell. He liked her, but there was an itch, he couldn't ignore it. One that told him if he kept scratching he'd uncover something . . . else.

He toggled off when he heard the knock at his door.

'Yeah.'

'I'm off,' Alma told him. 'Calls routed to your cell. Ash is on the desk till eight, Boyd's on the road.'

'That works.'

'Sylbie and Grover came in together, paid the fine.'

'Good.'

'I don't know if the cookie was worth it. Anyway, you were off shift ten minutes ago. Go home.'

'Might just. Thanks, Alma.'

He checked his calendar, noted he had his monthly meeting with the board of selectmen on Monday—joy. And he'd need to complete his quarterly reviews and inspections by the end of the month. He could go home, get some of that done. It wasn't like his social calendar was bursting with activity.

His own fault, he admitted. He could go by the pub, or just make a call to one of his friends, see what was up. And he wasn't in the mood.

The incident with Sylbie had left him mildly depressed, irritable. And horny. And the horny portion just pissed him off.

Because after his baffled shock and annoyance, he'd been tempted. Just a little tempted.

Hard to blame himself for it, he thought, as he rose, wandered to the window. A man would have to be dead a year not to be tempted by a naked Sylbie.

Now he was edgy and itchy, and up until that walk down to Ozark Art, he'd been in a pretty

175

damn good mood. Soured now, he thought, as he'd deprived himself of quick, hot sex, fancy coffee and a cookie.

But Sylbie was right. He had changed. He hoped he never lost his taste for quick, hot sex, but he no longer wanted the price of guilt and emptiness that came after it when it just didn't matter a damn.

What he needed was a distraction. Maybe he'd drive out to Mya's, mooch some dinner, hang out with the kids. Nothing drove sex out of a man's mind surer than a couple of wild kids fighting over the Wii or PlayStation.

He shut down, once again grabbed his jacket. He called a good night to Ash on the way out. On impulse, he jogged over to the florist, nipped in with five minutes to spare till closing.

A bunch of tulips was a good trade for a meal and distraction, he figured.

He drove out of the town proper, started to make the turn toward his sister's big, noisy house near the river. He didn't know until he'd turned the other way that he'd changed his mind.

*   *   *

Abigail had a nice fire crackling. On the stove, a pot of *pasta e fagioli* soup simmered. She'd baked a pretty little round of olive bread, put together a mixed salad she intended to toss with raspberry vinaigrette.

All the work she'd earmarked for the day was complete. She'd spent ninety minutes on weights and cardio, exercised Bert.

She was going to treat herself to dinner and a movie—maybe even a double feature, with popcorn

176

for the follow-up.

Considering all the interruptions, she'd had a very good, very productive week. Her fee for the job she'd just completed would fatten her bank account and add to her peace of mind.

And Sunday? She'd give the computer a rest. She'd clean her weapons, work in her garden and greenhouse, maybe get a little hiking in. Then settle down with her leftover soup and read the evening away.

For her, it encompassed a perfect weekend.

'I think action/adventure with a comedy to follow,' she said to Bert as she gave the soup another stir. 'And wine. The chief of police was right. It's a very nice one. It won't be cool enough for a fire in the evenings much longer, so we should take advantage. I think we should—'

They both came to alert when her system beeped. 'Someone's coming,' she murmured, and rested her hand on the weapon at her hip.

Her brows drew together when she saw the cruiser coming up her drive. 'Why is he here again?'

She moved to her computer, zoomed in to make certain Brooks was behind the wheel, and alone. After a moment's thought, she unstrapped the holster. He'd ask more questions if he saw her wearing it inside on a Saturday evening.

She stowed it in a drawer, waited until he parked. At least he'd parked beside her car, not behind it, this time.

She walked to the door, unlocked it, lifted the bar. She rested her hand on the pistol under the table as she opened the door a few inches.

And her frown deepened when she saw the tulips.

177

'Why are you sorry this time?'

'I'm not sorry. Oh, the flowers. Funny thing. I was going to use them to bribe my sister into feeding me, then I ended up driving here.'

His eyes seemed more amber in the quieting light, and the casual smile he offered didn't quite ring true.

'To use them to bribe me?'

'I hadn't thought that far. Will they get me in the door?'

She opened the door a few more inches. 'They're very pretty. You should go give them to your sister.'

'Probably, but I'm giving them to you. I had a crappy day. It didn't start out that way, but it ended up in the crapper. I was going over to Mya's to use her family to get me out of the mood. Then I figured it wouldn't work.'

'It's not likely that being here will change your mood.'

'It already has.' He gave her an easy smile that almost—almost—reached his eyes. 'Something smells really good, besides you.'

'I don't know why you'd come here.'

'I'm not sure, either. You can close the door on me. You still get the flowers.'

No one had given her flowers before, and she nearly said so before she caught herself. 'I was going to have a glass of the wine you brought, and now you've brought flowers. You make me feel obligated.'

'I'll take it, which shows how crappy my day ended up.'

She stepped back, closed and locked the door behind him. And when she turned, he held the flowers out to her.

'Thank you, even though you bought them for your sister.'

'You're welcome, even though.'

'They'll need water.'

He followed her, and the cooking smells, back to the kitchen.

'It's a good night for soup and a fire,' he commented, hoping he'd get a share of both. 'We may get a little frost tonight. Then tomorrow, it's shooting up toward seventy. Have you ever been through a tornado?'

'I'm prepared.' She took a pottery pitcher in hues of green and brown from a cabinet.

'Is that from one of our shops?'

'Yes. The local artists are very good.'

She got a container of flower food from beneath the sink, added a small scoop before filling the pitcher with water. He sat, said nothing while she arranged the tulips.

She set them on the counter, then studied him the way he might study a suspect. 'You can have a glass of wine.'

'I'd appreciate it.'

She retrieved the bottle, glasses, poured some out. 'You seem to want to tell me about this problem with your day. I don't know why you would, as I'm not part of your circle.'

'Could be that's why. Another why is I realized you were a part of it, indirectly.'

'How could I be?'

'I'll tell you.' He sampled the wine, but she neither sipped nor sat. So he shrugged. 'Okay. I had an unusual and uncomfortable incident with a woman today. Back in high school, she was the love of my life. Know what I mean?'

179

Abigail had an image, clear as glass, of Ilya Volkov's face. He was as close as she came, she supposed, and that wasn't close at all. 'Not really.'

'No heartbreaking crushes for you?'

'I took accelerated courses, so I was ahead of my age group in school.'

'Still. Anyway, about me.' He lifted his glass, toasted her, drank. 'She was my first. The first always has a little hold on you, right?'

'You mean first sexual consummation. I don't have any emotional attachment to my first sexual partner.'

'You're a tough audience, Abigail. When she dumped me—for a college freshman, football captain—she dumped me hard. I'm talking kick-in-the-balls, fist-in-the-teeth hard.'

'I don't understand why someone chooses to hurt a previous partner before moving on to another. I'm sorry she chose to.'

'I got over it, or figured I had. Then I moved to Little Rock, did ten years. When I came back, the woman in question was in the process of shedding husband number two.'

'I see.'

He realized how it all sounded, how he made Sylbie sound—all from his perspective. 'She's not as hard-hearted as I'm making her, but I'm still a little pissed off, and that colors it. So when I came back, took the job here, I was busy for the first couple months. Settling in, and my father wasn't well.'

'I'm sorry. I hope he's better.'

'He is, thanks. He's good. A little while back, Sylbie and I revisited the past, we'll say.'

'You had sex with her.'

'I did, a time or two. A couple weeks ago, we

180

had an encore. But it just wasn't there for me.' He studied his wine with a frown. 'Maybe you can't go back.'

'Why would you, if what was back was a mistake?'

'Good point. But, you know, sex. I decided I had to resist yet another repeat performance, and I'd have to tell her—which I should have done straight out instead of evading, avoiding. This afternoon, she . . . well, what she did was have the guy who runs the shop where she has some of her art displayed, and where she works part-time, call me down there. Officially.'

His conversational style, Abigail thought, was like his mother's. Personal, rambling. Fascinating. 'He reported a crime?'

'A dispute, which required my intervention. Instead, she's there alone, with the idea we'll make some use of the back room.'

'To have sex?'

'Yeah. I'm reasonably sure that was the plan, particularly since when I didn't jump on that idea, she dropped her dress. She just'—he flicked out a hand—'dropped it, and she's standing there in her skin and red shoes.'

'She's confident, and was probably certain of your agreement.'

'Confident on some levels, and I didn't agree. I was . . .'

'You said it was awkward and uncomfortable.'

'It was all that. Not that I didn't . . .'

'You were aroused. It's natural.'

'Like a reflex. But mostly? It just pissed me off. I was on duty, for God's sake, and she sweet-talked an easy mark to call me down.'

181

Abigail considered it a fascinating example of human dynamics and miscommunication. 'It appears she might not fully understand how seriously you take your duties.'

'I'm not a horny teenager. I'm the chief of the goddamn police.'

The spike of his temper, and the guilt so clearly wrapped around it, added another level of interest. 'You're still angry with her, and with yourself for the natural reflex.'

'I guess I am. I had to tell her I didn't want her— partly because of ground I already covered here, partly because, for Christ's sake, she didn't show an ounce of respect for either of us. Another part was knowing I was going to have to slap poor Grover back for making the call, scare the shit out of him so he didn't pull a stunt like that again.'

'That's several parts.'

'And I've got one more. I realized when I was looking at this beautiful, naked woman I'd once loved the way you love when you're sixteen, I didn't want her for all the reasons I just said. And because I want you.'

She turned away, stirred the soup again. It was fitting, she supposed, as he stirred something in her.

'I said I wouldn't have sex with you. Do you think I said that to pique your interest?'

'No. I think you say just what's on your mind, except what you've got behind locked doors in there. But I figure you wouldn't have brought it up if you hadn't had some level of want in there yourself.'

She turned back, remained standing across the counter from him. 'It was probably unwise for you

182

to come here when you're still a little angry and most likely experiencing some residual arousal from this incident.'

'God, I like the way you talk. And you're right, it wasn't the smartest move.'

'If I reconsidered because—'

She broke off when he lifted a hand. 'Do me a favor? Don't reconsider right yet. If you changed your mind on it, I'd be hard-pressed to pass it up. If you didn't, well, I'd just be depressed. I didn't come by for sex, though, like I said, hard-pressed. Let's just take it off the table for tonight. I'd be willing to settle for some of that soup, some conversation.'

She didn't want to like him, didn't want to find herself engaged by a man—a police officer—who talked his way past her guard and sat in her kitchen, drawing out her interest with a personal story.

Logically, she should tell him to go. But she didn't want to, and wondered what would happen if she did something just a little foolish.

'I planned to watch a movie with dinner.'

'I like movies.'

'I was going to watch *Steel Magnolias*.'

He let out a long, long sigh. 'I probably deserve that.'

When she smiled, it seemed to him the whole room lit up.

'Actually, I was going to watch *Live Free or Die Hard*.'

'I should've brought you more flowers.'

*　　　*　　　*

He discovered she was a damn good cook, and that he liked raspberry vinaigrette just fine. He also

183

learned she watched a movie with quiet intensity—no chatter.

That was fine with him, especially since the dog appeared accustomed enough to his presence to curl up and sleep at Abigail's feet. Though Brooks had no doubt if he made the wrong move, Bert would be up, alert, and have him pinned with those unblinking eyes, if not the teeth.

He relaxed himself. Good food, a good movie, a simmering fire and a quiet woman. When the credits rolled, she rose to gather the dishes.

As expected, the dog came to attention, shot Brooks a look that said: I'm watching you, buddy.

'I'll take care of that.'

'No. I have my own way.'

'I'll help you take them back, then.' He stacked bowls before she could decline. 'You turned my mood around, Abigail,' he said as they walked back to the kitchen.

'I'm glad I could help.' She set dishes on the counter, turned to him. 'You should go now.'

He had to laugh. 'Okay. Listen, why don't I pay you back for the mood changer. Take you out to dinner.'

'We just had dinner.'

'Some other time.'

'I don't go out to dinner.'

'Ever?'

'As a rule, I'm more comfortable here.'

'I'll bring dinner, then. I'm very skilled at picking up pizza.'

She liked pizza. 'It's not necessary.'

'Neither was letting me have soup and Bruce Willis. Consider it balancing the scales. I bet you like things nice and balanced.'

184

'I'm not good company.'

'You're wrong about that. I'll call you.'

'I haven't given you any contact numbers.'

'Abigail.' He brushed a finger down her cheek, a gesture so casually intimate her pulse scrambled. 'I'm a cop.'

She couldn't forget that, she reminded herself. Couldn't afford to forget that. 'I'll walk you out.'

'Do you have to remind the dog I'm a friend every time I kiss you?' he asked when she'd unlocked the door.

'Not unless I give him a different command.'

'Okay.'

This time he put his hands on her hips, stepped in to her. He took her mouth as those hands skimmed up her body, awakening nerves, kindling needs.

She did forget, for a moment. With the night air cool, his mouth warm, she forgot everything in the pleasure of the contact. Let herself take that pleasure, let her body press against his. Parted lips, a tease of tongue and teeth, that lovely liquid weight in the belly.

She wished—she wished for his flesh under her hands, his flesh sliding hot and damp against hers. Wished, wished for his hands, his mouth on her breasts, on her body. And for the good, strong thrust of him inside her.

Yearned for that primal human contact as she hadn't allowed herself to yearn for nearly a year.

When he broke the kiss, her mind and body waged war. If she let her body win . . .

Then he said, 'Good night, Abigail.'

'Good night.'

'Take it easy, Bert.' He stepped out, and she

185

welcomed the cool rush of air. Then he paused, looked back at her with those changeable eyes, that easy, effortless smile. 'Wine, conversation, dinner, a movie and a good-night kiss. Definitely a second date.'

'It—'

'You could look up the definition. I'd say we hit it. I'm looking forward to date number three.'

When she shut the door without a word, he grinned.

Arousal, he thought, as he grinned his way to his truck, wasn't always just a reflex. Sometimes it was a result.

11

After his Monday meeting with the selectmen, where he always felt a little bit like a fraud, Brooks headed over to Lindy's with Russ Conroy. Old friend, current selectman, and just-announced mayoral candidate for the fall election.

'Mayor Conroy.'

'That's the plan. Vote early, vote often.'

Brooks shook his head. They'd gone through school together from kindergarten right through high school graduation. They'd played ball together, with Russ on the mound, Brooks at third. They'd lied and bitched about girls, then women— and if it hadn't been a lie on Russ's side, they'd lost their virginity within the same week.

He'd served as best man at Russ's wedding three years before, and stood as godfather for their daughter when Cecily was born some eighteen months later.

He'd seen Russ, a redheaded runt with a face full of freckles and teeth too big for his head, go from grumbling general dogsbody at the pretty hotel the Conroys owned to the buff, compact manager of same.

His love-'em-and-leave-'em, let's-take-a-road-trip-to-Key-West friend had become a canny businessman, a loving husband and a devoted to the point of giddy father.

But he'd never expected there'd come a day when he'd cast his vote for Mayor Russell Conroy.

'Why is that the plan?'

'I'd be good at it.' Russ pulled open the door to the diner, wagged a finger at the waitress as he aimed for a booth. 'Bickford's been good to me. It gave me a home, a living, and more, it gave me Seline and CeeCee. I want a chance at helping it grow—and stay stable, to pump up the tourist trade here and there.'

'You would be good at it.' Brooks sat back as Kim served them coffee without being asked, and as Russ chatted her up.

He'd probably been born for it, Brooks realized.

'Mayor Conroy,' Brooks murmured as he lifted his coffee.

'Chief Gleason.'

'Ain't it a kick in the nuts? We're the grown-ups. Especially you, Daddy.'

'Daddy times two, come September.'

'Again? Really?'

Pride and pleasure shone on Russ's face. 'As real as it gets.'

'Hey, congratulations, Russ. You do good work in that department.'

'We're keeping it quiet for another month, but word's getting out.' He leaned forward a bit. In the Monday-morning quiet of the diner, ears were always pricked for gossip. 'Seline's sick as three dogs in the morning. A couple of the other teachers—including your dad—noticed she was, well, we'll say glowing some.'

'He didn't say a word to me, and I saw him for a bit yesterday.'

'She asked him not to. Your dad's a vault.'

'He is that.'

'So, with me being an old married man and father of one and a bump, I have to live vicariously.' Russ wiggled red eyebrows. 'Hot date this past weekend?'

'I got called in just before eleven to help break up a fight at Beaters. Justin Blake, apparently taking on all comers.'

'Boy's a troublemaker.'

'That plus belligerent, spoiled and still underage. I'm adding substance-abuse problems. His daddy didn't appreciate me putting his firstborn in a cell.'

'Lincoln's an older troublemaker, with the money to back it up. I'm surprised they served the kid at Beaters.'

'According to all the witnesses I talked to, they didn't. He shoved his way in, already lit, then got rowdy when they wouldn't serve him and tried to haul him out. Anyway, Blake dragged himself and his lawyer down to the station.'

'Doesn't sound like a fun-filled Saturday night for you.'

'Or most of Sunday,' Brooks added. 'But the kid's out on bail. He'll have to go to alcohol school, do some community service, pay a fine and

188

damages. Barely nineteen, and booted out of two colleges, already with two DUIs and more moving violations than I can count. He can't drive, legally, for another year, but it doesn't seem to stop him from getting drunk or high, then going someplace else to pick a fight.'

'Ah, youth.'

Brooks gestured with his coffee. 'We were never that stupid, or that arrogant.'

'We were pretty stupid, but no, not that. We never got behind the wheel after we got piss-faced on beer we were too young to buy and drink.' Russ sat back, shoved a flop of his carrot-juice mop off his forehead. 'You need a Saturday night off, son. You know Seline's got a list of eligible friends she's dying to pair up with you.'

'I'll kill you first, and as chief of police, I know how to get away with it.'

'Just saying. Unless you're still bumping hips with Sylbie.'

'That's done. Good and done.'

'Then—'

'Actually, I've spent some time recently with Abigail Lowery.'

'No shit?' Eyes bright, Russ edged forward again. 'Do tell, and I mean do.'

'I've got to get to work.'

'You can't drop that and not follow through.'

'Let's just say she's interesting, mysterious, sexy without trying to be. She's got a dog who looks big enough and smart enough to operate heavy machinery. And she can handle a Glock.'

'Then why's she spending time with you?'

'I keep getting in her way. I've got to get to work. Pay for the coffee, and I'll vote for you.'

'That's what I like to hear. Hey, come on over for dinner, bring the lady.'

'I'm still working on her getting used to letting me into the house,' Brooks said as he slid out of the booth. 'Getting her out of it's going to take more doing.'

*   *   *

In the late afternoon, Brooks took some personal time and ran the errands to complete a mission. By the time he'd finished them and drove to his parents' house, his father had changed from his work clothes to his gardening clothes.

Sunny and Loren worked on one of the front beds, plugging in young, colorful annuals.

Both of them wore hats, his father's a battered ball cap that went back to Brooks's third-base days, his mother's a wide-brimmed straw with a clutch of red flowers tucked in its ribbon.

He loved the way they worked together, hip to hip, with music spilling out of the screened windows and doors—all wide open, though there was still a chill to the air.

When Brooks pulled in, Loren pushed to his feet, rising up on his long legs. Healthy color in his face, Brooks thought, easy smile, hair curling out from under the cap showing plenty of gray but still thick.

One day, maybe, he'd stop seeing his father as he'd been in the hospital before the bypass. Stop seeing him pale and gray and old and a little afraid.

His mother got to her feet as well, planted her hands on her hips. Brooks remembered the fear in her eyes, too. She'd talked a good game as they'd waited and paced and prayed. But the fear had lived in her eyes.

Now they looked like they were supposed to, he thought. Grubby from gardening, happy to see him, and still hip to hip.

He got out, hoped to hell he hadn't made a big mistake, and retrieved the travel crate from the back of the car.

'Hey, there,' his father began.

'Hey, back. Hi, Ma.'

'What have you got there?'

'I brought you a present.' As he spoke, the contents of the crate woke with a yip that trembled with nerves and joy.

'Oh.' Sunny actually put her hands behind her back. 'Brooks, I told you, I'm not ready for—'

'He comes with a return policy. You know Petie out at the county pound? He's bending the rules just a little so you can have a look at the pup here, and he at you, before all the papers I filled out get finalized.'

'Brooks, I just can't . . . Oh, God, look at that face.'

'Petie says it looks like he's got some shepherd and some retriever in him, and God knows what else. But he's got a sweet nature, and some balls. The literal ones have to go, that's the rules, but he's a brave little bastard.'

'Oh, Brooks. Loren, do something.'

'We ought to let him out, don't you think?' Loren put an arm around Sunny's shoulders. 'At least take a real look at him.'

'Some help you are. All right, let him out of there. It's not right he has to be in a cage like a criminal.'

191

'That's the thing.' Brooks set the crate down, opened the door and scooped out the bundle of wiggling, licking, yipping delight. 'He's about ten weeks old. If he doesn't find a home in another month, say, it's curtains. The green mile. Riding the lightning.'

Deliberately, Sunny folded her arms. 'Stop.'

'Dead dog walking,' Brooks added as his mother sighed and his father struggled not to laugh. 'What?' Brooks held the dog's nose up to his ear. 'You sure? Okay. He says he wants me to tell you ... "Nobody knows the trouble I've seen,"' Brooks sang in somber tones.

'Oh, give me that pup.' Sunny stepped forward, gathered up the dog, who trembled with the force of love at first sight as he lapped at her face. 'Oh, damn it. Damn it. Damn it,' she said a third time, with the words soft and muffled against the pup's fur.

Beside her, Loren gave his son a thumbs-up before he ruffled the dog's ears. 'Has he had his supper?'

'Not yet, but I've got everything you need in the car. That is, if Ma's willing to save his life.'

'I should've at least tried out spanking with you.' She held the pup up so his paws ran in the air and his tail wagged. 'Loren, he's going to dig in the flower beds and poop on the floor. He'll chew everything he can get those milk teeth on.'

'Oh, yeah.' Loren reached over, tickled the pup's belly. 'He's going to be a whole world of trouble.'

She brought the pup down, hugged him to her. 'Come here, you brat.'

'You talking to me?' Brooks asked her.

'You're the only brat I see in my front yard.'

192

When he was close enough, she grabbed his ear, pulled him in. 'Thank you.' Then she laid her head on Brooks's shoulder and cried a little. 'Love finds a way. I didn't think I had it in me to do this again, feel this again. But love finds a way.'

She sniffled, straightened. 'I'm going to take him around back, show him where he's supposed to do his business. Y'all can get his stuff out of the car.'

'What made you bring her a puppy?' Loren asked.

'Actually, somebody put the idea in my head, and I ran with it.'

'It's a good run. Let's get his gear.'

'I thought he should have his own, so it wouldn't seem like a replacement. So I got it all,' Brooks said as they started unloading. 'Toys, bed, chew bones, leash, collar, bowls, puppy chow. Got these papers. He has to see the vet for the rest of his shots and the—' He made snipping motions with his fingers. 'I'll take the copy back to Petie tomorrow.'

'We'll take care of it. This means the world to her, and to me. I've missed having a dog. I bet he perks up old Chuck, too.'

'Might at least get that cat off the couch a couple times a day.'

'Might. Your mama's going to be busy with that pup for a while. How about I toss some burgers on the grill?'

'I say—hell,' he said when his radio squawked. 'Chief Gleason.'

'Hey, Brooks, are you down at your folks' yet?'

'Yeah, right in the yard,' he told Alma.

'Mrs. Willowby's reporting an intruder again.'

'Okay, I'm two minutes away. I'll take it.'

When he clicked off, he shrugged. 'Old Mrs.

193

Willowby reports an intruder about once a week. The house settles, the faucet drips, the sun shines the wrong way on the window, they're coming for her. I'll have to stay for weak tea and stale cookies after I go through the house.'

'Then we'll wait to throw the burgers on.'

'That'd be great. Shouldn't take but about thirty minutes.'

'We're not going anywhere.'

*   *   *

Once or twice a week, when her workload allowed for the time, Abigail gave a few hours an evening to personal business. In the normal course of things, she paid any bills that weren't on auto-payments as they came in, did her online shopping as the need— or sometimes just the whim—demanded. She followed the news, a handful of blogs on a weekly or daily basis, and even allowed a certain amount of time each day for games.

Since she'd designed and programmed one and hoped to do more one day, she felt she needed to keep abreast with current trends and technology.

But once or twice a week, she went hacking.

She checked on her mother by hacking into bank accounts, brokerage accounts, the hospital work schedule.

She knew Dr. Susan L. Fitch planned to take a three-week vacation in May to tour Provence. She knew which hotels Susan had booked, which private charter service she and her companion of the last several months—one Walter P. Fennington III— would use.

She knew quite a bit about her mother's life,

activities, finances.

They had neither seen each other nor spoken since the night Susan had left her with Terry and John at the first safe house in Chicago.

But she checked, off and on, out of curiosity, and to reassure herself the Volkovs had taken no reprisals in that area.

Why would they? Abigail wondered. They had moles in law enforcement. And those moles knew Susan Fitch knew nothing, cared to know nothing about the daughter she'd so meticulously conceived, then walked away from.

She checked on John's family. She hoped he'd be happy his wife had remarried eight years after his death. He'd be happy his children were well and apparently happy. She knew where they lived, worked, attended school. Just as she knew Terry's parents had moved to Sarasota.

She'd programmed an auto-search so any mention in any media outlet of the Volkovs popped on her computer. She followed them carefully. Ilya was engaged; a fall wedding was planned. His fiancée was from a wealthy family with ties to another *bratva*. She considered it as a kind of merger, though she imagined Ilya was pleased enough, as the woman was very beautiful.

Hacking into Ilya's computers regularly took more effort, more time and a great deal of research. But she didn't mind. On every visit, she copied and downloaded all of his files, e-mails, stored them, reviewed all the sites he visited.

People like him thought they were careful, but they weren't. She knew his business nearly as well, she imagined, as he did. She knew his life, his fiancée's, his girlfriends', how he spent his money, where he bought his clothes, his shoes.

Everything.

And she knew the Volkovs still looked for her.

She wasn't a priority, but from what she could extrapolate, she was more than a loose end. Elizabeth Fitch was a principle.

She was to be found and eliminated. As long as Sergei Volkov served as head of the *bratva,* she would remain a target. And she believed, absolutely, she would remain one when Ilya officially took his place.

She knew Yakov Korotkii continued as enforcer. She'd compiled a list, one she added to on these visits, of people she believed he'd terminated. She knew—as she'd hacked those agencies as well—that the FBI, the U.S. Marshals Service and Interpol, among others, had similar lists.

But nothing stuck to Korotkii. He was, perhaps because of her, a highly favored and well-protected tool.

She also knew the FBI and the marshals continued to look for her. Or for Elizabeth Fitch.

She remained a witness in the murders of Julie Masters and Alexi Gurevich, and also a person of interest in the deaths of John Barrow and Theresa Norton.

John had spoken the truth, protected her to the end. She could trust no one. To the Volkovs she was a target to be terminated out of pride and principle as much as any potential testimony she might give. To the authorities she was witness to the murder of two federal marshals, or, depending on the analysis, a fugitive who may have, out of desperation, boredom, madness, incapacitated one federal marshal, killed another, wounded one more, as Cosgrove had been shot in the hip during the melée.

Some theorized she'd initiated the gas explosion to cover up her crimes while she fled.

The plan to eliminate her had been in place, she imagined, for days, even weeks, before her seventeenth birthday. Keegan and Cosgrove had initiated it.

She had been meant to die along with John and Terry in the explosion.

She rarely thought of those first few months on the run, that first year in hiding, all the terror and grief. But she'd found her way.

She had a life now, and she meant to keep it.

With the dog at her feet, she tiptoed into Ilya's accounts. He changed his passwords routinely, updated his security, his firewalls.

But she'd spent a decade studying, developing, programming systems—their ins, their outs. Whatever he built, she could break. It gave her a great deal of satisfaction to invade him, to peer into his private world, shatter his privacy.

Her only regret was he'd never know.

He'd never fear as she had feared.

But she cost him.

Every now and again, when she had enough, when she was sure of the data and her own safety, she found a way to leak bits of information to an agent with the FBI—one she'd thoroughly researched, one she felt she knew as well as she knew herself.

Whoever she happened to be at the moment.

She signed the brief, data-heavy memos *tvoi drug*. Russian for 'your friend.' There were files, profiles, searches, queries, on *tvoi drug*. Most believed the

197

informant male, and connected within the Volkov *bratva.*

Tvoi drug had cost lives. Abigail hoped she'd saved some. Her greatest achievement, on her gauge, had been compiling enough information to generate a raid on a warehouse in South Chicago, and dismantle and destroy the forced prostitution ring operating out of it.

Now she studied recent activity. Codes, cryptic phrases, false names. She passed over information on basic computer scams. If the federals couldn't handle those on their own, they didn't deserve any help.

But the money laundering, she considered.

Scraping away at the Volkovs' bottom line offered satisfaction. Maybe not the deep and visceral satisfaction of knowing she'd played some small part in freeing more than twenty girls from sexual slavery, but diminished funds made their business more difficult to operate.

Yes, the money laundering would be her new personal project. She'd consider it a kind of wedding gift to Ilya.

She set about compiling snatches of information from e-mails—Ilya's, the accountant's, a handful of other contacts. It amazed her, always, what people revealed with keystrokes, how careless they were. While she worked, she thought in Russian, entrenched herself in it. So much so that when her phone rang, she muttered a mild Russian oath.

She expected no calls, but a few clients seemed to prefer phone conversations or texts over e-mails. She glanced at the display. Frowned.

Brooks had managed to dig up her cell phone number. Not really that hard, but it would've taken

198

some time and effort.

Why?

Cautious, she answered.

'Hello.'

'Hey. It's Brooks.'

'Yes, I know.'

'What do you like on your pizza?'

'I . . . It doesn't matter.'

'Pizza toppings matter, Abigail. They're vital to the pie.'

She supposed he had a point. And she wished everything about him didn't appeal and confuse. 'I like black olives and hot peppers, particularly.'

'That's a go. Any objection to pepperoni?'

'No.'

'Perfect. I'll be by in about a half-hour.'

'I didn't ask you to come by.'

'Yeah, I noticed. You really have to start doing that.'

'I'm working.'

'It's going on seven. Let's take a break. Besides, I have news for you.'

'What news?'

'It comes with the pizza. About a half-hour. See you.'

She set the phone down, studied it.

She wasn't prepared. Why did he always interrupt and insert himself when she wasn't prepared? Now she'd have to close up the work.

And she'd planned to have chicken stir-fry for dinner.

He'd expect conversation, and she wasn't sure she had any more. Between him and his mother, she was out of what struck her as appropriate small talk.

199

Still, she wondered what he'd meant by news.

Resigned, she shut down the work, then reluctantly put her gun and holster in the drawer.

She assumed he'd also expect a drink, so she considered her nicely balanced selection of wines and chose a good Chianti.

Then she stopped, stared at the bottle.

She was having dinner with him again. That made twice in one week, and that didn't count the huckleberry pie.

She was dating the chief of police.

'For God's sake. How did he *do* this? I don't date. I can't date.'

She set the wine down and did something else she didn't do. She paced. She needed to find a solution, a resolution to this . . . situation. Clearly refusing to see him would only make him more determined and suspicious. In any case, her attempts in that area had failed.

She understood the concept of pursuit and conquer. The male felt challenged, driven to persuade, capture, conquer. Perhaps she should reconsider having sex with him. With sex the pursuit would end, the challenge would be removed. His interest would begin to wane.

Those were logical reasons.

It would also include the benefit of eliminating this yearning. Once her own physical needs were met, his challenge met, his interest faded, she would have no reason to think of him at inopportune times. Everything would go back to normal and routine.

She considered the theory valid.

They'd have sex, then each would get on with their own separate lives and agendas.

Relieved, pleased with her qualified decision, she went upstairs, Bert trailing, to make certain there was nothing in her bedroom, bathroom, or indeed anywhere on the second floor, that would catch his eye.

He'd have no reason to ask about the second bedroom, and the door was secured. She took another moment, asking herself if breaking her own precedents—good precedents—and having an intimate encounter with a local, in her own home, made the best sense.

She believed it did. She believed she was capable of handling the one-time abnormality.

She glanced toward her bedroom station when her security signaled. Murmured to Bert to stand down.

Brooks was prompt, she thought, as she watched him drive toward the house.

She liked pizza, she decided, as she started downstairs. She liked sex. As she unlocked the door, she assured herself the plan was sound, and both parties would complete it amiably.

12

There she was, he thought, her canine companion at her side and those eyes of hers so carefully guarded he just knew they held secrets.

She didn't project annoyance this time, and still she watched every move he made when he climbed out of the truck with the pizza and a six-pack of Rolling Rock.

They kept watching him when he stepped onto

the porch, leaned in and kissed her.

'Hi.'

'Hi.' She stepped back, then went through the locking-up routine. 'You brought beer. I have wine breathing, but—'

'That'll work, too. We'll just put this in the fridge.' He passed her the six-pack, then pulled a rawhide bone out of his pocket. 'Something for Bert, if it's okay.'

The gift touched her. Ploy or not, she thought it showed kindness. 'He won't take it from you.'

'You give it to him, then.'

He handed her the bone, saw Bert's eyes click between the two of them, the rawhide. But the dog didn't move a muscle.

'It was very nice of you. He likes them.' She turned to the dog, murmured a command. Bert's butt hit the floor.

'That wasn't French.'

'Italian.' She gave Bert the bone, followed it with another command.

'He speaks Italian, too. That's some sophisticated dog. He's smiling.'

'Dogs don't smile.'

'Give me a break, look at those eyes. He's smiling. Where do you want the pizza?'

'The kitchen's best. You're in a good mood.'

'I'm about to have pizza with a pretty woman, one who goes for hot peppers, a personal favorite. And she opened wine. I'm off duty until eight hundred hours. I'd be stupid not to be in a good mood.'

'You're not stupid.' She got down wineglasses. 'And though your job includes a high-stress factor, you rarely appear stressed. That I've observed.'

'I like the job.'

'But if your father hadn't become ill, you'd still be in Little Rock.'

'Yeah, probably. I was meant to come home, take this job and settle back here.'

She shook her head as she got out plates. It occurred to her she did have more conversation. 'There's no such thing as predestination or fate or destiny. Life is a series of choices and circumstance, action and the reaction, and results of other people's choices. Your father's illness influenced you to choose this position at this time. I think it was a loving and loyal choice, but it wasn't meant.'

He poured the wine himself. 'I believe in choice, and in fate.'

'How? We can't have choice and free will and still be fated.'

'It's a puzzle, isn't it?'

He looked so natural in her kitchen, in her space, with his jeans and T-shirt, his high-top sneakers and battered leather jacket. Should she be concerned about that?

'Why don't we eat out on the back porch? It's a pretty night.'

That threw her. She never ate outside, and never went outside without a weapon.

'Look at the wheels turn.' He flicked a finger down her temple. 'You've been cooped up working most of the day, I imagine. I can't believe you bought this place if you don't appreciate a soft spring night.'

Just another choice, she thought. 'All right.' She opened the drawer, took out her holster. 'I don't go outside without my gun.'

'Okay.' The Glock 19 again, apparently a

203

favorite. 'I wish you'd tell me what you're afraid of.'

'I'm not afraid.' If it was a lie, it was a small one. She considered herself too well prepared and secured for real fear. 'I prefer to have a gun when I'm outside.'

'All right.' He waited while she put it on, unlocked the kitchen door. 'But when you decide to tell me, I'll find a way to help you.'

'How do you know I'm not a criminal? A fugitive from justice?'

'Do you believe in instinct?'

'Yes, of course. It's—'

'You don't have to explain. Just put it down to instinct.'

She had a little table on the porch, a single chair. Brooks set the pizza down, went inside for her desk chair.

'It's nice out here, the view, the air. You've started your garden.' He took the desk chair, sipped his wine. 'What do you have in the greenhouse?'

'Plants. Flowers, some vegetables. I have some small fruit trees. They do very well in the greenhouse environment.'

'I bet.'

At her signal, Bert lay down by her feet and began to gnaw on his bone. 'He's smiling again.'

This time she shook her head but smiled a little, too. 'You have a fanciful nature.'

'Maybe it offsets that stress.' He took the pizza she served him, balanced the plate on his lap, then, stretching out his legs, held his silence.

She did the same.

'You're not going to ask,' he decided. 'That's some control you've got there, Abigail.'

'Excuse me?'

204

'I said I had news, but you're not going to ask about it. Most people wouldn't have waited three minutes to ask.'

'Maybe it was another ploy.'

'Not this time.' He waited a few beats, sighed hugely. 'Now you're not going to ask because you're messing with me.'

Her smile bloomed again, and damned if he didn't feel a sense of victory every time he made those lips curve. 'All right, all right, if you're going to nag about it, I'll tell you. I took your advice. Rescued a pup from the pound for my mother.'

'Is she pleased?'

'She cried, in a good way. My sister texted me today that I was a suck-up, and Ma still likes her better. That's the middle of us. She was kidding,' he added, when Abigail frowned. 'We like to rag on each other. After an intense debate, during which I ate my burger and kept my mouth shut, the happy parents named their new child, because, believe me, he'll be treated like one, Plato. My dad wanted Bob or Sid, but my mother claims the puppy looked philosophic and very bright, and deserves an important name.'

'It's a good name. Names with strong consonant sounds are easier to use in training. It's good news. Happy news.'

'I think so.' He pulled his phone off his belt. 'Got a picture of him.' He scrolled through, offered it.

'He's very handsome, and has bright, alert eyes.' And it softened her to look into them, imagine him in a good, loving home. 'You're a good son.'

'They make it easy to be. How about your parents?'

'There's only my mother. We're estranged.'

'I'm sorry. Where is she?'

'We haven't communicated in several years.'

Off limits, Brooks deduced. Way off limits. 'I end up communicating with my parents damn near every day. One of the ups, or downs, depending on your viewpoint, of living in a small town.'

'I think in your case it must be an advantage, and a comfort.'

'Yeah. I took it for granted when I was growing up, but that's what kids do. Take for granted. When I lived in Little Rock, I talked or e-mailed a lot. And I came up every month or so, to see them, my sisters, my friends who still live here. But I never thought about moving back.'

'You were happy in Little Rock, and with your work there.'

'Yeah, I was. But when my father got sick, I not only felt I had to come back, I realized I wanted to.'

He pointed a finger at her. 'Fated.'

She gave that little head shake and smile he was growing very fond of. 'You have a close nuclear family.'

'You could say that. How's the pizza?'

'It's very good. When I make my own, I make a whole wheat crust, but I like this better.'

'Make your own? Like from a box?'

'If it's in a box, it's not making your own.'

'Most everything I make's out of a box. You make pizza from scratch?'

'Yes, when I want it.'

'Even my mother doesn't do that.' He put another slice on her plate, one on his, then topped off their wine. 'Maybe you'll show me the greenhouse later.'

'I'm not growing marijuana.'

206

He laughed, so quick, so delighted, it made her jump a little. 'Wouldn't that be interesting? But it's not what I was thinking. I grew up with gardeners, so I'm interested. Not to say we don't have a few around these parts growing some weed, for personal use or as a second income. My own mother did until she started having kids. And she'd still argue at the blink of an eye for legalizing it.'

'Legalizing, inspecting and taxing marijuana would eliminate the funds spent on the attempt to enforce the current laws, and generate considerable revenue.'

'There's that viewpoint thing again.'

The dog shifted, sat up, stared at Abigail. *'Allez,'* she said, and he climbed off the porch, headed for a tree.

'Back to French. Did that dog just ask permission to pee?'

'He wouldn't leave the porch without my permission.' She shifted herself, took a sip of wine. 'I've reconsidered.'

'Too late, you're already into your second slice.'

'Not the pizza. I've reconsidered having sex with you.'

He was grateful he'd just swallowed or he'd have choked. 'Is that a fact?'

'Yes. After weighing the pros and cons, I've decided sex with you would be mutually satisfying. You're attractive and pleasant. And clean. You kiss very well, and while I've found that's not always a reliable gauge for skill in bed, it often follows. If you're agreeable, we can finish dinner, I'll show you the greenhouse, then we can go in and have sex. I'm on birth control, but I would require you wear a condom.'

He was damn near speechless. 'That's an offer, all right.'

'You don't accept?' She hadn't factored in a refusal. 'I thought you wanted me, physically. You don't?'

He put his plate down, got to his feet. Too wound up to give a damn what the dog thought— or did—Brooks pulled Abigail up, gave her a good, hard yank against him.

No soft kiss this time, no easy exploration. This exploded, firebombing shrapnel through her senses. Her balance swayed, crumbled. She had to cling to him or fall.

'Wait. Wait.'

Perhaps it was the tremble in her voice—or the low, warning growl from the dog—but though he didn't let her go, he eased up.

'*Ami. Ami.*' Her hand trembled like her voice as she laid it briefly on Brooks's cheek. Then she added a hand signal for the dog. '*Ami,* Bert. Pillow.'

When the dog sat, Abigail let out a shaky breath. 'He thought you were hurting me.'

'Was I?'

'No. But I'd like to sit down.'

'Look at me.'

She took that breath again, then lifted her gaze to his. 'You're angry.'

'No, I'm not. I'm not sure what I am, but I'm not mad.'

'You don't want me.'

'Do I have to answer that question again, and if so, will I need an ambulance when your dog gets done with me?'

'I . . . oh. Oh.' He heard the humiliation in the sound as she closed her eyes and nodded. 'I understand. I was too blunt, too matter-of-fact. I should have waited for you to approach the subject, or, failing that, I shouldn't have been so calculating. I'd really like to sit down.'

He let her go, sat beside her. 'First, I've got nothing but good feelings about the idea you're willing to go to bed with me. The problem, on my side, is having the feeling you're handling it like a chore you want to cross off your to-do list.'

Exactly true, she thought, in delivery and intent. 'I'm sorry. I thought it was the right approach. You're not angry, but you're at least a little insulted. I am sorry.' She gathered enough courage to look at him. 'I know approach matters to some people. I know that. This was as poorly presented and demeaning as the woman in Ozark Art.'

'I wouldn't go that far. And I hoped you'd reconsider at some point.'

'I wasn't going to, then . . . I was nervous, and I mishandled it.'

'Nervous?'

'This isn't how I usually . . . I don't know how to explain.'

'Not without telling me more than you want to. All right. Let's try this. We'll finish this glass of wine, and you'll show me the greenhouse. We'll see how things go from there.'

'I'm not good with seeing how things go.'

'I'm real good at it. Let's give it a try. If you don't like how they go, we can always do things your way. I figure I can't lose.'

'You mean you'd have sex either way.'

He laughed again, reached out and took her hand for a squeeze. 'What a woman. Let's just see—damn it.' He broke off when his cell phone rang. 'Hold that thought. Yeah, Ash, what's the problem?'

She saw his face change as he listened, saw it go quiet and a little hard. 'No, you did right. I'm on my way. You wait, you hear? Wait until I get there.

'I'm sorry,' he said to Abigail as he closed the phone.

'It's all right.' But she didn't look at him as she rose to pick up the plates.

'This kind of thing is part of the package,' he began.

'I understand that, of course. But you're off duty.'

'So I must be using it as an excuse? No.' Gently, he laid a hand on her arm. 'No, Abigail. This particular problem is one I ordered whoever got the call on it—which was inevitable—to contact me. On or off duty. I need to handle this situation.'

'I see. I do understand.'

'I'd like to come back.'

'You don't have to feel—'

'Abigail, I'd like to come back, if I can. If I can't, I'll call you. I'm not sure which it's going to be.'

'Because you have to see how it goes.'

'That's exactly right. I have to go.' He leaned down, kissed her. 'I'd rather stay.'

She believed him, and the belief warmed something inside her as he strode off the porch and around the house toward his car.

So tonight, the job sucked, Brooks thought, as he drove toward Tybal and Missy Crew's. But he'd given this situation considerable thought since the last time Ty had drunk himself mean. Tonight, one way or another, Brooks intended to fix it.

*   *   *

Every window in the Crews' house glowed up like Christmas, while neighbors gathered on the lawns as if the domestic disturbance qualified as a party. Ash kept them back from the house where bluegrass blasted through the wide-open door and the occasional crash rang out.

As Brooks got out of his car, Jill Harris—house on the left—walked over.

'Somebody's got to go in there before he wrecks what's left of that place.'

'Is Missy in there?'

'She ran out, barefoot, crying, her mouth bleeding. I can't keep making these calls if nothing's going to be done about it.'

'Will you file a complaint?'

'I have to live next door.' At five-foot-nothing, Jill folded her arms across her pink cardigan. 'I tried talking to Missy about it once, while she sat in my kitchen holding a bag of my frozen peas to her black eye. She ended up calling me a dried-up old bitch who couldn't mind her own business. Now she doesn't speak to me. You think I want him banging on my door one drunken night?'

'All right, Ms. Harris. Come on, Ash.'

'Do you want to send someone out to find Missy?'

'No. She's around here somewhere, or she hightailed it over to her sister's. She knows we'll respond.'

Part of him wondered if she'd come to enjoy the drama of it all, and he didn't like the wondering.

'She'll wait for us to haul him off,' Brooks continued, 'then she'll come back home, wait till

211

morning to come tell us she slipped on the soap or some shit. I want you to stand by, but don't talk to him. I don't want you to say anything.'

'I can do that.'

Brooks didn't have to knock, as Missy had left the door wide open when she fled. He stayed on the stoop, called out.

'I don't know as he can hear,' Ash began.

'He'll hear. We're not going inside. We're staying out here, where we've got better than a dozen witnesses.'

'To what?'

'To what happens next. Ty! You got company at the door.'

'I'm busy!' Brooks watched a lamp fly across the living room. 'I'm redecorating.'

'I see that. Need a minute of your time.'

'Come on in, then. Join the fuckin' party!'

'I come in there, I'm hauling you to jail. If you come out here, we'll just have us a conversation.'

'Chrissake. Can't a man get some chores done in his own home?' Ty stumbled to the door, big, glassy-eyed, blood pockmarking his face where Brooks assumed flying glass had nicked it. 'Hey, there, Ash. Now, what can I do for you officers of the goddamn law tonight?'

'Looks like you've been sucking down that Rebel Yell pretty hard,' Brooks said, before Ash forgot himself and responded.

'No law against it. I'm in my own home sweet fucking home. I ain't driving. I ain't operating heavy machinery.' He cracked himself up, had to bend over and wheeze as the laugh took his breath away.

'Where's Missy?'

'Hell if I know. I come home. There's no supper

212

on the table. But she had time to whine. Whine, whine, whine, nag, nag, nag. Where I been, what I been doing and who I'm doing it with.'

'Is that when you hit her?'

The glassy eyes went sly. 'You know how clumsy she is. And when she's on the whining and nagging she can't see straight. Stupid bitch walked right into a door. Then she takes off.' He gestured, spotted the neighbors.

'Buncha assholes got nothing better to do than stand around outside. I'm in my house.' Ty pointed to his own feet to prove a point.

'Redecorating.'

'That is *key-rect*!'

'Maybe if you spent less time redecorating and more time fucking your wife, she wouldn't walk into walls and take off.'

'I'm gonna get me some paint and . . . What'd you say?'

'You heard me.' Beside him, Ash goggled, but Brooks kept his eyes trained on Tybal. 'I guess you can't get that pea-shooter you call a dick up anymore.'

Ty swayed back and forth on his size-fourteen boots, blinked his bloodshot eyes. 'You better shut your fucking mouth.'

'Then again, when you're equipped with a cock the size of a gherkin, what's the point in trying to get some wood?'

'Get off my property, you fucker.' Ty shoved him, and that was enough. But Brooks wanted to nail it shut.

'That the best you got?' Brooks put a sneer on his face. 'I guess it figures a dickless wonder does the pushy shove like a girl. Next thing, you'll be

213

pulling my hair and crying.'

Though he was prepared for the punch and Ty was teetering drunk, it still carried some weight. Brooks tasted blood as Ash let out a wondrous *Jesus Christ* beside him.

And on a roar, Ty charged.

Brooks sidestepped, turned his foot just enough that Ty tripped over it and went flying into the yard.

'Now you've done it. You're under arrest for assaulting an officer.'

'I'll kill you.' Scrambling to his feet, Ty came at Brooks, fists flying.

'Add resisting arrest.' Brooks dodged or blocked most of the blows. 'You want to give me a hand securing the prisoner, Ash?'

'Yes, sir.' Breaking out of his openmouthed shock, Ash ran forward.

'You keep your hands off me, you pissant cocksucker.' He swung at Ash, went wide, but connected with his shoulder.

'That'll be a second count of assaulting an officer. I think it's clear we'll be throwing drunk and disorderly into the mix.'

Between the two of them, they got Ty down on the ground, cuffed him. As they hauled a struggling, cursing Ty up, Brooks scanned the faces on neighboring lawns.

'I'm sending a deputy out shortly,' he said, raising his voice. 'He'll get statements from y'all. I don't want any bullshit, you hear? You say what you saw. Anybody doesn't, I'm charging with obstruction of justice. Don't test me.'

He put a hand on Ty's head, boosted him into the back of the cruiser, then swiped the back of his hand over his bloody lip. 'Deputy Hyderman, you follow me in.'

'Yes, sir, Chief.'

He ignored Ty's rantings as he drove to the station, did his best to ignore his aching jaw as well. The warning look he shot Ash had the deputy keeping his mouth shut as they loaded Ty into a cell.

'I want a lawyer. I'm suing your ass, then I'm kicking it for saying that shit.'

'What shit?' Brooks locked the cell door.

'That shit about I ain't got a dick, and I can't get it up to do Missy. You fucker.'

'Damn, Ty, you must be drunker than you look. I haven't seen your dick since the showers in high school PE, and I can't say I paid it much mind then. I never said anything about it.'

'You lying sack, you said it was the size of a—a—something small.'

'You're drunk, you had the music blasting. You don't know what you heard. Deputy, did I say anything to impinge the prisoner's manhood?'

'I . . . ah. I didn't hear anything.'

'I'm going to have Deputy Fitzwater go out and take statements from the witnesses. Here's what's going to happen now, Ty, and this time you should listen good. You can get a lawyer, all right. You'll need one. I'm filing charges for assault, for resisting, for D-and-D and for creating a goddamn public nuisance. You're going to jail, and not just overnight. Not this time.'

'Bullshit.'

'Assault on a police officer? That's a felony, Ty. You got two counts, plus the resisting. You could do five years.'

His rage-red face went white. 'Bullshit.' And the

215

word shook.

'You think about that. A lawyer might get that down to, oh, eighteen months in, with probation. But you'll do real time for it, that's a promise.'

'You can't send me to jail. I've got to make a living.'

'What you've been doing the last couple years? I don't call it living.'

He thought of Tybal out in center field—fast on his feet, an arm like a rocket. Of Ty and Missy shining all through high school.

And told himself what he'd done, what he would do, was for that bright, shiny couple.

'You think about that tonight, Ty. Think about spending the next year or two, or more, down in Little Rock. Or the chance I might give you of spending that time on probation, contingent on attendance and completion of alcohol rehabilitation, anger management and marriage counseling.'

'I don't know what you're talking about.' Ty dropped down on the bunk, putting his head in his hands. 'I feel sick.'

'You are sick. You think about it.' Brooks stepped back, secured the door to the cells.

'You baited him.'

'What're you talking about, Ash?'

'Come on, Chief, he can't hear us out here. You baited him into the assault.'

'Ash, I'm going to say this once. Sooner or later, it wasn't just going to be Missy with a split lip or black eye. The neighbors, they'd get tired of calling us in. Maybe one of them would get it into his head to stop it himself. Or Missy would get tired of getting smacked and pick up one of the guns they've got in that house. Or he'd get tired of having her run out and hit her hard enough she couldn't run anymore.'

'He never broke up the place like he was doing tonight.'

'No. He's escalating. I don't want to get called out there to deal with one—or both—of their bodies.'

'Can you do like you said? Make him go to rehab and stuff?'

'Yeah, I'm going to make sure of it. Officially? What you heard me say to him tonight was the same as you've heard me say before. Did he hit Missy, where was she, what was the problem, and so on. You got that?'

'I got it.'

'All right, then, I'm going to write it up, have Boyd go on out there to get those witness statements, and check to make sure Missy's back home.'

'She'll come in tomorrow, like always.'

Yeah, she would, Brooks thought. But this time she'd have to make a different choice. 'And I'll deal with her. You can go on home.'

'No, sir. I'll stay here tonight.'

'You caught it last time.'

'I'll stay. You should ice down that jaw. You took a pretty good shot. In the morning, maybe you could bring in some of those sticky buns from the bakery.'

'I can do that. Fancy coffee, too?'

'They got that one with the chocolate in it and the whipped cream on top.'

'I know the one. How's that shoulder?'

'It's not bad. Probably bruise up some, but that's

217

more weight on it. Tybal's okay when he's not drinking. Maybe, if what you did sticks, he'll be okay.'

*   *   *

It took longer than he'd hoped, but Abigail's lights were still on when he got back to her house. The four Motrin he'd swallowed took the throbbing in his jaw down to an annoying ache. That would've been good, but the lessening there made him aware of the few other spots Ty had landed a fist or a boot.

Should just go home, he told himself as he eased out of the car. He should go home, take an hour-long hot shower, drink two fingers of whiskey and go to bed.

The whole business with Ty had ruined his mood, anyway.

He'd just ask her for a rain check, since he'd driven out here.

She opened the door before he knocked, stood there in that braced and ready way of hers, studying his face.

'What happened?'

'Long story.'

'You need an ice pack,' she said as she stepped back.

The first time, he thought, she'd let him in without him asking or maneuvering. He went in.

'It took a while. Sorry.'

'I did some work.' She and the dog turned, walked back to the kitchen. She opened the freezer, got out an instant cold compress and offered it.

'People usually go for the frozen peas.'

'These are more efficient, and less wasteful.'

218

He sat, laid it against his jaw. 'Get punched in the face often?'

'No. Do you?'

'It's been a while. I forgot how much it fucking hurts. You wouldn't have any whiskey handy, would you?'

Saying nothing, she turned to a cupboard. She took out a bottle of Jameson—and right there he wanted to kiss her feet—and poured him two fingers in a thick lowball glass.

'Thanks.' The first slow sip eased the rawness in his mood. 'Anything you don't have handy?'

'Things I don't feel I have any use for.'

'There you go.'

'Do you want to tell me the long story?'

'Honey, I'm from the Ozarks. Long stories are a way of life.'

'All right.' She got out a second glass, poured more whiskey, and sat.

'God, you're a restful woman.'

'Not really.'

'Right now you are, and I sure need it.' He sat back, ignoring twinges, and took a slow sip of whiskey. 'So, Tybal and Missy. Back in our high school days, they were the golden couple. You know what I'm saying?'

'They were important in that culture.'

'King and queen. He was the all-star athlete. Quarterback with magic hands. Center fielder with a bullet arm. She was head cheerleader, pretty as a strawberry parfait. He went to Arkansas State, mostly on an athletic scholarship, and she went along. From what I hear, they sparkled pretty good there, too. Up until junior year, when he messed up his knee on a play. All the talk of him going pro, that blew up. Ended up coming back home. They broke up, got back together, broke up, that sort of thing. Then they got married.'

He sipped more whiskey. Between that, the Motrin and the restfulness of the woman, he felt better.

'He coached high school football awhile, but it didn't go well. He didn't have the wiring for it, I guess. So he went to work in construction. Missy, she tried some modeling, but that didn't work out. She works at the Flower Pot. They never prepared, I'm thinking, for things not to keep on sparkling, so dealing with the dull took a toll. Ty, he started paying that toll with Rebel Yell.'

'He yells?'

'No, honey, it's a whiskey not nearly as nice as what you poured me. My predecessor in this job let me know about the problem. The DUIs, the bar fights, and the D-and-Ds—that's—'

'Domestic disputes. He becomes violent and abusive when he drinks.'

'That's right. The last year or so, it's been worse.'

'Why hasn't he been arrested?'

'He has been, then he ends up with a warning or community service. Missy won't press charges when he smacks her around, and denies it ever happened. She fell, she slipped, she walked into a door.'

'She enables him.'

'That she does. And the fact is people gave them a blind eye on the trouble. The kind of shine they had lasts a long time in a small town like this. But I spent some time away, so maybe I see it—them— differently. Since repeated attempts at getting them into therapy, rehab, counseling have failed, I went another way.'

220

'That resulted in your injury.'

'You could say. When my deputy called to report they were at it—which means Ty came home drunk, hit her, she ran out—I got Ty to come out on his stoop, in full view of the fourteen people outside to watch the show. He had music blasting to accompany his wrecking of every breakable in the house he could get his hands on. This was a plus, as nobody but Ty and my deputy could hear me incite this drunken *asshole* to violence by questioning the size and virility of his penis. If that hadn't worked, I was prepared to suggest that his long-suffering and idiotic wife might find the size and virility of my penis more to her liking.'

On a long breath, he shook his head. 'I'm glad it didn't come to that. He punched me in the face in front of witnesses, and is now contemplating serving time for a felony or two.'

'That was very good strategy. Men are sensitive about their genitalia.'

He choked a little on the whiskey, then rubbed his hand over his face on a laugh. 'God knows we are.' Then he sobered, took a small sip. 'God knows we are that.'

'Your method wasn't conventional, but the result was good. But you feel sorry and a little sad. Why?'

'He was a friend once. Not best, not close to best, but a friend of mine. I liked them, and I guess I liked seeing that sparkle, too. I'm sorry to see them brought low like this. I'm sorry to be a part of bringing them low.'

'You're wrong. It'll be up to them to address and seek help for their problems, but as long as they were both unable to do that, they'd never resolve those problems. What you did gives him

221

only two choices. Jail or help. It's more likely that, when sober and faced with those choices and consequences, he'll choose help. As she appears to be codependent, so will she. I would think your actions fall well within the function and spirit of your job description. As well as within the parameters of friendship.'

He set the whiskey he hadn't finished aside. 'I was telling myself I should just go home with my mood and my aches and annoyances. I'm awfully glad I didn't.'

He reached out, took her hands. 'Let me take you to bed, Abigail.'

She kept her eyes on his. 'All right.'

13

All right.

He wondered that he should find it so sweet, so disarming, she kept it just that simple.

All right.

He rose, drew her to her feet. 'Maybe you could show me the way.'

'You mean to the bedroom.'

'Yeah. I know my way around what we'll be doing there.'

The smile flickered in her eyes, around her mouth. 'I'd be disappointed if that wasn't true.'

He kept her hand as they walked back to the living room, up the stairs. 'Considering what we'll be doing, and I hope you don't question my size and virility for the question, but how does Bert handle the process?'

'He's very well trained, so theoretically he won't interfere.'

Brooks glanced back at the dog. 'Theoretically's a tricky word. And by interfere, do you mean he won't rip my throat out?'

'He shouldn't.'

At the door to the bedroom, Brooks turned her around, narrowed his eyes as he studied her. 'I'm trying to figure out if you're being funny.'

'Humor can smooth over awkwardness, if there is any. I can't tell. But if Bert thought you hurt me, or tried to, his first response would be to protect me—to stop you. He's seen you touch me, and I've instructed him you're a friend, and to stand down. He sees I've brought you up here without duress, that I touch you.'

She laid a hand on Brooks's chest, then glanced at the dog, gave him an order.

'What language was that?' Brooks asked when the dog walked over to a generous dog bed, circled three times and laid down with a windy sigh.

'Farsi.'

'Seriously? You and Bert speak Farsi?'

'Not very well, but I'm working on it. I told him to rest. I don't want to put him out of the room. He wouldn't understand.'

'Okay. Is that a stuffed bear in his bed?'

'Dogs are pack animals.'

'Uh-huh, and a stuffed teddy bear is Bert's pack?'

'It comforts him. I'd like to turn down the bed.'

'I'll give you a hand.'

'No. I have my—'

'Own way. Fine.' He wandered over, studied the computer station set up very like the one on the

223

first floor.

'It makes you wonder.' She folded the simple duvet onto the padded bench at the foot of the bed. 'I'm in the business. I believe strongly in security, and feel a separate obligation to use and test products and systems.'

'I think that's true. But that's not all.' He turned around, watched with appreciation when she took a condom from the nightstand drawer and set it on the table by the bed. 'And we don't need to talk about it now. Is it okay if I put my weapon on the desk here?'

'Yes. Should I undress?'

'No. I have *my* own way.'

After he took off his gun, set it down, he crossed to her, trailed a hand down her hair, her cheek, her shoulder. 'I like finding out for myself what's under there.'

He kissed her, testing, teasing, his fingers still skimming, over her face, down her side, up her back. Light and easy as he could feel her holding back, holding in.

'You have good hands.'

'I haven't put them to much use where you're concerned yet.'

'But you will. I'd like to see,' she said as she began to unbutton his shirt. 'You don't wear a uniform like your deputies.'

'I got out of the habit. Didn't much feel like picking it up again.'

'I like that you don't. You wear your authority in a different way.' She parted his shirt, spread her hands over his chest. 'You're in very good shape.'

'Thanks.'

And lifted her eyes to his. 'So am I.'

'I've noticed.'

'I'm very strong for my build, and have exceptional endurance.'

'You're the sexiest thing, in the strangest ways.' He peeled her shirt up and away.

'I—'

'Ssh.' He laid his lips on hers as he boosted her onto the bed.

The dog didn't make a sound, but Brooks could feel the guarded stare boring into his back as he lowered himself to Abigail.

Her skin was soft, warm and smooth, the muscles of her arms, her shoulders taut. And though her mouth met and answered his avidly, those eyes stayed as watchful as her dog's.

'Close your eyes,' he murmured, nibbling his way to her throat and back.

'I like to see,' she repeated.

'Close your eyes for a minute, and just feel.'

He waited until she did, then closed his own. Then let himself sink, just a little deeper.

She felt. Nerve endings, pressure points, textures, all the more erotic with her eyes closed. A kind of trade-off for control.

She was safe, she reminded herself. She was capable. And she needed.

'Don't think.' He skimmed his teeth over her jaw. 'Just feel.'

She wasn't sure she knew how not to think. But she kept her silence since he seemed to prefer it, tried to let her mind relax.

Different, everything was different here, with him. She wanted to analyze why, but it was so pleasant to only experience.

Just this once, she told herself.

She softened under him, just a little. Just enough. He glided his lips along the subtle swell of her breast over the simple line of her bra, slid his tongue under the cotton, heard her breath catch. So he lingered there, stirring her while his hands roamed.

She'd opened one of the windows partway so the night breeze fluttered through, carrying the scent of the woods, the steady music of the creek.

Moonshine shimmered in hazy beams.

He flipped open the button of her pants, eased them down a few inches and felt the ridge of a tiny scar high on the blade of her hip.

He took his time, wanted time, to discover her, the angles and curves and dips, the simple clean scent of her skin, the way the muscles of her belly quivered when his lips brushed there.

Her response was just as simple, the give, the touch, the fluid rise of her legs and hips as he continued to undress her.

And then.

She erupted under him, jackknifing up, a whip of those long, firm legs, a twist of that compact body, and she was over him. Her mouth clamped down on his, ripped his dreamy languor to shreds and scorched the shreds to ashes. Her breath came on a tear as she scraped her teeth over his shoulder, slithered down, lithe and lethal as a snake, to nip at his chest while her hands tugged at his belt.

He levered up to drag her mouth back to his, to feed on the heat that radiated from her. Urgent now, urgent and hungry.

She arched back, limber as a bowstring, and pressed his face to her breast.

'I need.' He heard her moan it as she straddled

226

him and rocked until he dug his fingers into her hips to keep from imploding. 'I need.'

She was a madness of drive and movement. Caught in the storm of her, he let himself be blown, be battered, as they ravaged each other.

Too much, but not enough, she thought frantically as all those needs clawed and bit. She had to take, had to have, before this terrible pleasure broke her to pieces. His body, so strong, so tough, incited so many wants, his mouth and hands so many sensations. He could take her to that moment of relief and release.

Desperate, she grabbed the condom, ripped it open.

'Let me,' she whispered, stunned that her hands weren't quite steady as she covered him.

She rose over him. In the soft bedroom light he could see the intensity of her eyes, the glow of her skin. Then she took him in. For one breathless moment, everything stopped. Sight, sound, movement. Those fierce eyes stayed locked on his as their bodies joined.

He thought, Eye of the storm, then she swept him away.

She rode him as if her life hung in the balance, with urgent, focused speed. He raced with her, beat for crazed beat, with his heart drumming those frenzied strokes.

When she broke on a half-sob, half-cry, those fascinating eyes closed, that dazzling body bowed, as her arms lifted to wrap around her head in a picture of utter, wanton pleasure.

Those eyes sprang open again when he yanked her down, rolled her under him. Her mouth yielded, soft and swollen when he captured it, when he swallowed her quick, surprised cry as he thrust into her.

Now he rode, driving her up again, pleasing himself ruthlessly as she quaked, as she clung. He felt the orgasm rip through her, felt her nails bite into his back. And let his own release rend him to tatters.

It took him a moment—or two—to realize he'd collapsed on her, his breath whooping out like a marathon runner's after a dive across the finish line.

He rolled off, sprawled out on his back, hoping if he ended up having a heart attack she had it in her to do the CPR.

He managed one raw and reverent 'Wow.'

Glancing over, he saw Bert had remained in his bed but stood and stared.

'I don't know if your dog's curious or just plain jealous, but you might want to let him know you're okay.'

She gave Bert the command for rest. While he settled down, he kept his eyes on the bed.

'Are you okay?' Brooks asked when she said nothing more.

'Yes. It's been several months since I had sex. I realized I rushed you.'

'From my point of view, I think we timed it just right. Jesus, you've got some body there, Abigail. About as perfect as they come.'

'I like yours very much. It's very well proportioned, with excellent muscle tone.'

That just tickled the hell right out of him, so he shifted over to give her a kiss. His grin faded as he looked in those eyes. A man who'd grown up with a mother and two sisters knew when female tears were just below the surface.

'What's wrong?'

'Nothing. The sex was excellent. Thank you.'

'Jesus Christ, Abigail.'

'I'm thirsty,' she said quickly. 'Do you want some water?'

He laid a hand on her arm as she began to roll out of bed. 'Abigail.'

'I need a moment, and some water.'

She walked out without putting a stitch on. That surprised him, as he'd pegged her as the shy type in that area. Then again, the woman was a puzzle through and through.

'You know the secrets,' he said to Bert. 'Too bad you can't talk.'

Though she had water stored on the second floor, she walked down to the kitchen. She did need that moment.

She understood that sex and the immediate aftermath comprised a very vulnerable time, for body and mind. She'd prided herself on being able to fully participate, and recover her control and faculties quickly. Immediately, really.

Why was she shaken and . . . she wasn't entirely sure what she was experiencing. It might have been because she knew him on a more personal level than the others she'd chosen as bedmates. But all she could be certain of was the experience had been unlike anything she'd known.

Why did it make her weepy? If she'd been alone, she would have curled up in bed and cried this inexplicable feeling away.

She wasn't being rational, or smart. The sex had been very, very good. He'd enjoyed it, too. She liked his company, and maybe that was part of the

229

worry. But she was so *damned* tired of the worry.

'Just something I do,' she murmured, and got two bottles of cold water from the refrigerator.

She gnawed on it all the way back upstairs, where Brooks sat propped up in her bed, watching her.

'I don't know how to behave.' She blurted it out—there!—and handed him a bottle of water.

'Is there some standard you're reaching for?'

'Normal.'

'Normal.' He nodded, twisted off the cap, took a couple deep gulps. 'Okay, I can help with that. Get back in bed.'

'I'd like to have sex with you again, but—'

'Do you want me to show you normal?'

'Yes.'

'Then get back in bed.'

'All right.'

She laid down beside him, tried not to stiffen when he pulled her to him. But instead of initiating sex, he tucked her in so her head rested on his shoulder and her body curled toward his.

'This is pretty normal, according to my standards. Or would be if you'd relax.'

'It's nice.' She read books, she watched movies. She knew this sort of arrangement took place. But she'd never tried it before. Never wanted to. 'It's comfortable, and your body's warm.'

'After the heat we generated, I don't think I'll cool off until I'm dead a week.'

'That's a joke, and a compliment.' She tipped her head up to look at him, smiled. 'So, ha, ha, thank you.'

'There you go, being funny again.' Taking her hand, he laid it on his heart. 'And when I'm too weak to laugh. You turned me inside out, Abigail.

That's another compliment,' he added, when she didn't respond.

'I need to think of one for you.'

'Well, if you've got to think about it.'

'I didn't mean—' She looked up again, stricken, then caught that gleam in his eyes. 'You were teasing me.'

'See, this is the part, on my scale of normal, where we tell each other how amazing we were. You especially tell me.'

'Because a man's ego is often correlated with his sexual prowess.'

'That's one way of putting it. Things like you saw God or the earth moved are clichés for a reason.'

'The earth is in constant motion, so it's not a good compliment. A better one would be the earth stopped moving, even though that would be impossible, and a disaster if it were possible.'

'I'll still take it as a compliment.'

His hand stroked up and down her back, the way she sometimes stroked Bert. No wonder the dog loved it. Her heartbeat slowed to the rhythm, and everything inside her uncoiled.

Normal, she thought, was as lovely as she'd always imagined.

'Tell me one thing,' he said. 'Just one thing about you. It doesn't have to be important,' he added when she tensed. 'It doesn't have to be a secret. Just anything. It could be your favorite color.'

'I don't have one, because there are too many. Unless you mean primary colors.'

'Okay, color's too complicated. When you were a kid, what did you want to be when you grew up? I'll go first. I wanted to be Wolverine.'

'You wanted to be a wolverine? That's very

231

strange.'

'Not *a* wolverine. Wolverine—X-Men.'

'Oh. I know who that is. The mutant superhero from the graphic novels and movies.'

'That's the one.'

'But how could you be him when he already existed and his existence is fictional?'

'I was ten, Abigail.'

'Oh.'

'How about you?'

'I was supposed to be a doctor.'

'Supposed to be?' He waited a moment. 'You didn't want to be a doctor.'

'No.'

'Then you didn't answer the question. What did you want to be?'

'I was supposed to be a doctor, and thought I'd have to be, so when I was ten, I didn't think about being anything else. It's not a good answer. Yours was better.'

'It's not a competition. Anyway, you can be Storm. She's hot.'

'Halle Berry's character from the movies. She's very beautiful. She controls the weather. But Wolverine doesn't have sex with her. He has feelings for Jane, the doctor, and she in turn is torn between her feelings for Cyclops and Wolverine.'

'You know your X-Men relationship dynamics.'

'I saw the movie.'

'How many times?'

'Once, several years ago. It was interesting that Wolverine doesn't remember his past, and his reluctant protective instincts for the girl Rogue added dimension. He's a good character for a young boy to emulate. The writers seeded a

232

difficult field for Rogue, as her mutation makes it impossible for her to safely touch another person, skin to skin. The scene with her boyfriend in the beginning was very sad.'

'You remember a lot of the details for seeing it once.'

'I have an eidetic memory. I sometimes read books or watch movies a second or third time, but not because I don't remember them.'

He shifted to look down at her. 'There, you told me something. So you keep everything stored up here.' He tapped her temple. 'Why isn't your head a lot bigger?'

She laughed, then stopped, uncertain. 'That was a joke?'

'Yeah.' He brushed the hair away from her cheek, touched his lips there. 'Have you ever made pancakes?'

'Yes.'

'Good, because you'd remember how to make them.'

'You're hungry? You want pancakes?'

'In the morning.' He glided his hands up her body, in, grazing her nipples with his thumbs.

'You want to stay here, sleep here, tonight?'

'How else am I going to get those pancakes you're making me?'

'I don't sleep with people. I've never slept with a man overnight.'

His hands hesitated for a fraction of a second, then continued their glide. 'Then you don't know if you snore.'

'I don't snore!'

'I'll let you know.'

There were so many reasons why she couldn't—

shouldn't—allow it. But he was kissing her again, touching her again, stirring her again.

She'd tell him no. After.

*   *   *

She woke just before dawn, lay very still. She could hear him breathing—slow, steady. A different, softer sound than Bert. Bert did snore. A little.

She'd fallen asleep, actually fallen to sleep, after they'd had sex a second time. She hadn't told him to go, and she'd intended to. She hadn't made her last check of the house and the monitors. She hadn't put her weapon on the nightstand beside her.

She'd just gotten into that comfortable, normal position, and somehow slipped into sleep while he talked to her.

Not only rude, she decided, but frightening. How could she have let her guard down so completely with him? With anyone?

What did she do now? She had a routine, and one that didn't include an overnight guest.

She had to let Bert out, feed him, check the monitors, her business e-mail and texts.

What did she do now?

She supposed she'd make pancakes.

When she eased out of bed, the dog's breathing changed. She saw his eyes open in the half-light, and his tail give its customary morning thump.

She whispered the command for outside in German as she retrieved her robe and Bert stretched. Together, they padded quietly out of the room and downstairs.

When the door closed, Brooks opened his eyes,

234

smiled. He should've figured her for an early riser. Himself, he wouldn't have minded another hour, but considering the big picture, he could push himself out of bed.

And maybe he could talk her back into it once she'd let the dog out to do his morning thing. He rolled out, headed for the bathroom. On cue, the minute he emptied his bladder, he thought about coffee. Then he rubbed his tongue over his teeth.

He didn't feel right about poking around to see if she had a spare toothbrush, but he couldn't see the harm in digging out a squirt of toothpaste.

He opened the drawer of the little vanity, saw the neatly rolled tube of Crest, and her Sig.

Who the hell kept a semiauto in the drawer with the dental floss and toothpaste? A fully loaded one, he noted, when he checked.

She'd told him one thing the night before, he reminded himself. He'd just have to persuade her to tell him more.

He scrubbed Crest over his teeth with his finger, then went back in for his pants. When he got downstairs he smelled fresh coffee, heard the mutter of the morning news.

She stood at the counter, stirring what he hoped was pancake batter in a dark blue bowl.

'Morning.'

'Good morning. I made coffee.'

'I smelled it in my sleep. You don't snore.'

'I told you I—' She broke off when his lips met hers.

'Just verifying,' he said, as he picked up one of the mugs she'd set out. 'I borrowed a squirt of toothpaste.' He poured his coffee, and hers, watched her gaze lift to his. 'Do you want to tell me

235

why you have a Sig in your toothpaste drawer?'

'No. I have a license.'

'I know, I checked. You have several licenses. Got sugar? Oh, yeah, right here.' He dipped the spoon she'd put beside the mug in the sugar bowl, added two generous servings. 'I could keep checking, this and that and the other. I'm good at digging. But I won't. I won't do any more checking unless I tell you so first.'

'You won't check as long as I have sex with you.'

His eyes burned green with hints of molten gold as he lowered the mug. 'Don't insult both of us. I won't check because I won't go behind your back, because we're—whatever we are at this point. I'd like to sleep with you again, but that's not a condition. I want to keep seeing you because we enjoy each other, in and out of bed. Is that accurate?'

'Yes.'

'I don't like to lie. Not that I haven't and won't in the line. But outside the job, I don't lie. I won't lie to you, Abigail, and checking on you without you knowing seems like kin to a lie.'

'Why should I believe you?'

'That's up to you. All I can do is tell you. This is damn good coffee, and not just because I didn't have to make it myself. Pancakes?'

'Yes.'

'Now you look even prettier than you did ten seconds ago. Am I going to find another gun when I get out dishes and such to set the table?'

'Yes.'

'You're the most interesting woman of my acquaintance.' He opened the cupboard where he'd seen her take out plates for pizza.

'I thought you'd just stop.'

'Stop what?'

'Once we had sex, I thought you'd stop wanting to be here, stop wondering.'

He opened the drawer for flatware, noted the Glock. 'You might have forgotten, but the earth stopped moving.' He set out the flatware as she ladled batter onto her griddle. 'It's not just sex, Abigail. It'd be easier if it were. But there's . . . something. I don't know what the hell it is yet, but there's something. So, we ride it out, see what happens.'

'I don't know how to *do* that. I told you.'

He picked up his coffee again, stepped over to kiss her on the cheek. 'It looks to me like you're doing it just fine. Where's the syrup?'

Abigail

What is character but the determination of incident?
What is incident but the illustration of character?

HENRY JAMES

14

Waking up with Brooks, making breakfast, simply dealing with the jolt in her routine, threw Abigail off schedule. He'd taken his time with breakfast. He always seemed to have something to talk about, and keeping up jumbled her thoughts out of order. By the time he'd left, she was more than an hour behind on her plans for the day, not to mention the time she'd lost the night before.

Now instead of arriving at the market as soon as it opened, she needed to complete her research and documentation of the Volkovs' Chicago-to-Atlantic City money-laundering operation. If she didn't get the data to her FBI connection within the next two days, they'd miss the month's major delivery.

These things took time, she thought, as she settled down to work. Time to gather, to decrypt, to correlate, to send. Her information had to be pure and absolutely accurate.

And maybe this time something would stick to Ilya. Maybe this time he'd pay. Or at least, as before, she'd have caused him trouble, frustration, money and men.

In her fantasies her work brought the Volkovs to ruin, exposed them, stripped them clean. Korotkii, Ilya—all of them—spent the rest of their lives in prison. Keegan and Cosgrove were discovered, disgraced and convicted.

And when she let those fantasies spin out, somehow they all knew she was responsible for making them pay.

Still, it wasn't enough. Julie would always be dead at eighteen. John and Terry would always be murdered trying to keep her safe.

It was better to be realistic, and to do what she could whenever she could to chip away at their profits, their routines, their equilibrium.

She worked until afternoon before she was satisfied. Better to step away for an hour or two, she decided, and come back fresh for a last check of the data before she sent it in.

She'd do the marketing now, even though it was the wrong time of day. Just the wrong time. Then she'd come home, take Bert out for some exercise and training.

Then she'd recheck the data, program her series of bounces to her contact's e-mail. After that, she'd do some hard-and-sweaty training of her own, as she'd want that physical outlet after completing her task.

With the evening free, she'd put a few hours into work on the virus she'd begun developing over the last eighteen months.

She changed her weapon, strapping on her more compact Glock, covered it with a hoodie. Soon the temperatures would rise too high for a jacket, and she'd have to use an ankle holster.

As she checked and reset her alarm, let Bert out to put him on guard, she considered acquiring a new gun. She could treat herself to some weapon research that evening.

The idea relaxed her, and she admitted she found it pleasant to drive into town in the afternoon sunlight, to watch the way that light played through the tender, unfurling leaves.

She caught glimpses of the delicate drape of

toothwort, the bold yellow of trout lily catching the dappled sun along the stream bank just before the water took a quick, tumbling fall over rocks. Among those tender green leaves, wild plum added color and drama.

Everything seemed so fresh and new and hopeful. Spring revived, she thought, offered that new beginning of the cycle. It was her first full spring in this new place, this place she so much wanted to be her home.

Twelve years. Couldn't it be enough? Couldn't this be her place to stay? To plant her garden and tend it, watch it grow and harvest. To do her work, pay her debt—and just live.

Why should they find her here, in these hills, in this quiet? How could they ever connect Abigail Lowery with that young girl who'd been so foolish, so careless—and such an easy target?

As long as she stayed prepared, stayed vigilant, remained unexceptional—invisible—she could make a home and a life.

Stay safe. As long as she stayed safe, she could continue to chip away at the Volkovs and pay that debt.

She liked the town so much, she thought, as she turned onto Shop Street. She loved the pretty streets and busy shops, the color sliding into it all with pots and barrels of sunstruck daffodils and candy-colored tulips. Tourists added more movement, strangers passing through. Some very likely returned, another holiday or short visit. But they came for the quiet, the landscape, the hiking, the local lore and crafts. Not for nightclubs and urban action, the sort of entertainment that lured men like Ilya.

243

Her confidence remained high that she'd never see him or anyone connected to him strolling along the streets here, fishing in the rivers, hiking in the hills.

And surely if anyone from the U.S. Marshals, the FBI, even the Chicago police, visited here, she wouldn't be recognized. She was out of place, and a dozen years older, her hair a different color and style.

If they looked, they might see. But there was no reason to look for Elizabeth Fitch here in the pretty tourist town in the Ozarks.

If the day came, she knew how to run, how to change, how to bury herself in another place.

But it wouldn't be today, she promised herself, as she parked near the market. And every day it wasn't today was a gift.

She got out of the car, hit the key to lock it. Even as she heard the lock click into place, she saw Brooks crossing the street toward her.

She didn't know what to do with the quick rise of her pulse, the little flutter of . . . something in her belly. He even walked as if he had all the time in the world, she thought, and still managed to cover ground quickly. He stood beside her before she could decide what to do, or say.

'This is either really good timing or really good luck.' He took her hand—he was always touching her—and just covered her with his smile.

'I'm going to the market.'

'Yeah, I figured. Take a walk with me first. You're just what I need.'

'For what?'

'In general, let's say. Rough morning, and I haven't shaken it all the way off.'

244

'I need supplies.'

'Got any appointments later?'

'Appointments?' People were looking at them. She could feel the glances on the back of her neck. 'No.'

'Good. Let's walk down toward the park. I'm taking half an hour. You don't usually go shopping this late in the afternoon.'

'I like mornings.' But she'd have to mix it up more, she realized. Routines should never be noticed.

'Do anything interesting this morning?'

Somehow they were walking, and he still had her hand. What was she supposed to do about that? 'I'm sorry, what?'

'This morning, did you do anything interesting?'

She thought of money laundering, Russian mobs, the FBI. 'Not particularly.'

'Now you ask if I did anything.'

'Oh. All right. Did you?'

'I spent a lot of it being yelled at or lectured to. As expected, Missy came in to claim she'd tripped, and wanted me to release Ty. She wasn't happy with the charges against him, or the consequences of them. Now that he's sober, Ty's actually taking it better than she is.'

When Brooks lifted a hand in a wave to someone across the street, Abigail fought back a wince.

This was *not* being invisible.

'After she finished yelling at me,' Brooks continued, 'she did a lot of crying. When I let them talk to each other, they both did a lot of crying. After that, she hunted up and hauled in a lawyer, one who's been a pissant his entire life. That's where the lecturing came into my day. He seems to feel I'm exceeding my authority by offering the rehab and counseling in lieu of a trial and possible jail time.'

'It isn't within your authority to set a plea bargain.'

'You're both right, so I informed the pissant that was fine. Ty could stay put until we went before the judge, held a bail hearing and so on. And how he could risk spending the next several years in jail.

'How you doing, Ms. Harris?' he called out to a tiny woman watering a tub of mixed bulbs outside Read More Books.

'I'm doing, Brooks. How about you?'

'Can't complain. Where was I?' he asked Abigail.

She could feel the tiny woman's eyes on her as she continued down the sidewalk, hand in hand with Brooks.

'You told the pissant lawyer Ty could risk spending the next several years in jail. I really need to—'

'That's right. So, at that point, Missy and Ty started yelling at each other. Personally, I don't understand people who stay together when they've got so much animosity and contempt for each other they can call each other those kind of names. But Ty got worked up enough to turn it on me, vow to finish what he started last night and kick my ass.'

'It all sounds dramatic and distressing.'

'Can't say otherwise. Ty's vow didn't please the pissant, as it made his claim of diminished capacity or whatever the hell he was going for break apart like rotten lumber under a hammer. He was less pleased yet when Ty reached through the bars and got a hand around his pissant throat.

'Hey, Caliope. Those roses look mighty pretty.'

A woman in a long, colorful skirt, a huge straw hat and flowered gardening gloves waved from her yard. 'I knew you were going to say that.'

He laughed. 'Alma's daughter. She's a psychic.'

Abigail started to explain how doubtful it was that the lady with the gorgeous rosebushes had psychic ability, but Brooks was already continuing the story.

'I will admit my reflexes might have been just a tad slow pulling Ty off the pissant, due to all the yelling and lecturing.'

Her head might've been spinning a little, but she followed well enough. 'You let your prisoner choke his lawyer, and found it satisfying, as you'd have liked to choke him yourself.'

Brooks gave her arm a swing and grinned at her. 'Though it doesn't reflect well on me, that's about the truth of it. The pissant quit then and there— and Ty's sentiments toward him, delivered at the top of his lungs as said pissant retreated, were suggestions of self-gratification I don't believe the pissant can manage. Missy ran out after the pissant, screaming and sobbing. And as a result of drama and distress, I'm taking half an hour with a pretty woman.'

'I believe there are people who think the rules, or the law, shouldn't apply to their particular situation because they're poor or they're rich, they're sad or sick or sorry. Or whatever justification most fits their individual makeup and circumstance.'

'I can't argue with that.'

'But the court system often gives credence to that attitude by making deals to those who've broken the rules and the law for just those reasons.'

'I can't argue that, either, but the law, and the

system, have to breathe some.'

'I don't understand.'

'Law needs some room, some flexibility, to consider the human factor, the circumstances.' At the toot-toot of a horn, he glanced toward the street, waved at a man with a huge black beard driving a rusty pickup. 'The man who steals a loaf of bread,' Brooks continued without missing a beat, 'because he's starving and desperate shouldn't be treated the same as the one who steals it planning to sell it at a profit.'

'Perhaps. But if the law had more uniformity, those who steal for profit would have fewer opportunities to repeat the offense.'

He grinned down at her in a way that made her wonder if she'd said something charming or foolish. 'Ever think about being a cop?'

'Not exactly. I really should go back and—'

'Brooks! Bring that girl on over here.'

With a jolt, Abigail swung around, stared at the house with the dragons and mermaids and fairies. And saw Brooks's mother climbing down a run of scaffolding. She wore paint-splattered bib overalls and paint-splattered sneakers. A bright red kerchief covered her hair.

The minute her feet hit the ground, the puppy who'd begun to yip and dance at her voice leaped so high he executed a midair flip before he tumbled into a sprawl.

The woman laughed, scooped him up as she unsnapped his lead.

'Come on!' she called again. 'Come on and introduce Abigail to your little brother.'

'Her favorite son right now, too,' Brooks told Abigail. 'Let's say hey.'

'I really should get back to the market.'

'Haven't I been yelled at and lectured to enough for one day?' He sent Abigail a pitiful, pained look. 'Have some pity, will you?'

She couldn't be invisible if people noticed her, she thought, and it was worse if she made it obvious that she wanted to be invisible. Though she wished Brooks would let go of her hand—it seemed too intimate—she crossed the short distance to the yard of what she thought of as the magic house.

'I was hoping you'd drop by for a visit,' Sunny said to Abigail.

'Actually, I was—'

'I talked her into a walk before she did her marketing.'

'No point wasting a day like this indoors. Meet Plato.'

'He's very handsome.'

'And a rascal. I do love a rascal,' Sunny said, nuzzling the puppy, then Brooks. 'He's smart, too.'

'Me or the dog?'

Sunny laughed, patted Brooks on the cheek. 'Both. This one sits when he's told, but he won't stay put yet. Watch. Plato, now, you sit.'

Sunny set the dog down, kept a hand on his rump as she dug in her pocket for a tiny dog treat with her free hand. 'Sit now. There you go, a genius!' She let the dog gobble the treat when his butt hit the grass.

And he was up and jumping, wriggling two seconds later, then scrabbled his paws on Abigail's shins.

'We're working on manners.'

'He's just a baby yet.' Unable to resist, Abigail crouched down, smiling when Plato tried to crawl

249

on her knees, laughing when he leaped and licked. 'He has happy eyes.' She closed his jaws gently when he tried to nip and chew. 'None of that now. Yes, you're very handsome and happy.'

As if overcome by the compliment, he flopped down, rolled over to expose his belly.

'And he has good taste,' Sunny remarked, as Abigail gave Plato a belly rub. 'Both my boys do. You have happy eyes yourself today, Abigail.'

'I like dogs.' But she looked at the house, shifted the focus. 'Your house is so interesting and colorful. It must be rewarding to share your art with whoever passes by.'

'Keeps me off the streets and out of trouble. Mostly.'

'It's wonderful. I've enjoyed seeing what you've done and continue to do since I moved here. I like that it doesn't make sense.'

When Sunny laughed, Abigail felt the heat rise up the back of her neck. 'I didn't say that correctly. I meant—'

'I know exactly what you meant, and you're exactly right. I like that, too. Y'all come on in. I made some peach sun tea this morning, and I've got some of those ginger cookies with the lemon icing you like, Brooks.'

'I could use a cookie.' Reaching down, he skimmed a hand over Abigail's hair.

'Thank you very much, but I need to get to the market, and home to my own dog.' Abigail picked up the puppy as she rose, handing his wriggling body to Sunny. 'It was nice to see you again, and to meet Plato.'

She moved as quickly as she could, trying to judge the line between busy and running away.

They'd charmed her, seduced her. The man, the mother, even the little dog. She'd let herself be swept along. Conversation, invitations, pie, sex.

People had seen her walking with Brooks. Holding hands with him. Talking to his mother. And people would talk about it. Her.

Just because she wasn't part of a social network didn't mean she was oblivious to how it worked.

She couldn't be the unexceptional, hardly noticed woman who lived *on* the fabric of Bickford if she became part *of* the fabric through Brooks.

Why wasn't he behaving per the basic male profile? They'd had sex. He'd conquered. Now he should move on to the next challenge.

When someone grabbed her arm, she reacted without thought. Pure instinct had her swinging around, leading with a backfist fired by waist and hip, the follow-through of jab already primed.

Brooks slapped a hand on her fist a half-inch before it connected, had to brace, push back.

'Whoa.' He managed, barely, to block the jab as well. 'Excellent reflexes, Xena.'

'I'm sorry.' The simple trip to the market took on the quality of a nightmare. 'You startled me.'

'At least. Fortunately, my reflexes are pretty good. Otherwise I'd be sporting another bruise on my face.'

'I'm very sorry.' She spoke stiffly now. 'You came up from behind and grabbed me.'

'Got it.' As if to soothe, he stroked a hand down her hair. 'Baby, you're going to have to tell me who hurt you eventually.'

'Don't talk to me that way. This isn't going the way it's supposed to. You had sex.'

'I think that's we, and yeah. Why don't you clue

251

me in on how it's supposed to go?'

'You're supposed to go away.' Agitated, she pushed a hand through her hair, glanced around. 'I can't discuss this now, here. I don't understand why it needs to be discussed. You're not supposed to be interested now.'

'For someone as smart as you are, you can be thick as a brick. I had sex with you because I'm interested. And since we slept together, I'm more interested.'

'Why? No, don't answer. You always have answers. You confuse me. I don't want to feel like this.'

'Like what?'

'I don't know! I need to go to the market, and I need to go home, and I need to finish my work, and—'

'You need to take a breath.' He laid his hands on her shoulders now. 'Take a breath, Abigail.'

'I need to take a breath.' She closed her eyes, fighting the panic attack. Oh God, oh God, why hadn't she stayed home?

'Good, just take another breath. Take it easy, that's the way. Now, here's what we're going to do.'

'Don't tell me what we're going to do. There's not supposed to be any *we*.'

'Apparently, there is. How about here's what I suggest we do? Why don't we go over to my office. You can sit down, have some water.'

She shook her head. 'I have to go to the market.'

'Okay, you go on to the market. Later, should be around six or six-thirty, I'll come out. I'll bring a couple of steaks and grill them up. We'll have some dinner, see if we can sort this out.'

'We don't need to have dinner or sort anything

out. I just need to—'

Very gently, very quietly, he laid his lips on hers. When he lifted his head, her breath shuddered out.

'I've got the sense that's what you don't want to feel. But you do, and I do. So we ought to sort it out.'

'You won't go away.'

'Let's see how it sorts out. If it comes down to that, I'll go away. I'm not going to hurt you, Abigail, and I'm going to do my best not to make you unhappy. But when two people feel something, they ought to respect that enough to try to figure it out.'

'You don't understand.'

'No, honey, I don't. But I want to. Let's get you to the market.'

'I don't want you to walk me back there. I want to be alone.'

'All right. I'll see you tonight.'

One more conversation, she told herself, as she hurried away. One more where she'd remain calm and rational. She'd simply explain that she wasn't interested in or inclined toward a relationship. Her work kept her too busy for the distractions of dinners and company and overnight guests.

She would be firm; he would be sensible.

They'd end whatever this was that should never have begun amicably.

And everything would be quiet again.

As soon as she got home, she'd practice what she'd say and how she'd say it.

She'd be prepared.

*   *   *

She put off the practice, reminding herself her

253

priority was, and would always be, the work. Maybe compartmentalizing proved a little trickier than she expected, but she carefully reviewed all the data she'd gathered, made a few small adjustments. And composed her e-mail.

Information you may find useful. Thank you for your attention and any action deemed appropriate.

Tvoi drug

Using the system she'd already devised for the message, she routed it through various locations, shut down the temporary account. As she often did, she thought she would have enjoyed communicating with her FBI contact, exchanging thoughts and opinions, but she had to settle for gleaning information from the occasional memo or file she hacked.

After shutting down, she locked her copy of the data away.

'We'll walk,' she told Bert. 'I'll practice what I need to say to Brooks while we do. Tomorrow, everything goes back to the way it should be. We have to work for a living, too, right?'

As she pocketed her keys, Bert rubbed his body against her leg. 'I met another dog today. He's very sweet. I think you'd like him.'

When she stepped outside, Bert fell in at her heels. 'You'd like a friend. Next year I'll get a puppy. You'll help me train him, and he'll be good company for both of us. That's all we need, isn't it? It's all we need.'

With Bert, she walked around to look at her

254

young vegetable garden. 'It needs some tending, and it's time to think about putting in some more flowers. Past time. I've been distracted, but we'll get back on schedule. I need to do more work on the virus. One day, Bert, when the time's right and I've perfected it, we're going to infect the Volkovs like a plague.'

She sighed. 'But I can't think about that now. I have to think about this situation.'

She unzipped her hoodie as they moved into the woods, laid her hand briefly on the butt of her gun.

The wild plums popped, fragrant petals among the tender haze of green, and the willow someone had planted years before dipped its lacy fingers toward the busy water of the stream. Wood violets spread a carpet of rich purple.

In the quiet, in the scent, in the color, she calmed as they walked through sunlight and shade.

Quivering in anticipation, Bert shot her a look, and on her go joyfully scrambled off the slope of the bank to splash in the water. It made her laugh, as always, to watch the big bruiser of a dog play like a toddler in a wading pool.

She gave him his moment while she scanned the woods. Birds called, a musical lift accompanied by the rat-a-tat of a woodpecker hunting for lunch. The sun through the filter of young leaves cast a dreamy light.

It would brighten as they walked, she knew, and the view would open to the hills. She loved looking out from the high ground, studying the rise and fall of the land. And here, in soft light and shadow, with the birdcall and the mutter of the stream, the splashing dog—here, she thought, was more home than the house.

She'd buy a bench. Yes, she'd go online later and find something organic and woodsy. Something that looked as if it might have grown there. Of course, benches didn't grow, but it would have that illusion. And she could sit where the world opened to the hills, while her dog played in the stream. Maybe one day she'd feel secure enough to bring a book. Sit on the bench in her woods with the hills outstretched beyond, and read while Bert splashed.

But she had to stop thinking about the future. She had to deal with the right now, or the coming evening.

'All right.' She signaled the dog, kept her distance as he raced out to shake a storm of water in the air. '"Brooks,"' she began, while they walked, '"while I find you attractive and certainly enjoyed having sex with you, I'm not in a position to pursue a relationship"—no, "I'm not willing to engage in a relationship." That's firmer. "I'm not willing to engage in a relationship." He'll ask why. That's his pattern, so I have to have an answer ready. "My work is my priority, and involves not only a great deal of time but requires my focus."'

She repeated it, trying different inflections.

'It should be enough, but he's tenacious. I should say something about appreciating his interest. I don't want to make him angry or upset, or to damage his pride. "I appreciate your interest. It's flattering." Flattering is good. Yes.'

She took a long breath, relieved the panic didn't come again.

'Yes,' she repeated. 'I could say, "I'm flattered by your interest." And I am. It's easier to sound sincere if you are sincere. "I'm flattered by your interest, and I've enjoyed our conversations."

256

Should I bring up the sex again? God. God! How do people do this? Why do they? It's all so complicated and fraught.'

She lifted her face to the sun, breathing in the warmth and light as she came out of the trees. And looking out over the hills, she wondered. So many people out there, with so many connections, all those interpersonal relationships. Parent, child, sibling, friend, lover, teacher, employer, neighbor.

How did they all do it? How did they mix and mingle and juggle all those needs and dynamics? All those expectations and feelings?

It was easier to live quietly and alone, with your own schedule, your own goals, meeting your own expectations and needs, without constantly being required to add others to the mix.

It's what her mother had done, and certainly Susan Fitch was successful on all fronts. Yes, the daughter had been a disappointment in the end, but then again, that's what happened when you added another individual.

'I'm not my mother,' Abigail murmured, as she laid a hand on Bert's head. 'I don't want to be. But even if I wanted relationships and complications, I can't. It's not possible. So, let's try it all again. "While I find you attractive,"' she began.

She worked on the content, tone, structure of the speech, even the body language, for nearly an hour, fine-tuning it as she and Bert walked home again.

Assuming the discussion and dinner should be civilized, she opened a bottle of Shiraz. And had a half-glass to steady her nerves. By six-thirty she had to order herself not to pace, or pour another half-glass of wine.

When he drove up at six-forty-five, her nerves

257

had taken the time to build again. She repeated her prepared speech in her head, using it to calm herself as she went to the door.

15

He really was pleasant to look at, she thought. It might take some time for the chemical reaction she experienced around him to dissipate.

'Sorry, I'm late.' With a grocery bag tucked in his arm, he walked to the porch. 'I had a couple things come up.'

'It's all right.'

'Hey, Bert.' Casually, Brooks rubbed a hand over Bert's head as he walked into the house, then he shifted his angle, laid his lips on Abigail's. 'How're you doing?'

'I'm fine, thank you. I can take the bag to the kitchen.'

'I've got it.' He nodded toward the wine on the counter as he set the bag down. 'Nice.'

'You said steak. This should go well with red meat.'

'Good, because I've got a couple of fat New York strips in here.'

'You didn't say what you wanted to have with the steaks, so I wasn't sure what to fix.'

'Nothing. I've got it.' He pulled out two boat-sized potatoes and a bag of salad mix.

'What is that?' Abigail tapped the bag.

'Salad. It's a bag o' salad.'

'Bag o' salad.' Despite the nerves, her lips curved. 'I have plenty of fresh vegetables for salad.'

'That you have to chop up and so on. The beauty of bag o' salad is it's already done. Why don't you sit down? I'll get the potatoes on.'

She didn't think she should sit. She hadn't practiced sitting down. 'Would you like to have our discussion before dinner?'

'Do we only get one?'

'I'm sorry?'

He glanced back at her as he took the potatoes to the sink to scrub. 'Only one discussion? How about we talk before dinner, during, even after.'

'Well, yes, of course. But the discussion of the situation. Should we have that now, or would you prefer to wait until dinner?'

'What situation?'

'You and I . . . This social connection. The interpersonal relationship.'

He set the potatoes on the counter, and with a smile so warm it made something inside her ache, he took her face in his hands. 'Interpersonal relationship. I'm next door to crazy about you.' He kissed her, strong, long, until the ache spread. 'Would you mind pouring me some of that wine?'

'I . . . yes. No, I mean, I don't mind pouring the wine. We need to discuss—'

'You know, "discuss" sounds like we're going to get into politics.' He frowned at the oven for a moment, then set it to bake the potatoes. 'Why don't we stick with talk?'

'All right. We need to talk.'

'About our social connection and interpersonal relationship.'

In reflex, her back stiffened. 'You're making fun of me.'

'A little. These are going to take a little while.

259

Maybe we could go sit down. I could build us a fire.'

Too cozy, she thought. 'Brooks.'

'So you can say it.'

'Say it?'

'My name. It's about the first time you've used it.'

That couldn't be true. Could it? 'You're confusing me. I haven't even started and you're confusing me.'

'You're worried about what's happening between us. Is that right?'

Relieved to begin, she took a breath. 'While I find you attractive, and I enjoyed having sex with you, I'm not willing to engage in a relationship.'

'You already have.'

'I—what?'

'This is a relationship, Abigail, so you've already engaged in one.'

'I didn't intend to. I'm not willing to continue to engage in a relationship.'

'Why's that?'

'I'm flattered by your interest, and I've enjoyed our conversations. However, my work requires a great deal of time, and complete focus. I prefer not to be distracted, and believe you require a more amenable and socially oriented companion.'

He took a sip of wine. 'Did you practice that?' He pointed at her. 'You did.'

Every inch of her body stiffened with mortification. 'I fail to see why the fact that I wanted to be certain I articulated my thoughts and opinions clearly is amusing to you.'

The arctic tone of her voice did nothing to dim his grin. 'I guess you'd have to be standing on my side of the room.'

'That's just another way to say point of view, which is your rationale for a great deal.'

'Yeah, it counts a lot to my way of thinking. Abigail, I figure you had to work on that little speech awhile, because most of it's just bullshit.'

'If you're incapable of having a rational discussion, you should go.'

Wineglass in hand, body angled back to the counter, he remained as relaxed as she was rigid. 'You weren't planning a discussion. You were going to orate your practiced speech, then I was just supposed to mosey along. If you want me out, Abigail, then I think you're going to have to tell me what's bothering you, what you're afraid of, and what you feel.'

'I said I wasn't interested.'

'But you're not being truthful. I don't want to be with a woman who doesn't want to be with me. So if that's the case here, tell me, give me enough courtesy and respect to explain it, and I'll grill up the steaks. We'll have a decent meal, and I'll go. That's about as fair as I can make it.'

'I told you. My work—'

'Abigail.'

There was a world of patience in the word, and it lit a fire under her.

'Why doesn't anything go the way it's supposed to with you? Why can't you respond logically? I can't have a discussion with someone who refuses to be rational.'

'At the risk of setting you off, from where I'm standing I'm being about as rational as anyone could.'

'Then stop.'

'Stop being rational?'

261

She threw out her hands. 'I can't think!'

'Answer this. Do you have feelings for me?'

'I don't want to.'

'I take that as a yes, qualified. Why don't you want to?'

'I don't know what to do with them. With you. With this. I just want it to be quiet again. I just want my routine. I think that's reasonable.' Her voice pitched toward panic again, but she couldn't stop it from rising. 'It's not quiet when you're here, and everything's off schedule and unpredictable. I can't even go to the market because then I'm walking with you and talking to your mother and playing with a puppy, and your mother's offering me peach sun tea. I just want to be left alone. I know how to be alone.'

'Let's get some air.'

'I don't want air!'

'Honey, you're shaking, and you're having trouble getting your breath. Let's just take a minute, get some air, settle it down.'

'Don't take care of me! I've been taking care of myself since I was seventeen. I don't need anyone.'

Brooks unlocked the back door. 'Come on, Bert.' And, taking Abigail's hand, pulled her outside. 'If that's the case, then it's long past time you had someone willing to look out for you now and again who gives a goddamn. Now, fucking breathe.'

'Don't swear at me.'

'Breathe, and I won't have to.'

She pulled away from him, leaned against the porch post. Tears came along with the breath, so she pressed her face to the wood.

'You want me on my knees, that's the way to do it.' Rubbing his hands over his face, Brooks dug for

262

composure. 'Abigail, if I'm responsible for making you this unhappy, you've got my word I'll leave you be. But I wish to God you'd let me help you.'

'You can't help me.'

'How do you know?'

She turned her face toward his. 'Why do you care?'

'I'd say you haven't had enough social interaction or interpersonal relationships if you don't understand why anyone would.'

'You're making fun of me again.'

'Not this time.' He didn't touch her, but his voice was a gentle stroke over raw nerves. 'I've got feelings for you. I haven't sorted them all out yet, but I like having them.'

She shook her head. 'It's just a chemical reaction.'

'So you've said. I took chemistry in high school. Sucked at it. Am I making you this unhappy?'

She wanted to say yes, because she believed he'd go and stay away. But she couldn't lie when he looked in her eyes. 'No. It makes me happy when I see you. I don't want to be happy because of you.'

'So being happy makes you unhappy.'

'I know that doesn't sound rational, but it's accurate. I'm sorry I behaved that way.'

'Don't apologize.'

He dug into his pocket, came up with a folded blue bandanna. 'Here you go, now.'

Despising herself, she sniffled. 'Thank you.'

'I'm going to ask you a question. If you're not ready to answer, say so. But don't lie to me. Is this about a husband, ex-husband, boyfriend, something on those lines, who hurt you?'

'No. No. There's no one like that. No one's hurt

263

me.'

'You got hurt all over you. Are you saying no one physically hurt you?'

'Yes.' Calmer, she dabbed at her eyes with the soft, faded cloth, then stared out at her greenhouse. 'I can take care of myself. I don't have husbands or boyfriends or relationships.'

'You've got one now—the relationship.' Stepping over, he took her chin in one hand, brushed at the drying tears on her cheeks with the other. 'You're going to have to put that big brain of yours to work on how to deal with it.'

'I'm not like other people, Brooks.'

'You're unique. Why shouldn't you be?'

'You don't understand.'

'Then help me understand.'

How much could she tell him? If he understood, just enough, maybe it would end it.

'I want my wine.'

'I'll get it.' Before she could comment, he'd stepped back inside. She took the moment to align her thoughts. No point in wishing for more time to prepare, she told herself.

'I don't need you to do things for me,' she began, when he came out with their wine. 'It's important to me that I do for myself.'

'The wine? Seriously?' He took his own to the porch steps, sat. 'Manners are important, too. Simple courtesies. My mother's a very capable, independent woman, but I'd've gotten her glass of wine. From what I've seen, what I know, you're as capable as they come. That doesn't mean I can't do you a courtesy.'

'It's stupid.' A little lost, she looked down at the cloth, turned it in her hands. 'I hate being stupid.

And it wasn't what I was going to say, anyway.'

'Why don't you sit down here and say what you're going to say?'

She hesitated, then signaled to Bert that he could go into the yard, and sat.

'I am capable of most things, but I don't believe I'm capable of maintaining a relationship.'

'Because?'

'When my mother decided she wanted a child, she researched donors.'

'So she wasn't involved with anyone.'

'No. No one she wanted to procreate with.'

Procreate, Brooks thought. That was a telling word.

'She'd reached a point in her life where she wanted a child. That's not accurate,' Abigail decided. 'She wanted an offspring, and she had very specific, very detailed, requirements for the donor. My mother is a very intelligent woman, and naturally she wanted to produce an intelligent . . . offspring. She required high intellect, good health, including family medical history. She had physical requirements, in appearance and body type, stamina.'

'I get the picture.'

'When she'd determined the donor, she scheduled the conception date, through artificial insemination, to correlate with her own personal and professional calendar. Naturally, she arranged the finest prenatal care available, and I was born through a scheduled cesarean section, and proved very healthy, of the proper weight and size. She had, of course, already arranged for a nurse, so I was given excellent care, and tested and examined regularly to be certain my development was strong.'

The birdsong, so happy, seemed out of place, as did the sudden jeweled whirl of a hummingbird toward a pot of scarlet dianthus.

'Do you know all this because you found out, or because she told you?'

'She told me. I always knew. The knowledge was part of my education. Education, along with my physical health, were priorities. My mother is exceptionally beautiful, and she had some disappointment in that while my features are pleasing enough, my coloring good, I didn't reach the level in appearance she'd hoped for, but I made up for it with intellect and motor skills and retention. Overall, she was very satisfied.'

'Oh, baby.'

She hunched in when he put his arm around her shoulders. 'Don't feel sorry for me.'

'You're just going to have to swallow that one.'

'I'm telling you this so you understand my basic genetic makeup. My mother, while satisfied with me on the whole, never loved me or wished to. She never accepted I might have my own goals or desires or plans. Hers, for me, were again very specific and detailed. For a very long time I thought she didn't love me because I was lacking in some area, but I came to understand she simply didn't love. She has no capacity or aptitude for love, and no skills at displaying affection. Factoring genetics and environment, I also lack the capacity. I may not have the skills for relationships, but I understand emotions and affection are primary needs in developing and maintaining them.'

Brooks thought, What a load of crap. But he structured his response more carefully. 'Let me get this straight. Because your mother's cold, selfish and appears to have all the finer feelings of a sand flea, you're genetically predestined to be the same.'

'That's very harsh.'

'I can be harsher.'

'There's no need. When factoring both genetics and environment, what's often termed nature and nurture—'

'I know what the hell it is.'

'Now you're angry.'

'That's a mild term for it, but not with you. Let me ask you something else. If you're so genetically incapable of love and affection, how come you love that dog, and he loves you back. And don't try to pass it off as training.'

'We need each other.'

'Need's one part of it. If he got hurt or sick and couldn't function as a guard dog, would you get rid of him?'

'Of course not.'

'Because it would be cold and selfish and downright mean, and you're none of that. And because you love him.'

'He's a dog, not a person. There are people who feel strongly for and about animals, and don't have the same feelings for or about people.'

'You feel something for me.'

With no helpful answer, Abigail stared down into her wine.

'What about your father?'

'Donor.'

'Okay, what about the donor? If she didn't tell you specifically who he was, you found out. You're too smart to let that slide.'

'She wouldn't give me his name or certain details. When I was twelve I . . . accessed the

267

information.'

'She kept files.'

'My conclusion was—is—she felt it important to keep track of his health, any potential problem areas. So yes, she kept files. I hacked into them.'

'At twelve.'

'I've always had an interest in computers. He's a physicist. Very successful and respected. He was in his early twenties when he donated, several years younger than my mother at the time.'

'Does he know about you?'

'No. It's not done.'

'You could have contacted him.'

'Why? Why would I disrupt his life, his family? We have a biological connection and nothing more.'

'He has a family.'

'Yes, he married at thirty-one. At the time I accessed the information, he had one child and was expecting another. He has three children now. I'm not one of them. I'm the result of a donation.'

'Is he still married?'

'Yes.'

'So he can develop and maintain a relationship. You've got his genes, too.'

For a moment, a long moment, she watched the flight of the hummingbird—that sapphire blur—until it whizzed out of sight.

'Why would you want to be with someone whose skills and aptitude for personal connections are stunted?'

'Maybe I like the idea of watching them grow, and being part of it. Then there's the fact I'm hung up on you. Factor those together.'

'There are other reasons I shouldn't let this

continue. I can't tell you what they are.'

'Yet. I know you're on the run from something, something that scares you enough you need that dog, all this security, all those guns. Whatever it is has you behind locks, actual and metaphorical. When you trust me enough, when you figure out that needing help isn't the same as being weak and needy, you'll tell me. But for now, I should fire up that grill.'

She got to her feet when he did. 'How much of your interest in me is wondering what's behind the locks?'

She needed honesty, maybe more than most, so he'd give her honesty. 'It started out that way. I still wonder, partly because a cop always wonders. But mostly now? When you opened those locks, even a little, Abigail, you got me. You got me,' he repeated, taking her hand, pressing it to his heart.

She looked at her hand, felt that strong, steady beat. And let herself go, let herself lay her cheek there. When his arms came around her, she squeezed her eyes shut and the emotions rose so fast, so hard and fast. To be held like this on a cool spring night by someone who cared.

It was like a miracle, even for someone who didn't believe in them.

'I still don't know what to do with this, with you. With any of it.'

'Let's see how it goes.'

'I can try. Will you stay tonight?'

He pressed his lips to the crown of her head. 'Thought you'd never ask.'

She stepped back, steadied herself by looking into his eyes. 'I'll go make a dressing for the bag o' salad.'

And saw that quick flash of humor light his face. 'That'd be great.'

When she went inside, he walked over, took the cover off her grill. Oh, she had him, all right, he thought, more than was comfortable. But he believed he'd get used to it, just like he believed easing open those locks, a little at a time, would be worth the effort.

* * *

In Chicago, only two blocks from the club where Ilya had met Elizabeth Fitch one summer night, he toured the dingy apartment that housed one of their most profitable computer scam operations. He often oversaw this area himself, so while his presence generated some nerves, work continued smoothly.

Several operators worked computers, blasting out spam advertising job offers for work at home, Canadian pharmacies, online dating, free downloads. Some would generate fees—handled by phone operators who conned those naive or desperate enough to call in. Others would simply steal credit card information, which could be translated into quick profit or identity theft.

Here, the overhead was low, the profit rich and regular.

He'd personally designed a variation on the tried-and-true Nigerian scam that continued to be their top moneymaker.

It brought him considerable pride.

He enjoyed the work, and considered it an intellectual exercise. Business was good, increased from the previous year. No amount of warnings posted online, touted on the nightly news exposés, curbed the hunger in human nature for easy money.

And the only weapons needed to strip the foolish from their wallets were a computer and a phone.

He accepted violence, inflicted it when necessary, ordered it when it was warranted. But he preferred bloodless crime.

He considered himself a businessman, and would soon take a wife, make a family of his own. He would teach his sons to be businessmen, and to leave the blood to others. Men like Korotkii would always be useful, but he had higher plans for the sons he'd make.

He enjoyed hearing the phones ring, and the 'operators' read the prepared script, improvising when necessary. 'Yes, you can earn money at home! Increase your income, set your own schedule. For a small fee, we'll provide you with all you need.'

Of course, they'd provide nothing of use, but the fee would already be deposited. The mark would be out just under forty American dollars. Really, a small price for a lesson learned.

He spoke briefly with the supervisor, made a note of the day's take, then strode for the door.

He enjoyed, too, the communal breath of relief behind him as he stepped out the door.

He'd been born for power, and wore it as naturally as his favored Versace suits.

He walked out of the apartment building to his waiting car. He slipped into the back, said nothing to the driver. As the SUV pulled away from the curb, he texted his mistress. He expected her to be ready for him in two hours. Then he texted his fiancée. He'd be late but hoped to be finished with his meeting and other business by midnight.

The car pulled to the curb again outside the restaurant, closed tonight for a private party.

His father insisted on this face-to-face meeting every month, though, in Ilya's opinion, so much could have been accomplished more efficiently through Skype and conference calls.

Still, Ilya saw some value to the personal connections, and there would be good food, good vodka, and the company of men.

Inside, he handed off his cashmere topcoat to the pretty, sloe-eyed brunette. When time allowed, he'd like to fuck her while she wore those black-framed glasses.

His father already sat with several others at the big table set in the main dining room. Sergei's smile spread wide when he saw his son.

'Come, sit, sit. You are late.'

'I had some business.' Ilya bent down, kissed his father's cheeks, then his uncle's. 'I have the numbers for the Fifty-first Street operation. I wanted to give them to you tonight. You'll be pleased.'

'Very good.' Sergei poured Ilya's vodka himself before lifting his glass. At seventy, he remained robust, a man who enjoyed life's pleasures and rewards to the fullest.

'To family,' he toasted. 'To friends and good business.'

They discussed business while they ate, and always at these meetings ate traditional Russian food. Ilya spooned up borscht as he listened to reports from brigadiers and trusted soldiers. Out of respect, he asked questions only when he received his father's nod. Over braised spring lamb, Ilya reported on the businesses he oversaw personally.

Problems were discussed—the arrest of a soldier on drug charges, a whore who'd required discipline, the interrogation and dispatch of a suspected informant.

'Misha will speak,' Sergei announced, 'on the business of our people inside the police.'

Ilya pushed his plate aside. Too much food in the belly and he wouldn't enjoy his mistress fully. He looked at his cousin as he sipped his wine.

'Pickto says he hasn't yet been able to find how the information on some of our business is being fed to the FBI.'

'Then why do we pay him?' Sergei demanded.

'Yes, Uncle, I asked just that. He has warned us on some occasions in time for us to take steps to protect our interests, but he can't identify the contact within the Bureau, or the method of information. He believes the contact is one of three people, but they keep a tight lid on this. He asks for more time, and resources.'

'More money.'

'For bribes, he says.'

Misha, now the father of four, continued to eat with gusto. Ilya knew his cousin didn't have a mistress to satisfy. 'I don't question his loyalty, but I begin to think he, and the two others we have in place, aren't high enough on the food chain to meet our needs.'

'We will look into these three people. Ilya, you and Misha will take this business. Whoever this FBI police is, whoever the informant, we will end it. This costs us money, men, time. And offends.'

Now Sergei pushed aside his plate. 'This brings me to old business. We don't forget Elizabeth Fitch.'

273

'There's no contact with her mother,' Ilya began. 'None with the police that we have ever found. If she continues to live, she lives in fear. She's no threat.'

'As long as she lives, she's a threat. And again, an insult. This Keegan, we pay him, and he's useful. But he doesn't find her. The others, they cannot find her. She is one woman.' He banged his fist on the table. 'How can we hold our pride if we are defeated by one woman?'

'We won't stop looking,' Ilya assured him.

'No, we will never stop. It's a matter of honor. Yakov?'

'Yes, Uncle.' The years sat lightly on Korotkii, as they did on a man who enjoyed his work.

'Speak to Keegan. Remind him why this is important. And speak to Pickto as well. Money is motivation, yes. So is fear. Make them afraid.'

'Yes, Uncle.'

'Good. This is good. Now.' Sergei clapped his hands together. 'We will have dessert.'

16

It seemed easy, almost natural. She wondered if she'd crossed some boundary and now lived in the normal she'd always yearned for. She didn't know how it could possibly last, so every moment of that easy, natural normal glittered bright and precious as diamonds.

He was with her almost every evening. Sometimes she cooked, sometimes he brought food. They might sit outside or take a walk to her favorite spot overlooking the hills. He helped her in the garden, taught her to play gin rummy on a rainy night, then feigned disgust when she beat him every game.

He made her laugh.

When he touched her in the dark, all the worries, all the doubts, brewing inside her just dropped away. Every time she woke with him in bed beside her, the happy jolt of surprise stayed with her for hours.

She learned of the townspeople from him, putting pictures together in her mind from the funny stories or offhand comments he made. The clerk who often waited on her at the market stood as undisputed champion of the pie-eating contest held every July Fourth in the park. The manager of the bank was an amateur magician who performed at kids' parties. Brooks's oldest, closest friend was expecting his second child.

Brooks might be called away in the evening, and twice he had to handle a call in the middle of the night. Whenever she found herself alone, the house felt different. Not like it did during the day when her work, her routine, flowed along, but as if something essential was missing.

When it did, she tried to ignore the nagging sensation that when it all ended, nothing would ever feel completely balanced and whole again. So she focused on the moment, the hour, the day, the night. Then the next.

She tried to relax and see how it would go.

Together, they stood studying the flower bed they'd just finished. Most of the plants she'd nurtured along in her greenhouse, and seeing them in place as she'd pictured in her head brought her pleasure.

Having help, she discovered, didn't diminish that pleasure at all.

She liked feeling a little grubby, a little sweaty, a little tired, and knowing the spinach lasagna she'd put together earlier only had to slip into the oven.

'It looks very attractive.'

'It looks great,' he corrected.

'It looks great. But it'll look better in another few weeks. It was nice having help.'

He shot her a grin. 'Really?'

'Really. Would you like a beer?'

'I'm on call, so better not. Could use a Coke.'

'All right.'

So simple, she thought, as she went inside. She liked getting him a drink, fixing him a meal. Cooking for someone besides herself, she'd discovered, brought serious satisfaction. Just as she liked him suggesting he bring home a pizza or Chinese or toss some burgers on the grill.

She'd thought it would feel crowded—the house, her life, her routine—with him in it, but somehow it felt bigger. She'd worried that her work—the business and her personal agendas—would suffer with someone else taking up her time and space, but she'd been very productive the last couple weeks. So many of the little tasks or chores took less time, as he pitched in to help or just did them himself.

They weren't living together, she reminded herself, as she poured the Coke over ice. She couldn't let it go that far. But he had a toiletry kit in the bathroom, a few clothes in the closet.

She liked looking at them when he wasn't around. Just looking at his shirt, his razor, a pair of socks.

They served as tangible evidence he was in her life.

Or the life she was trying to build.

She glanced out the window as she heard the dog's bark, Brooks's laughter.

Bert chased the yellow tennis ball as if his world relied on its capture. The play equaled not only fun but good exercise. Still, it was odd to watch the dog respond so easily to the man.

Ami, she thought.

Yes, they'd become friends.

She picked up her glass of ice water, carried it and his Coke outside.

'Thanks. That dog would chase a ball to Texas if I could throw it that far.'

'He enjoys the run, and it's good for him. He likes it when you throw the ball, because you can throw it farther than I can.'

'He's giving me a workout. I won't need any infield practice on Saturday at this rate.'

When the phone rang, it relieved her. He wouldn't ask again, he wouldn't pressure her. But she knew he'd like her to come to the park on Saturday where he played softball.

She wasn't ready, and didn't know if she'd ever be ready, to face all the people who'd come, who'd talk to her or about her.

She picked up the wet, mangled tennis ball, threw it so Bert could continue his game.

She heard Brooks say, 'I'm on my way.' Then, when he stuck the phone back on his belt, 'Crap.'

'There's some trouble?'

'Spoiled rich kid gets high, trashes hotel suite, slugs hotel manager.'

277

'Oh. Your friend Russ Conroy?'

'Yeah. Justin Blake equals spoiled rich kid. He tried to fight with hotel security, and is now being held by same until I get there. I'm sorry.'

'It's your job.'

'And this one's going to take a while, as it involves a belligerent troublemaking asshole; his annoying, enabling and influential father; and the long-suffering lawyer the kid's behavior keeps in Gucci loafers and Chivas Regal. I may not make it back tonight.'

'It's all right.'

'Easy for you to say, you're not missing lasagna.'

'I'll keep some for you. It holds well.'

'Thanks. I'll call you either way. I've got to wash up some before I head in.' He took her hands, leaned in to kiss her. 'I'll miss you.'

She liked to think he would—a little, anyway. Being missed by someone was another first in her life.

The dog trotted up as Brooks went inside, then simply stood, panting a little, the ball clamped in his mouth, his eyes on the door.

'He'll come back if he can,' Abigail said. 'We have to be all right without him, too. It's important we're all right on our own.'

As she threw the ball again, she thought she'd just make a salad for her dinner. Eating the lasagna by herself seemed too lonely.

*   *   *

The Inn of the Ozarks stood on a gentle hill just inside the town limits. The four-story Victorian had been built by a successful bootlegger back in

278

the twenties as a country home. His success had come to a hard stop just days before the end of Prohibition, when a rival had shot him with a Henry rifle while the man took a turn on his veranda with a Cuban and a glass of moonshine.

The widow had never returned to the house, and for some years thereafter, it fell into disrepair. The oldest son, who liked to play the ponies, sold it the minute it came into his hands.

Russ's grandfather rebuilt and redesigned it largely on his own, and opened it as a hotel in the spring of 1948. While not a raging success during Cecil Conroy's day, it held its own. As the artist community took shape in the seventies and eighties, it graced many canvases, one of which had the good fortune to catch the eye of a wealthy collector in New York.

Inspired by the painting, the collector, as well as some of his friends and associates, began to make the hotel the base for getaways, business/pleasure interludes and assignations.

As a result, by the turn of the century, the hotel had earned a face-lift and the addition of a spa and an indoor pool.

Its fourth floor included the perk of twenty-four-hour butler service, and held the most prestigious suite in the building.

With Russ beside him, Brooks stood in that suite, with its pale gold walls, its dark-toned, gleaming antiques, its glowing local art.

Glass sparkled on the polished chestnut floor from the broken prisms of the once grand parlor chandelier. The heavy blown-glass vase that had surely been thrown into the sixty-inch flat-screen TV lay shattered on the handwoven rug that bore stains from the contents of one of three empty bottles of red wine. The remains of a Tiffany lamp shone on the debris of dishes, wasted food, overflowing soap dishes filled with butts and a scattering of porn DVDs.

The blue-and-gold silk of the sofa fabric bore cigarette burns like ugly eyes.

'And you should see the bedroom,' Russ commented around a split and puffy lip. 'Motherfuckers.'

'I'm sorry about this, Russ.'

'The master bath's jet tub's stained with this wine, with piss. One of them broke the faucet clean off. Don't ask about the toilet.'

'We're going to need pictures, before and after. Can you ballpark the monetary damage, just to give me a picture?'

'More than seventy-five thousand, probably closer to a hundred. Jesus, I don't know, Brooks. Could be more once we get under what we can see. And smell.'

'How many were in here?'

'Three. Girls in and out, too. They booked it under Justin's father's name, used his card at check-in. Justin and a girl. That was last evening. Sometime last night—we'll check the lobby security tapes—the other two boys—that's his usual crew, Chad Cartwright, Doyle Parsins—and two more girls came in. Justin told the desk to let them up. No law against having guests in your room. They stayed the night. The desk and security fielded a few complaints about noise from the other guests. Best I can tell the girls left this afternoon, and the other three spent the day smoking weed, ordering room service, watching porn. About six we started getting complaints again—yelling, crashing, wild laughter, banging. They had the damn door barricaded, wouldn't open it for the floor manager. I came up. Jesus, you could smell the weed in the damn hall.'

Brooks just nodded, let Russ spill it out. His friend's hands still shook some from what Brooks understood was rage and a kind of grief.

'I told that little fuckhead if he didn't unblock the doors I'd be calling the police and his father. Nothing against the fear and awe you generate, Brooks, but I think it was the threat to call his old man—and the rest of their parents—that got me in. Then that *cocksucker* sneered at me. Sneered, and told me to fuck off. The room was paid for. I could see what they'd done here, or some of it. See the other two sprawled out on the floor. I was too mad to let loose, you know what I mean.'

'I do.'

'I told the floor manager who was with me to get security. That's when that piece of shit sucker punched me.' Gingerly, he rubbed a fingertip over his abused lip. 'Carolee—you know Carolee.'

'I do.'

'She grabbed her walkie, called for Ben, told him to bring a couple of the bigger bellhops. She thinks on her feet. I've got the fuckwit up against the door now, and the other two are so wasted they're pissing themselves laughing. And he humps at the door, gives Carolee this shit-eating grin and tells her she oughta come on in, how he'll fuck some life into her.'

'Jesus Christ.'

Struggling to calm, Russ pressed his fingers to his eyes. 'He just wouldn't quit, Brooks. Ben and the

281

others came on the run, and that's when he starts kicking, trying to punch, starts screaming. Carolee called the station, and Boyd came right quick. He sent for Ash for backup, and we all figured they should let you know.'

'Figured right. He likely stole the credit card from his father, but the parents, they'll back him up, say they let him use it. Can't prove otherwise, but the damage here, the assaults . . .'

Brooks realized he needed to calm a bit himself. 'I'm going to have Boyd come in with Alma; she takes good pictures. She'll document all of this, and Boyd's going to do an official search, in her presence and yours or Carolee's, for illegal substances. Even if they smoked and snorted everything they had, there'll be trace. And God damn, I can see the joints mixed in with cigarettes in those soap dishes. His daddy won't buy that vicious moron out of this one. Not if you press charges.'

'You can bet your ass on that.'

'Good. I'm going to call them in now. If you put Carolee on this, you can ride in with me. You can make an official statement, press charges. You get your insurance people on this, get me a good, solid inventory and assessment of damages.'

Russ nodded. The high color in his face began to fade to a sickly white that wasn't much better. 'I already called them.'

'All right, then. You need some time first?'

'No.' Russ covered his face with his hands, scrubbed hard. 'God, I feel sick. I've got to tell my parents. It makes me sick what they did here, but I don't need time.'

'Then let's get started.'

282

Brooks thought he could have written it himself in three acts. Justin Blake goes on one of his personal rampages, the authorities are called and take the arrogant shithead into custody. Before you could say you have the right to remain silent, Lincoln Blake strides in, lawyer in tow.

In the time Brooks drove to the hotel, surveyed the worst of the damage, spoke with Russ, then drove to the station, Lincoln Blake had already arrived with his lawyer.

Blake pushed to his feet.

He cut an imposing figure with his broad chest in a well-cut suit, his bull neck caged in a striped tie. Cool blue eyes peered out above a sharp nose.

He wore his slate-gray hair cut military short, though rumor was Blake had successfully dodged the draft, when there'd been a draft to dodge.

'Russell, I understand my son and his friends may be responsible for a little breakage at your hotel. I want to assure that if this proves to be the case, we'll take care of it. Don't you worry, now.'

'Mr. Blake, I'll apologize for being rude, though it doesn't feel sincere at this moment, but I don't want to talk to you. Brooks, I'm going to go sit in your office, if that's all right.'

'Go ahead.'

'Now, Russell,' Blake began, but Russ kept walking. Blake's face set hard. 'A hotelier should understand that a certain percentage of overhead has to be earmarked for breakage and overuse.'

'Mr. Blake, I don't much want to talk to you now, either.'

As Brooks topped him in height, Blake couldn't look down his nose, but the sentiment was clear.

'You're a paid employee of this town, and you

283

won't last a year in this position with that attitude.'

'I'll take my chances. I assume you're going to tell me Justin had permission to use your credit card for the suite at the hotel, for all the room service and miscellaneous charges.'

'Of course.'

'Then that's your business. The rest is mine.'

'I want my son released immediately. We'll pay for any damages incurred, naturally.'

'Then you ought to know those damages are going to approach, if not exceed, six figures. Yeah.' Brooks nodded when Blake's eyes rounded, as his face reddened. 'They did a number on those rooms.'

'If Russell Conroy or his father, whom I have always respected, think for one short minute they can inflate this business to exploit—'

'Two of my officers are at the hotel right now, documenting the damages. The insurance agent is also on his way to do the same. I've just come from there and seen it for myself. My officers will also be doing a search for illegal substances, as the place reeked of marijuana. I don't know where your son or his friends got the red wine or the brandy, the beer and the other assorted alcohol, the containers of which were all over the damn place, but they are all under the legal drinking age. Added to it, your son assaulted Russ—don't you bluster at me this time,' Brooks snapped. 'He assaulted Russ, in front of witnesses. He also assaulted the security guard, in front of witnesses.'

'I want to speak to my son. Now.'

'No. I will speak with him, and his lawyer can be present and speak with him. But while he's under the legal drinking age, he is also legally an adult.

284

It may not make much sense, but that's the law. You'll speak to him when I'm done with him. And, Mr. Blake, you can't buy the Conroys off like you have the others. They won't be bought. This time, Justin's going to pay for what's he's done.'

'Push too hard, Gleason, you push on this and you'll lose your job.'

'Like I said, I'll take my chances. Now, I assume Justin asked for a lawyer, but I'm going to check. Until I know he's engaged that right, nobody talks to him.'

Brooks walked over to Jeff Noelle, one of his part-time deputies, who was doing his best to look invisible. 'Did he ask for a lawyer, Jeff? Do you know?'

'Yessir. He was bitching about a lawyer when Ash and Boyd brought them all in, and yelling at the other two prisoners to keep their mouths shut.'

'All right, then.' Brooks walked back. 'You've got a client, Harry.'

'I'd like to speak with my client privately at this time.'

'Sure. Jeff, you take Mr. Darnell to his client.'

'Yessir, Chief.'

Ignoring Blake, Brooks walked to his office, shut the door. 'Justin lawyered up, as expected. They'll have their confab, then I'll talk to him. Want some coffee?'

'No. I got some water. I don't think I can stomach anything else.'

'I'm going to take your official statement. We're going to do this by all the steps, Russ. I'm going to warn you Blake's going to try to pressure you and your family to take a payoff, let the kid slide.'

Color, nearly as red as his hair, rode up on Russ's

cheeks. 'There isn't enough money in the world. My mama bought that chandelier in Waterford, Ireland, had it shipped all the way back here just for that parlor. It was her pride and joy. For that alone, Brooks.'

'I know it. I'm going to record this.'

'Okay.' Russ closed his eyes a moment, nodded. 'Okay.'

When they'd finished, Brooks took a long study of his friend's face. That angry color had faded so the freckles stood out like mottling on the sick pallor of his face. 'I'd like to have Jeff drive you home, but you're going to want to go back to the hotel.'

'I have to.'

'I know it. He'll take you. I'm going to be a while here. I'll come over to your place when I'm done, if you want.'

'I'd appreciate it, Brooks. If you could call anyway, let me know how you think things stand.'

'I will, and I'll come to where you are after I do. I don't want anybody cleaning up that mess yet, all right?'

'How long do you think—never mind.' Russ held up a hand. 'All right.'

'I told Boyd to put police tape on the door. I know it's not what you'd like, but the tougher we make this, the better chance we have of getting it all the way through if the Blakes decide to go to court.'

'You do what you have to do.'

'There's one last thing.' Brooks opened a drawer and took out a digital camera. 'Say shit.'

Russ let out a little laugh, sighed. Then scowled at the camera. 'Shit.'

When Brooks left his office, he noted Blake was

no longer in the outer area. Probably gone off to hound the mayor, or burn up the cell towers with calls to the state rep, the freaking governor.

'It's a sorry shame,' Alma said, and handed Brooks an envelope. 'I took a boatload of pictures, like you said. About broke my heart, too.'

'This won't.' Boyd held up a trio of evidence bags. 'We got your marijuana, your cocaine and some Oxy to round it off.'

'That'll work. Did you log it in?'

'All nice and official. We got the video camera like you said we should, and Ash ran it while I did the search. Can't document much clearer.'

'Good work, all of you. Is Harry still back there?'

'He hasn't come out.'

'I'm going back, starting with the ringleader. Boyd, why don't you take Chad Cartwright, and Ash, you talk to Doyle Parsins. You remind them of their rights again, you hear? And you get everything on record. If either of them says "lawyer," you stop.'

'They didn't ask for one yet, or for a call, either,' Ash told him. 'Last I checked, both of them were passed out back there.'

'Give them a wake-up call.'

Brooks went back to the tiny conference room. He banged on the door, shoved it open. 'It's time you and I had a talk, Justin.'

Justin continued to sprawl in the chair, one arm thrown carelessly over its back. He only curled his lip.

'Chief, if I could have a word with you.' Harry got up, murmured something to Justin that had the boy jerk a shrug.

Harry came out, closed the door. He was a

287

head shorter than Brooks and about fifteen years his senior. Back in the day, Harry had coached Brooks's Little League team to a championship.

'Brooks, I realize that between the three of these young men there was some damage done to the hotel suite, and I understand there was some underage drinking. The fact is, they'll make good on the damages, if indeed there are any, and my client is permitted an independent assessor in that matter. And we both know the drinking's not going to go anywhere. Slap on the wrist, some counseling maybe. As for the claim of assault, Justin tells me Russ was understandably upset, and there was some mutual pushy-shovy. Now—'

Brooks pulled the digital print of Russ's split and swollen lip out of his file. 'Does that look like pushy-shovy to you?'

Harry stared down at the photo, then just sighed, raked his hands through his short thatch of brown hair.

'Don't you ever get tired of doing this dance?'

Harry waved a hand, shook his head. 'I've got to do my job, Brooks.'

'You know there are days I think my job sucks. Yours sucks more.' Brooks opened the door. He took out a tape recorder, put it on the table.

He noted the night had taken some of the shine off Justin's gold and bronzed prince-of-the-city looks. Good, Brooks thought, looking into the cocky, bloodshot eyes.

'Were you read your rights, Justin?'

'Yeah. I've got the right to say fuck you.'

'Justin,' Harry warned.

'Freedom of speech.'

'I'll exercise that same right. You want to look at

288

these, counselor.' Brooks poured the photos on the table as he sat.

As Harry studied them, Brooks studied the boy.

Justin Blake, the only child of Lincoln and Genny Blake, had been born into money, prestige and good looks. Chiseled features, sulky mouth, sizzling blue eyes and thick sun-kissed hair likely ensured he'd had his pick of girls through his high school years.

He might have made something of himself, Brooks considered—maybe he still would—but up to this point the money, prestige and good looks had translated into arrogance, a mean temperament and a vicious disrespect for any kind of authority.

'Justin Blake, you're charged with destruction of property, vandalism, underage drinking and three counts of assault.'

'Big fucking deal.'

'Oh, it will be. As will the possession charges. We have the weed, the coke and the Oxy you and your fellow morons had in the suite.'

Justin only smirked. 'I don't know what you're talking about.'

'We've got your prints on file already. I'll just bet we're going to find them on that bag of weed, the bag of blow, maybe even on the pills. You're on probation, and one of the terms of that probation is no drugs, no drinking, no trouble. You did the hat trick.'

'My father'll have me out of here in an hour. If Harry wants to earn his big, fat fee, he'll have the rest fixed before morning.'

'No, and no. Not this time. Russell Conroy has just officially pressed charges. My deputies have

289

interviewed witnesses. We have, as you can see, photo documentation of the havoc you wreaked. We have the drugs, the alcohol and shortly we'll be picking up the girls you entertained last night. I just think it would be icing on the cake if any one of them happens to be under the age of eighteen, 'cause then I get to add statutory rape and contributing to the delinquency of a minor. But even without the icing, you're not getting probation, counseling and community service this time. You'll do some time.'

Justin lifted his middle finger. 'An hour.'

'In violation of your probation, and look at the time! It's after eight o'clock. Too late for a bail hearing tonight. You'll be a guest of our fine facilities until ten tomorrow morning, at which time we'll go before the judge and lay it all out.'

'Bullshit.'

'Chief Gleason,' Harry began, 'my client's parents are respected members of the community. I believe we can safely release Justin into their supervision for one night.'

Brooks leveled one look, hard as granite. 'That's not going to happen. He stays. I may not be able to stop the judge from granting bail tomorrow, but until then he's mine.'

'You're nothing. You're just some glorified rent-a-cop trying to swing his dick around. My father could buy and sell you a dozen times out of fucking petty cash. You can't do anything to me.'

'It'd be a shame if you thought of your own worth by your father's bank account—if I gave a rat's ass about your twisted inner child. What I can do to you is this. I can arrest you and charge you, which is already done. I can incarcerate you until such time a judge tells me different. I can—and believe me, I will—testify at your trial, should you choose to take this to trial, and detail every bit of your vicious, useless, destructive behavior.'

'I'd like another moment alone with my client.'

'You've had over a half-hour with him already.'

'Brooks, I need a moment with my client.'

'All right, then. When you're done, he's going in a cell.'

Brooks stepped out. It took less than ten seconds for the screaming to start. He knew it was small of him, and likely unprofessional on top of that, but damn if it didn't do his heart good to hear Justin throw a tantrum worthy of a two-year-old brat.

17

In the quiet house with the dog snoring at her feet, Abigail scanned the hacked FBI files. It pleased her that Special Agent Elyse Garrison had pursued the lead she'd leaked to her, built on it. The five-point-six million the FBI's operation had confiscated equaled a nice, solid chunk, enough to sting, in Abigail's opinion. As would the six arrests.

It was hardly enough to put the Volkovs out of business, but it would annoy them and drive them to dig deeper into their organization, trying to find the source of the leaks.

Satisfied, she closed the files, told herself she should go to bed. It was nearly midnight, and she'd contracted two new jobs that week. She needed to be fresh to begin work in the morning.

But she wasn't tired. What she was, Abigail

admitted, was restless. And what she was doing, under the cover of work and research, was waiting for her phone to ring.

How many times, she wondered, had she read a book or watched a movie where she'd been baffled by a woman waiting for a man to call? It seemed to her women who did so not only lacked a sense of self-esteem but were simply foolish.

Now she could only be baffled at herself.

She didn't like the sensation she experienced, this combination of nerves and anxiety. Faint, yes, but *there*.

She didn't even want this relationship, she reminded herself, and she certainly didn't want this uncomfortable and unattractive position she found herself in now.

She didn't require phone calls or dinner companionship or conversations . . . or any of it. All of those things interfered with her routine, upset her schedule, and, more important, could only lead to complications she couldn't risk.

Still, she had to admit it was nice to have those things, and to forget—even for minutes at a time—and simply *be* Abigail.

The Abigail he was attracted to, enjoyed being with.

But wasn't that falling into the same trap she'd sprung on herself years before? Convincing herself she could be what she wasn't, have what she couldn't?

It was good, better—no, best—he hadn't called. She could begin immediately readjusting herself, her life back to what it had been before he'd changed it.

She'd make herself some herbal tea. She'd take

it upstairs and read herself to sleep. That was sensible. That was who she was.

When she rose, the dog came awake instantly. He followed her into the kitchen and, when he saw her fill the kettle with water, sat to wait.

A good dog, she thought, as she set the kettle on the stove, a comfortable, well-secured house and satisfying work. Those were the only things she required to be content, and contentment was all she required.

And yet when her alarm signaled, she didn't feel her usual click of tension and readiness. Instead, she felt a quick surge of hope. Annoyed by it, she turned to her monitor to watch Brooks drive toward the house.

He presumed too much, she decided, coming to her door after midnight. She wished now she'd turned off the lights, gone to bed. If she had, at least he wouldn't have any reason to think she'd waited for him.

She'd tell him she was on her way to bed and too tired for company. Simple, and again sensible, she thought, as she went to the door.

She opened it as he got out of the car, and in the glare of her security lights saw in his face, in his movements, layers of exhaustion, anger, sadness.

'Sorry.' He stood for a moment at the base of the porch steps, bathed in that bright light. 'I should've called earlier. I should've gone on home.'

'You didn't.'

'No. Things got complicated.' He shoved a hand through his hair. 'And I was here before I thought about how late it is. You're still up.'

'Yes.' Her resolve thinned and tore as she studied his face. 'I was making tea. Do you want

293

tea?'

'Sounds good.' He came up the stairs. 'I'm sorry I didn't let you know I'd be this long.'

'You have work. I've been working, too.'

Saying nothing, he put his arms around her, pressed his face to her hair. Not for pleasure, she realized. It took her a moment to decipher the tenor of the embrace. He sought comfort. He'd come to her for comfort, and no one ever had.

She started to pat his back—there, there—but stopped. And closing her eyes, she tried to imagine what she'd want. She rubbed his back instead, small, light circles, until she heard him sigh.

'The kettle's boiling,' she told him, when she heard it whistle.

'Yeah.' But he held on for another moment before he stepped back.

'You should come in. I need to lock the door.'

'I'll get it.'

'No, I . . .' Wouldn't feel fully safe if she didn't lock up herself.

'Okay. I'll get the kettle.'

When she'd finished, she found him pouring hot water into the squat teapot where she'd already measured out leaves.

'Lemon balm, right? My mother does the same thing some nights.'

'It's relaxing.'

'I could use some relaxing.'

She got out a second cup, saucer. 'Is your friend all right?'

'Not really.'

'Oh.' Instantly shamed of her earlier annoyance, she turned. 'He was hurt?'

'Not physically other than a fist to the face, but

he's had that before. He's likely to again.'

In silence, she arranged the cups, the pot, the sugar bowl and spoons on the table. 'You should sit down. You look very tired. We'll have to share the tea strainer when it's steeped. I only have one.'

'That's fine.'

Unsure, she remained standing when he sat down. 'Do you want food? I have the lasagna. It can be heated.'

'No. No, but thanks.'

'You're so sad,' she blurted out.

'I guess that's some of it. Got a lot of pissed off in there, too. I've got to shake both off before I deal with tomorrow.'

'Do you want to tell me, or should I change the subject?'

He smiled a little. 'You should sit down, Abigail, and have your tea.'

'I don't know if I'm good at this,' she said, as she sat.

'Drinking tea?'

'Comforting. Or defusing. Since you're angry and sad, it should be both.'

He laid a hand over hers briefly, then poured out the tea. 'Let's find out. Russ's family's owned the hotel for three generations now. It's not just a business, not just a livelihood, to them.'

'It's an essential part of their family history, and their place in the community.'

'Yeah. There's pride and love there. Justin Blake, have you heard of the Blakes?'

'Yes. They're a very wealthy and influential local family.'

'Justin's a spoiled, troublemaking fuckwit with a string of DUIs, a bad attitude. He'd have a sheet as

295

long as my leg if his father didn't use that money or influence, or political pressure—whatever works—to get him off. The kid has no respect for the law or any other damn thing.'

'It would be difficult to develop one if he's allowed to behave badly with impunity. I'm sorry,' she said quickly, 'I'm supposed to listen.'

'There's no supposed. Anyway, his latest. He and a couple of the assholes he hangs with booked the best suite at the hotel and trashed it. Destroyed it.'

'Why?'

'For kicks, out of boredom, because they could. Pick one.' Brooks shrugged, then scrubbed his hands over his face. 'Russ went up this evening to deal with them when guests complained about the noise. Upshot is Justin punched him, took some swings at security, got himself arrested. And this time he won't slide through. It's looking like better than a hundred thousand in damages. Maybe more.'

'That's a great deal.'

'Yeah, it is, and Russ and his parents won't cave when Lincoln Blake pushes at them. I had a go-round with him and the kid tonight.'

'You won't cave, either.'

'No, I won't. Justin and his pals are spending the night in jail. They'll make bail tomorrow, Blake will see to it. But Justin's got two choices. He takes a plea and does time, or he stands trial and does time, but he goes down this time. And either way the Blakes pay every cent of the damages. Jesus, I'm pissed off.'

He shoved up, stalked to the window. 'I should've gone home.'

'You wouldn't be pissed off at home?'

'No, I'd be pissed off anywhere. That fat, self-satisfied, cigar-smoking fuckhead figures he can threaten me with my job, and I'll scare off?'

'The father?'

'Yeah, the father.'

'Can he have you fired?'

'If he can, they can shove the job. I don't want it if I can't fucking do it. Not if some overprivileged asshole can do whatever the hell he wants and I'm supposed to look the other way.'

'Money is power,' Abigail said quietly, 'but it's not the only power.'

'I guess we'll see. I went over to talk to Russ's parents, and Russ and Seline—his wife—after I dealt with the lawyer. She cried. Mrs. Conroy. This sweet, funny woman who always had peanut butter cookies in the jar, just broke down and cried. I should've found a way to put that little bastard away before it went this far.'

'It's useless to blame yourself for what this person did, or what his father has been able to do, especially when the pattern was set long before you took the position as chief of police. The rational thing to do is arrest him, which you have, and to compile evidence for the prosecutor to assist in getting a guilty verdict at trial. That wasn't sympathetic,' she realized.

Brooks sat back down, picked up his tea. 'Worked pretty well, though. I know the logic of it, Abigail.'

'But your friend and his family have been hurt. It's emotional as well as financial and physical and criminal. People should pay for their actions. There should be consequences. There should be justice.'

Her hand balled into a fist on the table for

a moment before she ordered herself to relax it. 'It's hard not to feel sad and angry and even hopeless when bad things happen, because fear and influence and money often outweigh justice.'

He leaned forward, laid a hand over hers. 'Who hurt you?'

She shook her head, said nothing.

'Not yet, then.'

'What will you do tomorrow?'

'I've got a seven-thirty meeting with the prosecutor to go over everything again. We'll have an arraignment, bail hearing. I expect they'll cut Justin and the others loose until trial. I don't figure he'll go for a plea straight off. Maybe, once it gets closer, maybe if the lawyers don't screw it up. The Conroys are just mad enough to go for a civil suit on top of it. I won't be discouraging that. It's time the pressure came from the other side.'

'Then you know what you have to do and how to do it. Are they violent?'

'The kid likes to bust things up.'

'I meant could or would they try to hurt you or your friend's family? Using violence as intimidation.'

'Can't say for sure, but I wouldn't go there. Money's Blake's weapon of choice.'

Abigail considered. 'I don't believe they can have you fired.'

'Don't you?'

'Objectively, your family is a fixture in the community. Liked and respected. You're also liked and respected in your own right. I assume as a multigenerational business family, with a key property in the community, your friend and his family are also valued. Their property was damaged

298

through reckless and selfish behavior, so sympathy and outrage will be on their side. Those things are also weapons. Extrapolating from what you've said tonight, I'd posit that the Blakes are somewhat feared but not well liked. There are likely many people in the community who'd be pleased if the son is punished for his actions.'

'Extrapolating. Now, how can you use words like that and still manage to make me feel a whole hell of a lot better?'

'Did I?'

This time he laid a hand over hers and left it there. 'You were right about the sad. I was, and pissed off, and frustrated, and we'll have to toss in a dash of feeling sorry for myself. Now I'm down to sorry and mad with a whole fat scoop of looking forward to kicking some ass—legally speaking.'

'That's good?'

'It's real good.' He gave her hand a squeeze. 'I should go.'

'I wish you'd stay.'

He turned her hand over so their fingers linked. 'Thank God.'

'We should go to bed.'

'Two minds, one thought.'

'It's late,' she said, as she rose to gather the tea things. 'You're tired. And, I think, still a little sad. Sex releases endorphins, so for the short term you'd feel . . .' She trailed off when she turned and found him grinning at her.

'I'm half in love with you,' he told her, 'and heading fast toward three-quarters.'

Something inside her burst like sunlight before it flooded away on a rise of panic. 'Don't do that.'

'I don't think it's something you do or don't. It's

something that happens or doesn't.'

'It's a mixture of sexual and physical attraction, along with novelty and the tension between mutual interests and conflicts of interest. People often mistake hormonal reaction and certain compatibilities for what they think of as love.'

He continued to smile as he got to his feet, but something about the glint in his eyes had her taking a cautious step back as he walked to her.

He put his hands on her shoulders, lowered his head to brush his lips over hers. He said, 'Hush,' and kissed her again. 'You don't want to tell me what I feel or don't, or I might click back up to pissed off. We don't want that, do we?'

'No, but—'

'Hush,' he repeated, with his lips whispering against hers. 'Pretty Abigail, so full of suspicion and intellect. And nerves.'

'I'm not nervous.'

'Nerves,' he repeated, skimming his thumbs along the sides of her breasts while his mouth continued to toy with hers. Rubbing, brushing, grazing. 'When you're not quite sure what's next, when you haven't worked out all the steps, or there's a little detour. I like the nerves.'

'Why?'

'And I like the curious why.' He tugged her shirt up and off, watching the surprise—and, yeah, just a few nerves—flicker in her eyes. 'I like knowing you haven't figured it—me, this—all out.' His hands glided up her sides, over her breasts, down. 'Action and reaction, right? I like your reactions.'

There were nerves, she admitted. They seemed to slither along her skin, under it, coil in her belly, squeeze around her heart to increase the beat.

Everything inside her body felt soft, then sharp, loose then tangled. How could she keep up?

'We should go upstairs.'

She felt his lips curve against her throat, and his fingers trail up her back. 'Why?' he murmured, and flicked open the catch of her bra. 'I like your kitchen.' He shifted his feet, toeing off his shoes. 'It's warm. And efficient. I love the way you feel under my hands. Abigail.'

She fell into the kiss, headfirst, a breathless tumble that left her dizzy and weak. Seduction. Though she'd never allowed herself to be seduced—it was unnecessary—her mind recognized the sensation. And her body surrendered to it.

Craving the feel of his skin, his muscles, his bones, she shot her hands under his shirt, found the warm, the solid, the smooth. Her breath caught on a gasp when he hitched her up so she sat on her own kitchen counter. Before the shock of that had fully registered, his mouth closed over her breast.

So hot, so wet, so strong, she let out a quick cry of stunned pleasure. Later she would think the orgasm that shot through her was as much a result of the shock as the sensation. But now it caught her unprepared, left her shuddering and defenseless.

'Brooks.' She wanted to tell him to wait, to wait until she steadied herself, but his mouth was on hers again, taking her under so fast, so deep, she could only shudder and yield.

She'd never been taken before, he realized. Not like this, where her surrender was complete, not when she couldn't separate some small part of herself to reach for control.

And God, he wanted to take her, to destroy that fascinating and innate control.

301

He yanked down her zipper and, half lifting her, peeled the jeans away. Giving her no time to recover, he closed his mouth over hers again, swallowing her instinctive protest. He stroked her, teasing and gentle. She was already hot, already wet, already balanced on the edge. He wanted her to ride that, hold that sensation until it overwhelmed and overcame.

He wanted to watch her as she did.

The air, so thick and sweet, made her feel drunk with every breath. The pleasure he brought her was so complete, so absolute, she seemed trapped in it, mired and steeped. He caught her nipple between his teeth, bringing her to an exquisite point just bordering on pain while he stroked that heat higher.

When she thought she couldn't bear it, couldn't contain it, everything went bright and free. She heard herself moan, the long, long throaty sound of it as her head dropped heavily on his shoulder.

She wanted to twine around him, curl inside him, but he angled her back, wrapped her trembling legs around his waist. And drove into her.

Fresh shock, fresh pleasure. Hard and fast and furious. A rising flood churning into the wild sweep of a tidal wave. He dragged her through it, drowned her in it, until that violent wave tossed her to the surface. She could only float there, wrecked, until he joined her.

Now, gradually, she felt his heart hammering against hers, and the rags of his breath tearing at her ear. She felt the smooth surface of the counter under her, the dazzle of the kitchen lights against her closed lids.

She needed a moment or two, just a moment or

two to find her balance again, then she could—

He shocked her again when he scooped her off the counter, into his arms.

'You don't have to—'

'Hush,' he said yet again, and carried her upstairs to bed.

*   *   *

She came down first in the morning and could only stop and stare. She'd left the lights on, a careless waste of energy. But she couldn't seem to get too worked up about it. Clothes scattered the floor, hers and his.

She studied the counter with a kind of baffled wonder. She'd never understood the appeal for sex in odd or unusual places. What was the point when a bed, even a couch would be more comfortable and conducive? Though she did enjoy sex in the shower on occasion.

Obviously she'd been too narrow in her viewpoint, though she wondered how long it might take before she could perform basic kitchen duties with equanimity.

For now, she started the coffee, then gathered up all the clothes, folded them neatly. By the time Brooks came down—naked—she'd set the kitchen to rights and started breakfast.

'Seem to have left my clothes down here.' Obviously amused, he picked up the jeans she'd folded, put them on. 'You didn't have to get up this early, make breakfast.'

'I like getting up early, and don't mind making breakfast. You have a difficult day ahead. You'll feel better if you have a meal. It's just an omelet

303

and some toast.'

When she turned, he'd pulled on his shirt and was looking at her, just looking at her, with those clever, changeable eyes.

'I wish you wouldn't look at me like that.'

'Like what?'

'I . . .' She turned away to pour the coffee. 'I don't know.'

He came up behind her, wrapped his arms around her waist loosely, pressed a kiss to the side of her neck. 'Rounding third and headed for home,' he murmured.

'That's a baseball term. We're not playing baseball. I don't know what that means.'

He turned her around, kissed her mouth lightly. 'Yes, you do. It's nothing to get panicked about.' He rubbed at the tension in her shoulders. 'We'll take it easy. What kind of omelets?'

'Three-cheese with some spinach and peppers.'

'Sounds great. I'll get the toast.'

He moved so easily around her kitchen, as if he belonged there. Panic tickled up her throat again. 'I'm not—' How did people put it? 'I'm not built for this.'

'For what?'

'For any of this.'

'I am.' He popped bread in the toaster, leaned on the counter. 'I wasn't sure about that, until you. But I'm built for all of this. From my point of view, so are you. So, we'll see.'

'I'm not who you think I am.'

He studied her, nodding slowly. 'Maybe not on all the details. Maybe not. But I'm looking at you, Abigail, I'm listening to you, and where it counts, you're who I think you are.'

'That's not . . .' She nearly told him that wasn't her real name. How could she become this involved, this reckless? 'That's not something you can know.'

'I know that's not what you were going to say. I'm good at reading people. It comes with the territory. I know you're scared of something, or someone. You've taken a hard hit or two along the way, and done what you can to shield up. Can't blame you for it.'

Light poured in the window at his back, shot a nimbus around his hair. Dark hair, still tumbled from the night, from her hands.

'I don't know what to say to you.'

'You've got a lot of secrets behind your eyes, and a hell of a lot of weight on your shoulders. I'm going to keep believing that one day you're going to share those secrets and that weight with me, and we'll figure out the rest once you do.'

She only shook her head, turned away to put the omelets on plates. 'We shouldn't be talking about this, especially now. You'll be late for your meeting, and I have two new contracts to work on.'

'Congratulations. Why don't I pick something up for dinner tonight?'

'I have the lasagna.'

'Even better.'

She put the plates down when the toast popped, then sat with a jerk of temper. 'I didn't invite you.'

'We're past that.'

'I don't know how to be past that.'

He brought the toast over, set a slice on her plate as he took his seat. 'This looks great.'

'You change the subject, or you agree rather than debate. Because you're so certain you'll get

305

your way in the end.'

'You're good at reading people, too.' He took a bite of omelet. 'Tastes great. You could make a living.'

'You're frustrating.'

'I know it, but I make up for it by being so good-looking.'

She didn't want to smile but couldn't help it. 'You're not that good-looking.'

He laughed and ate his breakfast.

When he'd gone, she considered her options.

She couldn't tell him, of course, but hypothetically, what were the probable results if she did?

She was wanted for questioning in the murders of two U.S. Marshals. As a law enforcement official, he'd be obligated to turn her in. It was highly doubtful she'd live to give testimony. The Volkovs would find a way to get to her and eliminate her, most likely through one of their law enforcement plants.

But, hypothetically again, if Brooks believed her, and believed her life would be forfeit should he do his duty, he would be less inclined to fulfill that duty.

She tried to imagine being able to talk to him about John and Terry, about Julie, and everything that had happened since those horrible nights. She simply couldn't imagine it, couldn't theorize on how it might feel to be able to talk to him, to anyone, to share the burden.

He was kind, she thought, and dedicated to justice, to doing the right thing for the right reasons. In many ways, in basic, vital ways, he reminded her of John.

If she told him, if he believed her, he might be, like John, driven to protect her, to help her. And wouldn't that put his life at risk?

Yet another reason to keep her own counsel, to go on as she'd gone on for a dozen years.

But everything had already changed, she reminded herself. Everything wasn't as it had been. He'd done that; she'd allowed it.

So if she told him, because the balance had already shifted, she would have to be prepared to go, to run again, change her name again—whether he believed her or not.

Therefore, logically, rationally, she couldn't tell him. Their relationship would gradually lessen in intensity until the balance shifted back again. Until her life was back to what it had been.

Her conclusions should have made her feel more confident, more calm and certain. Instead, they left her unhappy and unsettled.

18

The morning business went pretty much the way Brooks had figured, with a few extra points for the good guys.

He'd expected Justin and his idiot pals to make bail, and had calculated the judge would set it high enough to sting a little. He set it high enough to sting a lot.

Harry objected, of course—he had to do his job—but the judge held firm. The Conroys might not have been as deep in the pockets as the Blakes, but they were as well respected, and a hell of a lot more well liked.

Justin had kicked the wrong cat this time, in Brooks's opinion.

From his position in the courtroom, he watched Blake seethe, Justin sneer, and the two others being arraigned keep their heads and eyes down while their parents sat stone-faced.

He had to fight back a mile-wide grin when the judge agreed to the prosecutor's demand that all three under charges turn in their passports.

'This is insulting!' Blake surged to his feet at the judge's ruling, and this time Brooks did a happy dance in his head. 'I won't tolerate the insinuation my son would run away from these absurd charges. We want our day in court!'

'You're going to get that.' Judge Reingold, who played golf with Blake every Sunday, slapped his gavel down. 'And you're going to show respect in this courtroom, Lincoln. You sit down and keep your peace in here or I'll have you removed.'

'Don't think you can sit up there and threaten me. I helped put you in those robes.'

Behind his wire-framed glasses, Reingold's eyes glittered. 'And as long as I'm wearing them, you'll show them respect. Sit down, be quiet, or sure as God made little green apples, I'll hold you in contempt of court.'

Blake shoved Harry aside when the lawyer tried to intervene. 'I'll show you contempt.'

'You just did.' Reingold banged his gavel again. 'That's five hundred dollars. Bailiff, remove Mr. Blake from the courtroom before he makes it a thousand.'

Red-faced, teeth set, Blake turned on his heel and stalked out under his own power. He took a moment to pause, scald Brooks with a blistering stare.

Brooks sat through the rest of the legal wrangling, the instructions, the warnings, the scheduling. He waited until Justin and his friends were led back to their holding cells until their bail could be posted.

More than satisfied, Brooks had to control a little bounce in his step when he walked over to speak with Russ and his family. There was no doubt in his mind that having the entire Conroy family present—Russ's split lip, Mrs. Conroy fighting tears—had influenced Reingold's ruling.

'That pompous bully Blake made it worse for himself and those vicious boys.' Seline, dark eyes sparking in contrast to her usual easy-as-Sunday-morning temperament, kept her arm protectively around her mother-in-law's shoulders. 'I *loved* it. I only wished he'd opened his mouth again, so it cost him more.'

'I wasn't sure Stan would stand up against Lincoln.' Mick Conroy nodded toward the bench. 'I feel some better about it. I'm going to take your mom home,' he said to Russ.

'You want me to come?'

Hilly, her eyes still shadowed, the bright hair she'd passed to her son pulled back in a haphazard ponytail, shook her head. She kissed Russ's cheek. 'We'll be all right. Brooks.' She kissed Brooks's cheek in turn. 'We're grateful.'

'There's no need for that.'

'She's still sad,' Seline murmured, when her in-laws walked out. 'She can't find her mad through it. I want her to find that mad. She'll feel better when she does.'

'You're mad enough for all of us.'

Seline smiled a little. 'God knows. I've got to get to school. The kids've probably traumatized the morning substitute by now.'

She gave Brooks a hard hug, turned to Russ, held on to him for a long minute. 'Don't fret too much, cutie,' she told him.

'Let me buy you a cup of coffee,' Brooks said to Russ when they were alone.

'I should get to the hotel.'

'Take a few minutes, decompress.'

'I could use it. Okay. I'll meet you there.'

The minute Brooks walked into the diner, Kim grabbed a coffeepot and beelined toward him. She pointed at a booth, turned the mug on the tabletop over, poured.

'Well,' she said.

'Just coffee, thanks.'

She poked him on the shoulder. 'How'm I supposed to maintain my status as News Queen if you don't give me the dish? Do you want me to get demoted?'

'No, indeed. We can't have that. They made bail.'

Her mouth turned down, ferociously. 'I should've known Stan Reingold would play weasel for Lincoln Blake.'

'Now, I wouldn't say that, Kim. I expected them to make bail. I didn't expect the judge to set it as high as he did, and I can guarantee you Blake didn't, either.'

'That's something, then.'

'And he's confiscating their passports until after the trial.'

'Well, now.' Lips pursed, she gave a satisfied nod. 'I take it all back. That had to burn Blake's fat

310

ass.'

'Oh, I'd say he felt the heat. He mouthed off, and the judge fined him five hundred for contempt.'

This time she slapped Brooks's shoulder. 'You're shitting me.'

'Swear to God.'

'I take it all back double. Next time Stan Reingold comes in, I'm giving him pie on the house. You hear that, Lindy?' she called to the man at the grill. 'Stan Reingold fined Lincoln Blake five hundred for contempt.'

Spatula fisted at his hip, Lindy turned. 'About time contempt cost him, 'cause the sumbitch has plenty of it. That coffee's on me, Brooks.' Lindy lifted his chin toward the door. 'And his, too.'

Kim spotted Russ when he came in, turned the second mug over. 'You sit right on down here, sweetie.' She rose to her toes to kiss his cheek. 'And no charge for the coffee or anything else you want. You be sure to tell your folks that anybody worth spit in this town is sorry as hell about what happened, and behind them a hundred percent.'

'I will. Thanks, Kim. It means a lot.'

'You look tired out. How about a big wedge of that French apple pie you like to perk you up?'

'Couldn't right now. Maybe next time.'

'I'll leave you to talk, then, but you need anything, you just holler.'

Brooks pretended to sulk. 'She didn't offer me any damn pie.'

Russ managed a wan smile. 'She's got to feel sorry for you first. Did you know about the passports?'

'I knew we were going to request it, but I didn't figure Reingold would rule on our side. He

311

surprised me, and maybe that's on me.'

'He's let the Blake kid slide on plenty before today.'

'Yeah, he has, and I think he's feeling the weight of that. He may be Blake's golf buddy, but he can't—and I think won't—brush off this kind of thing. I believe His Honor was well and truly pissed this morning. And I believe Blake isn't going to let Harry talk his boy into a plea on this. He wants the trial because he absolutely believes he and his are too fucking important to bend to the law. That boy's going down, Russ, and he may go down harder than I expected. I'm not sorry about it.'

'Can't say as I am, either.'

Brooks shifted forward. 'I wanted to talk to you for a few minutes because I'm dead sure Blake's going to do whatever he can to buy you off or pressure you into dropping the assault charges. He gets that gone, he's going to figure it's mostly about money. Pay the two dollars, so to speak, try to manipulate community service and some rehab, a suspended sentence for the boy.'

Russ's bruised mouth set like stone. 'It's not going to happen, Brooks. Did you see my daddy this morning? He looks ten years older. I don't give a damn about taking the punch, and if it wasn't for the rest, I'd let it go. But I'm not going to shrug this off so that little bastard slides through this.'

'Good. If Blake starts hounding you, let me know. I'll mention harassment charges and restraining orders.'

Russ sat back, and his smile came easier. 'Which one of them are you really after?'

'It's two for one, as I see it. They both need a good, swift kick. I don't know if Justin was born an

312

asshole, but his daddy sure as hell helped make him a bigger one.' He stirred at his coffee but found he didn't have a taste for it. 'I didn't see his mama in court.'

'Word is Mrs. Blake's embarrassed and tired out. About done with it. And Blake's ordered her to keep it shut. He runs that house.'

'That may be, but he doesn't run this town.'

'Do you, Chief?'

'I protect and serve,' Brooks said, with a glance out the window. 'The Blakes are going to learn what that means. How about you, Mr. Mayor?'

'It may be tougher to win an election with Blake backing whoever I run against, but I'm in it.'

'New times.' Brooks lifted his mug in toast. 'Good times.'

'You're pretty sassy this morning, son. Is it all about Reingold's rulings?'

'That didn't suck, but I've got me a fascinating, beautiful woman I'm falling for. Falling hard.'

'Quick work.'

'In the blood. My mama and daddy barely did more than look at each other, and that was that. She's got me, Russ. Right here.' He tapped a fist on his heart.

'Sure it's not considerably lower where she's got you?'

'There, too. But, Jesus, Russ, she does it for me. I just think about her and I'm there. I look at her, and . . . I swear I could look at her for hours. Days.'

Brooks let out a half-laugh, edged with a little surprise. 'I'm done. I'm gone.'

'If you don't bring her over for dinner, Seline's going to see to it my life's not worth living.'

'I'll work on it. I figure I'm going to have the

313

women in my family making the same demand before much longer. Abigail's the type who needs to be eased in. Something in there,' he added. 'Something from before. She's not ready to let me in on that yet. I'm working on that, too.'

'So she hasn't figured out you'll just keep digging, nudging and chewing until you know what you want to know or get what you want to get?'

'I'm blinding her with affability and charm.'

'How long do you figure that'll last?'

'I've got a little more to spare. She needs help. She just doesn't know it, or isn't ready to take it. Yet.'

*   *   *

Abigail spent the morning happily at her computer, redesigning and personalizing the security system for a law firm in Rochester. She was particularly pleased with the results, as she'd gotten the job on referral, and had nearly lost it as the senior partner had balked when she'd refused to meet with him personally.

She believed he and the other partners would be more than satisfied with the system and her suggestions. If they weren't? It was the price she paid for doing business on her terms.

To give her mind a rest, she shifted gears into gardening.

She wanted to create a butterfly garden along the south corner of her cabin, and had read and researched how to best accomplish the goal. With Bert by her side, she gathered tools, loaded her wheelbarrow. It pleased her to see the little vegetable garden she'd already planted doing so

314

well, to smell the herbs soaking up the sunshine as she wheeled by. Her narrow stream bubbled along, and birds sang to its tune. Through the thickening trees, a frisky breeze danced and wild dogwood peeked out like flowery ghosts.

She was happy, she realized, as she marked off her plot with string and stakes. Really happy. With spring, with work, with her home. With Brooks.

Had she been really happy before? Surely there had been moments—at least during her childhood, in her brief time at Harvard, even moments after everything changed so completely—when she'd been happy.

But she couldn't remember ever feeling quite like this. Nervous. Brooks was right about the nerves, and she wasn't entirely sure she liked his being right. But over them and through them was a kind of lightness she didn't know quite what to do with.

As she switched on her tiller, she hummed along with its churning grind, with the bubbling brook, with the birdsong. No, she didn't know quite what to do with it, but if she could, she'd have held these moments, these feelings tight—so tight—forever.

She had satisfying work, had her gardening, which she enjoyed more than she'd ever imagined. She had a man she respected and enjoyed—more than she'd ever imagined—who would come to dinner, talk, laugh, *be* with her.

It couldn't last, but what was the point in projecting, in making herself *un*happy? Hold it tight, she reminded herself, as she added compost to her soil. For the moment.

She trundled her wheelbarrow back to the greenhouse, wandered through the smell of rich,

315

moist earth; burgeoning flowers; sharp, strong greens, selecting the plants she'd nurtured for this particular project.

Good, steady physical labor in the warm afternoon. That made her happy, too. Who knew she had such a capacity for happy?

She made four trips, her Glock against her hip, her dog trotting at her heels before she began to lay out the plan she'd sketched out on chilly winter nights.

The cardinal flowers and coneflowers, the sweet-scented heliotrope mixed with airy lantana, the flow of verbena, the charm of New England asters, the elegance of oriental lilies for nectar. She had the sunflowers and hollyhocks and milkweed for host plants to tempt the adults to lay their eggs, the young caterpillars to feed.

She arranged, rearranged, grouped, regrouped, gradually veering away from her initial, somewhat mathematical layout when she found the less rigid and exact pleased her eye.

In case, she took out her phone and took pictures from several angles before she picked up her trowel to dig the first hole.

An hour later, she stepped back and checked her progress before going inside for ice to add to the tea she'd left steeping in the sun.

'It's going to be beautiful,' she told Bert. 'And we'll be able to sit on the porch and watch the butterflies. I think we'll draw hummingbirds, too. I'll love seeing all this grow and bloom, the butterflies and birds. We're putting down roots, Bert. The deeper they go, the more I want them.'

She closed her eyes, lifted her face to the sun.

Oh, she loved the way the air sounded, loved the

way it smelled. She loved the rhythm of work and pleasure she'd found here, the quiet moments, the busy ones. She loved the feel of her dog leaning against her leg and the taste of tea cool on her throat.

She loved Brooks.

Her eyes popped open.

No, no, she'd just gotten caught up in the happy moments here. In this euphoria of having everything just as she wanted. And she'd let herself mix that with what he'd said to her that morning, how he looked at her.

Action and reaction, she told herself. Nothing more.

But what if it were more?

Her alarm beeped, stiffening her spine and shoulders as she laid a hand on the butt of the Glock.

She wasn't expecting a package.

She walked quickly to the monitor she'd set up on the porch. She remembered the car even before she made out the driver. Brooks's mother—dear God—and two other women.

Talking, laughing, as Sunny drove toward the house.

Before she could decide what to do, the car rounded the last curve. Sunny gave the horn a cheery toot-toot when she spotted Abigail.

'Hey, there!' Sunny shouted out the car window before the three of them piled out.

The woman in the front had to be Brooks's sister, Abigail thought. The coloring, the bone structure, the shape of the eyes and mouth were too similar not to be genetic.

'Look at this! Butterfly garden.'

317

'Yes. I've been working on it this afternoon.'

'Well, it's just going to be wonderful,' Sunny told her. 'Smell the heliotrope! I've got Plato in the car. Do you suppose Bert would like to meet him?'

'I . . . I suppose he would.'

'Mama's so busy worrying about introducing the dogs, she doesn't worry about the humans. I'm Mya, Brooks's sister, and our middle sister, Sybill.'

'It's nice to meet you both,' Abigail managed, as her hand was gripped and shaken.

'We blew the day off,' Mya beamed out, a lanky woman with a pixie cut in streaky brunette. 'Work, kids, men. We had ourselves a fancy ladies' lunch, and now we're heading in to do some shopping.'

'We thought you might like to come along with us,' Sybill said.

'Come along?' Baffled, off-balance, one eye on her dog, Abigail tried to keep up.

'Shopping,' Mya repeated. 'After, we're talking about frozen margaritas.'

The puppy bounced, rolled, nipped and generally went crazy around and over Bert, who sat, quivering, his gaze slanted toward Abigail.

'Ami. Jouer.'

Instantly, he hunkered, head down, tail up and wagging, and playfully knocked Plato into an ungainly roll.

'Aw, aren't they cute!' Sunny declared.

'He won't hurt the puppy.'

'Honey, I can see that. That big boy's gentle as a lamb, and God knows Plato can use a little running-around time. He's been in the car or on the leash all afternoon. Did you meet my two girls?'

'Yes.'

'We're trying to talk her into putting away

318

her trowel and coming along for shopping and margaritas.' Sybill offered Abigail a warm, easy smile that showed hints of dimples.

'Thank you for asking.' Abigail heard the stiffness in her voice when compared with the other women's ease. 'But I really need to finish planting. I got a later start than I'd planned.'

'Well, it looks just beautiful.' Sybill wandered over for a closer look. 'I didn't inherit Mama's or Daddy's green thumb, so I'm envious.'

'It was very nice of you to come over and invite me.'

'It was,' Mya agreed, 'but mostly Syb and I just wanted to get a close-up look at you and check out the woman who's got Brooks all tangled up.'

'Oh.'

'You're not the type I imagined would hook him so good and proper.'

'Oh' was all Abigail could think of, again.

'Something's in Mya's mind,' Sunny began, hooking an arm around her daughter, 'it just rolls right off her tongue.'

'I can be tactful and diplomatic, but it's not a natural state for me. Anyway, I meant it as a compliment, a good thing.'

'Thank you?'

Mya laughed. 'You're welcome. Mostly, see, Brooks—in the past—tended toward the looks without necessarily much substance to back it up. But here you are, pretty and natural, strong and smart enough to live out here on your own, clever enough to plant a well-designed garden—I did get the green thumb—and you run your own business, from what I'm told. And I guess since you've got that big gun on your hip, you know how to take care of yourself.'

'Yes, I do.'

'Have you ever shot anyone?'

'Mya. Don't mind her,' Sybill said. 'She's the oldest and has the biggest mouth. Are you sure you wouldn't like to come with us?'

'I really need to finish this garden, but thank you.'

'We'll have a cookout Sunday afternoon,' Sunny announced. 'Brooks'll bring you around.'

'Oh, thank you, but—'

'Nothing fancy. Just a backyard barbecue. And I've got some yellow flags I need to divide. I'll give you some. They'll like that sunny spot over by the brook. I'll round up that pup, and we'll see you Sunday.'

'You've been seeing Brooks for a while now,' Mya commented.

'I suppose.'

'You know how he just chips amiably away at you until he gets his way?'

'Yes.'

Mya winked and grinned. 'He comes by it naturally. We'll see you Sunday.'

'Don't worry.' Sybill surprised Abigail by taking her hand as her sister walked off to help their mother with the puppy. 'It'll be fine. Your dog's all right with kids around?'

'He wouldn't hurt anyone.' Unless I tell him to, she thought.

'You bring him along. You'll feel easier having your dog with you. We're pretty nice people, and inclined to like anyone who makes Brooks happy. You'll be fine,' she said, and gave Abigail's hand a squeeze before she released it and walked back to the car.

There was a lot of laughing and chattering, a lot of waving and honking. Shell-shocked, Abigail stood, her deliriously happy dog at her side, and politely lifted her hand as the O'Hara-Gleason women drove away.

It was like being rolled over by a steamroller made of flowers, Abigail thought. It didn't really hurt, it was all very pretty and sweet-smelling. But you were still flattened.

She wouldn't go, of course. It would be impossible on so many levels. Perhaps she'd write a polite note of regret to Brooks's mother.

She put her gardening gloves back on. She wanted to finish the bed; plus, she'd used finishing it as an excuse, so finish it she must and would.

She'd never been asked to go shopping and have margaritas, and wondered as she dug what it was like. She knew people shopped even when they didn't need anything. She didn't understand the appeal, but she knew others did.

She thought of that day, so long ago, in the mall with Julie. How much fun it had been, how exhilarating and liberating it had been to try on clothes and shoes with a friend.

Of course, they hadn't been friends. Not really friends. The entire interlude had been one of chance and circumstance and mutual need.

And that interlude had led to disaster and tragedy.

She knew, logically, the harmless rebellion of buying clothes and shoes hadn't caused the tragedy. Even her own reckless stupidity of forging the IDs, agreeing to go to the club hadn't caused the events that followed.

321

The Volkovs and Yakov Korotkii held that responsibility.

And yet, how could she not link them together, not feel the weight and the guilt even after all this time? The argument with her mother had lit the chain reaction that had ended with the explosion of the safe house. If not fully responsible, she had been one of the links in that chain.

And still, as she planted she wondered what it was like to ride in a car with women who laughed, to shop for unnecessary things, to drink margaritas and gossip.

And wondering took some of the bloom off the pleasure of the sounds and smells of her solitude.

She planted it all, added more, worked through the afternoon into soft evening wheeling bags of mulch to the bed. Filthy, sweaty, satisfied, she set up the sprinklers just as her alarm signaled again.

This time she saw Brooks driving toward the house.

She'd lost track of time, she realized. She'd meant to go in, put the lasagna on warm in the oven before he arrived. And had certainly hoped to have cleaned up at least a little.

'Well, look at that.' He got out, a bouquet of purple iris in his hand. 'These feel a little dinky now.'

'They're beautiful. It's the second time you brought me flowers. You're the only one who ever has.'

He made them both a silent promise to bring them often. He handed them to her, pulled out a rawhide for Bert. 'Didn't forget you, big guy. You must've worked half the day putting that bed in.'

'Not quite that long, but it took some time. I

322

want butterflies.'

'You're going to get them. It's pretty as it can be, Abigail. So are you.'

'I'm dirty,' she said, backing up when he bent to kiss her.

'I don't mind a bit. You know I'd've given you a hand with the planting. I'm good at it.'

'I got started, and caught up in it.'

'Why don't I get us some wine? We can sit out here and admire your work.'

'I need to shower and put the lasagna in to warm.'

'Go on, get your shower. I can put the food in, get the wine. From the looks of things you worked harder than I did today. Here.' He took the flowers back. 'I'll put them in water for you. What?' he said when she only stared at him.

'Nothing. I . . . I won't be long.'

Not sure what to do, he concluded, when offered the most basic and minimal help. But she'd taken it, he thought, as he went in, filled her vase. And without argument or excuses. That was a step forward.

He put the flowers on the counter, expecting she'd fuss with the arrangement later, and likely when he wasn't around. He switched the oven, set it low, slid the casserole in.

He took the wine and two glasses out on the front porch, and, after pouring, carried his own glass over to lean on the post, study her flowers.

He knew enough about gardening to be sure the job had taken her hours. Knew enough about gardening artfully to be sure she had a knack for color and texture and flow.

And he knew enough about people to be sure the

planting of it was another mark of ownership, of settling in. Her place, done her way.

A good sign.

When she stepped out, he turned to her. Her damp hair curled a little around her face, and she smelled as fresh as spring itself.

'It's my first spring back in the Ozarks,' he said, picking up her glass to offer it. 'I'm watching it come back to life. The hills greening up, the wildflowers bursting, the rivers streaming through it all. The light, the shadows, sunlight on fields of row crops freshly planted. All of it new again for another season. And I know there's nowhere else I want to be. This is home again, for the rest of it.'

'I feel that way. It's the first time I've felt that way. I like it.'

'It's good you do. I look at you, Abigail, smelling of that spring, your flowers blooming or waiting to, your eyes so serious, so goddamn beautiful, and I feel the same. There's nowhere else. No one else.'

'I don't know what to do with how you make me feel. And I'm afraid of what my life will be if this changes and I never feel this way again.'

'How do I make you feel?'

'Happy. So happy. And terrified and confused.'

'We'll work on the happy until you're easy and sure.'

She set down her wine, went to him, held on. 'I may never be.'

'You came outside without your gun.'

'You have yours.'

He smiled into her hair. 'That's something, then. That's trust, and a good start.'

She didn't know, couldn't analyze through all the feelings. 'We can sit on the steps, and you could tell

324

me what happened this morning.'

'We can do that.' He tipped her face back, kissed her lightly. ' 'Cause I'm feeling good about it.'

19

He filled her in while the shadows lengthened and her new garden soaked up the gentle shower from her sprinklers.

She'd always found the law fascinating, the ins and outs of the process, the illogic—and, in her opinion, often the bias—infused into the rules and codes and procedures by the human factor. Justice seemed so clear-cut to her, but the law that sought it, enforced it, was murky and slippery.

'I don't understand why, because they have money, they should be released.'

'Innocent till proven guilty.'

'But they *are* guilty,' she insisted, 'and it has been proven. They rented the room and caused the damage. Justin Blake assaulted your friend in front of witnesses.'

'They're entitled to their day in court.'

She shook her head. 'But now they're free to use money or intimidation against those witnesses and the others involved, or to run, or to craft delays. Your friends suffered a loss, and the people who caused it are free to go about their lives and business. The legal system is very flawed.'

'That may be, but without it, chaos.'

From her experience, chaos came with it.

'Consequences, punishment, justice, should be swift and constant, without the escape hatches of money, clever lawyers and illogical rulings.'

'I imagine most mobs think that when they get a rope.'

She frowned at him. 'You arrest people who break the law. You know they've broken the law when you do so. You should be frustrated, even angry, knowing one of them finds a way through a legal loophole or, due to human failure, isn't punished for the crime.'

'I'd rather see a guilty man go free than an innocent one go down. Sometimes there are reasons to break the law. I'm not talking about our three current assholes, but in general.'

Obviously relaxed, Brooks stretched out his legs, gave Bert a little rub with his foot. 'It's not always black and white, right and wrong. If you don't consider all the shades and circumstances, you haven't reached justice.'

'You believe that.' The muscles in her belly twisted, vibrated. 'That there can be reasons to break the law.'

'Sure there are. Self-defense, defense of others. Or something as simple as speeding. Your wife's in labor? I'm not going to cite you for breaking the speed limit on the way to the hospital.'

'You'd consider the circumstances.'

'Sure. Back when I was on patrol, we got called in on an assault. This guy went into a bar and beat the shit out of his uncle. We'll call him Uncle Harry. Now, we've got to take the guy in on the assault, but it turns out Uncle Harry's been messing with the guy's twelve-year-old daughter. Yeah, he should've just called the cops and Child Services on it, but was he wrong to break Uncle Harry's face? I don't think so. You have to look at the whole picture, weigh those circumstances. That's what the courts are supposed to do.'

'Point of view,' she murmured.

'Yeah. Point of view.' He trailed a finger down her arm. 'Have you broken the law, Abigail?'

It was a door, she knew, that he invited her to walk through. But what if it locked behind her? 'I've never had a speeding ticket, but I've exceeded the posted limit. I'm going to check the lasagna.'

When he wandered in a few minutes later, she was standing at the counter, slicing tomatoes.

'I harvested some tomatoes and basil from the greenhouse earlier.'

'You've been busy.'

'I like to be busy. I completed a contract a bit earlier than I projected, so I rewarded myself with gardening. And I had visitors.'

'Is that so?'

'Your mother and sisters.'

He was on the point of topping off her wine. 'Say what again?'

'They were out this way. They'd had what your mother called a fancy ladies' lunch, and were going shopping and to drink frozen margaritas. They invited me to join them.'

'Uh-huh.'

'Mya explained they essentially came by to check me out. I liked her honesty, though at the time it was somewhat unnerving.'

Brooks let out a sound that might've been a laugh. 'She can be.'

'They had Plato with them. Bert enjoyed playing with him.'

'I bet.'

'They laugh a lot.'

327

'Bert and Plato?'

'No.' And that made her laugh. 'Your mother and sisters. They seem very happy. They seem like friends as well as relatives.'

'I'd say they are. We are.'

'Your other sister, Sybill, has a kind and gentle way. You appear to have qualities of both of your siblings. You also share a strong physical resemblance, particularly with Mya.'

'Did Mya tell you embarrassing stories about me?'

'No, though I would have been interested. I suspect she was more curious about me. She said when it came to women, to relationships . . .' Abigail paused a moment as she layered slices of buffalo mozzarella with the tomatoes. 'In the past you tended toward the looks without necessarily much substance to back it up.'

Brooks watched her as she spoke, as she perfected the pattern on the dish. 'I bet that's word for word.'

'Paraphrasing can impart a different tenor, even a different meaning.'

'Can't argue.'

'Is it true?'

He considered, shrugged. 'I guess it is, now that I think about it.'

'I think it's flattering.' And it also spoke to the novelty she'd brought up that morning. Novelty wore off.

'What surprises me is they had you three to one, and took no for an answer.'

'I was obviously, and honestly, deeply involved with the garden.' She picked up the wine now, drank. 'Your mother did, however, invite me to an

328

impromptu backyard barbecue this Sunday.'

He laughed, lifted his glass in salute. 'See? They didn't take no for an answer.'

She hadn't considered that, and now saw Brooks was right. 'Your mother seemed to ignore my reasonable excuse to decline. I thought it might be better to write her a polite note of regret.'

'Why? She makes great potato salad.'

'I have my gardening and household chores on my schedule for Sunday.'

'Chicken.'

'I'm sure your mother makes very nice chicken, but—'

'No. You're a chicken.' He made a clucking sound that deepened her frown and stirred her temper.

'There's no need to be rude.'

'Sometimes honest is rude. Look, there's no reason to be nervous about hanging out in the backyard and eating potato salad. You'll have fun.'

'No, I won't, because I'll have neglected my schedule. And I don't know how to behave at a backyard barbecue. I don't know how to have conversations with all those people I don't know, or barely know, or how to meet the curiosity that would, I assume, be aimed at me because you and I have been having sex.'

'That's a lot of don't knows,' Brooks decided, 'but I can help you with all of it. I can give you a hand with the gardening and household chores beforehand. You do just fine with conversations, but I'll stick with you until you're comfortable. And they may be curious, but they're disposed to like you because I do, and my mother does. Plus, I'll make you a promise.'

329

He paused now, waited until she lifted her gaze to his.

'What promise?'

'You give it an hour, and if you're not having a good time, I'll make an excuse. I'll say I've got a call I have to handle, and we'll go.'

'You'd lie to your family?'

'Yeah, I would. They'd know I'm lying, and understand.'

There, she thought, one of the complications that tangled into social duties and interpersonal relationships. 'I think it's best to avoid all of that and just send a note of regret.'

'She'll just come fetch you.'

That stopped her slicing again. 'That's not true.'

'It's gospel, honey. She'll figure you're too shy or too stubborn. If she decides on shy, she'll mother you over there. If she decides on stubborn, she'll push you every mile from here to there.'

'I'm not shy or stubborn.'

'You're both, with some of that clucker tossed in.'

Deliberately, she brought the knife down on the board a little harder than necessary. 'I don't see the wisdom in insulting me when I'm preparing you a meal.'

'I don't see being shy or stubborn as insulting. And everybody's got a little clucker pecking around, depending on the circumstances.'

'What are your circumstances?'

'That's a change of subject, but I'll give it to you. Semiannual dentist visits, wolf spiders and karaoke.'

'Karaoke. That's funny.'

'Not when I do it. Anyway, take my word. Give it

330

an hour. An hour won't hurt you.'

'I'll think about it.'

'Good enough. I'm repeating myself from last night, but that sure smells good.'

'Hopefully tonight will be more quiet and peaceful than last.'

It proved to be, until shortly after two a.m.

When her alarm sounded, she rolled out of bed, reaching for the gun on her nightstand and gripped it before her feet hit the floor.

'Take it easy.' Brooks's voice stayed utterly calm. 'Ease it down, Abigail. You, too,' he said to the dog, who poised at her feet, a low growl in his throat.

'Someone's coming.'

'I got that. No, don't turn on the light. If it's somebody up to mischief, it's better if they don't know we know.'

'I don't recognize this car,' she said, as she turned to the monitor.

'I do. Shit.' His sigh was more fatigued than annoyed. 'It's Doyle Parsins, so that would be Justin Blake and his pal Chad Cartwright and Doyle. Let me get my pants on. I'll take care of it.'

'There are only two people in the car.'

Brooks jerked on his pants, grabbed his shirt, shrugging into it as he walked back to study the monitor. 'Either Chad got some sense and stayed home, or they dropped him off to circle around the back. Since I don't credit them with that many smarts, I'd say Chad skipped the party.'

Firmly, Brooks laid a hand on her shoulder. 'It's not about you, Abigail. Relax.'

'I don't relax when someone sneaks onto my property at two in the morning. It's not reasonable to expect me to relax.'

'Good point.' He took her arms, but loosely, rubbing his way up and down them. 'I'm just saying they're looking to cause me some grief. Not you. Most likely creeping up here—see there, they're pulling off some ways from the house. Planning on slashing my tires, maybe spray painting some obscenities on my car. Figuring I'll get a rude surprise come morning. Jesus, high as hot-air balloons, the both of them.'

'If they're under the influence of drugs, they're unlikely to be rational.'

'Rational isn't Justin's default position, straight or high.'

And coming here like this told Brooks he was escalating, as Tybal had been.

Watching them, he took the time to button his shirt. 'Go on and call nine-one-one. Ash is on call tonight. You just give him the situation. I'll go out and see to it.'

He pulled on boots in case he had to chase them down, strapped on his weapon.

'You and Bert stay inside.'

'I don't need or want to be protected from a pair of delinquents.'

'Abigail, I'm the one with the badge.' His tone brooked no argument. 'And I'm the one they're here to screw with. No point getting them riled up toward you. Call it in, and wait for me.'

He went downstairs in the backwash of her outdoor security lights, taking his time. The bust would be clearer, stick harder, if he walked out on them doing something, or about to, rather than just creeping around, muffling the snorting giggles of the drunk and/or high.

Abigail would get her view of justice now, he thought, as the pair of them would spend the time until their trial in jail.

He watched them through the window, and as he'd anticipated, they crouched beside his cruiser. Justin opened a bag, tossed a spray can to Doyle.

He let them get started. The cruiser would need a paint job, but the evidence would be unarguable.

Then he stepped to the front door, dealt with the locks, and walked out.

'You boys lost?'

Doyle dropped the can and fell back on his ass.

'Sorry to interrupt your field trip, but I believe the half-wit pair of you are trespassing. We'll add vandalism to that, and seeing as you've just vandalized police property, it's a tough one for you. And I'm just betting I'm going to find controlled substances and/or alcohol in your possession and in your bloodstream. To sum up, boys? You're royally fucked.'

Brooks shook his head when Doyle tried to scramble to his feet. 'You run, Doyle, I'll add on fleeing and resisting. I know where you live, you idiot, so stay down, stay put. Justin, you're going to want to let me see your hands.'

'You want to see my hands?'

Justin punched the knife he held into the rear tire, then surged to his feet. 'Gonna let the air out of you next, asshole.'

'Let me get this straight. You've got a knife. I've got a gun. See this?' Brooks drew it almost casually. 'And I'm the asshole? Justin, you are deeply, deeply stupid. Now, toss that knife down, then take a look at your marginally brighter friend. See how he's facedown with his hands linked behind his head?

333

Do that.'

In the security lights, Brooks noted Justin's pupils were the size of pinpricks.

'You're not going to shoot me. You haven't got the stomach for it.'

'I think he does.' With her favored Glock in her hand, Abigail stepped out from the side of the house. 'But if he doesn't shoot you, I will.'

'Hiding behind a woman now, Gleason?'

Brooks shifted, just a little. Not only to block Abigail if Justin was stupid enough to come for them with the knife, but because he wasn't sure, at all, she wouldn't shoot the moron.

'Do I look like I'm hiding?'

'I'd like to shoot him,' Abigail said, conversationally. 'He's trespassing, and he's armed, so I believe I'm within my rights. I could shoot him in the leg. I'm a very good shot, as you know.'

'Abigail.' Torn between amusement and concern, Brooks stepped forward. 'Drop that knife now, Justin, before this gets ugly.'

'You're not putting me in jail.'

'How many ways can you be wrong tonight?' Brooks wondered.

Justin lunged forward.

'Don't shoot him, for Christ's sake,' Brooks shouted. He blocked the knife hand with his left arm, swung up his right elbow and jabbed it into Justin's nose. He heard the satisfying crunch an instant before blood spurted. As the knife dropped, he simply gripped Justin by the collar, propelled him forward so he stumbled to his knees.

Out of patience, he shoved Justin down on his face, put a boot on his neck. 'Abigail, do me a favor and go up and get my cuffs, will you?'

'I have them.'

Brooks lifted his brows when she pulled them out of her back pocket. 'You're a planner. Toss them over.'

He caught them, knelt down to yank Justin's arms behind his back. 'Doyle, you keep still now, or Ms. Lowery might shoot you in the leg.'

'Yes, sir. I didn't know he was going to do that, I swear. We were just going to mess around with the cruiser. I swear to God.'

'Keep quiet, Doyle, you're too stupid to talk.' Brooks glanced up as he heard the siren. 'Jesus, what's he doing coming in hot?'

'I saw the knife when I was relating the situation. Your deputy became very concerned.'

'All right. Hell. Justin, you just came at a cop with a knife. That's assault with a deadly on a police officer. The prosecutor might even bump that to attempted murder when we add in the trash talk. You're done, boy, and it didn't have to go like this. You're under arrest for trespassing, vandalism, defacing police property and assault with a deadly weapon on a police officer. You have the right to remain silent.'

'You broke my fucking nose. I'll kill you for that.'

'Do yourself a favor, take that right to silence to heart.' He finished the Miranda as he spotted the lights from Ash's cruiser zipping down the road. 'Doyle? Where's Chad Cartwright?'

'He wouldn't come. Said he was in enough trouble, and his daddy's likely to kick his ass he gets in more.'

'A glimmer of sanity.' He got to his feet as Ash slammed out of his car.

'Chief! You all right? Jesus. You're bleeding.'

335

'What? Where? Shit.' Brooks looked down, hissed in disgust. 'That's Justin's nose blood. God damn it, I liked this shirt.'

'You should soak it in cold water and salt.'

Both Brooks and his deputy looked over to where Abigail stood, the dog at full alert at her side.

'Ma'am,' Ash said.

Sirens screamed out again.

'What the hell, Ash?'

'It'll be Boyd. When Ms. Lowery reported she saw a knife, and only had a visual on two when this bunch usually runs in three, I thought I should call Boyd in for backup. Are you sure he didn't cut you?'

'Yeah, I'm sure. He was stupid enough to try, so he's charged with assault on a police officer. I guess you and Boyd can take the pair of them in. I'll be along shortly.'

'All right, Chief. Sorry for the trouble, Ms. Lowery.'

'You didn't cause it, Deputy Hyderman.'

Brooks stepped over to her. 'Why don't you take Bert and go on inside? I'll be in in just a couple minutes.'

'Yes.' She signaled to the dog and went back the way she'd come.

In the kitchen, she rewarded Bert with one of his favorite cookies, then put on coffee. She considered a moment, then opened a container to put human cookies on a plate.

Somehow it seemed like the right thing to do. She sat at the table and watched Brooks and the others on the monitor. The boy he'd called Doyle cried a little, but she found she couldn't feel any

336

sympathy. Justin remained sullen, snarling like a bad dog, in her opinion, sneering out of eyes she expected would be swollen and bruised from the broken nose shortly.

Once the prisoners were secured in the back of the first deputy's cruiser, Brooks spoke to his men for another moment, then said something that made them laugh.

Breaking the tension, she deduced. Yes, that would be a sign of a good leader. She started to rise and go unlock the front door, but saw Brooks head toward the back as she had. Instead she walked over and poured his coffee, adding the sugar as he liked it.

He stepped in, saw the plate. 'Cookies?'

'I thought you might want something.'

'I might. I've got to go in and deal with this.'

'Yes, of course.'

He picked up his coffee, took a cookie. 'I don't have to ask if you're all right. Steady as a rock, right on through it.'

'He's a stupid, violent boy, but we were never in any real danger. You might have been cut, which would've been upsetting. Was he right?'

'Who, and about what?'

'Justin Blake, when he said you wouldn't shoot him.'

Biting into the cookie, Brooks leaned back in that easy way he had. 'Mostly. If I'd had to, yeah, but I didn't have to. Better all around. Would you have shot him?'

'Yes.' She didn't hesitate. 'I'd wondered if I could or would, as he's young and stupid, but yes. If he'd cut you, I would have. But you have excellent reflexes, and he telegraphed his move, and was slow

337

due, I suspect, to drugs or alcohol. You weren't afraid.'

'You gave me a moment, initially. I told you to stay inside.'

'And I told you I didn't need or want to be protected. It's my property, and I was armed.'

'As always.' He took another bite of the cookie.

'Added to that, though nothing registered on the monitor, I wanted to be sure there wasn't a third who might have flanked you.'

'I appreciate it.'

'You should soak that shirt before the stain sets.'

'I've got a spare at the station. Abigail, I'm going to need for you to give a statement. You can come in, or I can send one of my men to take it here.'

'Oh. Yes, of course. I couldn't give you the statement under the circumstances.'

'No.'

'I think I'd prefer to go in. I could do it now.'

'Morning's fine.'

'If I came in now, it would be done. I'd rather it be done. I'll change and drive in now.'

'I can wait for you.'

'That's all right. You should go now, do what you need to do.'

'Yeah. The way you handled this makes me think you've handled trouble before. I'm hoping you'll trust me enough to tell me about that someday soon.'

Wanting the link, she curled her fingers around his wrists for a moment. 'If I could tell anyone, it would be you.'

'Okay, then.' He set the coffee down, took her face in his hands and kissed her. 'Thanks for the backup. And the cookie.'

'You're welcome.'

*　　*　　*

Thirty minutes behind Brooks, Abigail walked into the station. The older deputy—Boyd Fitzwater, she remembered—immediately got up from his desk and came around to meet her.

'Ms. Lowery, we sure appreciate you coming in like this. The chief's in his office, talking to the prosecutor and all. I'm going to take your statement.'

'Yes.'

'You want some coffee, something cold?'

'No, thank you.'

'We can sit down right here. Should be quiet. Ash is back with the paramedic we called in to treat the Blake boy's nose.' He smiled when he said it. 'It's busted good.'

'I'm sure a broken nose is preferable to a bullet. I believe Chief Gleason would have been justified in firing his weapon when Justin lunged toward him with the knife.'

'I'm not going to argue. But if we could start this from the beginning. I'm going to record it so we get it all straight. I'll be taking notes, too. All right with you?'

'Of course.'

'All righty, then.' Boyd switched on a tape recorder, read off the date, the time, the names of all involved. 'Ms. Lowery, why don't you just tell me what happened tonight?'

'At two-oh-seven a.m., my perimeter alarm signaled a breach.'

She spoke clearly, precisely.

'As Chief Gleason had indicated, Justin Blake most usually traveled with two individuals. I wanted to be certain there wasn't indeed a third man who might have circled around. My alarms didn't register, but I felt it best to be certain. After I spoke with Deputy Hyderman on the phone, I took my dog and went out the back of the house. My dog showed no sign of detecting anyone in that area, so I continued around to the front, where I saw Chief Gleason and the two trespassers. One, identified as Doyle Parsins, was already on the ground, and Justin Blake continued to crouch by the left-rear tire of Chief Gleason's police cruiser.'

'Did you hear anybody say anything?'

'Oh, yes, quite clearly. It was a quiet night. Chief Gleason said to Justin, "You're going to want to show me your hands." I should add that at this time, Chief Gleason's weapon was secured in his holster. Justin responded, "You want to see my hands?" and drove the knife he held in his right hand into the left-rear tire.'

She continued, giving Boyd a word-for-word, move-by-move statement. Boyd interrupted once or twice to clarify.

'That's really detailed.'

'I have an eidetic memory—you might call it photographic,' she added, though it always irked her to explain with that inaccuracy.

'That's really helpful, Ms. Lowery.'

'I hope so. He would have killed Brooks if he could have.'

Though he reached over to turn off the tape recorder, Boyd lifted his hand from it, sat back. 'Ma'am?'

'Justin Blake. He would have stabbed Chief

Gleason, and he would have killed him if he could have. His intent was very clear, as was his anger and, I think, his fear. It's what he knows, you see? To hurt or eliminate what gets in his way, what interferes. There are people who simply believe their own wants and wishes are above everything and everyone else.'

She'd seen murder, she thought. The boy didn't remind her of the cold, mechanical Korotkii. He lacked that efficiency and dispassion. But he'd made her think of Ilya, of the hot rage on Ilya's face when he'd cursed and kicked his dead cousin.

'He might not have killed or caused serious physical harm before tonight. I think if he had, he wouldn't have been so inept at this attempt. But if it hadn't been this, tonight, it would have been someone else, another night, someone without Chief Gleason's resources, reflexes and equanimity. There would have been more to clean up than a broken nose.'

'Yes, ma'am.'

'I'm sorry. It was upsetting. More than I realized. My opinion isn't relevant. If that's all you need, I'd like to go home.'

'I can get somebody to drive you.'

'No, I'm fine to drive. Thank you, Deputy, you've been very kind.'

She started for the door, paused when Brooks called her name. He crossed over, laid a hand on her arm. 'Be a minute,' he told Boyd, then led her outside.

'Are you okay?'

'Yes. I told you.'

'And you just told Boyd it was more upsetting than you realized.'

341

'It was, but that doesn't mean I'm not all right. I am tired, though. I think I'll go home and get some more sleep.'

'Good. I'll call or swing by later, just to see how you are.'

'You can't worry about me. I don't need it.' Didn't want it, any more than she wanted Justin Blake to remind her of Ilya Volkov. 'Did you soak your shirt, cold water and salt?'

'I trashed it. I'd see his blood on there whether it was there or not. I don't much care for that shirt anymore.'

She thought of a pretty sweater, stained with blood. 'I understand. You're tired, too.' She let herself touch his face. 'I hope you can get a little sleep.'

'I wouldn't mind it. You drive safe, Abigail.' He kissed her forehead, then her lips, before stepping over to open her car door. 'You were right, what you said in there. It was only a matter of time before he pulled a knife or a gun, picked up a bat, before he did somebody serious harm.'

'I know.'

'You don't have to worry about him anymore.'

'Then I won't.' Leading with emotion, she threw her arms around him, held tight. 'I'm very glad you have good reflexes.'

She slid into the car and drove away.

20

Just past three that afternoon, Abigail watched on her monitor as a dark Mercedes sedan cruised toward her house. The look of it sent a quick tingle up her spine. She didn't recognize the car, the driver—late thirties, early forties, broad shoulders, short, dark hair—or the passenger—fiftyish, dark gray hair, wide face.

She keyed the license plate into her system, reminding herself she was prepared—for anything. Her quick search through DMV records popped Lincoln Blake as the owner, and her shoulders relaxed.

An annoying interruption but not a threat.

Blake looked prosperous, she noted, when he got out of the passenger side. It struck her that he looked *deliberately* prosperous in his perfectly cut suit and city shoes. The second man also wore a suit, and carried a briefcase.

She believed she saw a slight bulge on his right hip that disturbed the line of his jacket. He carried a weapon.

Well, she thought, so did she.

She considered ignoring the knock on her door. She wasn't under any obligation to answer, to speak with the father of the boy who'd tried to kill Brooks. But she also considered the fact that a man like Blake, from everything she'd heard and intuited about him, wouldn't simply walk away. In any case, she was a little curious.

With Bert at her side, she opened the front door.

'Miss Lowery.' Blake offered a wide smile and his hand. 'Forgive the intrusion. I'm Lincoln Blake, one of your neighbors.'

'Your home is several miles away, in fact, on the other side of Bickford. Therefore, you don't live close enough to my property to be considered a neighbor.'

343

'We're all neighbors here,' Blake said jovially. 'This is my personal assistant, Mark. I'd like to apologize for my son's inadvertent trespass on your property last night. May we come in, discuss this situation?'

'No.'

It always puzzled her why people looked so surprised, even annoyed, when they asked a question and the response was negative.

'Now, Miss Lowery, I came out here to offer my apologies, as I understand my son caused you some inconvenience, and to sort this all out. It'll be helpful if we could be comfortable while we talk this out.'

'I'm comfortable. Thank you for your apology, Mr. Blake, though it hardly applies, as it was your son who came on my property without permission in the middle of the night, and who attempted to stab Chief Gleason. I believe the police are sorting all this out, and we really don't have anything to discuss at this point.'

'Now, that's just why I came by. I dislike trying to have a conversation through a doorway.'

'I dislike having strangers in my house. I'd like you to go now. You can discuss this with the police.'

'I'm not finished.' He jabbed out a finger. 'I understand you're *friendly* with Brooks Gleason, and that—'

'Yes, we are friendly. He wouldn't have been here at two in the morning when your son and your son's friend came illegally onto my property with the intent to deface Chief Gleason's police cruiser if we weren't friendly. However, my relationship with Chief Gleason doesn't alter the facts.'

'One fact is you haven't lived here long. You're

not fully aware of my position in this community, or the history behind it.'

She wondered, sincerely, why he thought any of that was relevant, but didn't bother to ask.

'I'm aware, and your position and history don't alter the facts of what transpired here early this morning. It was very disturbing to be awakened in that manner, and to witness your son attack Chief Gleason with a knife.'

'Fact.' Blake slapped an index finger on his open palm. 'It was the middle of the night, and therefore dark. I have no doubt Brooks Gleason goaded my boy, threatened him. Justin was simply defending himself.'

'That's inaccurate,' Abigail said calmly. 'My security lights were on. I have excellent vision and was less than ten feet away during the attempted assault. Chief Gleason clearly asked your son to show his hands, and when your son did so it was, first, to puncture the cruiser's tire and, second, to threaten Brooks with the knife.'

'My son—'

'I haven't finished correcting your inaccuracies,' she pointed out, and stunned Blake into momentary silence.

'Only then, when your son threatened him verbally and with gestures, did Brooks draw his weapon. And still your son would not drop the knife. Instead, even when I stepped out with my own weapon, your son lunged at Brooks with the knife. In my opinion, Brooks would have been fully justified in shooting your son at that time, but he chose to disarm him hand to hand at a greater risk to his own safety.'

'Nobody knows you around here. You're an odd,

345

solitary woman with no background or history in the community. If and when you tell that ridiculous story in court, my lawyers will rip your testimony to bits and humiliate you.'

'I don't think so, but I'm sure your lawyers will do their jobs. If that's all, I'd like you to leave.'

'You just wait a damn minute.' Blake stepped forward, and Bert quivered, growled.

'You're upsetting my dog,' Abigail said coldly. 'And if your assistant attempts to draw his sidearm, I'll release my dog. I can assure you he'll move faster than he can draw his weapon. I'm also armed, as you can plainly see. I'm a very good shot. I don't like strangers coming to my home, trying to intimidate and threaten me. I don't like men who raise violent, angry young men.'

Like Sergei Volkov, she thought.

'I don't like you, Mr. Blake, and I'll ask you to leave for the last time.'

'I came here to settle this with you, to apologize and offer you compensation for the inconvenience.'

'Compensation?'

'Ten thousand dollars. A generous apology for a mishap, for a misunderstanding.'

'It certainly would be,' Abigail agreed.

'The money's yours, in cash, for your agreement that this was, indeed, a misunderstanding.'

'Your proposal is I accept ten thousand dollars in cash from you to misrepresent what happened here this morning?'

'Don't be stubborn. My proposal is you accept the cash in my assistant's briefcase as an apology, and you simply agree what occurred here was a misunderstanding. You'll also have my word that my son will never step foot on your property again.'

346

'First, your word can hardly regulate your son's behavior. Second, it would be your son, not you, who owes me an apology for this morning. And last, your proposal constitutes a bribe, an exchange of money for my misrepresenting the facts. I believe attempting to bribe a witness in a criminal investigation is a crime. The simplest solution, and certainly the best outcome for you, is for me to say no, thank you. And good-bye.'

She stepped back, shut the door, clicked the locks in place.

He actually beat on the door with his fist. It didn't surprise her, Abigail realized. His son had inherited that same unstable temperament and illusion of entitlement. With her hand resting lightly on the butt of her gun, she walked back to the kitchen monitor, watched the assistant attempt to calm his employer down.

She didn't want to call the police. More trouble, more interruptions, more ugly behavior.

It had shaken her a little, there was no shame in admitting it. But she'd stood up to the intimidation, the threats. No panic, she thought now, no urge to run.

She didn't believe in fate, in anything being *meant*, but if she did, maybe—theoretically—she'd been meant to go through these two experiences, the reminder of Ilya, and now of his father, to prove to herself she could and would stand up.

She wouldn't run again. If she believed in fate.

'We'll give him two minutes, from now, to regain some composure and leave. If he doesn't, we'll go out again.'

But this time, she determined, her weapon would be in her hand, not in her holster.

347

As she meant it literally, she set the timer on her watch, and continued to observe him on the monitor.

His blood pressure must be at dangerous levels, she thought, as his face darkened, his eyes literally bulged. She could see the rapid rise and fall of his prosperous chest as he shouted at his assistant.

She hoped she wouldn't have to call for medical assistance as well as the authorities.

All she wanted to do was finish her work and spend a little time working in her gardens. This man's difficulties weren't hers.

At the one-minute, forty-two-second mark, Blake stormed back to the car. Abigail let out a small sigh of relief as the assistant made the three-quarter turn and drove away.

All these years, she thought. Was it irony she was once again a witness to a crime, and once again the subject of threats and intimidation?

No, she didn't believe in fate, and yet . . . it certainly felt as though fate had decided to twist her life, and circle it right back to where she'd begun.

It was something to think about.

She looked at her work, sighed again.

'I think we'll take a walk,' she said to Bert. 'I'm too annoyed to work right now.'

Her mood leveled out in the air, calmed when she walked through the trees, studied the progress of wildflowers, considered again her private seating area with its view of the hills. She would start a search for the proper bench very soon.

She felt . . . happy, she realized, when she received a text from Brooks.

How about I pick up some Chinese? Don't cook. You're probably tired.

She considered, texted back.

I'm not tired, but I like Chinese food. Thank you.

Moments later, she got another text.

You're welcome.

It made her laugh, picked up her mood a few more notches. Since she was already out, she gave Bert a full hour of exercise, then went back home to work with a clear mind.

She lost track of time, a rarity for her, and was prepared to be annoyed when her alarm beeped again. If that disagreeable man had come back, she wouldn't be so polite, she determined.

Her mood shifted yet again when she saw Brooks's cruiser. A check of the time showed her she'd worked past six.

No gardening today, she thought, and put the lack of that pleasure on the head of the disagreeable man and his stony-faced assistant.

But she shut down and went to the door happy—again—at the prospect of having dinner with Brooks.

Her smile of greeting turned to concern when she saw his face.

'You didn't sleep.'

'We had a lot going on.'

'You look very tired. Here, let me take some of that. You brought a great deal of food for two people.'

'You know what they say about Chinese food.'

'It's not really true. You won't be hungry an hour later if you eat properly. I see you brought *pijin* to go with it.'

'I did?'

'Chinese beer,' she said, as she led the way in. 'Chinese villagers brewed beer as far back as 7,000

B.C.'

'I don't think the Zhujiang I picked up is that old.'

'That's a joke. It was used—not the beer you bought—in rituals. It wasn't until the seventeenth century that modern beer brewing was introduced to China.'

'Good to know.'

'You sound tired, too. You should sit, have one of the beers. I slept another two hours, and had an hour's walk. I feel rested. I'll take care of the food.'

'I just told them to load me up. I didn't know what you wanted, especially.'

'I'm not fussy.' She opened cartons. 'I'm sorry you had a difficult day. You can tell me about it if you like.'

'Lawyers, arguments, accusations, threats.' He opened a beer, sat at her counter. 'Paperwork, meetings. You don't have to put all that in bowls. The beauty of Chinese is you can eat right out of the carton.'

'Which is rushed and less soothing.' She believed he required soothing. 'I can fix your plate if you tell me what you'd like.'

'Whatever. I'm not fussy, either.'

'We should take a walk after dinner, then you should try a warm bath and try to sleep. You seem very tense, and you rarely are.'

'I guess I'm just annoyed at having lawyers in my face, who try to push and intimidate me and my deputies.'

'Yes, he's a very annoying man.' She scooped rice out of the bowl, ladled sweet-and-sour pork over it, added a dumpling, some noodles, some butterfly shrimp. 'I had to walk off my own mood after he

350

left this afternoon.'

'Left? Here? Blake came here?'

'This afternoon, with his assistant. Ostensibly to apologize for his son's "inadvertent" trespassing. But that was just a ruse, not well disguised. He was displeased when I wouldn't let him come in to discuss the situation.'

'I bet he was. He doesn't like being refused. It's good you didn't open the door.'

'I did open the door, but wouldn't invite him in.' She decided she'd try the beer straight out of the bottle, as Brooks did. 'Are you aware his assistant carries a gun?'

'Yeah. Are you telling me he pulled a weapon on you?'

'Oh, no. No, don't be upset.' She'd meant to soothe and had accomplished the opposite. 'Of course he didn't. I just noticed the line of his suit, and then his body language when Bert growled.'

Brooks took a long pull of beer. 'Why don't you tell me what was said and done?'

'You are upset,' she murmured. 'I shouldn't have mentioned it.'

'Yes, you should have.'

'It wasn't anything important, really. He said he'd come to apologize, then was clearly put out when I refused to invite them in. He termed what happened a misunderstanding, and indicated it was of your doing. I disabused him of that, as I was a witness. He implied I didn't understand his position in the community, and that my relationship with you made my standing as witness suspicious. Not in those words, but that was the meaning. Do you want me to relay the exact conversation?'

'Not just yet. The gist is fine.'

351

'The gist. All right. He was displeased and angry as I told him to leave—and warned him and his assistant that if the assistant drew his weapon on Bert, I would release Bert, who would disarm the assistant handily. And reminded them I was also armed.'

'Jesus Christ.'

'I was—clearly. It seemed best to point out the obvious. Mr. Blake reiterated he'd come to apologize, and added he'd come to offer compensation. In the amount of ten thousand dollars if I accepted it and agreed that what had happened was a misunderstanding. It annoyed me.'

'How many times did you ask them to leave?'

'Three. I didn't bother to ask again, simply said good-bye and closed the door. He did bang on the door for nearly two minutes after that. He's very rude. Then his assistant convinced him to get back in the car.'

Brooks pushed back from the counter, paced the kitchen. 'Why didn't you call me?'

'There wasn't any need. It was relatively simple to deal with. Irritating, but simple. I—'

She broke off because when he turned to her, the controlled rage on his face snapped her throat closed.

'Listen to me. Two men you don't know come to your door, one of them's armed. They refuse to leave when you tell them to, multiple times. What's the logical thing to do?'

'Close the door. I did.'

'No, Abigail. The logical thing to do is close the door, then call the police.'

'I don't agree. I'm sorry if that makes you angry, but I don't. They left.' She decided to avoid more anger by not mentioning she'd intended to go back out, weapon drawn, at the two-minute mark.

Later, she'd wonder if the avoidance equaled one of those interpersonal relationship tangles.

'I was armed, Brooks, and Bert was on alert. I wasn't in any danger. In fact, Blake became so agitated, I would have called both you and medical assistance if he hadn't left when he did.'

'Do you want to press charges?'

'No. You're angry with me. I don't want you to be angry with me. I did exactly as I felt best at that time, under those circumstances. If your ego's threatened because I didn't call for help—'

'Maybe some. Yeah, I'll own that. And I'm not going to say it's not a relief to me knowing I'm with a woman who can handle herself. But I know Blake. He tried to bully and intimidate you.'

'Yes, he tried. He failed.'

'Trying's enough. And he attempted to bribe you.'

'I told him his attempt to bribe a witness in a criminal matter was illegal.'

'I bet you did.' Brooks shoved a hand through his hair, sat again. 'You don't know him. You don't know the kind of enemy you made today, and believe me, you made one.'

'I think I do know,' she said quietly. 'I think I know very well. But making him an enemy isn't my fault, or yours.'

'Maybe not. But it's what it is.'

'You're going to confront him over it.'

'You're damn right I am.'

'Won't that just increase the level of animosity?'

'Maybe. But if I don't deal with it, he'll see it as a weak spot. He could come back, try again, figuring you didn't mention it, are just angling for a bigger payoff.'

'I made my position very clear.'

'If you understand the kind of person you're dealing with, you'll realize that it doesn't matter a damn.'

Twelve years of running, she thought. Yes, she understood. 'You're right, but it mattered to me on a very personal level that I made my position clear.'

'Okay, that's done. Now I'm telling you, if he comes back, don't open the door to him. Call me.'

'Subjugate my ego to yours?'

'No. Maybe. Shit, I don't know about that part, and don't much care.'

She smiled a little. 'That would be another discussion.'

The way he took a breath told her he was trying to cool his temper.

'I'm telling you because he'll only be more intimidating and bullying if he comes back. I'm telling you because I want him to understand action will be taken if he tries to harass you, or anyone else. I asked the same of Russ, his wife, his parents, told my deputies to tell their families.'

She nodded, felt less annoyed. 'I see.'

'He's in a rage, Abigail. His money and his position, as he sees it, aren't making this one go away. His son's behind bars, and very likely to be behind them for a very long time.'

'He loves his son.'

'I don't know about that, either, honest to God. But I know his ego's bound up in it. Nobody's going to put his boy in jail. Nobody's going to sully the Blake name. He's going to put everything he's got into fighting this, and if that means pushing at you, he'll push.'

'I'm not afraid of him. It also matters to me I'm not afraid of him.'

'I can see that. I don't want you to be afraid, but I want you to call me if he comes here again, if he tries to talk to you on the street, if he or anybody associated with him contacts you in any way. You're a witness, and you're damn well under my protection.'

'Don't say that.' Her heart literally skipped. 'I don't want to be under anyone's protection.'

'It is what it is.'

'No. No, no.' Now panic spurted, fast and hot. 'I'll contact you if he comes here again, because it's unethical for him to try to influence me to lie and it's illegal for him to bribe me to lie. But I don't want or need protection.'

'Calm down, now.'

'I'm responsible for myself. I can't be with you if you don't understand and agree I'm responsible for myself.'

She'd taken several steps back, and the dog had ranged himself in front of her.

'Abigail, you may be—you are, as far as I can tell—capable of handling most anything that comes at you. But I'm duty bound to protect everybody within my jurisdiction. That includes you. And I don't like you using my feeling for you as a weapon to get your own way.'

'I'm not doing that.'

'You damn well are.'

'I'm not—' She broke off, searched for calm, for sense. 'It's not what I meant to do. I apologize.'

'Screw apologize. Don't ever use what I feel as a hammer.'

355

'You're so angry with me. I didn't mean to use your feelings. I didn't. I'm clumsy in this kind of situation. I've never been in this kind of situation. I don't know what to do, what to say or how to say it. I just don't want you to feel particular responsibility for me. I don't know how to explain how uneasy it would make me if you did.'

'Why don't you try?'

'You're angry and tired, and your dinner's gone cold.' It appalled her to feel tears running down her cheeks. 'I never meant for any of this to happen. I never thought you'd be so upset about Blake. I'm not doing the right thing, but I don't know what is. I don't mean to cry. I know tears are another weapon, and I don't mean them as one.'

'I know you don't.'

'I'll—warm up the food.'

'It's fine.' He rose, got a fork from the drawer, then sat again. 'Fine,' he repeated after he'd scooped some up, sampled.

'You should use the chopsticks.'

'Never got the hang of them.'

'I could teach you.'

'I'll take you up on that some other time. Sit down and eat.'

'I— You're still angry. You're pushing it down because I cried. So the tears are a weapon.'

'Yeah, I'm angry, and pushing it down some because you're crying and obviously torn up about things you won't tell me, or feel you can't. I'm pushing it down some because I'm in love with you.'

The tears she'd nearly had under control flooded back, hot and fast as the panic. On a sob she stumbled to the door, fought the locks open, rushed out.

'Abigail.'

'Don't. Don't. I don't know what to do. I need to think, to find some *composure*. You should go until I can speak rationally.'

'Do you think I'd leave you alone when you're twisted up like this? I tell you I love you, and it feels like I broke your heart.'

She turned, her hand fisted over her heart, her eyes drenched with tears and emotion. 'No one ever said that to me. In my life, no one's ever said those words to me.'

'I'm making you a promise right here that you'll hear them from me every day.'

'No—no, don't promise. Don't. I don't know what I'm feeling. How do I know it's not just hearing those words? It's overwhelming to hear them, to look at you, and to see you mean them. Or it seems you do. How do I know?'

'You can't know everything. Sometimes you have to trust. Sometimes you have to just feel.'

'I want it.' She kept her hand clutched over her heart, as if opening her fingers would allow it all to fly away. 'I want it more than I can stand.'

'Then take it. It's right here.'

'It's not right. It's not fair to you. You don't understand; you can't.'

'Abigail.'

'That's not even my name!'

She slapped a hand over her mouth, sobbed against it. He only stepped to her, brushed tears from her cheek.

'I know.'

Every ounce of color draining, she stumbled back, gripped the porch rail. 'How could you know?'

'You're running or hiding from something, or someone. Maybe some of both. You're too damn smart to run and hide under your real name. I like Abigail, but I've known it's not who you are right along. The name's not the issue. Your trusting me enough to tell me is. And it looks like we're getting there.'

'Does anyone else know?'

'Scares the hell out of you. I don't like that. I don't see why anyone else would know, or care. Have you let anyone else get as close as you've let me?'

'No. Never.'

'Look at me now.' He spoke quietly as he moved to her. 'Listen to me.'

'I am.'

'I'm going to tell you I won't let you down. You're going to come to believe that, and we'll go from there. Let's try this part again. I'm in love with you.' He eased her into a kiss, kept it soft until she'd stopped trembling. 'There, that wasn't so hard. You're in love with me. I can see it, and I can feel it. Why don't you try the words?'

'I don't know. I want to know.'

'Just try them out, see how it feels. I won't hold you to it.'

'I . . . I'm in love with you. Oh, God.' She closed her eyes. 'It feels real.'

'Say it again, and kiss me.'

'I'm in love with you.' She didn't ease in, but flung herself. Starving for that knowledge, the gift, the light of it. Love. Being loved, giving it.

She hadn't believed in love. She hadn't believed in miracles.

Yet here was love. Here was her miracle.

'I don't know what to do now.'

'We're doing fine.'

She breathed in, out. Even that felt different. Freer. Fuller. 'I want to heat up the food. I want to teach you how to use chopsticks, and have dinner with you. Can we do that? Can we just be for a while?'

'Sure, we can.' If she needed a little time, he could give it. 'But I'm not promising anything on the chopsticks.'

'You changed everything.'

'Good or bad?'

She held on another minute. 'I don't know. But you changed it.'

21

Dealing with the meal settled her down—the simplicity and routine. He didn't pressure her for more. That, she understood, was his skill and his weapon. He knew how to wait. And he knew how to change the tone, to give her room, to help her relax so her thoughts weren't tied up in knots of tension.

His clumsiness with the chopsticks, though she suspected at least some of it was deliberate, made her laugh.

She'd laughed more since he'd come into her life than she had in the whole of it before him.

That alone might be worth the risk.

She could refuse it, ask for more time. He would give it to her, and she could use it to research another location, another identity, make plans to run again.

359

And if she ran again, she'd never know what might have been. She'd never feel what she felt now, with him. She'd never again allow herself to try.

She could—would—find contentment, security. She had before. But she'd never know love.

Her choice was to take the rational route—leave, stay safe. Or to risk it all, that safety, her freedom, even her life, for love.

'Can we walk?' she asked him.

'Sure.'

'I know you're tired,' she began, as they stepped outside. 'We should wait to talk about . . . everything.'

'Tomorrow's as good as today.'

'I don't know if I'll have the courage tomorrow.'

'Then tell me what you're afraid of.'

'So many things. But now, most of all? That if I tell you everything, you won't feel the same about me—and for me.'

Brooks reached down, picked up a stick, threw it. Bert looked at Abigail, got her signal and chased after it. 'Love doesn't turn on and off like a light switch.'

'I don't know. I've never been in love. I'm afraid to lose it, and you. And this. All of this. You have a duty, but more, you have a code. I knew a man like you, more like you than I realized at first. He died protecting me.'

'From whom?'

'It's complicated.'

'Okay. Did he love you?'

'Not the way I think you mean. It wasn't romantic or sexual. It was duty. But he cared about me, beyond that. He was the first person who cared for me.' She pressed a hand to her heart. 'Not for what I represented or what I accomplished, or what I was expected to be. But who I was.'

'You said you don't know who your father was, so not your father. A cop? Duty. Were you in witness protection, Abigail?'

Her hand trembled. Did he see it or just sense it? she wondered. But he took it in his, warmed and stilled it.

'I was being protected. I would have been given a new identity, a new life, but . . . it all went very wrong.'

'How long ago?'

'I was sixteen.'

'Sixteen?'

'I turned seventeen on the day . . .' John's blood on her hands. 'I'm not telling you the way I should. I never even imagined telling anyone.'

'Why don't you tell me the beginning?'

'I'm not sure where it is. Maybe it was when I realized I didn't want to be a doctor, and I knew that for certain in my first semester of pre-med.'

'After things went very wrong?'

'No. I'd completed pre-med, the requirement for medical school, by then. If I'd continued, per my mother's agenda, I'd have continued into medical school the next fall.'

'You said you were sixteen.'

'Yes. I'm very smart. I took accelerated courses throughout my education. My first term at Harvard I lived with a family she selected. They were very strict. She paid them to be. Then I had one term on my own, in a dorm, but carefully supervised. I think my rebellion started the day I bought my first pair of jeans and a hoodie. It was thrilling.'

'Back up. You were, at sixteen, in Harvard, in pre-med, and bought your first pair of jeans?'

'My mother bought or supervised the acquiring of my wardrobe.' Because it still seemed huge to her, she smiled. 'It was horrible. You wouldn't have looked at me. I wanted, so much, to be like the other girls. I wanted to talk on the phone and text about boys. I wanted to look the way the girls my age looked. And God, God, I didn't want to be a doctor. I wanted to apply to the FBI, to work in their cyber-crimes unit.'

'I should've figured,' he murmured.

'I monitored courses, studied online. If she'd known . . . I don't know what she would have done.'

She stopped at the view where she'd wanted a bench, and wondered if she'd ever have reason to buy one now. Now that it was too late to stop in the telling.

'She'd promised me the summer off from studies. A trip, a week in New York, then the beach. She'd promised, and that had gotten me through the last term. But she'd made arrangements for me to participate in one of her associate's summer programs. Intense study, lab work. It would have looked well on my record, accelerated my degree. And I—for the first time in my life—defied her.'

'About damn time.'

'Maybe, but it started a terrible chain of events. She was packing. She was covering for another associate, and keynoting at a conference. She'd be gone a week. And we argued. No, not accurate.' Annoyed with herself, Abigail shook her head.

At such times, accuracy was vital.

'She didn't argue. There was simply her way, and she had no doubt I'd fall in line. She concluded my behavior, my demands, my attitude, was a normal phase. I'm sure she noted it down for my files. And she left me. The cook had been given two weeks off, so I was alone in the house. She left without a word while I was sulking in my room. I don't know why I was so shocked she'd leave that way, but I was, sincerely shocked. Then I was angry, and maybe exhilarated. I took her car keys, and I drove to the mall.'

'To the mall?'

'It sounds so silly, doesn't it? My first real taste of freedom, and I went to the mall. But I had a fantasy about roaming the mall with a pack of girlfriends, giggling about boys, helping each other try on clothes. And I ran into Julie. We'd gone to school together for a while. She was a year or so older, and so popular, so pretty. I think she spoke to me that day because she'd broken up with her boyfriend and was at loose ends. Everything just happened from there.'

She told him about shopping, how it made her feel. About the hair dye, the plans to make fake IDs and go to the club.

'That's a lot of teenage rebellion in one day.'

'I think it was stored up.'

'I bet. You could make passable IDs at sixteen?'

'Excellent ones. I was very interested in identity theft and cyber crimes. I believed I'd have a career as an investigator.'

'It wouldn't surprise me.'

'It's flattering you'd say so. It mattered so much once. That day, in the mall, I took Julie's picture, and I took my own later. I cut my hair, and I dyed it black. Very black, and I bought makeup, used it the way Julie showed me. And I'd studied the other

363

girls in college, so I knew how to apply it.'

'Hold on a minute, I'm trying to picture you with short, black hair.' He studied her, narrowed his eyes. 'A little Goth, a little funky.'

'I'm not sure, but I looked very different from the way my mother wanted me to look. I suppose that was the point.'

'Sure it was, and the other point is you were entitled to it. Every kid is.'

'Maybe that's true. I should've stopped there. It should've been enough. The clothes, the hair and makeup. And the program she'd assigned me to started that Monday, and I'd made up my mind not to go. She would have been furious, and that should've been enough. But I didn't stop there.'

'You were on a roll,' he commented. 'You created the fake IDs and got into a club.'

'Yes. Julie picked the club. I didn't know anything about them, but I looked up the one she wanted, so I knew it was owned by a family rumored—known, really—to be Russian Mafia. The Volkovs.'

'Rings a dim bell. We didn't deal with the Russians as a rule in Little Rock. Some Irish, some Italian Mob types.'

'Sergei Volkov was—is—the *pakhan,* the boss of the Volkov *bratva.* He and his brother owned the club. I learned later it was run primarily by Sergei's son, Ilya. His cousin Alexi worked there— ostensibly. Primarily, again, I learned later, Alexi drank there, did drugs and women there. I didn't know or understand any of that when we met him.

'We drank Cosmopolitans, Julie and I. They were popular because of the television show *Sex and the City.* We drank and danced, and it was the most exciting night of my life. And Alexi Gurevich came to our table.'

She told him everything, how the club had looked to her, sounded. How Ilya had come, how he'd looked at her, talked to her. How she'd been kissed for the first time in her life, and by a Russian gangster.

'We were so young, and so foolish,' she continued. 'I didn't want to go to Alexi's house, but I didn't know how *not* to go. I felt ill, and when Ilya had to stay back, promising to meet us later, it was worse. Alexi's house wasn't far from my mother's, really. I imagined just going home, lying down. I'd never been drunk before. It had stopped being pleasant.'

'It'll do that.'

'Did you ever . . . when you were a teenager?'

'Russ and I got drunk and sick together a few times before we hit the legal age, and a few times after.'

'It was my first and last time, and I've never had another Cosmopolitan. Even looking at them makes me vaguely ill.' And a little afraid, she admitted to herself. 'He had a beautiful home with a river view. Furnished with too much deliberation, I thought. Too consciously trendy. He made more drinks, put on music, but I felt ill, and I used the bathroom off the kitchen to be sick. Sicker than I'd ever been in my life. All I wanted to do—'

'Was curl up on the floor and die?'

'Yes. Yes.' She laughed a little. 'I suppose it's something a lot of people experience at least once. I still didn't feel well when I came out, and I saw . . . Julie and Alexi were having sex on the sofa. I was fascinated and horrified at the same time, and so embarrassed. I went out through the kitchen to the terrace. It felt better in the air. I sat on a chair and fell asleep. And the voices woke me.'

'You're cold.' Because she'd started to shiver, Brooks put an arm around her shoulders.

'I was cold that night, with the breeze off the water, or the sickness, or—with what happened next. This feels the same. I'd like to walk back. It may be easier to tell you when we're walking.'

'Okay.'

'I planned to put a bench here, something organic. Something that looks like it just grew here. I like the view, and it's so quiet, with just the stream gurgling and the birds. See how Bert likes to play in the water? It feels like it's all mine. Silly.'

'It's not.'

Silly, she repeated in her head.

'That night, I looked through the glass of the sliding doors, and I saw two men with Alexi. I didn't see Julie. They were speaking Russian at first, but I'd studied Russian. I like languages, and I have an aptitude for them. I understood. The man, his name was Korotkii. Yakov Korotkii accused Alexi of taking money from the family. They argued, and at first Alexi was very arrogant. But that didn't last. They said he'd informed to the police because he'd been arrested for drugs. The other man, he was big, forced Alexi to his knees, and Alexi became afraid. He tried to bargain, to threaten, then to beg. Would you hold my hand?'

He took it, squeezed gently. 'Stop when you need to stop.'

'It needs to be finished. Korotkii shot him once, then twice at the temple. He shot him the way you might start your car or put on your shirt. An ordinary thing. Then Julie came out. She wasn't dressed, she'd been sick. She barely spoke, barely saw, and Korotkii shot her, like a reflex, like you swat at a gnat. God. God.'

'Here, now, lean on me.' He released her hand but only to wrap an arm around her, tuck her in as they walked.

'He was angry, though, Korotkii, because he hadn't known she was there, because his information hadn't included her. Or me. They didn't know about me, huddled outside the sliding door, frozen. Just frozen.'

She shouldn't have come outside, Abigail thought. Her legs didn't feel steady, and her stomach had begun to churn. She wished she could sit, wished she couldn't—still—see and hear and feel it all so clearly.

'That's enough now,' Brooks murmured. 'Let's get you back inside.'

'Ilya came. He'd kissed me, my first. He was so beautiful, and he'd kissed me and made me feel like I was real. I don't think I'd ever felt quite real. Except when I'd bought the jeans and the hoodie, then when I dyed my hair. Then when Ilya Volkov kissed me.

'That's not relevant.'

'Yes, it is.'

'He came in, and he was angry. Not that his cousin had been murdered, but because Korotkii was supposed to assassinate Alexi the next night. And I knew the man, the first man who'd kissed me, would kill me. He knew I was there, and they'd find me and kill me. He cursed Alexi, he kicked him, and kicked him. He was already dead, but Ilya was so angry, he kicked him.

367

'I saw that in Justin Blake last night. I saw what I saw in Ilya in him. It's more terrifying than any weapon.'

She smelled her garden now, just a hint of it—spice and sweet—on the air. It comforted as much as Brooks's arm around her.

'So I ran. I'd taken off my new shoes, but I didn't think of that. I ran without paying attention to where. Just blind terror, running, sure they'd catch me and kill me because I'd defied my mother, done what I wanted to do, and Julie was dead. She was just eighteen.'

'All right. It's all right now.'

'It's not all right, and not all. It's not nearly all. I fell, and my purse flew out of my hand. I didn't even know I still had it. My phone was in my purse. I called the police. They came, the police, and found me. I told them what happened. I talked to two detectives. They were kind to me, Detectives Griffith and Riley. They helped me.'

'Okay, give me your keys.'

'My keys?'

'We'll go inside now. I need your keys.'

She fished them out, handed them to him. 'They took me to a house, a safe house. They stayed with me, and then John came. Deputy U.S. Marshal John Barrow, and Deputy U.S. Marshal Theresa Norton. You're like him, like John. Patient, insightful and kind.'

'We're going to sit down. I'm going to start a fire, make you some tea.'

'It's too late in the season for a fire.'

'I want a fire. Okay?'

'Of course.' She sat obediently. 'I feel a little strange.'

368

'Just sit there, rest a little till I'm done.'

'They called my mother. She came back. She didn't want me to testify, or to stay in the safe house the marshals had waiting, or to go into witness protection.'

'She was worried about you,' Brooks said, as he set the kindling.

'No. She wanted me to start the summer project, to go back to Harvard, to be the youngest neurosurgeon ever on staff at Chicago's Silva Memorial Hospital. I was ruining her agenda, and she'd gone to so much time and effort. When I wouldn't go with her, she walked out, as she had the day it all began. I've never spoken to her again.'

Brooks sat back on his heels. 'She doesn't deserve a word, not one word from you.' He struck a match to the paper he'd crumbled, watched it flame up, catch the kindling. He felt like that, he realized, ready to flash and burn. That was the last thing she needed.

'I'm going to make that tea. Just rest for a few minutes.'

'I want to tell you all of it.'

'You will, but you take a break now.'

'Are you going to call the marshals? The FBI?'

'Abigail.' He took her face in his hands. 'I'm going to make you tea. Trust me.'

He wanted to strike something, break something to pieces, to punch his fist into something hard that would bloody it. She'd been abused as surely as if she'd been found with bruises and broken bones, by a mother who could walk away from a traumatized, terrified child.

He put the kettle on. She needed to get warm again, feel safe and quiet again. He'd needed to know what she told him, but he wished he'd let it go, let it slide away, from both of them.

Still, as the kettle heated, he took out his notebook, wrote down all the names she'd given him. Then tucked the notebook away again, made her tea.

She sat very straight on the couch, very pale and very straight, her eyes shadowed. 'Thank you.'

He sat beside her. 'I need to say some things to you before you go on with this.'

She stared into her tea, braced. 'All right.'

'None of this was your fault.'

Her lips quivered before she firmed them. 'I have some responsibility. I was young, yes, but no one forced me to make the IDs or go to the club.'

'That's just bullshit, because neither of those things make you responsible for what happened after. Your mother's a monster.'

Her head snapped up, her shadowed eyes went huge. 'My—that—she—'

'Worse. She's a fucking robot, and she tried to make you one, too. She let you know from the get-go she'd "created" you to her specs. So you're smart and beautiful and healthy, and you owe her for that. More bullshit.'

'My genetic makeup—'

'Shut up. I'm not done. She made you dress as she wanted, made you study what she wanted, and I'll lay odds made you associate with people she chose, read what she chose, eat what she de-fucking-creed. Am I wrong?'

Abigail could only shake her head.

'She may never have raised her hand to you, may have kept you clothed, fed, with a nice roof over your head, but honey, you were abused for the first

370

sixteen years of your life. A lot of kids would have run away or worse. You cut your hair and snuck into a club. You want to blame somebody other than the shooter and his boss for what happened, blame her.'

'But—'

'Have you ever had any therapy?'

'I'm not crazy.'

'No, you're not. I'm just asking.'

'I was in therapy as long as I remember until I left home. She engaged one of the top child therapists in Chicago.'

'You never had any choice on that, either.'

'No,' Abigail said with a sigh. 'No, choices weren't on her agenda.'

He took her face, laid his lips on hers. 'You're a miracle, Abigail. That you could come from something that cold-blooded, that coldhearted, and be who and what you are. You remember that. You can tell me the rest when you're ready.'

'Will you kiss me again?'

'You don't have to ask me twice.'

Again, he took her face in his hands, leaned in to lay his lips warmly on hers. She curled her fingers around his wrists to hold him, hold there a moment longer.

She wasn't sure he'd want to kiss her once she'd told the whole of it.

She told him about John, about Terry, the house itself, the routine of it, the legal delays. Stalling a bit, she admitted. She told him about Bill Cosgrove teaching her poker, and Lynda doing her hair.

'It was, in a terrible way, the best time of my life. I watched television, listened to music, studied, cooked, learned, had people to talk to. John and

Terry—I know it was a job, but they were family to me.

'Then my birthday came. I didn't think they knew, or would think anything of it. But they had presents for me, and a cake. John gave me earrings. I'd gotten my ears pierced that day at the mall with Julie, and he gave me my first real pair of earrings. And Terry gave me a sweater; it was so pretty. I went up to my room to put the earrings and the sweater on. I was so happy.'

She paused for a moment, working out how to explain to him what she'd never fully explained to herself.

'It wasn't like the day in the mall. The happiness wasn't fueled by rebellion and novelty and lies. It was so deep, so strong. I knew I'd wear that sweater set, those earrings, on the day I testified in court. That while I couldn't bring Julie back, I would have a part in getting justice for her. And when it was done, I'd become who I wanted to be. Whatever name they gave me, I'd be free to be myself.

'And then . . . I don't know everything that happened. I can only speculate. I've put it together so many ways. The most logical is that Bill Cosgrove and the agent who substituted for Lynda that night, his name is Keegan, came in through the kitchen, as usual. I think Terry was in there alone, and John in the living room. She must have sensed or suspected something. I don't know what or why. They killed her, or at that point disabled her. But she managed to call out to John first, so he was alerted. But he couldn't get to me, couldn't get to the stairs without exposing himself.

'I heard the gunfire. Everything happened so fast. I ran out of the bedroom and saw John. When

372

John got to me he was shot, several times. He was bleeding, from the leg, the abdomen. He pushed me back in the bedroom, and he collapsed. I couldn't stop the bleeding.'

She looked down at her hands. 'I couldn't stop it. I knew what to do, but I couldn't help. He didn't have much time. There wasn't much time. He told me to run. To take what I could and get out through the window. I couldn't trust the police. If they had Cosgrove and the other, they'd have more. The Volkovs. I didn't want to leave him like that. But I went out the window, with the money I had, with my laptop, some clothes, with his ankle weapon. I was going to try to call for help. Maybe if help came he wouldn't die. I didn't know if Terry was alive or dead. I'd barely gotten a block away when the house exploded. I think they'd planned to blow it up, with me in it. They'd have taken over from John and Terry, staged something and blown up the house.'

'Where did you go?'

'I went home. My mother would be at work, and the cook would have gone for the day. I still had my key. I went home so I could hide until my mother got home. And I found she'd boxed up all my things. Some were already gone. I don't know why that upset me so much, considering.'

'I do.'

'Well. I opened her safe, and I took money from her. Ten thousand dollars. It was wrong, but I stole from my mother, and I left. I've never been back. I walked, tried to think. It had been storming, but now it was just rain. Just rainy and dark. I knew John and Terry were dead, and the last thing he'd told me to do was run. I saw a pickup truck with

Indiana plates outside a coffee shop. I got in the back, under the tarp. I fell asleep somewhere along the drive, and when I woke up, I was in Terre Haute. I found a motel, paid cash. I went to a drugstore and bought bright red hair dye. It turned my hair orange, but I looked different. I slept again, a long time. Then I turned on the television. And I saw on CNN the report about John and Terry, about the house. About me. They thought I'd been in the house. They were looking for our remains. I nearly called the police. I had Detective Griffith's card, but I was afraid. I decided I'd wait, buy a cell phone, a disposable, in case. I waited another day, eating in the room, barely leaving it, watching the news, trying to find out more through the Internet.'

She paused, took a long breath. 'Then I found out more. They didn't think I was in the house. They knew I wasn't. There was speculation someone had abducted me, and other speculation that I'd snapped, shot John and Terry, blown up the house. Cosgrove and Keegan had each other to back up the story, how they'd gotten there just seconds too late. And Cosgrove was wounded.'

'John got a piece of him? What about ballistics?'

'It was through-and-through. They said the lights went off, and they couldn't be sure who fired at them, but Keegan got Cosgrove out. The house exploded as he called it all in.

'So I ran. I took a bus to Indianapolis. I got supplies, another motel, and I made new identification, and with it and some of the cash I bought a used car from a junk dealer that got me to Nashville. I waited tables there for three months. Then I changed my hair again, my ID again, and moved on.'

374

She drew another breath. 'There wasn't much on the news anymore, and I wasn't quite able to hack into the files—the U.S. Marshals and FBI. I went to MIT on a forged ID and transcripts, and monitored classes on computer science, and anything else that seemed helpful. I connected with a student there, a boy. He knew a lot about hacking. More than I did. I learned from him. I slept with him, then I left him. I think he cared for me a little, but I left him with only a quick note once I'd learned all he could teach me. I moved around every few months, a year at the most. Changed IDs, modified my appearance. The details aren't really important.'

She paused again. 'I'm wanted for questioning in the murder of two U.S. Marshals.'

He said nothing, just pushed to his feet, walked over to the window.

And the world dropped away for Abigail. He would be finished with her now, she thought. Everything would be finished now.

'Have you kept tabs on Cosgrove and Keegan over the years?'

'Yes. Keegan has been promoted several times.'

'Good, you know where they are, what they're doing. That'll save time and work.'

'I don't understand.'

He turned back to her. 'You don't think we're going to let those two bastards get away with murdering two good cops and implicating you? For keeping you running since the day you turned seventeen? For doing all that so another murderer and his murdering, thieving, son-of-a-bitching friends and associates could walk on killing an innocent girl?'

She could only stare at him. 'You believe me.'

375

'Jesus, of course I believe you. I'd believe you even if I wasn't in love with you, it's so obvious you're telling the truth.'

'You still love me.'

'Listen up.' He stalked back over to her, pulled her to her feet. 'I expect—no, I demand— more respect than that from you. I'm not some weak-spined half-ass fuckhead who slithers off when everything's not just exactly perfect. I loved you an hour ago. I love you now. I'm going to keep right on loving you, so get used to it and stop expecting me to let you down. It's insulting, and it's pissing me off.'

'I'm sorry.'

'Good. You should be.' He yanked her in for a kiss, let her go. 'Where'd you learn to shoot?'

'John taught me initially. I lived in Arizona for a time, and took lessons from an old man. He was a conspiracy theorist and a survivalist. He was interesting but not entirely stable. But he liked me, and was very knowledgeable. I spent time at a number of universities, under assumed names. I needed to learn.'

'What's in the locked room upstairs?'

'I'll show you.'

She led him up, unlocked the triple locks. 'It's a safe room,' she said, as she opened the door.

And a frigging arsenal, he noted. Handguns, long guns, knives. Shelves of packaged food, bottled water, a computer setup as elaborate as her station downstairs, a chem toilet, clothes, wigs, hair dye, batteries, he saw, as he wandered. Flashlights, dog food, books, a freaking grappling hook, tools.

'Did you set this up yourself?'

'Yes. I needed to learn, as I said. I learned. I

have several alternate IDs and passports in here, in a lockbox. Cash, credit cards, and the laminate and paper I need to make still more IDs, if necessary. It's against the law.'

'Oh, yeah. I'll arrest you later. Okay, you know how to protect yourself, and you think ahead. You've been at this how long now?'

'Twelve years.'

'Long enough. Time to stop running.'

'I want to. Today, I thought . . .'

'What?'

'It's not rational.'

'Jesus, Abigail.' Despite it all, he had to laugh. 'Be irrational.'

'It seemed like a circle. Seeing Ilya in Justin Blake, seeing what I thought of Sergei Volkov in Lincoln Blake. Seeing so much of what I admired in John in you. And finding I could stand up to the Blakes, I could do the right thing and not panic or run. It seemed like I could make the running stop, but I don't know if I can.'

'You can. I want another beer. I want to think. We'll figure this out, and we'll fix it.'

'Brooks—'

'Beer, thinking, figuring and fixing. You've stopped being alone, Abigail. You'll have to get used to that, too. What's your real name, anyway?'

She took a breath. 'Elizabeth.' Her voice sounded rusty on the word. 'Elizabeth Fitch.'

He angled his head. 'You don't strike me as an Elizabeth.'

'For a little while, I was Liz.'

'Yeah, I can see that. I'm partial to Abigail, but I can see Liz. So.' He stepped forward, took her hand. 'Nice to meet you, Liz.'

22

It wore her out, Brooks realized, as he sat drinking his beer and thinking. The telling of it and, he imagined, the reliving of it. She'd wedged herself into the corner of the couch, drooping. So he kept his silence, let her drift away awhile while the fire went to simmer and the breeze kicked up against the windows.

Storm coming on, he thought.

Twelve years on the run. She'd turned seventeen and had, or believed she'd had, nothing and no one to depend on but herself.

He pictured himself at seventeen, considered his biggest worry or problem at the time. Wishing he'd had a mightier bat, a faster glove, he remembered, to drive him toward his fantasy of living up to his name as a hot major-league third baseman.

And longing—lusting—for Sylbie.

And that, he concluded, had been pretty much that.

Some schoolwork stress, fights with the longed-for Sylbie, annoyance with parental demands and rules. But he'd had parents, family, home, friends, structure.

He couldn't imagine what it had been like for her, being seventeen and in constant fear for her life. Witnessing cold-blooded murder, watching the man who'd given her a sense of security, even family, bleeding to death and trying so damn hard to obey his dying request.

John Barrow told her to run, no question saving her life with the order. And she'd never stopped.

He shifted, studying her while she slept. Time to stop running, he thought. Time to trust someone to help, to make it right.

Sergei and Ilya Volkov, Yakov Korotkii, Alexi Gurevich.

He needed to do some research on the players, or utilize Abigail's research. He imagined anything that was or could be known about them was in her files. And in her head.

Marshals Cosgrove and Keegan—same deal.

A dirty cop earned a cell shared by those he'd sent over, in Brooks's opinion. A dirty cop who killed another cop for profit or gain? There was a special circle of hell reserved for them. He wanted a part in putting Cosgrove and Keegan dead center of that circle.

He had some ideas, yeah, a few ideas, on that. He wanted to chew on them some, do that research, let it all sift around. After a dozen years, a few days, even weeks, of studying and formulating wouldn't hurt. And he expected she'd need some of that time to adjust to the new situation. He'd need it to convince her to let him do what needed to be done, once he'd settled on exactly what that would be.

For now, he figured the best thing would be to cart her on up to bed. They could both sleep on it awhile.

He got up, started to lift her. And she kneed him dead in the balls.

He swore he felt them tickle his throat, then stick there when her elbow jabbed his larynx. He felt his own eyes roll up and back as he dropped like a stone. Airless.

'Oh God, oh God! Brooks. I'm sorry.'

Since the only sound he could make was a

379

wheeze, he gave it up after one attempt. He'd just lie there for the moment, maybe forever.

'I must have fallen asleep. You startled me.' She tried to turn him over, brushed his hair from his face. The dog licked it sympathetically. 'Can you breathe? Are you breathing? You're breathing.'

He coughed, and that burned like fire to match the inferno raging in his crotch. 'Shit,' he managed, and coughed again.

'I'm going to get you water and ice. Just take slow breaths.'

She must have told the dog to stay with him, as Bert laid down so they were eye to eye. 'What the fuck?' When that hissed out of him, Bert licked his face again.

He managed to swallow, then roll cautiously to his hands and knees. He stayed there another moment, wondering if he'd complete the cycle and puke. He'd made it to sitting on the floor, stomach contents intact, when Abigail rushed back in with the cold pack and a glass of water.

'Don't you put that on my balls. It's bad enough.' He took the water, and though the first couple of sips ripped like drinking broken razor blades, the rawness slowly eased. 'What the fuck?' he said again.

'It was reflex. I'm so sorry. You're so pale. I'm so sorry. I fell asleep, and I was back there, at Alexi's. Ilya found me, and . . . I think you touched me, and I thought it was Ilya, so I reacted.'

'I'll say. God help him if he tries for you. We may never have kids now.'

'A minor insult of this kind to the genitalia doesn't affect fertility,' she began, then looked away. She went considerably pale herself. 'I'm very

380

sorry,' she repeated.

'I'll live. Next time I start to carry you up to bed, I'll wear a cup. Now you may have to carry me.'

'I'll help you.' She kissed him gently on the cheek.

'I'd say that's not where it hurts, but if you kiss me where it does and I have the normal reaction, it may kill me.' He waved her away, pushed to his feet. 'It's not so bad.' He cleared his throat, winced.

'I'll help you upstairs.'

'I've got it. I'm just going to . . . check things out. For my own peace of mind.'

'All right. I'll let Bert out before I come up.'

When she came up, he'd stripped down to his boxers but stood by her monitor, studying it.

'Is everything . . . um.'

'Yeah. That's some aim you've got, killer.'

'It's a particularly vulnerable area in a man.'

'I can attest. I'm going to want you to show me how this system works sometime soon. How you switch from view to view, zoom in, pan out and so on.'

'It's very simple. Do you want me to show you now?'

'Tomorrow's soon enough. I figure you've got plenty of data on the Volkovs, and the agents in their pocket. I'm going to want to review that.'

'Yes.'

He caught the tone. 'What?'

'I haven't told you everything.'

'Now would be a good time for that.'

'I'd like to clean up first.'

'Okay.' And get her thoughts together, he concluded.

She took a nightshirt from the drawer. 'I'll

381

just be a minute,' she told him, and went into the bathroom.

He wondered how much more there could be as he heard the water running, and decided there was no point in speculating. Instead, he turned down the bed, lowered the lights.

When she came out, she got two bottles of water out of her cold box. She offered him one, then sat on the side of the bed. 'I think, if I were you, I'd wonder why I'd never tried to go to the authorities, tell everything that happened.'

'You didn't know who to trust.'

'That's true, at least initially. And I was afraid. For a long time I had nightmares and flashbacks, panic attacks. I still have occasional anxiety attacks. Well, you've seen. And even above that—though it took me time to understand it, I believed I had to do what John told me. He died protecting me. It all happened so quickly, so violently, and was so urgent, so insistent. I realize now we were both very much in the moment. And in that moment, my survival hinged on escape.'

'If you hadn't run, you'd be dead. That's clear.'

'Yes, I've never questioned that. In those first day, weeks, it was all panic. Get away, stay away, stay concealed. If the Volkovs found me, they'd kill me. If the authorities found me, and they were involved with the Volkovs, they'd kill me. If they weren't involved, they might arrest me for murder. So I ran, and I hid, the way I told you.'

'No one could blame you for that.'

'Maybe not. I was young and traumatized. No matter what the intellect, seventeen is still immature, undeveloped. But after some time had passed, I began to think more clearly, think beyond the moment. There had to be others like John and Terry. Others who'd believe me, who'd listen, do whatever they could to protect me. How could I keep running, hiding? How could I do nothing when I was the only one who'd seen Julie's murder, who knew the truth of how John and Terry had died?

'So I hacked into the FBI's and U.S. Marshals' databases.'

'You—you can do that?'

'I do it routinely, but I learned a considerable amount in the first year or two after I went into hiding. Some from the boy I told you about, some on my own. I wanted to learn everything I could about Cosgrove and Keegan, about Lynda Peski, too. She'd called in sick that day. Was that true? Was she another Volkov mole? Her medical records showed she'd been treated for food poisoning, so—'

'You accessed her medical records?'

'I've broken many laws. You said sometimes it's necessary to break the law.'

He rubbed his forehead. 'Yeah, I did. Let's put that on the shelf. You were, what, about nineteen or twenty, and capable of hacking into the files of government agencies?'

'I would have been a very good cyber investigator.'

'Law enforcement's loss.'

'I believed, and still believe, Lynda Peski wasn't part of it. I can't be sure, even now, but there's nothing to indicate she was anything but a marshal in good standing—retired now, married with two children. I suspect Cosgrove put something in her food to make her ill that day. But I can't prove it, and I didn't feel safe contacting her. I believed, and still believe, Detectives Griffith and Riley are good, honest police officers. But I hesitated, as they're Chicago police, not federal, and federal often takes over from the local police. Added to that, I worried I'd put their lives in danger. It seemed more productive, safer, to research and study. At the same time, I needed money. I had fifteen thousand when I ran, but there are expenses in flight, in generating documents, in transportation and clothing and so on. As my primary skill was in computers, I worked on programming. I developed some software, sold it. It was lucrative.'

'Is that so?'

'Yes, and I developed a computer game, actually three connecting games. It was more lucrative.'

'What game?'

'It's called Street Wars. My research indicated most game players are male and enjoy battle- or war-type games. I—'

'I've played that game.' Eyes narrowed, he pointed at her. 'Russ and I used to have marathon tournaments whenever I came home from Little Rock. It's bloody and brutal. And really cool.'

'My target demographic enjoys brutal and bloody in their gaming. Having three was also key. If the first gains popularity, the target audience will want, and pay, for a follow-up. I was able to sell the three-part package outright for a considerable amount. It seemed less complicated, under my circumstances, than a royalty-based contract.'

'You rich?'

'Yes. I have a great deal of money, which I add to with my current security business.'

He smiled at her. 'I like having a rich girlfriend.'

'I've never been anyone's girlfriend.'

'Well, I'm sewing you into that. Because you're rich.'

He made her smile. 'You said you loved me before you knew I was rich. It's less complicated and stressful to relocate, to arrange private transportation, if necessary, to equip and secure a new location, if there's money. I didn't want to steal it.'

'And you could have?'

'Oh, yes, of course. I accessed Cosgrove's and Keegan's bank accounts, found what I believe are payments from the Volkovs. I could have siphoned funds from them. Even from the Volkovs themselves.'

'Wait.' Now he held up a hand, circled around. 'You've hacked into the Volkovs' network?'

'Yes. I'll explain. I secured the money I made in several different accounts, under various identifications. I felt safer, less afraid with money, and with the information I'd gathered. I wanted more time. I'd started to study a particular FBI agent. I wanted to follow her, review her files, reports, her evaluations for at least a year before contact. I'd moved to New York. I felt safe there. So many people, all so busy. Too busy to pay attention to me. And by that time I could work almost entirely out of my brownstone.'

She thought back on it, a bit wistfully. 'I had a very nice house in SoHo. It was there I considered getting a dog. For security, and companionship. I'd started my security business, and at that time dealt face-to-face with clients. I would go to them, evaluate their system, their needs.'

'When was this?'

'I located in New York six years ago. I was twenty-three, but my identification claimed I was twenty-six. Older is better in these cases. I started fairly small, designing and installing security systems for homes and small businesses, business computer networks. It gave me considerable time for my research. And in researching I found the agent I felt might be the one. I wanted what I wanted at sixteen. Friends, relationships, normal. And I wanted to do the right thing, for Julie, for John and Terry.

'I was there more than a year, the longest I'd stayed in one place. I thought about buying a home in the country, because I realized, though I enjoyed the convenience of the city, I preferred the quiet. But it felt safe there, in SoHo. All those people, the busy pace. And I'd landed a big account, a law firm. I'd done the personal security for one of the associates, and he'd recommended me. Six more months, I told myself. I'd stay in New York, complete the new contract, continue my research. Then, if I felt absolutely sure of this agent, I'd contact her and begin the process.'

'What happened?'

'I was nearly there, nearly ready. I'd completed the contract, and that had netted me another for one of the clients of the firm. My first corporation. It was good work, exhilarating, challenging. I believed, absolutely, my life was about to begin again. And I came out of the client's building. Houston Street, downtown. I was thinking how I'd go home, change, go to the market and buy myself a good bottle of wine to celebrate. I was thinking the six months I'd set to contact the agent was nearly up. I was thinking of getting a dog, of where

I'd want to live when I could really live again. I was thinking of anything but the Volkovs. And he was just there.'

'Who?'

'Ilya. Ilya Volkov and another man—his cousin, I found out later. They got out of a car just as I started for the curb to hail a cab. I almost walked into him. All those people, all that city, and I nearly walked into the man I'd run from for nearly eight years. He looked right at me, and I froze just as I had on the terrace that night. He started to smile, as a man does at a woman who's staring at him, I suppose. And then he knew me, and the smile went away.'

'He recognized you? Are you sure?'

'He said my name. "Liz. Here you are." Just like that. He reached for me, he nearly had my arm. His fingers brushed my sleeve before I jerked away, and I ran. He came after me. I heard him shouting in Russian; I heard the car gun away from the curb. I thought, He'll shoot me in the back, or catch me and drag me into that car.'

She pressed a hand to her heart, rubbed it there as the beat began to thud as it had that day in New York.

'I ran into the street. It was crazy; I was nearly run over. I didn't care. Anything would be better. I lost my shoes. It was like that night again, running in my bare feet. But I was smarter now. Panicked at first, but more prepared. I knew the streets. I'd studied them, and I'd pulled away when I'd run into traffic, and his driver couldn't make the turn. I don't know how far I'd run before I realized I'd gotten away. I got on a crosstown bus, then I got in a cab.'

Too warm now, she thought, and crossed to a window to open it. 'I didn't have any shoes, but no one seemed to notice or care. It was a benefit of a large city.'

'I guess I'm a country boy, as that doesn't strike me as a benefit.'

'It was that day. When I got home, I got out my go bag. I would have run again with only that, but I calmed down, packed up what I felt I'd need. I wasn't sure how much time I had. If he'd seen which building I'd come out of, if he'd managed to dig out the name I was using, find my address. I kept a car, in another name, in a garage. It was, I'd thought, worth the expense. And it proved to be true. I called a private car service, had it take me to the garage. They might trace me there, but that would take time. By then I'd be gone, I'd buy a new car, change my ID.'

'Where did you go?'

'I stayed mobile for weeks. Motels, paid cash. I watched Ilya's e-mail. I learned they hadn't been able to trace me for several days. I didn't have to leave so quickly after all. And they weren't able to trace me once I left the brownstone. No one had seen, or paid attention to, me leaving. But I learned a lesson. I'd gotten careless. I'd let myself plan for a normal life, even in some way to live one. They'd never stop coming after me, so I had to accept the way it was. And do what I could to get justice for John and Terry and Julie another way.

'I'm tied in to the Volkovs' network— e-mail, e-files, even text messaging. When I have something that seems worthwhile, I leak the data anonymously to the FBI agent I studied and cleared to my specifications. I don't know how much

388

longer it'll be safe to use her as contact. If Volkov's people connect her, they may eliminate her. I think, logically, they'd try to use her to find the source of the leaks before they eliminate her. But that may be worse. They could torture her, and she couldn't tell them because she doesn't know. I'd be safe, but she wouldn't. Neither will you, if you involve yourself.'

'You'd have made a good cop, cyber or otherwise, to my way of thinking. But I am a cop. You're just a cop's rich girlfriend.'

'Don't joke. If they connect you to me, in any way, they'll kill you. But not just you. They'll kill your family. Your mother, your father, your sisters, their children. Everyone you care about.'

'I'll take care of my family, Abigail. I guess we'll stick with Abigail for now.' He stroked a hand over her hair. 'I'll have to get used to Liz when this is finished.'

'It's never going to be finished.'

'You're wrong. I want you to promise me something.' To keep their eyes level, he shifted his hand to cup her chin. 'I want your word on this. You won't run out on me. You won't run figuring you're doing what's best for me and mine.'

'I don't want to make a promise I might break.'

'Your word. I'm going to trust your word, and you're going to trust mine. You promise me that, and I'll promise you I won't do anything without your full knowledge and approval. That's no easy promise for me to make, but I'll make it.'

'You won't do anything unless I agree?'

'That's my promise. Now I want yours. You won't run.'

'What if they find me, the way Ilya did in New York?'

'If you have to run, you run to me.'

'You're like John. They killed John.'

'Because he didn't know what was coming. Now, if you look me in the eyes and tell me you're seriously worried the Russian Mafia's going to infiltrate the Bickford Police Department, we'll pack up Bert and whatever else we need and head out tonight. Name the place.'

'I don't think that.'

'Good. Then promise me.'

'You won't do anything without telling me. I won't run without telling you.'

'I guess that's close enough. You've had enough for tonight. We're going to get some sleep. I'm going to think about all this. I may have more questions, but they can wait. And after I've thought on it awhile, we'll talk about what we'll do. That's "we." You're not alone anymore. You're not going to be alone anymore.'

He urged her into bed, pulling her close after he turned off the light. 'There. That feels right. Maybe I do have one question for tonight.'

'All right.'

'Did you hack into our system at the station?'

She sighed, and in the dark didn't see him smile at the sound. 'I felt it was important to know details about local law enforcement. The security on your network isn't very good.'

'Maybe I should talk to the selectmen about hiring you to fix that.'

'I'm very expensive. But under the circumstances I could offer you a large discount on my usual fee.' She sighed again. 'I'd secure your personal computer for free.'

'Jesus.' He had to laugh. 'You're in my personal

e-mail and all that?'

'I'm sorry. You kept coming here and asking questions. You'd looked up information on me. Well, the information I generated, but it was disturbing.'

'I guess it was.'

'You should be careful, calling the current mayor a fuckwit, even in correspondence with your good friend. You can't be sure who might see your personal e-mail.'

'He is a fuckwit, but I'll keep that in mind.' He turned his head, kissed the top of her head. 'I love you.'

She pressed her face to the side of his throat. 'It sounds lovely in bed, in the dark, when everything's quiet.'

'Because it's true. And it'll be true in the morning.'

She closed her eyes, held the words to her as he held her. And hoped, in the morning, he'd give them to her again.

Elizabeth

Let justice be done,
though the heavens fall.

Lord Mansfield

23

Roland Babbett checked into the Inn of the Ozarks on a spring afternoon that simmered hot and close as August. In his room with its engaging view of the hills, he set up his laptop on the glossy old desk. He appreciated the amenities—the complimentary Wi-Fi, the flat-screen TV, the carefully (he imagined) selected furnishings, and the generous shower.

A great deal of the time he worked out of crap motels with piss-trickle showers and stingy slivers of soap, or out of his car, where the facilities ran to a Mason jar he could empty of urine periodically.

Such was the life of a private investigator.

He enjoyed it, even the crap motels and Mason jars. Two years as a cop had taught him he didn't work all that well with rules and regs. But he'd been a pretty good cop, and that had segued into a job with Stuben-Pryce Investigations. In the nearly ten years he'd worked there, he'd proven himself reliable, inventive and dogged. Qualities appreciated by the firm.

He also enjoyed his bonuses, and hoped to net another on this job.

He unpacked—cargo shorts and pants, tees, sweats, rough boots. He'd selected the wardrobe to go with his cover as a freelance photographer, one that would allow him to wander the town, the outskirts, take photographs, talk to locals.

He didn't like the client. Roland considered Lincoln Blake a first-degree asshole, and the fruit of Blake's loins a raw pimple on society's ass.

But work was work, and Blake generated a lot of income, being a nosy, pushy, scheming first-degree asshole. When the boss said go, Roland went. Especially since he had one kid in private school, another who'd enroll in the fall and—surprise—a third on the way.

He loved his family, and the pay from Stuben-Pryce, plus bonuses, gave them a good life, which included a hefty mortgage on their new four-bedroom in West Little Rock.

So asshole or not, the client was king. If Blake wanted to know all there was to know—especially the dirt—on one Abigail Lowery, Roland would find out all there was to know. The same for Brooks Gleason, Bickford's police chief, and according to the client, Lowery's lover.

The client claimed the two in question, along with the Conroys—the owners of the hotel with the very nice view and amenities—had set up his son in order to extort money. Blake fervently, and loudly, denied his boy had caused the extensive damage to the hotel's premier suite as claimed, nor had he assaulted Russell Conroy, nor had he pulled a knife on the chief of police.

Roland, nobody's fool, fervently but quietly believed the butt pimple had done all that and more. But he'd do his job, earn his salary. And pay his bills.

He checked his camera gear, his recorder, his notebook and lock picks. Then called his wife on his cell phone to let her know he'd arrived safe and sound.

He told her he wished she were there and meant it. The room boasted a king four-poster. Pregnancy turned Jen into a sexual dynamo.

As he packed up for his first walk about town, he promised himself he'd make a return trip, with Jen, after the baby came, and her parents were still dazzled enough to take on three kids for a long weekend.

He shouldered the camera bag, hung the Nikon around his neck on a strap decorated with peace signs. Wearing cargo shorts, Rockports and an R.E.M. T-shirt, he slipped on sunglasses, checked himself out in the mirror.

He hadn't shaved that morning, deliberately, and thought the scruff added to the look. He liked pulled-on personas and, given the choice, kept them fairly close to his own. Natural, easy.

He considered himself to be a personable guy. He could talk to anyone about anything, as vital a tool as his computer. He wasn't bad-looking, he thought, as he added a Greenpeace ball cap to his ensemble.

Though he was starting to worry about male pattern baldness. His brother, only two years older than Roland's thirty-four, already showed a fist-sized patch of bare scalp at the crown of his head.

He thought fleetingly of picking up some Rogaine—why not try preemptive measures—as he walked out of his room.

He'd wrangled a room on the top floor, though the reservation clerk had offered another, due to construction noise. But he'd brushed off the warning and inconvenience. This way, he should be able to get a look at the suite the client's son hadn't trashed, if you believed first-class assholes.

He strolled down the hall, noted the door, firmly shut, a sign apologizing for the inconvenience due to unexpected repairs. The noise, somewhat muffled, sounded more like demo than repair.

He'd check it out later, when the crew and staff weren't around.

For now, he took the stairs down, since he was also mildly concerned about encroaching middle-age paunch, and walked outside into the heat.

Pretty little town, he thought. Jen would like it—the shops, the art. He'd pick up something for her and the kids, including the as yet unnamed and unknown surprise, before he left.

Plenty of tourists, he noted. A guy with a camera blended right in. He made use of it, taking a few shots of the hotel, zooming in on the windows of the suite in question, with their curtains tightly shut.

He had a good eye for a picture. He thought when the time came to retire from private investigating, he'd try photography as a working hobby. He wandered, framed in, shot. An interesting window, a close-up of flowers in a half whiskey barrel. To the casual eye he'd look like someone meandering, without specific destination.

But he had the salient addresses in his head. Lowery's place would require a drive, but he could walk past the police chief's apartment, and the house where his parents still lived. Just getting a feel for the place, the people, Roland thought and spent some time studying the windows of Brooks Gleason's apartment above a busy diner.

Shades up, he noted. Nothing to see here. He wandered around the back, took some pictures of flowerpots as he studied the rear entrance.

Decent locks but nothing major, should he feel the need to do a little snooping inside. He'd avoid that, if possible.

With the town map in his hand, courtesy of the hotel, he strolled down the sidewalk.

And stopped, absolutely charmed and bedazzled by the mural house. He checked the address, and confirmed it was indeed the residence of the police chief's parents. Information already gathered told him the mother was an artist, the father a high school teacher.

He had to assume the woman with the rainbow kerchief over her hair currently standing on scaffolding in paint-splattered bib overalls was the subject's mother.

Leashed to the base of the scaffolding, a puppy curled in the shade and snoozed.

As much for his own interest as the job, Roland took a few pictures, moved closer. When he got to the edge of the yard, the puppy woke in a yappy frenzy.

And the woman looked down. She tipped her head. 'Help you?'

'I'm sorry to interrupt. I was just walking around, and . . . this is just amazing. Did you paint all of this?'

'I did. Visiting?'

'I'm spending a few days in town. I'm a photographer, and I'm taking a few weeks in the Ozarks. I want to put a show together.'

'You won't lack for subject matter around here. All right, Plato, I'm coming.'

She climbed down nimbly, unclipped the dog, who instantly raced over to sniff at Roland. 'Good dog.' He hunkered down to give the dog a rub. 'I guess I woke him up.'

'He's a fierce guard dog, as you can see. Sunny

399

O'Hara,' she added, offering a hand dotted with paint.

'Roland Babbett. Would it be all right if I took some pictures of the house? It's wonderful.'

'You go ahead. Where are you from, Roland?'

'Little Rock.'

'My son lived there some years. He was a police detective. Brooks Gleason.'

'Can't say I know the name, but I try to stay out of trouble.'

She grinned along with him. 'That's good, because he's chief of police here now.'

'It feels like a nice town. I hope he doesn't stay too busy.'

'Oh, well, there's always this and that. Where are you staying?'

'I'm splurging, since I'll do a lot of camping on the second part of this trip. I'm at the Inn of the Ozarks.'

'Couldn't do better; it's one of the brightest jewels in Bickford's treasure box. We had some trouble there a few days ago, as it happens. Town troublemaker and a couple of his minions tore up the Ozarks Suite.'

'Is that what it is? I'm on that floor, and they told me there'd be some noise. Repairs going on.'

'A lot of them. You may want to get yourself on another floor.'

'Oh, I don't mind it. I can sleep through anything.' Casual and friendly, he let his camera dangle by its strap. 'I'm sorry to hear about the trouble, though. It's a really beautiful hotel. The architecture, the furnishings. It has the feel of a family home—with benefits. Why'd they tear it up?'

'Some people just like to break things, I guess.'

'That's a shame. I guess even nice little towns have troublemakers. I'll try to steer clear of him while I'm here.'

'He's in jail, and likely to be there awhile. You'll find most people who live here are friendly. We depend on tourists, and artists like yourself. That's a serious camera you've got there.'

'My baby.' He tapped it. He really wanted the pictures, nearly as much as the information she so breezily passed on. 'I still do film now and then, but digital's my primary choice.'

'If you get anything you want to sell, you can take it into Shop Street Gallery. They buy a lot of local photography.'

'I appreciate the tip. A couple sales'll keep me in hot dogs and beans for the next few weeks.'

He chatted with her for a few more minutes, then walked back toward the center of town. If Sunny O'Hara was anything to go by, Roland thought, the client wasn't going to be pleased with the report.

He headed for the diner. Diners and waitresses were usually good information sources. He chose a booth with a good view of the comings and goings, set his camera carefully on the tabletop.

He was tempted to take a picture of the waitress—he really did love saturating himself in the persona, and she had a good, interesting face.

'Coffee, please.'

'How about some pie to go with it? Cherry's especially good today.'

'Cherry pie?' He thought of encroaching middle-age paunch. So he'd do fifty extra crunches tonight. 'I don't think I can say no.'

'Warmed up? Vanilla-bean ice cream?'

Okay, seventy-five extra crunches. 'Yes, ma'am.

I don't know anybody strong enough to say no to that. If it's as good as it sounds, I'm going to be in here every day while I'm in town.'

'It is. Visiting?' she said, in nearly the same easy tone as Sunny.

He gave her the same cover, even showed her a few pictures he'd taken of the mural house.

'You never know what she'll paint on it next. Those are right nice pictures, too.'

'Thanks.'

'I'll put your order in.'

He doctored his coffee while he waited, studied his guidebook like a good tourist. She brought back a generous wedge of pie with ice cream gently melting on the laced crust. 'Sounds good, looks good.' Roland forked off a bite. 'Tastes even better. Thanks, Kim.'

'You enjoy, now.' She glanced over, and so did he, as Brooks walked in. 'Hey there, Chief.' When she gestured to the booth directly in front of him, Roland decided to double her tip.

'Just coffee.'

'You ain't heard about the cherry pie à la mode. I got it on good authority nobody can say no.' She sent Roland a wink as she spoke, and he toasted her with a forkful.

'It'd be wasted on me right now. Lawyers.'

'Well, sweetie, that calls for two scoops of vanilla-bean on the pie.'

'Next time. I just came in for a decent cup of coffee, and some breathing room to review my notes.'

'All right, then. Blake's lawyers?' she asked, as she poured the coffee.

'New ones. Harry got the ax, and between you

and me, I think he's doing a dance of joy at the firing. Blake hired on a firm from up north.'

'Yankee lawyers?' Kim's mouth twisted in derision. 'I shouldn't be surprised.'

'Armani suits and Louis Vuitton briefcases, at least according to the paralegal Big John Simpson's got doing research on the case. They've got motions on top of motions. Want a change of venue for one thing. The judge doesn't like them, so that's something.'

'Want to get him away from here, away from where people know what a nasty piece of work that Blake boy is.'

'Can't say I blame them. But here or on Pluto, fact's fact. The trouble is facts aren't always enough in a courtroom.'

On one step back she slapped both fists on her hips. 'You don't think he'll get off? Not after what he did.'

'I'm not going to think it, because if he gets out of this whistling, the next time, I know in my gut, he's likely to kill somebody.'

'Well, my Jesus, Brooks.'

'Sorry.' Brooks rubbed at his tired eyes. 'I should've taken my crappy mood to my office.'

'You sit right there and have your coffee, and you don't let all this weigh on you.' She leaned down, kissed the top of his head. 'You did your job, and everybody knows it. You can't do more than your job.'

'Feels like I ought to. Anyway . . . just the coffee.'

'You holler if you want anything else.' Shaking her head, she walked away, topping off Roland's coffee as she went.

Roland sat, mulling. Nothing the cop said struck

him as false. He despised the 'nasty piece of work' himself. But as the wise and wonderful Kim had said, you couldn't do more than your job.

His was to find anything that might tip the scales in the client's favor.

He nearly choked on his pie when the vision walked in.

He knew small southern towns could produce some beauties, and in his personal opinion, southern women had a way of nurturing that beauty like hothouse roses. Maybe it was the weather, the air, the chance to wear all those thin summer dresses like the one the vision wore now. Maybe it was the slower pace or some secret mothers passed to daughters.

Whatever it was, it worked.

He loved his wife, and had never in their twelve years together— ten-plus with rings on the finger— strayed. But a man was entitled to a little fantasy now and then when possibly the sexiest woman ever created sashayed into his line of sight.

She hip-swayed right up to Gleason's booth, slid in, like melted butter on warm toast.

'Not a good time, Sylbie.'

In Roland's world, it was always a good time for Sylbie.

'I just have a question. I'm not going to try to get you back or anything like that. I learned my lesson back in March.'

'I appreciate that, but it's a bad time right here and now.'

'You look tense and tired and out of sorts. I'm sorry about that. We were friends once.'

When he didn't speak, she looked away, let out a breath that had her delectable breasts rising, falling.

'I guess we weren't friends, and maybe that's my fault. I've been doing a lot of thinking since I humiliated myself for your benefit.'

'Let's not go there.'

'It's easy for you to say, since you weren't the one standing there naked.'

Roland felt himself going hard, and mentally apologized to his wife.

'It was a mistake, and some of it's on me for not talking it out with you. You're sorry. I'm sorry. Let's forget it.'

'I can't forget it until I know.'

'Know what?'

'Why her and not me? That's all. I need to know why you want to be with Abigail Lowery—everybody knows you are—and you don't want to be with me.'

Roland wanted to know, too, and not just for the client. He'd seen Lowery's photo, and she was attractive, sure. Pretty, maybe even beautiful in a quiet sort of way. But next to the stupendous Sylbie? She was no cherry pie à la mode.

'I don't know how to tell you.'

'Just tell me the truth. Is she better in bed than me?'

'Jesus Christ.'

'That's the wrong thing to ask.' On an impatient gesture, she pushed back a glorious fall of hair. 'I wasn't going to ask, even though I wonder. Just give me something, will you, that I can understand?'

'She makes me happy. When I'm with her I feel like that's where I'm supposed to be, where I've been wanting to be. And everything that matters makes sense. I don't know why one person falls in

405

love with another, Sylbie. They just do.'

'You're in love with her?'

'I'm in love with her.'

She stared down at the tabletop for a moment. 'Can I have a sip of your coffee?'

'Sure.'

She took it, grimaced, set it down again after one sip. 'You always drink it too sweet.'

'Bad habit.'

'Did you ever love me?'

'I wanted you. There were times I craved you like I was starved to death. The first time around, we were too young to know. The second? Maybe we were both trying to know. I couldn't make you happy. You couldn't make me happy. And nothing that really mattered made sense.'

'The sex did.'

He laughed a little. 'Okay, you're right about that. But sex, even good sex, can't be the start, finish and the whole in between.'

'I thought I'd figured that out after my first divorce, but I guess I didn't. And the second one . . . I never wanted to be the kind of woman with two divorces on her back.'

She turned to stare out the wide window. 'But I am.'

'Maybe you should think of it as two marriages. I figure people who try marriage more than once, they're optimists.'

'Optimists.' With a half-laugh, she shoved his coffee away. 'Sounds better than a loser.'

'You're not a loser, Sylbie.'

'I'm sort of seeing Grover.'

'You . . . oh.' Brooks picked up his coffee, gulped some down. 'Well.'

'I know. He's not the type I usually aim for. He's not handsome, and he's a little paunchy. But he's got a sweetness to him. You did, too, but I didn't appreciate it. I'm appreciating his. We're not sleeping together yet, but I feel good when I'm with him. I feel better about myself. I guess we're friends the way you and I never were.'

'That's good.'

'He makes me happy, and I didn't expect to be. I guess I'll find out if I can stay happy.'

'I hope you can.'

'So do I.' She slid out. 'I don't think I'm ready to say I hope you stay happy with Abigail Lowery, but I nearly am.'

'That's a start.'

'I'll see you around.'

She sashayed out. Roland decided he had a lot more mulling to do, but since he'd finished his pie, he needed to do it elsewhere. In any case, Gleason was leaving, laying money on the tabletop for the coffee.

Maybe he'd drive out toward Lowery's place, get the lay of the land.

*   *   *

Taking a break from work, Abigail paged through recipes online. It kept her from worrying. Nearly kept her from worrying. She knew Brooks would want to talk about what happened next when he came. She worried about what he thought should happen next.

So she worked, did laundry, worked, weeded the garden, worked, looked through recipes. She couldn't seem to settle, focus on one chore until she

407

completed it.

It wasn't like her.

She wished he'd come.

She wished she could be alone.

She wished she knew what she really wished. She hated this indecision, the gnawing anxiety. It wasn't productive.

When her alarm sounded, she spun in her chair, certain that telling Brooks—telling anyone—the story had brought the Volkovs to her door.

Illogical. Actually ridiculous, she admitted, but her pulse hammered as she watched the man in the ball cap on her monitor.

A good camera, she noted. Boots that had seen some wear. A backpack.

A hiker or tourist who'd wandered onto her property, despite the postings. That was it, probably.

When he took out binoculars, aimed them toward her cabin, the anxiety increased.

Who was he? What was he doing?

Coming closer. Still closer.

He stopped again, scanned with his compact field glasses, turning slowly until it seemed to Abigail he stared through them right at one of the cameras. Then he continued on, continuing the circle.

He took off his cap, scrubbed at his hair before taking out a water bottle and drinking deeply. Reaching into his pocket, he took out a compass, took a step, stumbled. He fumbled with the compass, dropped it. She saw his mouth move as he dived for it, snatched it off the ground.

He shook it, lifted his face to the sky, then sat on the ground, dropped his head to his knees.

He stayed as he was for several moments before

pushing to his feet. He mopped at his face, then continued toward her cabin.

After checking her weapon, Abigail took the dog outside, circled around.

She could hear him coming. Nothing stealthy in his approach, she thought, and he was muttering to himself, breathing fast, heavy. From the side of the greenhouse, she watched him come into view, heard him say, very clearly, 'Thank God,' as he arrowed straight toward her rear door.

He knocked, swiped sweat from his face, waited. He knocked again, more forcefully. 'Hello! Is anybody there? Please, let somebody be there.'

He walked down the porch, cupped his hand on the window glass.

And she stepped out, the dog by her side. 'What do you want?'

He jumped like a rabbit, spun around. 'Jeez, you scared the—' His eyes went huge when he saw the gun, and his hands shot straight up in the air. 'Jesus, don't shoot me. I'm lost. I got lost. I'm just looking for the way back to my car.'

'What were you doing in the woods, on my property? It's clearly posted.'

'I'm sorry. I'm sorry. I was taking photographs. I'm a photographer. I was just going to take a few shots, get the feel of things, and I got caught up, went in farther than I meant to. I'm sorry, I shouldn't have ignored the No Trespassing signs. You can call the cops. Just don't shoot me. My— my name's Roland Babbett. I'm staying at the Inn of the Ozarks. You can check.'

'Please take off your pack, set it down, step away from it.'

'Okay, sure.'

409

He wasn't wearing a gun—she'd seen him do a full circle and would have spotted it. But he might have a weapon in the pack.

'You can keep the pack,' he said, when he set it down. 'My wallet's in there. You can keep the money.'

'I don't want your money.'

'Listen, listen, I got lost. I dropped my compass and broke it. I saw the cabin through my binoculars when I was scanning around. I just came for some help. Call the police.'

'Where did you leave your car?'

'If I knew, I wouldn't be lost. I don't mean to be a smart-ass,' he added quickly. 'I drove out of Bickford, south out of town for about a mile, then I pulled over. The light was really good, the shadows. I wanted to take some shots. Photographs, I mean,' he said, with another wary look at the gun.

'You should respect private property.'

'Yes, you're right. I'm really sorry.'

She pointed. 'If you go that way, you'll come to the road. Turn left. You should find your car in about a quarter-mile.'

'Okay. Thanks. I'll just—'

'Take your pack,' she told him, as he started to step off the porch without it.

'Okay.' He picked it up, his eyes shifting from her face, to the gun, to the dog, back again. 'Thank you.'

'You're welcome.'

She watched him walk away, in quite a hurry, until he was out of sight. Back in the house, she continued to watch him on the monitor as he hiked at a half-jog up her road to the main one, tossing glances over his shoulders every few minutes.

She'd frightened him, she thought. Well, he'd frightened her. She supposed that made them even.

*   *   *

Roland knew exactly where his car was parked.

He hadn't been expecting the gun. He hadn't been expecting the cameras, either. He'd been told she had security, including cameras around the house. Nobody had mentioned she had them ranged back in the woods.

If he hadn't spotted one when he had, he'd have blown the job.

She'd bought the scared, lost hiker routine. Why not? He *had* been scared. She'd held the Glock like someone who knew how to use it. Like someone who would use it.

He had to admire that, now that he wasn't standing on the wrong side of it.

And the dog. He'd known about the dog, but *God damn*, that was one big bastard.

Then the locks on the back door. As good as they came, he mused, as he tossed the pack in the backseat. He was pretty damn good with the picks, but he'd never get through those. Moot point, as he couldn't get by the cameras, not without a whole lot of equipment.

That much security? Overkill.

The job just got a lot more interesting. Anybody with security like that, the big dog, the Glock, the 'tude?

She had something to hide. He loved finding out what people wanted to hide.

411

24

Brooks came into the kitchen with a clutch of white daisies with bright yellow buttons and a rawhide bone for Bert.

'You brought me flowers again.'

'My daddy brings my mama flowers once or twice a week, and I figured out it's because they make her smile, just like you are now.'

'I worried things wouldn't be right when you came tonight, that it would feel awkward after everything. And you brought me daisies.'

'Then you can stop worrying.'

She got a vase, wished she had a pretty little pitcher instead, and vowed to buy one the next time she went into town.

'Every time I come in here something smells good, in addition to you.'

'It's the rosemary,' she told him, as she arranged the flowers. 'It's very fragrant. I found a new recipe for chicken I wanted to try.'

'Happy to be your taste-tester.'

'It should go well with the *Pouilly-Fumé*.'

'If you say so.' He brushed her hair back, then indulged himself with a nuzzle of her neck. 'How'd your day go?'

'I was restless and distracted, but I finished some work. And I was interrupted by a lost hiker—a photographer. I don't understand why people don't respect boundary lines. There's so much land here open to the public, there's no need to come onto private property.'

'Grass is always greener. He came to the house?'

'Yes. He set off the alarm, and I saw him on the monitor. He dropped and broke his compass, and apparently saw the cabin through his binoculars.'

Brooks paused in the act of pouring their wine. 'Binoculars?'

She checked the chicken. 'Yes. I wondered if he'd seen the camera through them, but apparently he was looking for his way, or some help. I went outside, around the greenhouse, so I could come up behind him.'

'You went out, when some strange guy was coming to the house?'

'I know how to take care of myself. I've been doing it for a long time, remember? He was alone. I had my gun and Bert. He knocked, called out. And he was very disconcerted when I stepped out, with the gun.'

Brooks finished pouring the wine, took a long swallow. 'Yeah, I can see that.'

'I didn't mind frightening him. He shouldn't have come onto posted property. I questioned him briefly, then directed him to where, if he told me accurately, he'd left his car. He left quickly.'

'An armed woman with a big dog? He'd've been a fool not to. What was he doing out here?'

'Photography. He said his name was Roland Babbett, and he was staying at the Conroys' hotel.'

'That's easy enough to check on.' Brooks dug out his cell phone. 'What did he look like?'

'Mid-thirties. Between five-ten and five-eleven, about a hundred and seventy pounds. Medium complexion, light brown hair, brown eyes, prominent chin. He wore a brown cap with the Greenpeace logo, a black T-shirt with the name of the band R.E.M., khaki cargo shorts and hiking

413

boots. He had a navy backpack, and a Nikon camera on a strap. The strap had multicolored peace signs on it.'

'Yeah, you would've made a good cop,' Brooks replied. 'I saw him at the diner earlier today. Cherry pie à la mode.'

'What does that mean?'

'Nothing. Just curious. What time did he come here?'

'The alarm sounded at four-eighteen.'

'Yeah, that's curious. I see him at the diner in town going onto four o'clock. Less than a half-hour later, he's out here.'

Her hand tightened on the stem of her glass. 'You think they've found me.'

'Honey, did he look like Russian Mafia? And would it be their style to have some guy poking around up in your woods?'

'No.' Her shoulders relaxed. 'He wasn't armed. At least he wasn't wearing a weapon. The Volkovs wouldn't send a single unarmed man.'

'I think that's a pretty safe bet.' But he intended to be thorough, and punched in a number on his cell. 'Hey, Darla, how's it going? Uh-huh. Those spring colds can hit hard. You get some rest. Yeah, it's that time of year, all right. Listen, do you have a guest name of Roland Babbett registered? No problem. Uh-huh, hmmm. It takes all kinds, doesn't it? Uh-huh.' He rolled his eyes at Abigail. 'Yeah, Roland Babbett. What room's he in? Now, Darla, I'm not just anybody asking. I'm the chief of police. I'm just following up on something. You know I can call Russ and ask. Uh-huh. Is that so? Mmm-hmm. No, no trouble, just a routine thing. You take care of that cold, now, you hear? Bye.'

414

He picked up the wine again. 'Darla tends to run on a bit. He's there, all right. Took a room—requested it—right down the hall from the Ozarks Suite.'

'The one Justin Blake and his friends vandalized?'

'That would be right. Now, isn't it curious how I saw this Babbett in town, and he comes here, got a camera and binoculars, and he's staying down from that particular suite?'

'It could be a coincidence, but it feels designed.'

'Designed is a good word for it. Designed by Blake.' Leaning a hip on the counter, he picked up his wine. 'What do you bet if I scratched the surface some, I'd find out Roland Babbett is a high-priced private investigator?'

'I think I'd win the bet. He did see the camera, and he thought very quickly, pretending to be lost.' Duping her, she thought, with considerable annoyance. 'But I don't see what he gained by coming here.'

'A little legwork. Check out your setup here, get a feel. He had some luck today, spotting one of your cameras, using it to his advantage to make contact. I don't doubt the reception gave him a bad moment, but all in all, it worked for him. He had a conversation, a close-up look. Same thing earlier when I happened to go in for some coffee when he was in the diner. He got to sit there, eating his pie, and get a good look, and . . . shit.'

'I'm sorry?'

'I bet his ears were trained, too. I bet he caught damn near every word of my conversation with Sylbie. Which I wasn't going to bring up,' he added, when Abigail said nothing. 'And now it occurs to me that was the wrong way, because, I guess, it was an important conversation. And you were part of it.'

'You talked about me, with her?'

'And that tone, that look in your eye, was why I wasn't going to mention it.'

'I don't know what you mean.' She turned away to put the green beans she'd bought earlier in the week and had already prepped on the stove to steam. 'I don't have a tone.'

'You could cut brick with it. Not that I mind.' He didn't bother to hide the grin when he gave her a friendly poke at the base of the spine. 'It's sort of flattering.'

'I wouldn't be flattered. I don't care to have you talk about me with your former . . . connection.'

'Connect is what Sylbie and me never really did. She came in while I was having coffee, and she sat down. Partly to apologize for that, we'll say unfortunate, incident back in March. The other was to ask a question. She wanted to know why you and not her.'

Considering, Abigail took the chicken off the heat. 'It's a legitimate question, from her point of view. That's what you'd think. From mine, it's both awkward and annoying. A woman who looks like she does would be used to having anyone she wants, and wouldn't see me, fairly enough, in that same light. However true that might be, it's still annoying. You're flattered because I'm annoyed, and that only annoys me more.'

'Before you move to downright pissed, don't you want to know what I told her?'

'It's none of my business what you said in a private conversation.' She got out plates, set them

416

down sharply. 'Yes, I want to know.'

'I told her that when I'm with you, it feels right. It feels like where I'm supposed to be. It all makes sense. I said I didn't know why one person falls in love with another, just that they do.'

She turned back, eyes on his. 'You told her you loved me.'

'I did, because I do.'

'I'm less annoyed.'

'Good. Heading in the right direction. I didn't want to have the conversation with her, but after I had, I realized it was a good one. I think we understand each other better than we ever did, and that'll make it easier for both of us.'

'It would be easier for me if she weren't so physically gifted. And that's petty. I don't like being petty and shallow.'

'As I grew up with two sisters, I can safely say odds are strong she's thinking the same about you. But my point is this Roland Babbett got himself an earful.'

'None of it's applicable to the charges against Justin Blake, if indeed Babbett is a private investigator working for Justin's father.'

'No, but it's fuel. Just like you carrying a gun and having high-class security is fuel. How well will those bona fides of yours hold up?'

'My documents and available history will stand up to a standard police run. There would be no reason to question them.'

'A PI's not a cop,' Brooks pointed out.

'I believe they'll hold up to a rigorous check. I've never had any trouble.'

'Ever been arrested, brought in for questioning?'

'No, but I'm routinely checked by clients before

417

contract. Due to the sensitive nature of the work, and my fee, my documents and references are thoroughly checked by any new client.'

'That's good.' Satisfied, he nodded. 'That's good to know. My concern, and it's just a concern at this point, is this Babbett wouldn't be working for a client wanting to hire you, but one looking for dirt, for something he can use to discredit you or threaten you.'

'He'd have to be very skilled, and very determined.'

'Maybe we'll take some precautions.'

'You could intimidate him. You have authority, and weapons. You could confront him, intimidate him and make him leave.'

'Maybe I could, but that's the sort of thing that would tend to make him more curious once he's gone. Unless I have a lever.'

'I don't want to leave.'

'We're not going to let that happen.'

She hated this new stress, this additional complication that had nothing, *nothing,* to do with the Volkovs.

'If I'd stayed in the house, not answered the door, or simply given him directions—'

'I don't think that would've made much difference. He's doing a job. What we'll do—or you will, as I expect you're better and quicker—is find out what we can about him. See what kind of man we're up against here. Meanwhile . . . I'm going to want to borrow some of your cameras.'

'Why?'

'That precaution. Is it okay if the Bickford Police Department borrows some of your equipment for a day or two?'

'Yes.' She took a key ring out of her pocket. 'Borrow what you want.'

'Thanks. I'll have Ash or Boyd run out and get it, if that's okay. I need to make a couple calls to set up that precaution.'

'All right. I have to finish the meal.' Hopefully it would settle her nerves. 'I don't want to overcook the vegetables.'

She had to do something, keep doing something, so the panic couldn't push through. If she performed normal tasks—add fresh thyme and butter to the green beans, drizzle the wine sauce over the chicken, plate them with the roasted potatoes—she could cling to the illusion of normality.

She'd prepared and presented the meal very well, but she could barely force down a few bites.

She had a contingency plan. She always did. All the documents she needed for the next identity were inside her safe room, locked away. Waiting.

But she didn't want to use them, didn't want to become someone else again. That meant she'd have to fight to protect who she was now. What she had now.

'If this investigator is very skilled and very determined, it will still take time for him to discredit my documents and history,' she began. 'I need more time to plan and organize any sort of contact with Special Agent Garrison.'

'She's in Chicago?'

'I wanted someone in Chicago, where the Volkovs are based. She would have more incentive, and more access. Her response time would be quicker, once she learned to trust my information.'

'Good thinking.'

'But unless I can formulate an alternative, if I make direct contact, she'd be duty-bound to detain me. If that happens, I don't believe I'll have the time or opportunity to clear myself before I'm eliminated.'

He reached over, took both her hands. 'You're not going to be detained, and you're sure as hell not going to be eliminated. Look at me. Whatever it takes. And I've given some thought on alternatives and methods.'

'I've considered sending Special Agent Garrison an e-mail on her personal account, telling her who I am, relating the entire story, all the details. I can route it as I do the data I send her, and it wouldn't be possible to track. But it could leak. If the information I give her gets in the wrong hands, the Volkovs will know I'm not only still alive—'

'Ilya Volkov saw you. They know you're alive.'

'They knew I was alive five years ago in New York. I might have had an accident or contracted a terminal illness.'

'Okay, slim, but point taken.'

'They'll also know I've accessed their accounts, their electronics, and have given information to the FBI. Naturally, they'd take steps to block me from the access, which would cost me time and effort. They'd also be much more careful about what they put in e-mails and e-files. But more, it would make them very angry, and increase their effort to locate and eliminate me.

'They have very skilled techs. Part of their income is from computer fraud, scams, from identity theft.'

'You're better than their techs.'

'Yes, I am, but I've also had considerable time

to study and program, to break through firewalls, elude alerts. It would take time to do that again, with newer, stronger security in place. In their position, I'd lay traps. If I made a mistake, they might track me. Time, again, is important. If and when I contact the FBI, the process of taking Keegan and Cosgrove, identifying other moles, arresting Korotkii, Ilya—all of that would have to happen quickly.'

'Like dominoes falling,' he suggested.

'Yes, along those lines. Bureaucracies don't, in general, operate in a timely fashion. And before the process can begin, the agent, her superiors, would have to believe me.'

'They will.'

'The word of a fugitive, suspected at least by some of killing or certainly causing the deaths of two U.S. Marshals. Against the word of two other marshals, one of whom has been decorated and promoted.'

He covered her restless hand with his. 'The word of a woman who at sixteen handed them a top-level Mafia assassin on a damn platter. They're the ones who screwed up.'

'You're biased because you love me.'

'I love you, but I also have good instincts. You think the FBI, the marshals, the CPD wouldn't bend and twist to break the back of the Volkov organization? They'll deal with you, Abigail.'

It took an effort not to pull her hand from his. 'Are you asking me to trust them to protect me?'

'No. I'm asking you to trust yourself, and me, to do that.'

'I think I could.'

'Then what we need is, first, a conduit.'

'I don't understand.'

'Someone to speak for you, to make contact and open the door to negotiations.'

'You can't—'

'No,' he agreed, before she'd finished. 'I can't. I'm too close to you, emotionally and geographically. They'll check out the conduit. But they'd have no reason to connect me—or you—to my former captain on the Little Rock PD.'

'I don't know him.'

'I do. Just hear me out. Captain Joseph Anson. You can research him. He's a solid cop, decorated, a twenty-five-year man. He's got a wife—first and only—two kids. He's a good boss, a smart cop. By the book, but not so much that he can't skip a page if it's the right thing to do. He's trusted and respected in the department because he's trustworthy and respectable. And he's got balls.'

She got up, walked to the window to think it through. A conduit made good sense, would lay a reasonable buffer down. But . . .

'Why would he believe me?'

'He'll believe me.'

'Even if he did, why would Special Agent Garrison believe him?'

'Because of his record, his service, because he's clean. Because he'd have no reason to lie. He's a handful of years away from his thirty, away from retirement. Why would he risk that by lying to the feds?'

She nodded, seeing the logic. 'But why would he risk that by involving himself in this?'

'Because he's a good man, and a good cop.' Now Brooks rose, went to her. 'Because he's raised two daughters, and if he doesn't imagine them in your place, I'll put them there in his head.'

'You're asking me to trust a man I don't know, have never met.'

'I know it, and don't think for a minute I don't know how much that asks. If you can't do it, we'll find another way.'

She turned to the window again. Her gardens were doing so well. Her life had been so smooth, really, for the last year. And yet nothing had really grown until she'd opened the door to Brooks.

'Would you trust him with your life?'

'I would be. You're my life now.'

'Oh, God, you say that and I feel I'd wither away if I lost what I've found with you. You make me want to risk the quiet, Brooks, and I thought the quiet was all I ever wanted.'

'You can't keep running, Abigail.' Taking her shoulders, he turned her around to face him. 'You can't keep shutting yourself up, shutting yourself down.'

'I thought I could, but no, I can't. Not now. How would you do it?'

'Drive to Little Rock. We couldn't risk a phone call or an e-mail. It has to be face-to-face, not only so we don't leave a trail but because Anson's a face-to-face type. I could be there in under two hours, get this started, be back before morning.'

'Tonight?'

'What's the point in putting it off? There's a PI I guarantee is working on his laptop right now, scratching at that surface. We've got the advantage, why waste it?' He got to his feet. 'You take your laptop or that iPad of yours. Do your research on the captain on the way. If you're not satisfied, we turn around, come back.'

'You want me to go with you?'

'Always. But in this case I want him to see you, hear you. I want you to tell him the way you told me. You're scared. I don't blame you.' He took her arms. 'You want to take more time, to analyze, to calculate, work out details. But that's not what you did when you got out of that safe house. It's not what you did in New York when they chased after you. You went with instinct, and you beat them.'

'I'm going to take my alternate identification, and cash. My go bag. If this goes wrong, I can't come back here.'

'If it goes wrong, I'll go with you.'

'I know you mean that now—'

'Now's where we are. You take whatever you think you need.'

'I want to take Bert.'

Now he smiled. 'I wouldn't have it any other way.'

*   *   *

He drove her car. Neighbors wouldn't think much about an SUV in Anson's driveway, but they'd remember a Bickford police cruiser if a badge asked somewhere down the line.

While he drove, Bert did what dogs did in cars, hung his head out the back window with a dopey grin on his face, and Abigail worked on her laptop.

'Your Captain Anson has an excellent record.'

'He's a good cop.'

Advantage or disadvantage? Abigail wondered.

'If he agrees to help, will you know if he's telling the truth?'

'Yes. Trust me.'

424

'I am.' She looked out the side window at the blur of landscape. 'More than I have anyone else in a dozen years. If this goes through, and others believe me, it would lead to arrests, trials, my testimony. And there could be repercussions. You have to understand that.'

'We could go on the way things are, let it alone. And both of us—I think both of us—would never feel quite okay with it. Safer, but not quite okay.'

'Safe's been enough for a long time now.' She looked back at him, still in wonder how one person could change everything. 'It's not now. Still, it won't be enough to hurt the Volkov organization, to just damage it. To be okay and safe, we have to destroy it.'

'Working on it.'

'I have some ideas. But not all of them are strictly legal.'

She watched the grin move over his face. 'That doesn't surprise me. What do you have in mind?'

'I've been working on something, but I need to refine it a bit more. It's technical.'

He glanced over, and down at her laptop. 'Nerd stuff.'

'I suppose. Yes, nerd stuff. If we do this, I'll need to spend more time and effort on the programs I've been developing. In the meantime, and again, if your captain agrees, you have to decide on your communication. Once he makes contact with the FBI on this matter, they'll track his communications.'

'We're going to make a stop on the way, pick up some prepaid cell phones. That should cover it for the time being.'

'It should.'

He reached over, briefly laid his hand over hers. 'We're going to find a way.'

She believed him. It made no sense, defied all logic, and yet she believed him.

Her nerves ratcheted up when Brooks drove down the quiet street in the pretty neighborhood. Old leafy trees, green lawns, lights glowing against window glass.

Captain Anson might attempt to arrest her on the spot. He might insist on contacting the federals.

He might not be home, which would be anticlimactic and somehow more stressful.

He might—

'Relax,' Brooks said and stopped in front of a tidy two-story house with attached garage and a lovely red maple in the front yard.

'That's not possible.'

He shifted so they were face-to-face. 'In or out, Abigail? It's your choice.'

'In, but I can't relax about it.'

If she had to run, she wouldn't allow him to run with her. She wouldn't allow him to give up his life, his family, his world. She had an extra set of keys in her bag, and could be out and gone, if necessary. If that happened . . .

'Whatever happens, I need you to know these past weeks have been the best of my life. Being with you changed me. Nothing will be the same for me again, and I'm glad of it.'

'We're going to win this, starting now.'

'All right.' She ordered Bert to stay, and got out of the car.

After Brooks skirted the hood, he took her hand. She did her best to focus on that contact as her heart began to thud in her throat.

426

Lights glowed in the window, and she could smell spring, and the oncoming summer—the grass, the heliotrope, dianthus, some early roses. She felt the anxiety build, an anvil on her chest, and closed her eyes against it for a moment while Brooks knocked.

The man who answered boasted broad shoulders and heavily salted dark hair gone thin at the temples. He wore khakis and a blue golf-style shirt with reading glasses hanging from the pocket by the earpiece.

His feet were bare, and from somewhere behind him, Abigail heard the commentary of a ball game.

His eyes were a hard steel blue, until the smile burst onto his face.

'Son of a bitch, it's Chief Gleason at my door.'

'It's good to see you, Captain.'

'Son of a bitch,' Anson repeated, then gave Brooks a one-armed hug while he measured up Abigail. 'Are you going to introduce the lady?'

'Abigail Lowery, Captain Joe Anson.'

'Nice to meet you, Abigail. Man, Nadine's going to be sorry she missed you. She took her mom on a girl's trip—a spa thing—for her mom's birthday. She won't be back till Sunday. Well, come on in.'

The living room looked comfortable, Abigail thought, lived in and easy, with framed family photographs on a wall shelf and prettily potted houseplants on the windowsill.

'I was catching the game back in the den. Just let me switch that off.'

'Sorry to interrupt, to drop by like this.'

'No need. It's my second night baching it. I'm boring the hell out of myself.' He slipped into an alcove off the living room. Seconds later the sound went off, and an ancient yellow Lab followed Anson

427

creakily out of the den.

'He's harmless,' Anson said to Abigail.

'I like dogs. He has a very intelligent face.'

'Huck was always smart. Mostly blind now, and more'n half deaf, but he's still got his smarts. Why don't we go on back to the great room, have a seat? How's your dad doing, Brooks?'

'He's good. Really good.'

'That's good to hear. And the job?'

'I like it, Captain. I like where I am and who I am there.'

'He's a good cop,' Anson said to Abigail. 'I hated losing him. How about a beer?'

'I wouldn't say no.'

'I would,' Abigail said, then realized the simple truth sounded rude. 'I mean, if I could have some water.'

'Sure. I got some lemonade. It's not half bad.'

'That would be nice, thank you.'

At Anson's direction, they settled into a seating area off the large, open kitchen. At the back, wide glass doors led out to a patio, where she saw what she assumed was an enormous grill under a black cover, and several outdoor chairs and tables.

As Anson got the drinks, the old dog shuffled over, sniffed at her, then rested his head on her knee.

She stroked his head, rubbed his ears.

'If he bothers you, just tell him to go sit.'

'He isn't bothering me.'

'Abigail's got a dog. Great dog. Bert's out in the car.'

'What the hell did you leave him out there for? Go get him. We'll take this out back, let the two of them get acquainted and pal around.'

'Bert would like that. If you're sure, I'll go get him. I ordered him to stay, so he wouldn't get out of the car for Brooks.'

'You go ahead, and just bring him on around the back. Side gate's on the left.'

'Thank you.'

When she went out, Anson handed Brooks the beer, jerked a thumb toward the sliders. 'What's going on, Brooks?' he asked, as they stepped out.

'A lot.'

'Your lady covers it well, but she's got enough nerves lighting her up to power the whole city of Little Rock.'

'She's got reason for them. I talked her into coming here, to you, because she needs help. And because I'm in love with her.'

Anson let out a breath, took a long swallow of beer. 'What kind of trouble is she in?'

'I want her to tell you, and I need you to hear her out. All the way. I'm counting on you, Captain.'

'She's not from around here, or up where you come from, either.'

'No, but Bickford's her home now. We both want it to stay that way.'

They heard the gate open and shut. Huck's head went up—not at the sound, Anson knew—at the scent.

Anson's eyebrows lifted when Abigail walked around the house with Bert.

'That's one big, handsome bastard.'

'He's very well behaved,' Abigail assured him. *'Ami,'* she said when Huck, quivering, walked over to sniff the newcomer. *'Ami. Jouer.'*

Tails slashing the air, the dogs sniffed each other. Huck walked over to the fence line, lifted his leg.

Bert followed suit. Then they wrestled.

'Huck's got some life in him yet.' Anson offered Abigail the lemonade, gestured to a seat. 'Brooks said you had a story to tell me, Abigail.'

'Yes. I should start by saying my name isn't Abigail Lowery. Technically. It's Elizabeth Fitch. When I was sixteen I witnessed a man named Yakov Korotkii, who is a lieutenant in the Volkov crime organization, murder his cousin Alexi Gurevich and my friend Julie Masters.'

Anson sat back. After a moment, he glanced at Brooks. 'You did say a lot.'

Then he turned those steely eyes back on Abigail. 'Why don't you tell me about that?'

25

She couldn't know if he believed her. His face showed nothing, no surprise, no doubt, no understanding. As Brooks had, he interrupted the flow a few times with questions, then only nodded so she'd continue.

Before she finished, the dogs came back for rubs, and were both sprawled out, exhausted from the play, when she stopped.

'I remember some of what you're telling me,' Anson began. 'It was big news at the time, especially within law enforcement. Two U.S. Marshals killed, another wounded, the witness in a Mob-related double murder missing. Your name and face was all over the national media for some weeks, and there were a number of interagency memos on you.'

'Yes, I know.'

'As well as an outstanding warrant for fleeing a scene. A BOLO and APB. You're wanted for questioning in the matter of those agents' deaths, and the explosion of the safe house.'

Her fingers linked together, painfully tight, in her lap. 'Interoffice communication indicates that Keegan and Cosgrove have been taken at their word. Wanted for questioning is simply a ruse in order to charge me for murder, or accessory to murder.'

'How would you be privy to interoffice communication?'

Saying nothing, Brooks reached over, unlaced her fingers, kept his hand on hers.

'I'm a computer scientist, and specialize in security. I'm also a hacker.'

'And you're telling me you can access confidential files and memos inside the U.S. Marshals Service and the FBI?'

'Yes. I'm very skilled, and this has been a priority for me. Both Keegan and Cosgrove made statements which claim they came in, found Terry down in the kitchen and her weapon missing. As they began to call it in, they were fired on by persons unknown, and Cosgrove sustained a wound. As Keegan returned fire, the lights went out. Keegan was able to get Cosgrove outside, call in the incident. But before he could go back in for Terry, or to find me or John, the house exploded. He also claimed he believed he saw someone fleeing.'

'That about sums up what I remember from it,' Anson agreed.

'One of the prevailing theories is I grew

431

panicked, or perhaps bored, and contacted the Volkovs to make a deal. They tracked me to the safe house, and I fought with Terry as I tried to get out. Either I or persons unknown associated with the Volkovs shot John, fired on Keegan and Cosgrove, and I either escaped in the confusion or was taken. The assassins then blew up the house to cover the tracks—or I did it.'

'A sixteen-year-old girl getting the draw on two marshals *and* blowing up a house.' Brooks shook his head. 'I wouldn't buy it.'

'A highly intelligent girl who'd been trained personally by one of those marshals in firearms, who'd requested and received five thousand in cash from her trust fund, who'd forged IDs, had spent a summer while the legal wheel slowly turned, thinking about what would happen to her once she testified.' The logic of it stood firmly enough for Abigail. 'It's reasonable to believe that girl snapped, tried to make it all go away.'

'Reasonable,' Anson commented, 'when there's nothing to contradict the statements and timelines, such as a conflicting statement from an eyewitness.'

'I don't believe the theory I murdered John and Terry, or had a part in their murders, will hold,' Abigail told him. 'But I do believe if I'm taken in, that won't matter. I'll be dead within twenty-four hours. It might be staged as a suicide, but I favor direct elimination.'

'You're very cool about it,' Anson observed.

'I've had a number of years to consider what they'd do to me if they could.'

'Why come in now?'

She looked at Brooks. 'If I don't, nothing changes. And so much already has. Brooks asked

432

me to trust him, and in doing so, to trust you. I'm trying.'

'She's been feeding, anonymously, an FBI agent based in Chicago with intel on the Volkov organization.'

'And you have that intel because you're hacking into the Volkov network?' Puffing out his cheeks, Anson sat back. 'You must be one hell of a hacker.'

'Yes, I am. The Volkov organization is very computer-centric, and they believe they're very safe, very well shielded. They have excellent techs,' she added. 'I'm better than they are. Also, Ilya is consistently careless in this area. It's, in my opinion, a kind of arrogance. He uses e-mail and texts routinely for both business and personal correspondence.'

'They've made a number of arrests on that intel, Captain,' Brooks said.

'Who's your FBI contact?'

Abigail looked at Brooks, got his nod. 'Special Agent Elyse Garrison.'

'Why didn't you go to her with your story?'

'If it leaked—and I know there's at least one Volkov mole inside the Chicago office—she could be taken, tortured, killed. Killed outright. She could be used to lure me in. They haven't been able to trace the contact to me. Once they do, her life and mine are put at serious risk.'

'You want someone to make contact for you, someone who isn't—as far as any check would show—connected in any way to Elizabeth Fitch.'

'Someone,' Brooks continued, 'with a sterling record in law enforcement, someone with position and authority, credibility. Someone this Garrison is likely to believe.'

433

'And if I buy into this, I go to Chicago and make this contact, what then?'

'It opens the door for us to set up a meet between her and Abigail, at a location we choose.'

'I would continue to monitor law enforcement chatter and communications, so I'd know if they'd attempt a trap, or if any of the people I believe or suspect to be in league with the Volkovs learn of the communication.'

'You're crossing a lot of lines here.' He turned a cool, hard eye on Brooks. 'Both of you.'

'Tell me, Captain, what do you think her chances are of living to testify if she goes in straight, with the moles in place, the Volkovs whole?'

'I believe in the system, Brooks. I believe they'd protect her. But I can't blame her for not believing it. If it was someone I loved, I'm not sure I'd believe it, either.'

He exhaled deeply.

In the quiet yard with the dogs softly snoring, a little garden fountain gurgling, Abigail wondered the scrape of her nerves under her skin didn't screech like nails on a blackboard.

'We may be able to do this your way, smoke out Keegan and Cosgrove, and those like them,' Anson began. 'We may be able to make some key arrests that put a hard dent in the Volkov organization. And then? Are you willing to go into witness protection?' he asked Brooks. 'To give up where you like to be, who you like to be?'

'Yes.'

'No,' Abigail said immediately. 'No. I wouldn't have agreed to come here if I believed that would be a result. Elizabeth Fitch will meet Special Agent Garrison, will testify. Only three people know Elizabeth Fitch and Abigail Lowery are the same person, and that has to remain constant. If a connection is made between them, I'll disappear. I can do it.'

'Abigail.'

'No,' she said again, quietly, fiercely, to Brooks. 'You need to do the right thing, and you need to protect me. You can do both. I'm trusting you to do both. You have to trust me. I'll be Elizabeth again, for this, and then she's gone. She'll disappear, and Abigail can live her life. I know how to bring down the Volkovs, and in a way I believe they'll never fully recover from. It's not about guns and knives and blood. It's about keystrokes.'

'You're going to take them down with a computer?' Anson demanded.

Her eyes, calm and green, met his. 'That's exactly right. If I can do what I've theorized, and the authorities listen and act, this will be over. I'm putting my life in your hands, Captain Anson, because Brooks trusts and respects you without qualification.'

'Let's go in, have some coffee,' Anson said after a moment, 'and talk this through.'

*   *   *

She insisted on driving back. Brooks had barely slept in thirty-six hours, and would be on duty within another six. So he kicked back the seat and caught a little sleep on the drive.

And gave her time to go over everything, again.

Joseph Anson would go to Chicago, make contact. He would not use or reveal the name Abigail Lowery but tell Agent Garrison that

Elizabeth Fitch had come to him, told him the story, given him the agent's name. He'd relate information Abigail had previously funneled to Garrison.

If Garrison followed her previous pattern, she would report only to her direct superior. Then the process would begin.

So many things could go wrong.

But if they went right . . .

She could belong to the man sleeping beside her. She could learn what to do at backyard barbecues. She could become Abigail so that everything that happened from that point on would be real.

She would finally look out from the witness chair in the courtroom, stare into the eyes of Korotkii, Ilya, Sergei Volkov, and speak the truth. As Elizabeth.

No, as Liz, she thought. At least in her mind, she'd speak as Liz for Julie, John and Terry.

And she'd use everything she'd learned in the past twelve years to strip the bones of the Volkov organization clean.

*   *   *

He stirred as she turned toward her cabin.

'I've been thinking,' he said.

'I thought you were sleeping.'

'Some of both.' He brought the seat back up, scrubbed at his face with his hands. 'So I was thinking you should ask me to move in with you. I'm practically living here now,' he added, when she said nothing. 'But maybe you could make it official.'

'Do you want to live here so you can protect me?'

'That would be a side benefit. Other side benefits include having my stuff handy, some closet and drawer space, and easy access to sex. All of those are pluses, but the main reason I want to live here is because I love you and I want to be with you.'

She sat for a moment, looking at her cabin. Hers, she thought. The house, the gardens, the greenhouse, the little creek, the woods. She'd come to think of them as hers, to feel that belonging. For the first time, she'd come to think of a place as home.

Hers.

'If you moved in, you'd need security codes and keys.'

'They'd sure be handy.'

'I'd like to think about it, if that's all right.'

'Sure.'

The single word, so easy as he got out of the car, opened the back for the dog to jump out, told her he was confident he'd overcome any objections she might voice, and have his way.

It should have irritated her, she thought. It should even insult her. And yet it did neither. It simply reminded her who he was.

Theirs. She tried out the word, let herself wonder over it while they waited for Bert to relieve himself after the drive.

Theirs in the pretty, star-dazzled night, with the flowers glowing, the creek murmuring and the soft breeze urging the leaves to whisper an answer.

Their house, their gardens, their greenhouse and creek and woods.

Hers was safer. Quieter.

Theirs. Full of compromise and questions.

And promise.

She unlocked the front door, reset the alarm. 'Would you like to move in with me?'

'Well, that's a big step. I'm going to have to think about it.'

'You just said . . .' She turned into his grin, felt her lips curve in response as she locked up. 'You're teasing.'

'Caught me.' He laid his hands on her shoulders, turned her to face him again. 'But it is a big step for you, I know.'

'It's a more natural progression for you. You were raised in a traditional two-parent home.'

'Boy, my mother'd be pissed to be labeled traditional.' He put an arm around her shoulders to lead her upstairs. 'We'll keep that between you and me.'

'I never considered sharing a home with anyone. And I've only begun to believe it's possible for me to stay here, to have a home here.'

'Believe it, and keep believing it. No point sending negative thoughts out into the universe.'

'Optimistic or pessimistic thoughts don't influence events.'

'How do you know?' Playfully, he gave her hair a quick tug. 'You can't know what other people are thinking or wishing or believing unless they tell you. And what about the whole faith can move mountains deal?'

'I've never seen a mountain move, much less through faith.'

'Literal brain.' He tapped her forehead. 'What about volcanoes? A volcano moves the hell out of a mountain.'

'It's ludicrous to posit that a rupture in the earth's crust, the diverging and converging of

438

tectonic plates, the release of lava, gases and ash through those ruptures can be caused by faith—or the lack of it.'

'Did I posit? I don't know what got into me.' He saw her roll her eyes as she walked toward the bathroom. 'I made a volcano for a science project in sixth grade. It was very cool.'

For the first time she didn't shut the door, but continued to talk to him as she prepared for bed. 'It's a very good project for a young student.'

'Plus cool.' He walked in, picked up his toothbrush as she washed her face. 'I wanted to name it The Devil's Fart, but my father convinced me my grade could be adversely affected.'

'Wise.'

'I called it that in my head, though, so it made the whole baking soda, food coloring and vinegar lava spewing out of the flour paste over soda bottle cone more memorable. I bet you killed in science projects.'

'I did well.' It felt odd, but in an interesting way, to share the bathroom sink with him. 'I built an underwater volcano on converging tectonic plates to demonstrate how islands are formed.'

He lowered his toothbrush, narrowed his eyes at her in the mirror. 'Underwater volcano.'

'Yes. Hot water always rises to the surface of cold, and floats. With the baked clay model—'

'Baked clay.'

'Yes, and the remote controlled plates, I was able to create a very satisfying eruption.'

'How old were you?'

'Nine.'

'Show-off.'

'I did enjoy doing well in school. You're talking

439

about science projects so I'll relax and sleep better.'

'It's working for me.'

She found when she lay beside him in the dark, her mind drifting, it worked for her as well.

*   *   *

Brooks arrested Roland Babbett as his first official duty of the morning. He felt pretty damn good about knocking on Babbett's door at seven a.m. Better yet when the heavy-eyed, bed-headed Babbett opened the door.

'Roland Babbett?'

'Yeah. Is there a problem?'

'There is for you. I'm Chief Gleason of the Bickford town police, and this is my deputy Boyd Fitzwater. I have a warrant for your arrest.'

'Huh?'

'And another to search your room, belongings and vehicle. You're going to need to get dressed and come with us.'

'What's this about? Under arrest? That's crazy.'

'Not considering you're in possession of burglary tools, and used same at two-fifteen this morning to illegally enter the Ozarks Suite. Which is both locked and posted.'

Roland's eyes, not so heavy now, took a long study of Brooks's face. 'I want to make a phone call.'

'No problem. You can have your phone call once we're at the station. I'm going to give you a chance to get dressed, or we can take you in while you're in the hotel robe. It's a nice robe.'

'I'd like to get dressed.'

'Okay, then. Boyd, why don't you read Mr.

440

Babbett his rights while he puts some pants on.' Brooks held up the search warrant before he started wandering the room. 'Nice view. Mr. Conroy does it up right. You try the restaurant for dinner?'

'Room service.' Roland dragged on a pair of pants, pulled out a T-shirt. 'I had the steak.'

'How was it?'

'Bloody and good.'

'Yeah, they do it right.' He opened the navy backpack, poked through, then put the lock-pick set in an evidence bag. 'You visiting?'

Despite the circumstance, Roland snorted out a laugh. 'Everybody asks. You know by now I'm here on business.'

'Stuben-Pryce out of Little Rock.' As he sealed a mini tape recorder into a bag, Brooks's voice stayed smooth and easy as warm cream. 'I was on the job down there. You probably know that by now, too. That's a fancy firm, with fancy prices, Mr. Babbett.'

'We do good work.'

'I don't doubt it.' He shot Roland a friendly smile. 'Too bad you don't have better taste in clients.'

'Not my call. Do you mind if I brush my teeth, empty my bladder?'

'I'd mind if you didn't.'

Brooks continued to search the room while Boyd stood in the open bathroom doorway. 'We're a quiet town,' Brooks said conversationally. 'Oh, it can heat up some now and then, especially this time of year and on through the summer. A lot of tourists, a lot of conflicting personalities, you could say, stewing in all that heat. But we don't often run into PIs from fancy city firms doing some B-and-E

441

right in our landmark hotel.'

'I'm going to get my ass kicked over this.' In a gesture that mirrored his attitude, Roland spat toothpaste in the sink. 'Lose my bonus. I was hoping to bring my wife down for a kid-free break after she has the baby.'

'When's she due?'

'August fifteenth.'

'October's a pretty time in the Ozarks,' Brooks commented, as Roland came out. 'We'd be happy to have you, when you're visiting. Boyd, you can finish up with the search. I'll take Mr. Babbett in.'

'You're not going to cuff me?'

Brooks offered that friendly smile again. 'You want me to?'

'No. I appreciate it.'

'I don't figure you're going to run, and if you did? Where're you gonna go?'

He didn't run. Even if he'd had somewhere to run, he was made, his cover blown, the job in pieces.

At the station, Brooks gave him a cup of decent enough coffee, a phone and a few minutes of privacy—at a desk rather than in a cell.

After he made the call, Roland sat brooding.

'You finished up there?' Brooks asked him.

'Yeah. Finished.'

'Why don't we talk in my office? Jeff?' Brooks said to his part-timer. 'Don't go poking in or sending in any calls, all right? Not unless it's important.'

'Yes, sir, Chief.'

'Have a seat.' Brooks closed his office door, walked over to lean a hip on his desk. 'Well, I'm going to tell you straight. You're in some trouble here, Roland.'

'I got a lawyer coming down.'

'Fancy lawyer from the fancy firm, I expect. Still, we got you pretty cold on the B-and-E. Camera caught you in the hall, at the door, then the other cameras caught you poking around inside the suite. Got your lock picks.' As if sympathetic, Brooks let out a breath, shook his head. 'Even a fancy lawyer's going to have a time getting around that, don't you figure? Could mean a little jail time and put a hurt on your license. And a baby coming. I'd hate for your wife to visit you in jail in her condition.'

'Jail's doubtful, but the hurt on my license . . . Hell.' Roland pressed his fingers to his eyes. 'Might be okay there. It's the first ding on my record.'

Brooks lifted his shoulders, let them fall. 'Might be.'

'I'm not usually sloppy. I figured the look-around for a breeze. I didn't spot the cameras.'

'Don't be too hard on yourself. They weren't there until after you stopped by Abigail's.'

'Uh-huh.' Now, Roland's eyes met Brooks's in perfect understanding. 'She, her dog and her Glock scared the hell out of me.'

'You scared her. She's a city girl still,' Brooks lied cheerfully. 'Alone out there, no close neighbors. Add to that how she makes her living. I'm sure you know that already. Working security, always looking for how people get around it and do what they do? She's a bit jumpy.'

'You'd have to be to have security cameras in the woods.'

'Oh, she's always experimenting, running programs and what she calls scenarios. It happens you walked into one. Shook her up enough to have

443

her lock herself in the house till I got home. You know, in case you were some ax murderer instead of a lost photographer.'

'She didn't look shook up,' Roland muttered.

'Well, Abigail, she puts on a good front, and the dog helps her confidence. She told me about you, and I had to wonder. You gave her your real name.'

'ID was in my pack. She had the gun. I didn't want to annoy her with a lie if she checked my pack. But I didn't consider she, or you, would run me.'

'Cops. We're just naturally cynical and suspicious. So, Roland, here's the thing. I know who'd hire a PI from a fancy firm to poke around at Abigail, at me, at the Conroys and the hotel.'

'I can't confirm or deny without my legal counsel.'

'I'm not asking you to, I'm telling you. Lincoln Blake would do close to anything to get that asshole son of his off, including hiring out for somebody to plant false evidence, make false statements.'

Where he'd been slouched and sulky in his seat, Roland now straightened. 'Listen. I don't go there, not for any client, not for any fee. Neither does the firm. We wouldn't have the reputation we do otherwise.'

'Off the record, I'll say I believe that. But on it?' Brooks gave a careless shrug.

'Is there a deal coming along?'

'Might be. Russ Conroy's my oldest and closest friend. His parents are family to me, and his mama broke down and cried after she saw what that fucker and his friends did to that suite. It's considerably better now, but . . .'

Brooks picked up a file, handed it to Roland. 'We took those after Justin Blake and his idiot friends got done with the place.'

'Jesus,' Roland muttered, as he examined the photos.

'That kind of damage? That's not careless or stupid or childish. It's downright mean. That's just what Justin Blake is.'

Brooks reached over to hand the file back. 'And when the fucker managed to make bail, he comes out to the house of the woman I'm in love with, stoned, armed, in the middle of the night. He was stupid enough to take a jab at me with the knife he'd brought to slash my tires with. He upset my woman, and, Roland, that upsets me.

'You might see why she reacted the way she did when you came hiking on down to the house.'

'Yeah, maybe. Yeah.'

'Justin caused over a hundred thousand in damages to that suite, he punctured my tire, tried to puncture me, and scared my lady. And that's over and above him being a pain in my ass since I took this job. He's going down for what he's done, Roland. I will make it my mission in life to see to it. He's earned it, and if I gave a rat's flea-bitten ass, I'd say he needs it. He's got something twisted in him, the kind of thing we've both seen in others who end up dead or killing somebody.'

'I'd like to say something, off the record.'

'All right, then. Just between you and me.'

'I don't like working for Blake. He's a son of a bitch. There's nothing about his son you just said I don't agree with. I'll take my lumps on this if I have to, but I hate taking them on behalf of those two dicks.'

'I can't blame you a bit. So here's the deal, before the lawyer gets here. Go away, Roland. I

445

don't just mean leave town—though as I said you come back to visit with your wife, we'll be happy to see you. I mean go away from this. It's upsetting my friends, it's upsetting my lady. And you're wasting your time, because Justin Blake isn't going to slide his way out from this one. I don't blame anybody for doing a job they're hired to do—on the right side of the law, that is. But this can go pretty hard on you, and I can make it so your firm takes a hit. Maybe it's not much, considering, but I don't know why they'd want the bad publicity.'

'I have to turn in my reports.'

'You go right ahead on that. You didn't find anything on me, on Abigail, on the Conroys, because there's nothing to find. But if you keep poking at us, I'll find out, and it'll go different. You got far enough in this to know computers are Abigail's playground.'

'There's a threat buried in there.'

'I'm not burying a thing. I'm giving you the facts as I see them. I can let this go. You keep your clean record, you turn in your reports, and go home to your wife. Your lawyer's not going to cook you up a better deal.'

'Why are you?'

'For the reasons I just gave you, and one more. I don't much want to lock you up, Roland, that's another fact. If I'd gotten a different sense of you, if I thought you were the kind who enjoys working for a man like Blake, who'd edge over more than crossing a property line or going into a locked room to take a look around, you'd be in a cell right now. I'd work to keep you there.'

'I'd like to call my boss, give him the status.'

'Go ahead.' Brooks pushed off the desk.

'I met your mother.'

Brooks leaned back again. 'Did you?'

'I walked down—getting that sense, like you said. That house, it's amazing.'

'We're partial to it. Go ahead and make your call,' Brooks told him, and strolled out.

26

Abigail put everything else aside and focused entirely on the creation of the virus. She'd made numerous attempts to piggyback it on the worm she'd already constructed, but the results weren't satisfactory.

She could do considerable damage with the worm, but with the worm boring openings into the Volkov network, the virus that followed, spreading through those openings, would devastate.

To accomplish everything she needed, it had to be very fast, very complete, and trigger no alerts.

She'd always considered the project a kind of hobby, one she'd hoped would one day pay off.

Now it was a mission.

If she had time to build more equipment, or the luxury of hiring another skilled tech, or two . . . But she didn't, so speculating proved useless. This was only for her.

In any case, over time she'd developed her own programming language—the better to thwart anyone who attempted to hack into her files— and even if she could hire on, she'd have to teach someone her language and techniques.

Faster, more efficient, to do it herself.

She ran the next test, watched her codes fly by, and thought, No, no, no. It remained too unwieldy, too separate, took too long.

She sat back, her hair twisted up off her neck and secured with a pencil. As she studied the screen, she drank iced green tea for clarity of thinking.

The tea, the two yoga breaks she'd made herself take, the absolute quiet, didn't appear to help.

When her alarm sounded, and Bert went on alert, she checked her monitor. She hadn't expected Brooks so early, she thought, as she spotted his cruiser, then glanced at the time.

She'd worked straight through the morning and into the middle of the afternoon.

Six hours, she thought, with no appreciable progress.

Maybe it was beyond her after all.

She started to get up, to unlock the doors for him, then remembered she'd given him keys and the security codes. An uneasy step, she admitted, but the advantage right that moment was she didn't have to stop to let him in.

Still, there would be someone in the house, in her space. How was she supposed to concentrate on something this complex, this delicate, unless she was alone?

Which tore apart her fantasy of a state-of-the-art computer lab and a team of highly skilled techs. But that was only fantasy, because she always worked alone, until—

'Hey.' Brooks walked in, set a bag on the counter. 'How's it going?'

'Not as well as I'd like. I need to try another sequence, test again.'

'How long have you been at it?'

448

'It doesn't matter how long. It's not done.'

'Okay. I'll get out of your hair as soon as I put this stuff away. I brought some of my things over, so I'll deal with that upstairs. If you're not done when I am, I'll find something to do.'

'Mmm' was her only response. She tried not to tense up at the sound of the refrigerator, the cupboards opening and closing. When silence returned, she let out a cleansing breath and dived in again.

She forgot he was there. Over the next two hours, she lost herself in the codes and sequences. When the headache and eyestrain finally stopped her, she rose for medication, for fluids.

And remembered him.

She went upstairs. The quiet held so absolute she thought he must be napping, but she didn't find him in the bedroom. Curious, she opened the closet.

There were his clothes, hanging with hers. Shirts, pants. A suit.

She'd never seen him in a suit. She trailed her fingers over the sleeve as she studied the shoes and boots on the floor of the closet.

They shared a closet, she thought. So much more intimate and vital somehow than sharing a bed. Crossing over, she opened drawers in the bureau. She'd meant to reorganize to give him space, but had forgotten in the work.

He'd seen to it himself. She'd need to alter some of his choices, but that was a small thing.

Closing drawers, she stepped back, took a turn around the room. Should she buy another dresser, a chest of drawers?

Would they need one?

Would he stay?

449

A movement out the window caught her eye, and stepping closer, she saw him, hoeing at weeds in her vegetable patch. He'd mounded up her potato plants, something else she'd meant to do that day.

Sweat dampened his shirt, gleamed wetly on his arms, and a ball cap shaded his face.

And, oh, the thrill of it. The unexpected and staggering thrill of it. His clothes hung in the closet with hers as she stood at the bedroom window and watched him work the garden under a sky like bleached denim.

She spun away from the window, hugging herself, then ran downstairs.

In the kitchen, she found the food he'd brought in the fridge and the dozen lemons she'd bought a few days earlier.

She made fresh lemonade, filled two tall glasses with cracked ice and poured. She put the pitcher and glasses on a tray and carried it all outside.

'It's too hot to hoe,' she called out. 'You'll be dehydrated.'

'Nearly done.'

She walked out to him with the glasses as he finished the last row. 'It's fresh.'

While sweat tricked down his temples, he downed half the glass without pause. 'Thanks.'

'You've done so much work.'

Leaning on the hoe, he studied the garden. 'I'm hoping to sample those butter beans, come harvest. I'm fond of butter beans.'

'Those are lima beans.'

'You're standing in the South, honey.' After a roll of his shoulders, he downed the rest of his lemonade. 'I haven't worked a garden since I headed down to Little Rock. Didn't know I missed it.'

'Still, it's hot and close.' She touched his hand to bring his gaze back to her. 'I wasn't very welcoming before.'

'Work's allowed to get in the way now and again. Mine does, and will.'

'Mine, in this case, is frustrating. I thought I'd be closer.'

'Can't help you on that. I don't understand a damn thing you're doing. But I can work a garden, and I can grill up those steaks I picked up, so you can have more time at it.' He cocked his head as he studied her. 'But I'd say it's time for a break all around, and I sure as hell need a shower.'

'You're very sweaty,' she agreed, and took the hoe from him to carry it to her little garden shed. 'I can pick some of the lettuce, and a few other things, for a salad when you're done.'

'I'm thinking "we."'

'You've already done more than your share in the garden.'

'Not we in the garden.' He took her hand, pulling her along toward the house. 'We in the shower.'

'I really should—'

'Get wet with me.' He paused to take off his dirty boots, sweaty socks. 'Did I ever tell you about this swimming hole we used to frequent?'

'No.'

'It's not that far from here, a little higher in the hills. Really more a bend in the river than a pool, but it worked fine.'

Taking her glass, he set them both down on the counter as he moved her through the kitchen.

'Water's cool. The color of tobacco, I'd say, but clear. Russ and I and some others used to ride our

451

mountain bikes up there on those long, schoolless days of summer, strip down and cool off. The first time I skinny-dipped with a girl was there, at what we locals call Fiddlehead Pool, because there's fiddlehead ferns thick as thieves up there. I'll take you sometime.'

'That sounds very interesting, but right now—'

He'd managed to get her into the bedroom, began to back her toward the bath. 'You need to get naked and wet. Let me help you with that.'

'You appear to be very determined,' she commented, when he pulled her shirt over her head.

'Oh, I am. I am.' And flicked open the catch of her bra.

'Then I suppose there's no point in arguing.'

'No point at all.' Reaching behind her, he turned the shower on, then flipped open the button of her fly.

'Then I should cooperate.'

'That'd be the sensible thing.'

'I prefer doing the sensible thing.' She drew his shirt off, let it drop.

'Hallelujah.' But he started to hold her back when she would have moved into him. 'Let me rinse some of this sweat off first.'

'I don't mind it. It's basic and natural, and . . .' She pressed her lips to the side of his throat. 'Salty.'

'You about kill me, Abigail. That's God's truth.'

She wanted to, wanted to make him want and yearn and quiver as he made her. She embraced the musky scent of him, the good sweat of physical labor as she stripped off his pants, as he stripped off hers.

And the water ran cool over her head, down her

452

body.

'It feels good,' she murmured.

So good when his mouth took her mouth, when his hands took her body. When she tasted his hunger for her, felt his need for her.

She imagined them sinking into cool, tobacco-colored water in the bend of a river where fiddlehead ferns grew thick and green and moonlight shimmered in rays through a canopy of trees.

'I want to go to your swimming hole.'

'We will.'

'In the moonlight,' she said, as her head fell back, as his lips skimmed over the column of her throat. 'I've never been romantic, not before you. But you make me want moonlight, and wildflowers and whispers in the dark.'

'I'll give you all of it, and more.' He slicked her wet hair back, framed her face to lift it to his. 'And more.'

'Promises and secrets, and all the things I never understood. I want them with you. I love you so much. I love you. That's already more than I ever had.'

'More still.' He drew her into the kiss, long and slow and deep, as the water showered over them. He'd have given her the moon itself if he could, and an ocean of wildflowers.

Promises. He could give her those. A promise to love her, to help her find peace of mind, a safe haven.

And moments like this, alone, where they could tend to each other, pleasure each other. Shut the world and all its troubles, its pressures and its demands away.

She washed him, and he her—inch by inch. Arousing, lingering, prolonging. Now the scent of honey and almond rising up, the slick, slippery slide of hands, of bodies, the quick catch of breath, the long, low sigh.

So when he braced her, when he filled her, there was moonlight and wildflowers, there were whispers and promises. And more.

There was, she thought as she surrendered, everything.

*   *   *

The sensation of contentment stayed with her as she stood in the kitchen, contemplating doing something interesting with potatoes—Brooks liked potatoes—to go with the steak and salad. She glanced, a little guiltily, at her computer as she poured wine for both of them.

'I should try again, now that we've had our break.'

'Give your big brain a little rest. Let's sit down a minute. I've got a couple updates for you.'

'Updates? Why didn't you already tell me?'

'You were involved when I first got home,' he reminded her. 'Then I was distracted by shower sex.'

He sat at the counter, and since she'd already poured it for him, picked up his second glass of lemonade.

'I guess we'll take them in order. I had a talk with Roland Babbett. The cameras I borrowed from you did the trick, caught him going into the Ozarks Suite using B-and-E tools to do it.'

'You arrested him?'

454

'In a manner of speaking. I have to say I liked the guy, once we got things aired and ironed out.'

He ran it through for her, but she didn't sit. Instead, she kept her hands busy scrubbing then quartering small red-skinned potatoes.

'You told him he frightened me.'

'I may have colored your reaction a little differently than the reality of it, but I figure your pride can handle it.'

'You . . . prevaricated so he'd feel some sympathy toward me and less curiosity about the cameras, the gun and so on.'

'I like "prevaricated." It's an important word, and classier than "lied." '

'You believed him, too, believe he'll just leave and not pursue his investigation.'

'I do. He's a family man at the base of it, Abigail, and with his wife expecting their third child, he doesn't want to risk his livelihood on this or go through the upset and pressures of a trial. His firm isn't going to want to deal with the publicity we could generate, especially as one of their operatives saw photos of the damage on the hotel. And over that, he doesn't like Blake or the boy.'

'But he works for them.'

'Roundabout, yeah. I work for them, roundabout, as I'm a public official. Doesn't mean I have to like them, either.'

'You're right, of course.'

'I made him a good deal, one he can live with. He can turn in his reports, fulfill the contract with the client, move on.'

'If there's no more danger from that quarter, the logic you used to contact the authorities now, to move forward with testifying, doesn't hold.'

He reached out to still her hands for a moment, to bring her eyes to his. 'It does if you consider that down the road something like this may happen again. If you consider you're never going to feel rooted here, the way I think we both want you to, until you finish this.'

'That's true, but perhaps we could delay, take more time to . . .' She trailed off when he said nothing, only looked at her. 'Delay is an excuse. It's fear, not courage.'

'I'm never going to question your courage, or criticize the way you've coped.'

'That means a great deal to me. I want it over, Brooks. I do. And having taken appreciable steps toward that end is frightening, but it's also a relief.'

'Then I hope you'll be relieved to know Captain Anson's in Chicago. He intends to contact Agent Garrison tonight.'

'He called you?'

'Late this afternoon, on the drop phone.'

'I'm grateful to him.' She began mincing garlic, her eyes trained on her hands, on the knife, as the pressure built in her chest. 'I hope she'll believe him.'

'You picked a smart, capable, honest woman.'

'Yes, I was very careful in my selection.'

'Anson's a smart, capable, honest man. We couldn't do better.'

'We both made logical choices. It's good it's happening quickly. Delay isn't sensible once decisions are made, so it's best it's moving forward quickly.'

She poured olive oil, spooned some Dijon mustard with it in a bowl. After a distracted moment, she added a splash of balsamic vinegar.

'Except for my part.'

'You'll get there.'

'I'm not confident of that at this point.'

'I am, so take some of mine.' He watched her spoon a little Worcestershire in the bowl, then some Italian dressing he knew she used primarily for marinades. In went the garlic, some pepper, a little chopped fresh basil.

'What're you doing there, Abigail?'

'I'm going to coat the potatoes with this and roast them. I'm making it up,' she added, as she began to whisk the mixture. 'It's science, and science keeps me grounded. Experimenting is satisfying when the results are pleasing. Even when they aren't, the process of the experiment is interesting.'

He couldn't take his eyes off her.

She whisked, sniffed, narrowed her own eyes, added a little something more.

Pretty as a picture, he thought, with her hair still a little damp from the shower and pulled back in a short, glossy brown ponytail. She'd put on a sleeveless shirt of quiet gray and jeans that rolled up into casual cuffs just above her knees.

One of her nines sat at easy reach on the counter by the back door.

Her face, those wide green eyes, stayed so sober, so serious, as she put the potatoes into a large bowl, poured the experimental mixture over them, reached for a wooden spoon.

'Marry me, Abigail.'

She dropped the spoon. Bert sauntered over to sniff at it politely.

'Well, that just popped out,' he said, when she just stared at him.

'You were joking.' She picked up the spoon, set

457

it in the sink, lifted another from a pottery sleeve. 'Because I'm cooking, and it's a domestic area.'

'I'm not joking. I'd figured to set the scene a lot better when I asked you. That moonlight you want, flowers, maybe some champagne. A picnic's what I had in mind. A moonlight picnic up at the spot you like with the view of the hills. But I'm sitting here, looking at you, and it just popped out.'

He came around the counter, took the spoon, set it aside so he could take both her hands. 'So marry me, Abigail.'

'You're not thinking clearly. This isn't something we can consider, much less discuss, particularly when my situation remains in flux.'

'Things are always in flux. Not this,' he added. 'I swear to you we'll end this, we'll fix this. But there's always going to be something. And I think now's the perfect time, before it's ended, before it's fixed, because we should be able to promise each other when things outside aren't perfect.'

'If it goes wrong—'

'Then it goes wrong. We don't.'

'Marriage . . .' She drew her hands free, used them to stir the coating on the potatoes. 'It's a civil contract broken at least half the time with another document. People enter into it promising forever, when in reality—'

'I'm promising you forever.'

'You can't *know*.'

'I believe.'

'You—you've just moved in. Just hung clothes in the closet.'

'Noticed that, did you?'

'Yes. We've known each other less than three months.' She got out a casserole—and busy, busy,

458

busy—scooped and poured the coated potatoes into it. 'We have a very difficult situation to address. If you feel strongly about the subject, and continue to feel strongly, I'd be willing to discuss our views on the matter at some more rational time.'

'Delay is an excuse.'

She slammed the casserole into the oven, whirled on him. 'You think it's clever to throw my own words back at me.'

'I think it's apt.'

'And why do you make me lose my temper? I don't like to lose my temper. Why don't you lose yours?'

'I don't mind getting pissed.' He shrugged, picked up his lemonade again. 'I'm not right at the moment. I'm more interested in the way you're twisting yourself into knots because I love you and I want to marry you.'

'I'm not twisting myself into knots. I've very clearly given you my opinion on marriage, and—'

'No, you very clearly gave me your mother's opinion.'

Very carefully, she picked up a cloth towel, wiped her hands. 'That was uncalled for.'

'I don't think so, and it wasn't said to hurt you. You're giving me cold logic and statistics. That's your mother's way.'

'I'm a scientist.'

'Yeah, you are. You're also a giving, caring woman. One who wants moonlight and wildflowers. Tell me what that part of you wants, what that part of you feels, not what your mother pushed into your head as long as she could.'

'How can this be so easy for you?'

'Because you're the one. Because I've never felt

for anyone what I feel for you. I want a lifetime with you, Abigail. I want a home with you, family with you. I want to make children with you, raise them with you. If you truly don't want any of that with me, I'll give you the best I've got, and hope you change your mind. I just need you to tell me you don't want it.'

'I *do* want it! But I . . .'

'But?'

'I don't know! How can anyone think when they feel so much?'

'You can. You've got that big brain to go along with that big heart. Marry me, Abigail.'

He was right, of course. She could think. She could think of what her life had been like without him, and what it would be if she shoved those feelings down and relied only on the flat chill of logic.

'I couldn't put my real name on a marriage license.'

He cocked his brows. 'Well, in that case, forget it.'

The laugh rushed out of her. 'I don't want to forget it. I want to say yes.'

'So say yes.'

'Yes.' She closed her eyes, felt dizzy with delight. 'Yes,' and threw her arms around him.

'This is right,' he murmured, turned his lips to her damp cheek. 'I'm the luckiest man in the world.' He drew her back to kiss her lips, her other cheek. 'My mother says that women cry when they're happy because they're so filled with the feeling they want to let it out, share it. And teardrops spread that happiness.'

'It feels true. I hope the potatoes turn out well.'

460

On a laugh, he dropped his brow to hers. 'You're thinking about the potatoes? Now?'

'Because you asked me to marry you when I was creating the recipe. If it comes out well, it'll be a very special one. We'll pass the story to our children.'

'If they suck, we can still pass the story on.'

'But we won't enjoy the potatoes.'

'Jesus, I really love you.' He squeezed her until she gasped.

'I never believed I would have this, any of this, and now I have so much. We're going to make a life together, and create a family. We're mates.' She stepped back, gripped his hands. 'And more. We're going to merge our lives. It's amazing that people do. They remain individuals, with their own makeup, and still they become and function as a single unit. Yours, mine, but also, and most powerfully, ours.'

'It's a good word, "ours." Let's use it a lot.'

'I should go out and pick our lettuce for our salad so we can have our dinner.'

'We's another good word. We'll go out.'

'I like that better.' She started to turn for the door, went still as her thoughts aligned. 'Mated. Merged.'

'If you want to mate and merge again, better turn down those potatoes.'

'Not piggybacked, not layered or attached. Integrated. Merged. Separate makeups—individual codes—but merged into one entity.'

'I don't think you're talking about us anymore.'

'It's the answer. A blended threat, yes, I'd tried that, but it has to be more—different than combining. It has to be *mated*. Why didn't I think

461

of it before? I can do this. I believe I can do this. I need to try something.'

'Have at it. I can handle dinner. Except I don't know when to take those potatoes out.'

'Oh.' She looked at the clock, calculated. 'Mix and turn them in another fifteen minutes. They should be done thirty minutes after that.'

Within an hour she'd recalculated, rewritten codes, restructured the algorithm. She ran preliminary tests, noted the areas she'd need to adjust or enhance.

When she pulled her mind out of the work, she had no idea where Brooks and Bert were, but saw Brooks had left the oven on warm.

She found them both on the back porch, Brooks with a book, Bert with a rawhide.

'I've made you wait for dinner.'

'Just gotta throw the steaks on. How'd it go?'

'It needs work, and it's far from perfect. Even when I complete it, I'll need to Romulanize it.'

'Do what to it?'

'Oh, it's a term I use in my programming language. The Romulans are a fictional alien race. From *Star Trek*. I enjoy *Star Trek*.'

'Every nerd does.'

The way he used the word 'nerd' struck like an endearment, and never failed to make her smile. 'I don't know if that's true, but I do. The Romulans had a cloaking device, one that made their starship invisible.'

'So you need to make your virus thing invisible. Romulanize it.'

'Yes. Disguising it as benign—like a Trojan horse, for instance—is an option, but cloaked is better. And it's the right way. It's *going* to work.'

'Then we have a lot to celebrate.'

They had sunset, and what Abigail thought of as their engagement dinner.

At moonrise, the phone in Brooks's pocket rang. 'That's the captain.'

Abigail put her hands in her lap, linked her fingers, squeezed them. She made herself breathe slowly as she listened to Brooks's end of the conversation and interpreted what Anson told him.

'He made contact,' she said, when Brooks ended the call.

'He did. She was skeptical, suspicious. I'd think less of her if she hadn't been. She checked his credentials, asked a lot of questions. Grilled him, basically. She knows your case. I expect every agent and marshal in Chicago does. He can't swear she believed he didn't know where you are, but there's not a lot she can do about that, as there's no connection or communication between you.'

'But they'll need me to come in. They'll want to interview me, interview Elizabeth Fitch, in person.'

'You're in control of that.' His eyes on hers, he laid a hand over her tensed ones. 'You go when you're ready. They talked over two hours, and agreed to meet tomorrow. We'll know more then.'

'She's contacted her superior by now.'

'Ten minutes after Anson left, she came out, got in her car. Again, he can't swear she didn't make the tail, but he followed her to the assistant director's house. Anson called to let us know right after she went inside. He's on the move. Didn't figure it'd be smart to sit on the house.'

'They know I'm still alive now. They know I'm *tvoi drug*.'

'Both of those things are in your favor from their

463

point of view.'

'Logically.' She breathed deep. 'There's no turning back now.'

'For either of us.'

'I want to work, at least another hour or two.'

'Okay, but don't push it too hard. We've got a barbecue tomorrow.'

'Oh, but—'

'It's easy, and it's normal, and it's a break I figure both of us can use. A couple hours away from all this.' He stroked a hand down her hair. 'It'll be fine, Abigail. Trust me. And we've got news. We're engaged.'

'Oh, God.'

On a laugh, he gave a tug on the hair he'd just stroked. 'My family's going to do handsprings, I expect. I've got to take care of getting you a ring,' he added.

'Shouldn't you wait to tell them? If something goes wrong . . .'

'We're going to make sure nothing does.' He kissed her lightly. 'Don't work too late.'

Work, she thought, when he left her alone. At least there she knew what she was doing, what she was up against. No turning back, she reminded herself, as she sat at her station. For either of them, from any of it.

And still she felt more confident at the prospect of taking on the Russian Mafia than she did attending a backyard barbecue.

27

She jolted out of the dream and into the dark.

Not gunfire, she realized, but thunder. Not an explosion but bursts of lightning.

Just a storm, she thought. Just wind and rain.

'Bad dream?' Brooks murmured, and reached through the dark for her hand.

'The storm woke me.' But she slid out of bed, restless with it, to walk to the window. Wanting the rush of cool air, she opened it wide, let the wind sweep over her skin, through her hair.

'I did dream.' Through another sizzle of lightning, she watched the whip and sway of trees. 'You asked before if I had nightmares or flashbacks. I didn't really answer. I don't often, as much as I did, and the dreams are more a replaying than a nightmare.'

'Isn't that the same thing?'

'I suppose it is, basically.'

She stood where she was, the wind a gush of cool, the sky a black egg cracked by jagged snaps of lightning.

He waited for her to tell him, she knew. He owned such patience, but unlike her mother's, his offered kindness.

'I'm in my bedroom at the safe house. It's my birthday. I'm happy. I've just put on the earrings and the sweater John and Terry gave me as gifts. And in the dream I think, as I did then, how pretty they are. I think I'll wear them, for the good, strong feelings they give me, when I testify. Then I hear the gunshots.'

She left the window wide as she turned around to see him sitting up in bed, watching her.

Kindness, she thought again. She hoped she never took his innate kindness for granted.

'It happens very slowly in the dream, though it didn't happen slowly. I remember everything, every detail, every sound, every movement. If I had the skill, I could draw it, scene by scene, and replay it like an animated film.'

'It's hard on you to remember that clearly.'

'I . . .' She hadn't thought of that. 'I suppose it is. It was storming, like tonight. Thunder, lightning, wind, rain. The first shot startled me. Made my pulse skip, but I didn't fully believe it was a gunshot. Then the others, and there could be no mistake. I'm very frightened, very unsure, but I rush out to find John. But in this dream tonight, it wasn't John who pushed me back into the bedroom, who stumbled in behind me, already dying, blood running out of him, soaking the shirt I pressed to the wound. It wasn't John. It was you.'

'It's not hard to figure out.' She could see him in a snap of lightning, too, his eyes clear and calm on hers. 'Not hard to put in its place.'

'No, it's not. Stress, emotions, my going over and over all those events. What I felt for John and Terry, but particularly John, was a kind of love. I think, now that I understand such things better, I had a crush on him. Innocent, nonsexual, but powerful in its way. He swore to protect me, and I trusted him to do so. He had a badge, a weapon, a duty, as you do.'

She walked toward the bed but didn't sit. 'People say, to someone they love: I'd die for you. They don't expect to, of course, have no plans to. They

466

may believe it, or mean it, or it may simply be an expression of devotion. But I know what it means now, I understand that impossible depth of emotion now. And I know you would die for me. You'd put my life before yours to protect me. And that terrifies me.'

He took her hands in his, and his were as steady as his eyes. 'He had no warning. He didn't know the enemy. We do. We're not walking into an ambush, Abigail. We're setting one.'

'Yes.' Enough, she told herself. Enough. 'I want you to know, if you're hurt during the ambush, I'll be very disappointed.'

She surprised a laugh out of him. 'What if it's just a flesh wound?' He caught her hand, tugged her down.

'Very disappointed.' She turned to him, closed her eyes. 'And I won't be sympathetic.'

'You're a tough woman with hard lines. I guess I'll have to avoid flesh wounds.'

'That's for the best.'

She relaxed against him, listened to the storm blow its way west.

*   *   *

In the morning, with the sky clear and blue, and the temperatures rising, she worked for another hour.

'You need to give that a rest,' Brooks told her.

'Yes. I need to fine-tune. It's close, but not perfect. I don't want to do anything else until I consider a few options. I'm checking something else now. Unrelated.'

'I checked in with Anson. He's meeting Garrison and Assistant Director Cabot in about ninety

467

minutes.'

'I estimate I'll need another day on the program.' She glanced back briefly. 'I can't divulge to the authorities what I plan to do. It's illegal.'

'I got that much. Why don't you divulge it to me?'

'I'd rather wait until I've finished it, when I'm sure I can do what I hope to do.' She started to say more, then shook her head. 'It can wait. I'm not sure of the proper dress for this afternoon or—' She broke off, horrified, spun around in her chair. 'Why didn't you *tell* me?'

'What?' Her sudden and passionate distress had him bobbling the bowl of cereal he'd just poured. 'Tell you what?'

'I need to take a covered dish to your mother's. You know very well I'm not familiar with the rules. You should have told me.'

'There aren't any rules. It's just—'

'It says right here.' She jabbed a finger at her screen. 'Guests often bring a covered dish, perhaps a personal specialty.'

'Where does it say that?'

'On this site. I'm researching barbecue etiquette.'

'Jesus Christ.' Torn between amusement and absolute wonder, he dumped milk in the bowl. 'It's just a get-together, not a formal deal with etiquette. I picked up extra beer to take over. We'll grab a bottle of wine.'

'I have to make something, right away.' She flew into the kitchen, began searching her refrigerator, her cupboards.

He stood, watching her and shoveling in cereal. 'Abigail, chill it some. You don't need to make anything. There'll be plenty of food.'

'That's not the point! Orzo. I have everything I need to make orzo.'

'Okay, but what is the point?'

'Taking food in a covered dish I've prepared myself is a courtesy, and a sign of appreciation. If I hadn't checked, I wouldn't have known, because you didn't tell me.' She put a pot of water on the stove, added salt.

'I should have my ass whipped.'

'You think it's amusing.' She gathered sun-dried tomatoes, olive oil, black olives. 'I may not know precisely how this sort of thing functions, but I understand perfectly well your family's opinion of me will be important.'

'My mother and sisters already like you.'

'They may tend in that direction, until I rudely attend the barbecue without a covered dish. Just go out and pick a small head of radicchio out of the garden.'

'I'd be happy to, but I don't know what it looks like.'

She spared him a fulminating glance before storming out to pick it herself.

That sure took her mind off illegal computer viruses and stepping into the arms of the feds, he thought. And since she was on a tear, he thought it might be wise to stay out of her way for a couple of hours. When she stormed back in, he made a mental note that radicchio was the purple leafy stuff, in case it came up again.

'I need to go into the station for a couple hours,' he began.

'Good. Go away.'

'Need anything? I can pick whatever up on the way back.'

469

'I have everything.'

'I'll see you later, then.' Brooks rolled his eyes at Bert on his way out as if to say, Good luck dealing with her.

He'd barely gotten out the door when his phone rang.

'Gleason.'

'Hey, Chief. There's a little to-do over at Hillside Baptist,' Ash told him.

'I don't handle to-dos on my day off.'

'Well, it's a to-do with Mr. Blake and the Conroys, so I thought you might want in on it.'

'Hell. I'm rolling now.' He jumped in the car, backed it up with the phone at his ear. 'What level of to-do?'

'Shouted accusations and bitter insults, with a high probability of escalation. I'm rolling, too.'

'If you get there ahead of me, you start heading off that escalation.'

He thought, Hell—and hit the sirens and the gas when he swung onto the main road.

It didn't take him long, and he pulled up nearly nose-to-nose with Ash as they came in from opposite directions.

'You shaved off your . . .' It couldn't rightfully be called a beard, Brooks considered. 'Face hair.'

'Yeah, it got too hot.'

'Uh-huh.'

As Brooks had judged, the to-do had already bumped up to a scene, and a scene was one finger jab away from a ruckus, so he decided to wait to rag on Ash about the haze he'd scraped off his face.

Lincoln Blake and Mick Conroy might've been at the center of it, but they were surrounded by plenty of people in their Sunday best, lathered up

470

and taking sides on the newly mowed green slope in front of the red-brick church.

Even the Reverend Goode, holy book still in his hand, had gone beet-red straight back into the sweep of his snowy hair.

'Let's simmer down,' Brooks called out.

Some of the voices stilled; some of the chest bumpers eased back as Brooks moved through.

Blake had brought his stone-faced assistant, and Brooks had no doubt he was packing. Arkansas still had laws against guns in church—Christ knew for how long—but it was short odds some of those gathered on that green slope wore a weapon along with their tie and shined-up shoes.

Add guns, he thought, and a to-do could go from a scene to a ruckus to a bloodbath in a heartbeat.

'Y'all are standing in front of a church.' He led with disapproval, laced with a thin cover of disappointment. 'I expect most of you attended services this morning. I heard some language when I got here that's not fitting at such a time and place. Now, I'm going to ask y'all to show some respect.'

'It's Lincoln here started it.' Jill Harris folded her arms. 'Mick no sooner walked out the door than Lincoln got in his face.'

'A man's got a right to say his piece.' Mojean Parsins, Doyle's mother, squared off with the older woman. 'And you oughta keep that parrot nose of yours out of other people's business.'

'I could if you hadn'ta raised a hooligan.'

'Ladies.' Knowing he took his life in his hands—women were apt to leap and bite, and were as likely to be carrying as their men—Brooks stepped between them. 'It'd be best if you, and everybody else, went on home now.'

'You entrapped our boy, you and that Lowery woman. Lincoln told me just what you did. And the Conroys here, they're trying to make a killing off a bit of teenage mischief.'

Hilly Conroy elbowed her husband aside. From the look of her, Brooks decided she'd finally found her mad. 'Mojean Parsins, you know that's a lie. I've known you all your life, and I can see on your face you know that for a lie.'

'Don't you call me a liar! Your boy's run that hotel into the ground, and you're trying to make my boy pay for it.'

'You don't want to stack your son up against mine, Mojean. If you do, and you try spreading those lies, you'll be sorry for it.'

'You go to hell.'

'That's enough.' Mojean's husband, Clint, stepped forward. 'That's enough, Mojean. We're going home.'

'You need to stand up for your boy!'

'Why? You've been standing in front of him his whole life. I apologize, Hilly, Mick, for the part I played in making Doyle the embarrassment he is. Mojean, I'm going down to the car, and I'm driving home. You can come or stay, that's up to you. If you stay, I won't be home when you get there.'

'Don't you talk to me that—'

But he turned, walked away.

'Clint!' After a quick, wide-eyed look around, she trotted after him.

'This has about worn me out,' Jill commented. 'I'm going to walk on home.'

'Why don't Hilly and I give you a ride, Ms. Harris?' Mick stepped forward, took her arm. 'I'm sorry about this, Brooks.'

472

'You just take Ms. Harris on home.'

'This isn't finished, Conroy.'

Mick sent Blake a cold stare with weariness around the edges. 'I'm telling you for the final time, I'll do no business with you. Stay away from me, my family and my properties. Keep your assistant and his like away from me, my family and my properties.'

'If you think you can squeeze more money out of me, you're mistaken. I made you a fair offer.'

'Go on home,' Brooks told Mick, then turned to Blake.

Here he didn't bother with disapproval or disappointment. He arrowed straight into disgust, and let it show.

'I'm going to be talking to Mr. and Mrs. Conroy later.'

'Getting your stories lined up.'

'I'll be talking to Reverend and Mrs. Goode as well. Do you want to imply your minister and his wife are liars, too? The fact is, my deputies and I will be talking to everybody who witnessed or had part in this business this morning. If I find there's been any level of harassment on your part, I'm going to advise the Conroys to file a restraining order against you and whoever you've been using to dog them. You won't like it. You'll like it less if one's filed and you cross the line of it.'

'You can't bully me.'

'You'd know all about bullying, so you know that's not what I'm doing. I'm outlining the situation. You may want to talk it over with your lawyers before you do anything you might regret. For now, I'm telling you to move along. Your wife looks upset, and embarrassed.'

'My wife is none of your business.'

'That's the truth. It will be my business if you cause another ruckus.'

'Lincoln.' His color down again, his voice calm, Reverend Goode stepped forward. 'I understand you're in turmoil. I'm here if you want to unburden yourself. But I must ask you to take Genny home. She looks ill. I must ask you not to come back to this house of God with an unchristian purpose. Go home now, Lincoln, and tend to your wife. I'll pray for you and your family.'

'Keep your prayers.' Blake strode away, leaving his assistant to help Genny down the slope toward the waiting car.

'You're going to need some strong prayers, Reverend.'

Goode sighed. 'We do the best we can do.'

*　　*　　*

She changed clothes three times. It was completely unlike her to worry about wardrobe unless it was for the purpose of establishing identity or blending in. Her research indicated that attire would be casual, unless specifically stated. But that could include a casual dress or skirt, neither of which she currently owned.

Now she felt she needed to acquire some.

If they succeeded—no, *when* they succeeded, as it did no harm to employ Brooks's positive thoughts—she'd find use for a more expansive and varied wardrobe.

Now she settled on dark blue capris and a red shirt and sandals she'd rarely worn and only bought in a weak moment. She spent some time with makeup, also rarely worn since she'd become Abigail, as blending and going unnoticed had been the goal. But she had a good hand with it, if she said so herself.

She'd use that hand if—*when*—she transformed to Elizabeth, to cooperate with the authorities and give testimony against the Volkovs.

As she glanced to the monitor to watch Brooks come home, she put on John's earrings, worn when she felt a need for confidence.

She went downstairs, found Brooks in the kitchen, scowling down at a can of Coke.

'Something happened.'

'Unrelated.' He popped the top, guzzled. 'There was a to-do edging toward ruckus down at the Hillside Baptist Church.'

'Organized religion has an unfortunate history of fostering violence.'

He just rubbed the cold can over his forehead. 'This wasn't about religion. Blake's been hassling the Conroys—and he took that to church this morning. He takes something that public, makes a fool of himself, he's lost control. He's not going to leave this alone. I'm going to have to talk to the Conroys about taking some legal steps to . . .'

He finally focused on her. 'You look really good.'

'I have on makeup. I thought it was appropriate.'

'Really good.' When he smiled, the anger and stress she'd seen in his eyes warmed away.

'How do you do that? Relax so quickly?'

'I'm taking a pretty woman to a barbecue, and it sure takes the edge off my bad mood. Where's the stuff you made?'

She took it, then a six-pack of beer, out of the refrigerator. 'If you feel you should follow through

475

on the problem now, I'm sure your family will understand.'

'You're not getting out of this so easy. Colorful,' he commented, as he picked up the bowl. 'Ready?'

'I suppose.' She clipped a leash on Bert. 'You could brief me on the areas of interest of people who'll be there. It would help me make conversation.'

'Believe me, making conversation won't be an issue.' He snagged the beer on the way out. 'As soon as we announce we're getting married, every woman there's going to be all over you about wedding plans.'

'We don't have any.'

'Take my word on it, honey, you will before the day's over.'

She considered that while she rode with the bowl on her lap and her dog sniffing at every inch of the back of the cruiser.

'They may not be pleased.'

'With what? You and me?' He flicked her a quick glance. 'They'll be pleased.'

'I don't think they would, if they knew the full extent of the situation.'

'I wish I could tell them to prove you wrong, but it's better if we don't.'

'You seem so calm. I've learned to be calm when something has to change, but this is different. It's hard to be calm, to wait for Captain Anson to call, to wonder what the authorities will say and do. To think about testifying, about being so close with the program.'

'Whatever happens, we're together. That keeps me calm.'

She couldn't claim to be. Her stomach jumped,

her heart kicked, and with each passing mile she had to fight to keep her nerves concealed. She tried to think of it as going into a new community, stepping out for the first time with fresh identification. Nerves plagued her each time, but she knew how to conceal them, how to blend so anyone who noticed her saw exactly what she wanted them to see.

It had worked for a dozen years. It had worked until Brooks. He'd seen something else, something more, but she thought of that now as a blessing. If he hadn't, she wouldn't have this chance at a genuine life.

And the genuine life she might have would include backyard barbecues.

When he parked, she thought she had herself fully under control.

'Relax,' he told her.

'Do I look tense?'

'No, but you are. I'll take that; you get Bert.'

He tucked the bowl under his arm, hefted the six-pack, and with her hand steady on the leash, they walked toward the house. Toward the music and voices, toward the scent of grilling meat.

She recognized three of the women—Brooks's mother and his two sisters, but not the other women, the men, the children. The thought of being thrust into the midst of so many strangers dried her throat and thickened her heartbeat.

Before she could get her bearings, Sunny set down a platter and hurried over. 'There you are.'

'I had a little business to deal with,' Brooks told her.

'I heard.' Sunny tied Abigail's tongue into knots with a quick, hard hug before she gave Bert a casual

477

rub. 'Don't you look pretty. And what's this?'

'Orzo,' Abigail managed. 'I hope it's appropriate with your menu.'

'Since the menu's a lot of this with more of that, it'll fit right in. And it's beautiful. Go on and put that on the table, Brooks, and get Abigail a drink. We've already got the margarita blender going overtime.'

'I'll fix you up,' he told Abigail. 'Be right back.'

'My girl Mya—you met Mya and Sybill—makes killer margaritas. Why don't you let Bert off the leash so he can play with Plato?'

Abigail crouched down as the dogs sniffed and wagged at each other. *'Ils sont amis. Amis,* Bert. *C'est tout.'*

'He's all right with kids running around?' Sunny qualified.

'Yes. He's very gentle, very patient. He wouldn't attack unless I gave him the command. Or I was being assaulted.'

'We'll be sure nobody assaults you. Come on and meet Mick and Hilly Conroy. They're old friends, and that's their son, Russ—Brooks's best pal, with his wife, Seline, and their toddler, CeeCee. They've had a spot of trouble,' Sunny continued as she walked. 'I'm hoping to cheer them up.'

'It's an unfortunate situation. Brooks is very concerned.'

'We all are. Here's Abigail,' Sunny announced, when they joined the group.

'About time.' The younger woman had smooth olive skin that set off the bright green eyes she used to assess Abigail. 'I was beginning to think Brooks made you up.'

'No. He didn't.' I did, Abigail thought.

'This is Seline, and her CeeCee, and our Russ. Russ's parents, our friends Mick and Hilly.'

'I've seen you around town a time or two,' Hilly said. 'It's nice to meet you finally.'

'Thank you. I'm very sorry about your hotel. It's a beautiful building.'

'It's good of you to say.' Hilly tipped her head to her husband's arm, as if seeking comfort. 'We'll have it all back and better than ever. Right, Mick?'

'Count on it. I heard the Blake boy gave you some trouble, too.'

'He wanted to give Brooks trouble, but he didn't succeed. He appears to be a very angry, very stupid person with violent tendencies. He should pay the consequences.'

'We can all drink to that,' Mya said, as she strode over with a margarita in each hand. 'Daddy snagged Brooks a minute, so I'm delivering your drink.'

'Oh, thank you. It looks . . . frothy.' She tried a sip, discovered the tequila ran strong and smooth through the froth. 'It's very good.'

'Packs a nice kick, doesn't it?' As she spoke, Sunny put an arm around Abigail's shoulders. 'You were right about Bert.'

Following the direction, Abigail looked to see Bert sitting cooperatively while the puppy danced around him, a long-legged girl hugged his neck and a towheaded boy stroked his back.

'He's very well behaved,' Abigail assured her. 'And I think he's enjoying the attention.'

'He's big as a horse,' Seline commented.

Abigail started to disagree. After all, the average horse would be considerably bigger. Then had to remind herself not to be so literal.

'His size should intimidate intruders.'

'Scare the crap out of them,' Russ commented. 'Now that we've got a second coming along, I'm talking Seline into a Lab.'

'Poodle.'

'Girlie dog.'

'We're girls.' She gave her daughter a kiss on the cheek. 'You're outnumbered.'

'This one might even things up.' He tapped her belly with his finger. 'A guy needs a *dog*, not a little French toy.'

'Poodles are smart.'

'They are a highly intelligent breed,' Abigail agreed. 'Only the border collie is thought to be more intelligent. They're agile and, if properly trained, very skilled and obedient.'

'See?'

'A Lab's a *dog*. They're smart,' Russ added, appealing to Abigail.

'Yes, of course. They're the most popular breed in this country, and in Great Britain. They make excellent assistance dogs. They're loyal, and most have a well-developed play drive. They're excellent with young children.'

'Young children.' He snagged CeeCee, made the girl laugh as he tossed her in the air. 'We've got one of those, getting another.'

'Poodles are good with kids.'

When Seline turned to Abigail, Sunny laughed. 'Now you've done it. These two will tag you as referee in this battle. I'm going to save you, show you the gardens. Food's going to be ready in a few minutes.'

'Maybe they should consider a Labradoodle,' Abigail murmured, as Sunny steered her away.

It wasn't so difficult, she realized. For about

480

twenty minutes, she walked and talked the gardens, talked with Brooks's family and friends, answered excited questions regarding Bert from wide-eyed children.

By the time everyone crowded around picnic tables, she felt more at ease. And relaxed further when, with the food now the focus, the attention shifted away from her.

A backyard barbecue had its points, she thought. A casual setting for socialization, a variety of food prepared by a variety of hands. It was a kind of ritual, she realized, and somewhat tribal, with adults helping to serve or feed or tend to the children, their own and those belonging to others, with the dogs nearby and—despite her wince of disapproval—enjoying the food scraps tossed their way.

And she liked the margaritas with their frothy kick.

'Having a good time?' Brooks asked her.

'I am. You were right.'

'Hold that thought.' He leaned in to kiss her, then picked up his beer. 'I think you'll all be interested,' he began, without raising his voice over the conversations crisscrossing the table, 'Abigail and I are getting married.'

And those conversations, every one, stopped cold.

'What did you say?' Mya demanded.

'It's what she said that matters.' He took Abigail's hand. 'And she said yes.'

'Oh my God, Brooks!' Mya's face went brilliant with her smile. She grabbed her husband's hand, squeezed it, then leaped up to rush around the table and hug Brooks from behind. 'Oh my God.'

481

Then it seemed everyone spoke at once, to Brooks, to her, to each other. She didn't know who to answer, or what to say. Her heartbeat thickened again as, beside her, Brooks looked at his mother, and she at him.

'Ma,' he said.

Sunny nodded, let out a long sigh, then pushed to her feet. He rose as she did, as she reached out, folded him into her. 'My baby,' she murmured, then closed her eyes. When she opened them again, she looked directly at Abigail, held out a hand.

Unsure, Abigail got to her feet. 'Mrs.—'

Sunny just shook her head, gripped Abigail's hand, pulled her into the fold. 'I'm going to cry, just half a minute,' Sunny told them. 'I'm entitled. Then I'm going in and getting that bottle of champagne we had left over from New Year's Eve so we can toast this proper.'

She held tight, tight, then slowly eased back to kiss Brooks on both cheeks. To Abigail's surprise, Sunny took her face in her hands, laid her lips on each of Abigail's cheeks in turn.

'I'm glad of this. I'm going to get that champagne.'

'She needs a minute.' Loren stood, walked to his son. 'She's happy, but she needs a minute.'

He embraced his son, then turned to embrace Abigail. 'Welcome to the family.' He laughed, then squeezed, lifting her to her toes.

Everyone talked at once again, and Abigail found herself whirled between hugs, stumbling over the answers to questions about when, where, what about her dress.

She heard the pop of the champagne cork over the questions, the laughter, the congratulations.

She let herself lean against Brooks, looked up, met his eyes.

Family, she thought.

She could have family, and understood, now that she could touch it, that she'd do anything, everything, to keep it.

28

Wedding plans. Abigail saw them as a small, shiny snowball rolled down a mountain. It grew, and grew, and grew, gathering weight, speed, mass, until it produced an immense, messy, thunderous avalanche.

In the sunstruck afternoon in the Gleasons' backyard, that avalanche roared over her.

'So, are you thinking next spring?' Mya asked her.

'Spring? I . . .'

'No.' Under the picnic table, Brooks patted Abigail's thigh. 'I'm not waiting that long.'

'Spoken like a man who doesn't have the first clue what goes into doing a wedding. We had ten months for Sybill and Jake's—and worked like dogs to get it all done in time.'

'But it was beautiful,' Sybill reminded her.

'I assumed we'd just go to the courthouse,' Abigail began, and was rewarded with stereo gasps from the women.

'Bite your tongue.' Mya pointed at her.

Sybill gave her sister an elbow in the ribs. 'You want something simple.'

'Yes. Very simple.' She looked at Brooks.

483

'Simple, sure. I'm betting there's a lot of simple between a run to the courthouse and the diamond jubilee forming in Mya's mind. I'm thinking in the fall—time enough for a little fuss, not enough time to rent a circus tent.'

'That's less than six months! Less than six months to find the perfect dress, book the right venue, interview caterers, photographers—'

'Photographers?' Abigail interrupted.

'Of course. You can't have your uncle Andy taking your wedding photos.'

'I don't have an uncle Andy.' And she'd always avoided photographs. Ilya had recognized her in New York, in a matter of seconds, on the street. If a photo of her somehow got online or in a newspaper it could—likely would—lead to discovery and disaster.

'Which leads back to the guest list. I can help with our side. I have the list from mine, and from Syb's. How many do you estimate from your side?'

'There's no one.'

'Oh, but—' Mya didn't need an elbow jab or the warning look from Brooks to cut herself off. She rolled on as if 'no one' was perfectly normal. 'That sure keeps it simple. What we need is a planning session, a ladies' lunch—because you don't have anything to do about it,' she told Brooks with a wide grin. 'Weddings flow from the bride.'

'Fine with me.'

'I know this wonderful bridal boutique down in Little Rock,' Mya continued.

'White Wedding,' Seline put it. 'It *is* wonderful. I found my dress there.'

'What we need to do is take a day, all us girls, go down there, check it out, have lunch, brainstorm.

484

I'll have to check my calendar.' Mya dug out her phone, began to swipe screens. 'Maybe we can set it up for next week.'

'Next week,' Abigail managed.

'You always were a bossypants.' Sunny sat back, sipping a margarita. 'That's one of the things we love about her, Abigail, but it takes some getting used to. Why don't you give her a few days, Mya, to get settled in to being engaged?'

'I am bossy.' Mya laughed and tossed back her hair when her husband snorted into his beer. 'And when we're sisters? I'll be even worse.'

'She means it,' Sybill said.

Abigail heard the quiet hum of the vibrating phone in Brooks's pocket. When she looked down, he eased it out, checked the display. 'Sorry, need to take this.' His eyes met hers briefly as he stood up, walked some distance off.

It seemed surreal. Mya continued to talk about wedding boutiques, flowers, and plated meals or buffets, and all the while Brooks talked to Anson about decisions that would put her life on the line.

Like the snowball again, she thought, rolling, rolling, growing, picking up weight and mass until it took the mountain with it.

No stopping it now, she reminded herself. She was committed to pushing through.

'Are you all right?' Sybill asked her.

'Yes. Yes, I'm fine. It's just a little overwhelming.'

'And it's just getting started.'

'It is.' Abigail glanced over at Brooks. 'It's started.'

Brooks walked back, laid a hand on her shoulder. 'Sorry, I have to take care of this.'

485

'Go be a cop, then,' Mya advised. 'We can drop Abigail home on our way.'

'Oh.' For an instant, Abigail's mind went blank. 'Thank you, but I really need to get home to some work I left pending.'

'Then I'll call you tomorrow, or e-mail you. E-mail might be better, I can send you some links. Just give me your—'

'Mya.' Sunny arched her eyebrows. 'What happened to those few days to settle?'

'All right, all right. I can't help it if I was born to plan and organize parties. You e-mail me when you're settled.' Grabbing a paper napkin, Mya wrote down her e-mail address.

Abigail had a feeling it would take more than a few days. 'I will. Thank you so much for the afternoon.'

'Abigail.' Sunny crossed to her, hugged her hard, and whispered, 'Don't worry. I'll run interference with Mya for a week or two.'

It took some time. Apparently, people didn't just say good-bye at a barbecue. They hugged, or stretched out a conversation, made future plans, played with the dog. Even called out and waved once you got as far as the car.

'Before you tell me what Captain Anson said, I want to say your family is . . .'

'Loud, pushy?'

'No. Well, yes, but that's not what I want to say. Affectionate. Naturally so. I understand you better now, for having spent the afternoon with them. Your mother . . . Don't feel sorry for me. I don't like it.'

'Okay.'

'Your mother put her arm around my shoulders.

It was just a careless gesture. I doubt she gave it a thought, and has done the same, countless times, to others. But when she did that, to me, I felt—I thought—So this is what a mother does. She touches you, or holds you, just because. For no important reason. And then I thought, If there are children, I want to learn to be the kind of mother who can touch or hold without thinking, and for no important reason. I hope I have the chance to do that.'

'You will.'

'Anson talked with the FBI.'

'For most of the day. His take is, initially, at least, they'd hoped to do an end run around him, get to you. But he stuck with the out-of-left-field contact. They were careful what they passed on to him, but he's dead sure they'll be doing some surveillance on Cosgrove and Keegan.'

'Does he think they believed my story?'

'You'd laid it out, step-by-step, right down to what John said to you. And now you've been this very valuable source over the last couple years. Why would you lie about Cosgrove and Keegan?'

'It wouldn't be logical.'

'No, it wouldn't. They want to talk to you in person. They want you to come in. They promise you protection.'

'They want to question me, to make certain I wasn't complicit in John's and Terry's deaths. If and when they're sure of that, they'll want me to agree to testify against Korotkii.'

'Yeah, and they're going to want more. You've got an inside track on the Volkovs, access to data that can, likely would, put a lot of the organization in prison, fracture the rest.'

487

'As long as the data comes from an anonymous source, the authorities can use it. Once it's known the data's been obtained by illegal means, they won't be able to.'

'No, they wouldn't. They may be able to find a little wiggle room.'

She'd considered this, all of this. 'I won't give them the process, even if they grant me immunity for the hacking. I need the process to take down the network. They can't do what I hope to do, not technically nor legally. I'll be exposed again unless I can break their network and siphon off their funds.'

'Siphon off . . . You have that kind of access to their money?'

'I can have, to a great deal of it. I've been considering where to funnel it once I'm ready to transfer funds from various accounts. I thought substantial anonymous donations to charities that feel most appropriate.'

He glanced away from the road, gave her a long look. 'You're going to clean them out.'

'Yes. I thought you understood. If they have what's approximately one hundred and fifty million in accounts to draw from, they can easily rebuild. And then there's the real estate, but I have some ideas on how to dispose of that.'

'Dispose.'

'Tax difficulties, a transfer of deeds—some property the authorities can and will simply confiscate, as they've been used for illegal purposes. But others are rather cleverly masked. They won't be when I'm finished. It's not enough to testify, Brooks,' she said, when he pulled up at her cabin. 'Not enough to put Korotkii, potentially Ilya, even Sergei, in prison. With their resources, their money, they'll regroup, rebuild—and they'll know I caused the trouble. I don't intend for them to know how their network was compromised. And I don't intend to tell the authorities. They couldn't sanction what I plan to do.'

She stepped out of the car, looked at him over the roof. 'I won't go into a safe house again. I won't let them know where I am, even if and when I agree to testify. I don't trust their protection. I trust myself, and you.'

'Okay.' He opened the door for the dog, then held out a hand for hers. 'We find a location in Chicago when that time comes. You and me? We're the only ones who know where it is. We'll stay there. For the meet, you pick a place. A hotel, I'd think, maybe in Virginia or Maryland, and you don't tell them the location until you're in.'

'That's very good. You can't be with me.'

'Yes, I can. As long as they don't see me.'

It stopped now, every bit of it stopped, unless he was with her through it.

'I figure you can get eyes and ears in the hotel room so I can follow—and so we have a record, if we ever need one.'

'I hadn't thought of that. I should have, as that would be best.'

'You think, I think—that's how it's done.'

She turned to him, let herself move into him. 'It has to happen fast, when it starts. Everything will have to happen quickly, and in proper order.'

She wouldn't take him from his family if things went wrong. She'd learned that, too, at a backyard barbecue.

'I need to finish the program. This is only partially done without it.'

'You work on that, and I'll start some research myself. I'll find us a location for the meet.'

'Virginia,' she said. 'Fairfax County. It's far enough from D.C., and less than an hour from a small regional airport in Maryland. I'll charter a plane.'

'Charter? No shit.'

'Perhaps you forgot you have a rich girlfriend.'

He laughed. 'I don't know how that slipped my mind.'

'If they want to back up the meeting, have me followed, we'd be able to lose them on those roads, and they'd most likely look at Dulles Airport, or Reagan National.'

'That's a plan.' He kissed her. 'Go play with worms.'

*　　　*　　　*

He stayed out of her way, for the most part. But, Jesus, after a couple hours on the computer, a man wanted a beer on a Sunday evening. And some chips, which he'd had to sneak in, as she didn't have a single item of junk food in the place.

When he walked into the kitchen, she sat, hands in her lap, staring at her screen. He eased open the fridge, took out a beer, glanced her way, eased open the cabinet where he'd stashed the chips. Sour-cream-and-onion.

And she turned.

'I'll be out of your way in a second.'

'I did it.'

He studied her face, set the beer aside. 'You finished the program.'

'Yes. It works. Theoretically. I've tested it several

times. I can't actually run it into the network until it's time, so I can't be absolutely certain. But I am. Certain it will work.'

He grinned, came over, boosted her up by the elbows for a kiss. 'You're a genius.'

'Yes.'

'Then why don't you look happy?'

'I am. I'm . . . numb, I think. I believed I could do it, but when I did, I realized I hadn't really believed I could do it.' Because it ached a little, she pressed her fingers to her left temple. 'That doesn't make sense.'

'Yes, it does.'

'Brooks. I can take down their network, corrupt every file, every program. I can shut them down, no matter what operating system or computer any individual uses. I can do it, and, doing it immediately after I siphon the funds, they'll be ruined. Broken.'

Now she pressed her hand to her heart. 'And before I do that, I can give the authorities enough to shut down a string of operations, use that to prosecute other lieutenants and soldiers, until the Volkov *bratva* is in pieces they can never put back together.'

'Humpty Dumpty them.'

She let out a breathless laugh. 'Yes. Yes. I didn't really believe I could do it,' she murmured. 'If I had, I'd have done it before I agreed to testify.'

He kept his face blank. 'Do you want to step away from that?'

'You'd let me.' As he often did with her, she framed his face in her hands. 'I love you so much. You'd let me step away, even though it's against your code. But no, I won't. I can't. It's part of the

491

whole, part of who I want to be. Part of who you expect me to be.'

'I only expect you to be who you are.'

'I expect more now. I expect more of Elizabeth. I expect more of Abigail. And I want you to expect more of me now. My testimony, my data, the hacking, the supervirus. It's all one. When it's finished, Elizabeth can go with a clear conscience.'

She closed her eyes, then opened them, smiled into his. 'And Abigail can marry you with one. I want to marry you so much. I might even want to go to a wedding boutique.'

'Uh-oh.'

'I'm a little afraid of it, but I might.'

'*Now* you look happy.'

'I am. I'm very happy. As soon as we find a hotel, I could arrange for transportation. We could have your captain set up the meeting. We could start the next stage.'

'I've got the hotel. In Tysons Corner, Virginia. Middle-range, right off the highway.'

'I'd like to see the hotel's website, and a map of the area.'

'Figured you would. I've got them bookmarked on my laptop.'

'We could book the rooms, arrange the meeting for tomorrow or the day after. It's less time for the authorities to try to find me.'

'Day after. I need to rework the schedule so I'm covered.'

'That's better. I have to make arrangements for Bert.'

'My mother will take him.'

'Oh. But . . .' She hesitated, looked down at the dog. 'I thought a licensed kennel, with

492

professionals.'

'You're going to put him in jail?'

'A kennel isn't a jail.' Now she had two sets of hazel eyes staring at her. 'He did enjoy being over there this afternoon, but it seems like a lot to ask of your parents.'

'They'll love it. Plus, that's what family does. Get used to it. Go on and check out the hotel. I'll give her a call.'

'All right.'

Brooks pulled out his cell phone as Abigail left the kitchen. 'You owe me,' he said to Bert.

*   *   *

Everything in place, Abigail told herself. She stood in her safe room, carefully selecting what she'd need to take this next step.

She booked the hotel rooms under two different names, at two different times, from two different computers. Brooks would check in as Lucas Boman—the name of his first Little League coach. She'd create his ID the next day. Hers, which she'd give Anson to pass to the feds once she and Brooks were checked in, set up, would be Catherine Kingston, an ID she already had in her supply. She considered her collection of wigs, her supply of hair color.

'Going as a redhead?' Brooks commented, when she lifted a short, straight bob in golden red.

'My natural color tends toward auburn. I don't have a wig that matches my natural color.'

'Hold on.' Head angled, he studied her. 'You're a redhead?'

'Brown's more accurate, but with reddish tones.'

493

'Just want to mention I've seen the other area on you, and it's not brown with reddish tones.'

'It would be, but I'm thorough when I change appearance.'

'Interesting. Really interesting. Maybe you should've aimed for the CIA.'

'It didn't capture my interest. I think they'll expect me to alter my appearance somewhat for the meeting. This should be just enough, along with some slight changes with makeup, and some padding. Larger breasts.'

'You can hardly ever go wrong with larger breasts.'

'I believe my natural breasts are more than adequate.'

'Let's see.' He cupped them, considered. 'More than.'

'Obsession with breast size is as foolish as obsession with penis size.'

'I believe my natural penis is more than adequate.'

She laughed, turned toward the mirror.

'I guess you're not going to check to make sure.'

'Perhaps later.'

She put the wig on with such quick, skillful moves he knew she'd worn one often. 'It's a change.'

He preferred her longer hair, he thought, and the less studied style.

'Yes. I can work with this. I'll need to buy one closer to my natural color, a longer length I can style in several ways. I'll want to look like the photos they'd have of Elizabeth, even though they're dated. I can use contacts, change my eye color—just the tone of it—subtly. Fuller hips, larger breasts. A few shades deeper in skin tone with some

494

self-tanner. Yes, I can work with this,' she repeated.

She took the wig off, replaced it on its stand. 'Operatives in the CIA have to lie and deceive. It's necessary, I imagine, for the tasks they perform. I've done a lot of lying and deceiving for the last twelve years. I'd like to have a life where lying and deception aren't part of my every day. I can't put all the lies away, but . . .'

She turned to him. 'I'll have one person who knows the truth, who knows everything, whom I'll never lie to. That's a gift. You're a gift.'

'I've got one person who believes in me enough to tell me the truth, to trust me with everything. That's a gift, too.'

'Then we're both very lucky.' She crossed to him, took his hand. 'I think we should go to bed. I need to run a few tests to verify your penis is adequate.'

'Lucky for both of us I've always tested well.'

*   *   *

His cell phone rang at a quarter to two in the morning. Brooks did a half-roll to the side of the bed as he reached for it.

'Chief Gleason.'

'Hey there, Brooks, it's Lindy.'

'What's the problem, Lindy?'

'Well, that's what I need to talk about. I got Tybal here with me.'

'Shit.'

'Yeah, it's some shit, but not the kind you're thinking. You're going to want to hear what Ty has to say.'

Brooks shoved himself up to sit. 'Where are you?'

'Right now, we're in my truck about a half-mile from the Lowery place. Since your car isn't in town, I figured you're there.'

'That's like police work, Lindy. Why don't I meet both of you at your place?'

'Rather not do that under the shit we're talking about. It's going to be best if we come on over there, talk this out in private. People tend to see things in town, even at an hour like this. Maybe especially.'

'That's a point. Hold on.' He put his hand over the phone. 'I've got Lindy—from the diner?'

'Yes, I know who he is.'

'He's telling me he's with Tybal Crew, and they need to talk to me in private.'

'Here?'

'If it wasn't important, and didn't need to be private, Lindy wouldn't be calling me at two in the morning.'

'I'll get dressed.'

'I'll keep them downstairs, out of your way.'

'I think if someone needs to come here at this hour to talk to you, I should hear what they have to say.'

'All right, then.' He put the phone back to his ear. 'Is Ty sober?'

'He is now, or near enough.'

'Come on ahead.'

Shoving one hand through his hair, Brooks set the phone aside. 'I'm sorry about this.'

'Even days ago, I wouldn't have let anyone come here like this. But I don't feel nervous, not really. I feel more curious. Should I make coffee?'

'It wouldn't hurt my feelings.'

It pleased her to do it, to think that in her future

with Brooks, late-night calls, making coffee for people in trouble, would be part of the routine.

She hoped she'd make a good cop's wife.

Still, she was just as pleased to know that Bert, with orders to relax, lay in the corner of the kitchen. And she also took the precaution of turning her computer monitors to screen savers.

She wasn't quite sure how to address two men who visited in the middle of the night, but when she took coffee out to the living room, Brooks let them in the front door.

And Lindy, long gray braid dangling down the back of a faded Grateful Dead T-shirt, led the way.

'Ma'am.' He bobbed his head. 'I sure do apologize for disturbing you this time of night.' Then slapped a backfist into Tybal's gut.

'Yes, ma'am,' Tybal responded. 'Sorry to put you out.'

'I'm sure you have good reasons.'

'Damn well better,' Brooks muttered. 'Jesus, Ty, you're sweating Rebel Yell.'

'I'm sorry about that.' The tips of his ears went pink as he dipped his head. 'There's extenuating circumstances. I got my sixty-day chip, and now I gotta start over.'

'Everybody takes a slide, Ty,' Lindy told him. 'Your first day starts now.'

'I've been going to meetings.' Ty shuffled his feet and looked to Abigail like a scruffy, shamefaced bear. 'Lindy's my sponsor. I called him. I know how I shoulda called him before I took the drink, but I called him.'

'Okay. Okay, sit down, the pair of you,' Brooks ordered. 'And tell me what the hell you're doing here at two in the damn morning.'

'The thing about it is, Brooks, I'm supposed to kill you.' Ty wrung his ham-sized hands. 'I ain't gonna.'

'I'm relieved to hear it. Sit the hell down.'

'I didn't know what to do.' Ty sat on the couch, hung his head. 'Once I started thinking past the whiskey, I still didn't know. So I called Lindy, and he got me sobered up some, talked it all through with me. And he said how we needed to come tell you. Maybe Lindy could tell you some. I don't know how to start.'

'Drink some coffee, Ty, and I'll get it rolling for you. Seems like Lincoln Blake's wife left him.'

'When?' Brooks frowned as he picked up his own coffee. 'I just saw her this morning.'

'At the church, yeah. I heard about that, expect most everybody has by now. That's what did it, to my way of thinking. What I hear is after they got home, she just packed up a couple suitcases and walked out. Ms. Harris's granddaughter Carly was out and about, saw her putting the suitcases in the car and asked if she was going on a trip. Ms. Blake says, just as calm as you please, how she's leaving her husband and never coming back. Just got into the car and drove off. Seems like he holed up in his study the rest of the day.'

'That can't have set well,' Brooks commented. 'Blake's pride already took a hard hit this morning.'

'Earned it, didn't he? Anyways, Birdie Spitzer does some for them, and isn't one for gossip, be why she's hung on to the job, you ask me. She told me herself. I guess this was too juicy a grape not to squeeze some. Said there was some hollering, but there's some hollering per usual in that house, from him, anyhow. Then the missus left, and he shut himself up. Birdie knocked on the door sometime later, to see if he wanted his supper, and he yelled out for her to get the hell out of his house and not come back.'

'Blake fired Birdie?' Surprised, Brooks raised his eyebrows. 'She's worked in that house for twenty years.'

'Twenty-four, she says, come August. Guess that's another reason she carried the tale to the diner. She doesn't know if she's got a job or not, doesn't know as she wants it, should he expect her back, even so.'

'Now he's alone,' Abigail said quietly. 'I'm sorry. I shouldn't interrupt.'

'That's all right, and you got the truth of it. He's alone in that big house with his son in a cell and his wife gone. Speculating, I'd say he sat and brooded some on that, and came to the conclusion the reason for his situation rested right here on Brooks.'

'That's an inaccurate conclusion based on faulty criteria,' she began. 'Mr. Blake's conclusion, I mean, not yours.'

'Yes, ma'am.' Lindy grinned. 'That's a pretty way of saying he's full of shit, if you don't mind plain speaking.'

'No, I don't. Yes, he's full of shit.'

Brooks took a sip of coffee, shifted his attention to Ty. 'How much did he pay you to kill me, Ty?'

'Oh, well, God,' Abigail managed, and surged to her feet.

'Relax, honey, Ty isn't going to hurt anybody. Are you, Ty?'

'No, sir. No, ma'am. I come to tell you. Lindy said that was best, so here I am.'

499

'Tell me what happened with Blake.'

'Okay. See, he called me out there, to the house. I ain't never been in there, and it's sure something. Like out of a movie. I thought maybe he had some work for me, and I could sure use it. He had me come right into that study of his, and sit right down in this big leather chair. Offered me a drink. I said no, thanks. But he just poured it, set it there beside me. My brand, too. I got a weakness, Brooks.'

'I know it.'

'But I haven't had one drop since you arrested me, God's truth, not till tonight. I was kinda nervous, sitting there in that fancy house. He kept saying how one drink wouldn't hurt me. I was a man, wasn't I? I didn't take it.'

'All right, Ty.'

'But he kept saying it, and saying how he had some work, but he didn't hire pussies, and what was that word I told you, Lindy?'

'Eunuchs. Fucker—sorry, more plain speaking.'

'I agree with your opinion,' Abigail told him, then looked at Ty. 'He tied your weakness to your manhood, and tied both to your desire for work. It was cruel and manipulative.'

'It made me mad, but it felt true when he said it. How you tried to make me feel less of a man, Brooks, and how you humiliated me, and castrated—he said you'd castrated me, and it made me feel bad. Mad, too. And that glass of Rebel Yell was right there. I only meant to have the one, just to prove I could. But I had another, and I guess another after that.'

Ty's eyes filled, and when he lowered his head, his shoulders shook.

Abigail rose, left the room.

500

'I just kept drinking, 'cause the glass was right there, and it never seemed empty. I'm an alcoholic, and I know I can't have one drink and not take another.'

Carrying a tray of cookies, Abigail came back in. She set the plate on the table.

As he watched her take one, pass it to a teary Tybal, Brooks thought he loved her more than breath.

'He was cruel to you,' she said. 'He should be ashamed of what he did to you.'

'I kept drinking, and getting mad. He kept talking about what Brooks'd done, making me look weak and gutless in front of my own wife, how he was trying to run this town into the ground. Look how Brooks'd framed his son. Something had to be done about it.

'He kept talking, and I kept drinking. He said what was needed was somebody with guts and balls. He asked if I had guts, if I had balls. Goddamn right I do, that's what I said. Maybe I'd just go kick your ass, Brooks.'

Ty shook his head, hung it again. 'I've been going to meetings, and I've been going to group. I'm getting to understand when I've been drinking I just want to go beat hell out of something. I hurt Missy 'cause of it. And between what he said and the drink, I was wound up good and proper. It seemed like a good thing when he said how ass kicking wasn't enough. It had to be permanent. You'd killed my manhood, that's what you'd done. The only way to get it back was to kill you. Since he'd be grateful, he'd give me five thousand dollars. Like a reward, he said. He gave me half of it there and then.'

501

'He gave you money?' Brooks asked him.

'I took it, too. I'm ashamed to say, it was cash money and I took it. But I didn't keep it. Lindy's got it. What he said—Mr. Blake said—to do was go on home, get my gun. How I oughta wait till after dark, sit on out here, on the road. Then I oughta call you up, tell you there was trouble. And when you drove out, I'd just shoot you. I went home to get my gun. Missy wasn't there, as she's over to her sister's. I got my rifle, loaded it up, too, and I started thinking why the hell wasn't Missy home. Started thinking she'd earned herself a couple good smacks. I don't know how to explain, but I heard myself thinking those things, and it made me sick. It made me scared. I called Lindy, and he came over.'

'You did the right thing, Ty.'

'No, I didn't. I took the drink. I took the money.'

'And you called Lindy.'

'You have an illness, Mr. Crew,' Abigail said. 'He exploited your illness, used it against you.'

'Lindy said the same, thank you, ma'am. I'm ashamed to tell Missy. She's still some pissed at you, Brooks, but she's glad I'm not drinking. Things are better with us, and she knows it. She'll be more pissed if you put me in jail. Lindy said you wouldn't.'

'Lindy's right. I'm going to need the money, Lindy.'

'It's locked up in my truck.'

'And I'm going to need you to come in, make an official statement, Ty.'

'Missy's going to be pissed.'

'I think she might be a little pissed about the drinking, but when she hears it all, start to finish? I think she's going to be proud of you.'

502

'You think so?'

'I do. I'm proud of you. I'm glad you didn't try to kill me.'

'So'm I. What're you going to do, Brooks?'

'I'm going to put all this together, all right and tight, then I'm going to go arrest Blake for solicitation of murder for hire of a police officer.'

29

The next step, Abigail thought, when she got home from taking Bert to Sunny. It felt strange, and a little sad, she realized, to walk into the house without Bert. It's just for a short time, she reminded herself. A quick trip—that changed everything.

When Brooks came home, they'd drive to the airport, take the private plane to Virginia, check into their two rooms. She'd have plenty of time to set up the cameras and video feed.

Plenty of time to obsess, worry, overthink, if she let herself.

So she wouldn't. She focused on the task at hand and began to transform herself into Catherine Kingston.

When Brooks arrived, he called out, 'Where's my woman?' and made her smile.

She was someone's woman.

'I'm upstairs. Is everything all right?'

'As it can be. Blake's got his lawyers scrambling, and I expect a deal's coming along. He might even slip out of this, seeing as Ty was admittedly impaired, but even so, he'll be done in this town. I don't expect . . .' He trailed off as he got to the

503

doorway and saw her.

'I repeat, "Where's my woman?"'

'It's a good job,' she decided, studying herself in the mirror.

The hairstyle and the careful makeup sharpened the angle of her jaw. Contacts darkened the green of her eyes. The careful padding transformed her from slim to curvy.

'They'll probably ask the hotel for any security feeds, once they know the hotel. We'll be in by then, but they'll run them to see when I checked in, and if I came alone. That's the reason we take separate cabs from the airport, have different check-in times.'

'You look taller.' Eyeing her, he walked over, kissed her. 'Definitely taller.'

'I have lifts in my shoes. Just an inch, but it adds to the illusion. If any of this leaks to one of Volkov's moles, they shouldn't be able to match me. Abigail's not in the system, and that'll make it very hard to connect Catherine Kingston or Elizabeth Fitch to Abigail Lowery. I'm ready whenever you are.'

'I'll get the bags.'

He'd never flown private, and decided he could get used to it. No lines, no delays, no crowds, and the flight itself smooth and quiet.

And he liked the wide leather chairs positioned so he could face Abigail—or Catherine, he supposed—and the way the light played over her face as they winged north.

'They've started a fresh file on Cosgrove and Keegan,' Abigail told him, as she worked her laptop. 'They've applied for warrants to monitor their electronics and communications. They may

504

find something. Cosgrove especially tends to be careless. He gambles,' she added, 'both online and in casinos.'

'How's he do?'

'He loses more than he wins, from what I've gathered through his finances, and his gambling pattern, it was the gambling—and the losses—that allowed the Volkovs to pressure him into working for them while I was under protection.'

'Gambling problem,' Brooks speculated. 'And he caves when pressured. How would he respond to an anonymous source claiming to have information about his connection to the Volkovs?'

She glanced up, tipped down the large framed sunglasses she'd added to her illusion. 'That's an interesting question.'

'If he folds under pressure, blackmail might push him into making a mistake.'

'He's not as smart as Keegan, which is why he hasn't moved up the ranks as smoothly, I believe—in the marshals or the Volkov organization. I calculated the Volkovs would have eliminated him by now, but apparently he's seen as having some value.'

'Have you ever done any fishing?' Brooks asked her.

'No. It appears like a tedious pastime or occupation. I don't understand what fishing has to do with Cosgrove or the Volkovs.'

He pointed at her. 'First, I'm going to take you fishing sometime, and you'll see the difference between restful and tedious. Second, sometimes you hook a little fish and it can lead to a bigger catch.'

'I don't think . . . oh. It's a metaphor. Cosgrove is

505

the little fish.'

'There you go. Hooking him might be worth a try.'

'Yes, it might. Greed responds to greed, and his primary motivation is money. A threat, something with just enough information that proves the source has evidence. And if he uses his electronics or phones to communicate, they'd have enough to question him.'

'Which could lead to that bigger fish. And it'd add more weight to your testimony.' He held out the bag of pretzels he opened, but Abigail shook her head. 'What's your bait?'

'Because you need bait to hook even a little fish.'

With a nod, he bit into a pretzel. 'Wait till you drown your first worm.'

'I don't even like the sound of that. However, there was a woman in witness protection after testifying against her former boyfriend, a low-level gangster involved with the Volkovs' prostitution ring in Chicago. She was found raped and beaten to death in Akron, Ohio, three months after the conviction.'

'Was Cosgrove her handler?'

'No, he wasn't assigned to her, but everything I was able to gather at the time pointed to his being the one to pass her information on to his Volkov contact. I know enough to compose a believable and threatening message.'

'Another pebble in the river.'

'What river? The one with the fish?'

Laughing, he gave her foot a bump with his. 'Could be, except if we were sticking with that metaphor, you don't want to be tossing any pebbles. Might scare those fish away.'

'I'm confused.'

'In this metaphorical river, we toss the pebbles because we want a lot of ripples.'

'Oh. A pebble, then.' She considered this for a moment, then began to compose.

Anya Rinki testifies against Dimitri Bardov. July 8, 2008. Enters the Witness Protection Program. New ID: Sasha Simka. Transferred to Akron, Ohio; employed as sales clerk at Monique's Boutique.

Case assigned to Deputy U.S. Marshal Robyn Treacher. Case files accessed by William Cosgrove October 12 and 14, 2008—no log-in or official request for same on record.

Copy of e-mail from personal account of William Cosgrove to account of Igor Bardov, brother of Dimitri, sent October 15, 2008, attached.

$15,000 deposited in account for William Dwyer a/k/a William Cosgrove on October 16, 2008.

Anya Rinki, a/k/a Sasha Simka, found raped and murdered October 19, 2008.

This data will be e-mailed to Administrator Wayne Powell within forty-eight hours unless you agree to a payment of $50,000. Details on the remittance of same to be given in the next communication.

'I think that's a nicely formed pebble,' she said, and turned the screen so Brooks could read it.

His smile spread slowly before he shifted his gaze

from the screen to her face. 'Good shape, good weight. You had all those dates in your head?'

'They're accurate.'

'What's the content of the e-mail you're going to attach?'

'It said: "Sasha Simka, Akron, 539 Eastwood, Apartment 3-B."'

The smile faded as Brooks eased back from the computer screen. 'So Cosgrove killed her for fifteen thousand.'

'Yes, not personally beating her to death doesn't make him any less responsible. I believe he'll respond to this. I believe he'll agree to pay. As soon as I know the surveillance is in place, I'll send it.'

'What did they pay him for you?'

His tone, hard and cold, had her taking a moment to shut down her laptop. 'He owed fifty thousand in gambling debts. Ilya bought—they're called markers—he bought Cosgrove's markers, then used the debt to threaten him.'

'And when you weren't . . . eliminated?'

'They forgave half, and required him to work off the rest. The fee, even though I lived, was considerably more than the fee for Anya Rinki. You'd have to conclude Korotkii is worth more to Sergei Volkov than Dimitri Bardov.'

He spoke quietly now, and with absolute certainly. 'They'll pay, Abigail, for what they did to you, to Anya Rinki, to all the others. I swear it to you.'

'I don't want you to make a vow over something you may not be able to control.'

His gaze never wavered from hers. 'Whatever it takes, however long it takes.'

Because it touched her, and frightened her a

little, she glanced out the window. 'We're starting our descent.'

'Nervous?'

'No.' She took a moment to be sure. 'No, I'm not nervous about what happens next. It's surprising, really, how completely I was convinced I could never do this. And now how completely I'm convinced I can, and must. And the difference is . . .' She took his hand, linked fingers. 'This. Just this.'

'This'—he tightened his grip—'is pretty damn important.'

*   *   *

She checked in a full thirty minutes before Brooks, so by the time he knocked on her door she'd already positioned the cameras and mics in the sitting area of what the hotel called an executive suite. In his room—across the hall and two doors down—she set up the monitors, linked the equipment.

In just over an hour, she'd set, interfaced and tested the equipment.

'As soon as we make contact, the feds will put men on the hotel,' Brooks told her.

'I know. But the sooner the better.' Nothing more to do, she determined. No more precautions to take. 'Let's make the call.'

She had to wait alone, but found it comforting to know he could watch her. So she worked while she waited, and, when she had confirmation on the warrant on Cosgrove's and Keegan's electronics, programmed a time lag of two hours—long enough for the surveillance to be in place—to send her blackmail note.

509

A pebble in the river, she thought, and looked directly at the camera and smiled.

As she monitored activities, she knew exactly when the plane carrying Assistant Director Gregory Cabot and Special Agent Elyse Garrison cleared for takeoff to Dulles International.

'They're on their way now,' she said clearly, 'and should land at Dulles in about an hour and forty minutes.'

She checked her watch, calculated. 'I'd estimate they'll be in the hotel by ten. They may still opt to watch and wait until morning, but I think they'll come to me tonight, as it puts control in their hands, or they'd believe it would.'

She rose, wished she could open the curtains. But with the right equipment, the right angle from a neighboring building, they could watch her in the room.

'I think I'll order a meal. It would give them an opportunity to put an agent undercover as a room-service waiter, so they can get a visual of me and the room. The confirmation I'm here, alone, might be helpful.'

She ordered a salad, a large bottle of water, a pot of tea. Finding it oddly intimate, she continued a one-sided dialogue with Brooks as she switched the TV on, volume low, as she assumed someone alone in a hotel might do.

She checked her makeup, her wig—though she really wished she could remove both—and as an afterthought, rumpled the bed a little so it might look as if she'd stretched out with the television.

When the food arrived, she opened the door for the waiter, gestured toward the table in the sitting area.

He had dark hair, a compact build and what she thought of as quick eyes.

'Are you in town for business, miss?'

'Yes, I am.'

'I hope you have time for some fun while you're here. Enjoy your dinner,' he added, when she signed the bill. 'If you need anything, just pick up the phone.'

'I will. Thank you. In fact . . . perhaps you could arrange for more water, or coffee, if they prefer, when the assistant director and Special Agent Garrison arrive.'

'Excuse me?'

'Your shoes, your eyes and the weapon under the waiter's jacket. I hope you'd communicate to the assistant director and agent that I'm ready to speak with them tonight if that suits them.'

And that, she thought, telegraphed clearly that the control remained in *her* hands.

'It can wait until tomorrow if they prefer keeping me under surveillance longer, but I don't intend to go anywhere. It should save time to talk tonight. And thank you for bringing the meal. The salad looks very nice.'

He gave her a long look. 'Ma'am,' he said, and left her alone.

'That wasn't just impulse, and it wasn't showing off. Exactly. I felt if they understood I understand, we might move more smoothly through this process. The pebble dropped into the river while I was speaking to the FBI waiter,' she added. 'I think I'll eat. The salad does look nice.'

In his room, munching on some minibar nuts, Brooks just shook his head.

What a woman he had.

511

When she'd finished, she set the tray outside the door. Plenty of fingerprints, she mused, sufficient DNA as well. They could run her prints and save yet more time.

She sat, drinking her tea, monitoring her computer for alerts and thinking how much she wished to be home with Brooks, her dog, her gardens. She knew now, really knew, how lovely it was to wish for home.

When the knock came, she switched off the computer, rose, walked to the door to look out through the security peep at the lanky man and the athletically built woman.

'Yes?'

'Elizabeth Fitch?'

'Would you please hold your identification up so I can see it?' She knew their faces, of course, but it seemed foolish not to take this step. She opened the door. 'Please, come in.'

'Assistant Director Cabot.' He held out a hand.

'Yes, thank you for coming. And you, Special Agent Garrison. It's nice to meet you in person.'

'And you, Ms. Fitch.'

'Elizabeth, please, or Liz. We should sit down. If you'd like some coffee—'

'We were told you'd already offered.' Cabot smiled very slightly. 'It's on its way up. The agent you made is taking a lot of guff from his colleagues.'

'I'm sorry. I was expecting you'd send someone in if you had the opportunity. And I'm very observant.'

'You've managed to stay off the radar for a long time.'

'I wanted to stay alive.'

'And now?'

512

'I want to live. I've come to understand there's a difference.'

Cabot nodded. 'We'll want to record this meeting.'

'Yes, I'd prefer you did.'

'Set it up, Agent Garrison. I'll get that,' he said, at the knock on the door.

Garrison took a computer out of a case. 'I'd like to ask why you chose me as your contact.'

'Of course. You have an exemplary record. You come from a solid family base, and while you excelled in school, you also took time for extracurricular activities, formed lasting friendships. I concluded you were well rounded, intelligent and had a strong sense of right and wrong. Those were important qualities for my purposes. In addition, in studying your higher education and your record at Quantico, then in Chicago, I concluded that, while ambitious, you wished to succeed and advance on your own merits. You have a healthy respect for authority and the chain of command. You may shave the rules, but you respect them as a foundation for the system, and the system as a means to justice.'

'Wow.'

'I apologize, as some of my research on you included invasions of your privacy. I justified that by the desire to serve as a source on the Volkov organization. The ends justify the means. That's often no more than an excuse for doing the wrong thing, but in this case, at that time, I believed it was my only viable option.

'Would you like me to pour the coffee, Assistant Director?'

'I've got it.'

513

Abigail held her silence a moment as she took a self-evaluation. Nerves, yes, she admitted. Her pulse beat rapidly, but without the pressure of panic.

'I assume you verified my identity from prints on the room-service dishes.'

Again, Cabot nearly smiled. 'You assume correctly. Agent?'

'Yes, sir. We're set.'

'Will you state your name for the record?'

'I'm Elizabeth Fitch.'

'Ms. Fitch, you contacted the FBI, through a liaison, expressing a desire to give a statement regarding events that occurred in the summer and fall of 2000.'

'That's correct.'

'We have your written statement as provided, but again, for this record and in your own words, would you tell us about those events?'

'Yes. On June 3, 2000, I argued with my mother. This is important, as I had never to that point argued with her. My mother was—is still, I imagine—a dominant personality. I was a submissive one. But on that day I defied her wishes and her orders, and it set off the events that followed.'

As he listened to the retelling, Brooks's heart broke again for that young, desperate girl. She spoke carefully, but he knew her now. He knew those slight pauses when she struggled for composure, the subtle changes in inflection, in her breathing.

How many times would she have to say it all again? he wondered. To the prosecutors, to judge and jury. How many times would she have to relive

514

it all?

How many times would she have to start and stop, start and stop, as the listener interrupted with questions, with demands for clarification.

But she didn't waver.

'Marshals Cosgrove and Keegan both stated, and the preponderance of evidence supports those statements, that Marshal Norton was down when they entered the safe house for their shift, that they were fired upon and returned fire upon person or persons unknown. They were unable to access the second floor at that time. As Cosgrove was wounded, Keegan carried him out of the house. When he called for assistance, he observed an individual fleeing the scene. He was unable to determine the identity of the individual, as there was a rainstorm and visibility was impaired. At this time, the safe house exploded due to what was later discovered to be a deliberate sabotage of the gas furnace.'

'Yes.' Hoping she appeared calm, Abigail nodded at Cabot. 'That's an accurate synopsis of their statements. They lied.'

'It's your contention that two Deputy U.S. Marshals gave false reports?'

'It's my sworn statement that these two men, in collusion with the Volkov organization, killed Marshals Theresa Norton and John Barrow.'

'Ms. Fitch—'

'I'd like to finish. William Cosgrove and Steven Keegan, under the directive of the Volkov *bratva*, intended to kill me to prevent me from testifying against Yakov Korotkii and others. They rigged the explosion to cover themselves. It's my sworn statement that both these men continue on the

515

Volkov payroll.

'John Barrow died in my arms while trying to protect me. He gave his life for mine. He saved my life by telling me to run. If he hadn't, I would've died in that house.'

She rose, went to the open suitcase on the bed, took out a sealed bag.

'This is the sweater and the camisole Terry gave me for my birthday that evening. I went upstairs to put it on before Cosgrove and Keegan arrived. I was wearing it when I held John, bleeding from multiple gunshot wounds. This is his blood. It's John's blood.'

She paused when her voice broke, bore down hard.

She handed the bag to Garrison. 'John and Terry deserve justice, their families deserve the whole truth. It's taken me a long time to find the courage to tell that truth.'

'There isn't any concrete proof on the shooter from that day, but again, there is evidence that could be interpreted as a young girl, nerves stretched past the breaking point, who killed her protectors in an attempt to escape the situation.'

Abigail sat again, folded her hands in her lap. 'You don't believe that. You don't believe I could have attacked and killed two experienced marshals, wounded another, blown up a house, then escaped. It's certainly possible, but it's not logical.'

'John Barrow taught you how to handle and shoot a sidearm,' Garrison commented.

'Yes, and he taught me very well, considering the limited time we had. And yes, I asked for and received five thousand in cash from my trust,' she added, before Garrison could. 'I wanted the

516

security and the illusion of independence. I know the explosion damaged some evidence, but you would've been able to reconstruct. You would know Terry died in the kitchen, and John on the second floor. You would also know from their reports, and from the reports, interviews and statements from the Child Services representative assigned to me, that I exhibited no signs of that kind of stress.'

She took another moment before going on. 'If you've studied my background at all, if you know anything about my home life before that June, you'd understand that rather than stressed, I was, in fact, more content than I'd been in my life.'

'If Cosgrove and Keegan are responsible for the deaths of Marshals Norton and Barrow, they will be brought to justice. Your testimony in the murders of Alexi Gurevich and Julie Masters, and in the death of Deputy U.S. Marshals Norton and Barrow, is essential to the investigations. We'll need to place you in protective custody and transport you back to Chicago.'

'No.'

'Ms. Fitch, you're a material witness, and a suspect.'

'Suspect is stretching credulity, and we all know it. If you put me in protective custody, you're killing me. They will get to me, and through whoever you put in their way.'

'Elizabeth. Liz,' Garrison said, leaning forward. 'You've trusted me with key information that's led to arrests, to convictions. Trust me now. I'll personally take the lead in your protection.'

'I won't be responsible for your death, for your parents' grief. I promise you, if I live long enough I'll run again rather than testify. I'm good at hiding,

517

and you'll never have my testimony.'

'You have to believe we won't let anything happen to you.'

'No, I don't. Who else might you trust with my life? What about Agent Pickto?'

Garrison sat back. 'What about Pickto?'

'Special Agent Anthony Pickto, age thirty-eight, assigned to Chicago Bureau. Divorced, no children. His weakness is women. He enjoys them more when they're reluctant. He's funneled information on investigations in exchange for access to women the Volkovs bring to the States from Russia, then force into prostitution. They pay him, too, but that's secondary. He's digging for the FBI contact—you, Agent Garrison. He's getting closer. If he learns who's receiving the data that's led to these arrests, to these busts, you'll be taken. Questioned, tortured, raped. They'll threaten you with the torture and death of everyone you love, and perhaps will select one as an example to demonstrate how serious they are. When you're of no further use, they'll kill you. Agent Pickto reports to you, Assistant Director.'

'Yes,' Cabot confirmed, 'he does. You're making very serious accusations about an agent in good standing.'

'They're not accusations, they're facts. And only one of the reasons I won't put my life in your hands. I'll help you put these people away, help you break the Volkov organization, but I won't tell you where I am. If you don't know, you can't divulge the information under duress.' She reached into her pocket, took out a flash drive. 'Check the information I've correlated on Pickto, then ask yourself if, before reading it, checking it, you would have trusted my life, this agent's life, others under your command, others in the Marshals Service, to this man.

'You would never have found me, but I came to you. I'll give you everything you need, and all I'm asking is you let me live. Let Elizabeth Fitch live to help get justice for Julie and Terry and John. And when she's done, let her die.'

'I can't promise to do this your way. I have people to answer to.'

Impatience shimmered through. 'Do you think I'd have come to you if I didn't *know* you could authorize exactly what I'm asking? You have power, you have evidence, and considerable leverage. My way, and the Volkovs will be done in Chicago, in New York, New Jersey, Miami. You'll weed out agents and other law enforcement and judiciary officials who have worked for them—by choice or out of fear.'

No longer able to sit, pretend a calm she didn't feel, Abigail surged to her feet. 'I was sixteen, and yes, I had poor judgment. I was reckless. One night of my life, I broke the rules. But I don't deserve to die for it, any more than Julie did. If you take me in against my will, this will leak to the press. And they'll talk of that young girl, of twelve years in exile, in coming forward to offer help at great risk.'

'Is that a threat?'

'Yes, it's very much a threat. Your superiors wouldn't be pleased with the bad press, especially at a time they're working to break the Volkov *bratva*, especially when trusted FBI agents like Anthony Pickto are implicated. Perhaps explaining that to those you answer to will give you additional leverage.'

'Pause the recording, Agent Garrison.'

'Yes, sir.'

'I'm going to make a phone call.' With that, he strode out of the room.

Abigail sat again, folded her hands in her lap, cleared her throat. 'Ah, should I order more coffee?'

'No, thanks. I'm good. You play hardball, Liz.'

'I'm playing for my life.'

'Yeah. Pickto. You're sure?'

'I wouldn't impute someone's name, reputation and career otherwise.'

'Okay. He's been asking some questions. Nothing that bumped my radar, nothing out of line, but I've heard he's asked some questions about the last couple Volkov busts. And when I put those questions in this context, it bumps my radar, hard.'

'I'd have trusted him,' Garrison admitted.

'Of course.'

'You know, if he's ordered to bring you in, Cabot will have you locked down tight. I want you to know, if that happens, I *will* keep you safe.'

'If he takes me in, I'll get away, however tight he locks me down. I'll find a way. You'll never see or hear from me again.'

'I believe you,' Garrison murmured.

'I can be very resourceful.'

It took twenty minutes for Cabot to come back. He sat. 'I think we can work out a compromise.'

'Do you?'

'An elite two-man team, known only to me, to guard you in a location again known only by me.'

'And when they learn, and they will, you have the information, and they take your wife or one of your children, when they send you a hand or an ear, who

520

will you save?'

Cabot's fists balled on his knees. 'You think very little of our security.'

'I have your address, I know where your children go to school, where your wife works, where she prefers to shop. Do you think they can't access the same, won't use any means to access it when their organization is threatened?

'I'll cooperate. I'll speak with the prosecutors, with your superiors. I'll testify in court. But I won't go into a safe house again, and I won't go into witness protection once it's done. That's my price, and it's very little for the value I'm offering.'

'And if we move on this, push forward on this, and you run again?'

She reached over, picked up the bag holding the bloodstained sweater. 'Terry's sweater, John's blood. I've kept this for twelve years. Wherever I've gone, whoever I became, this was with me. I need to let it go, and at least some of the pain and guilt and grief. I can't until I do what I need to do for Julie, for John, for Terry. I'll keep in daily contact via computer. When it's announced I've been found, and I'll testify, they'll do everything they can to find out who knows where I am, who's protecting me. But they'll find nothing, because there won't be anything to find.

'And when I walk in the courtroom that day, it ends for them. It ends for all of us. That's the deal.'

When they left her, finally left her, she lay down on the bed.

'Will he keep his word?' She closed her eyes, imagined Brooks there with her instead of just watching. 'Will he? I'm so tired. I'm so glad you're here. Right here,' she said, and, fisting a hand, laid it on her heart.

Brooks watched her drift off, and thought if Cabot didn't keep his word there would be hell to pay. And he would exact the payment.

But for now he stood watch while she slept.

30

Brooks spotted the FBI shortly after he sat down for breakfast at the hotel's morning buffet. He barely glanced toward where Abigail sat, reading the newspaper at her single table. Casually scanning the room, he pretended to make and receive calls on his cell phone, just another busy man in transition. With the phone still at his ear, he headed out with his overnight bag.

And pulled the fire alarm on his way.

He paused, as any man might—surprised, mildly annoyed—and watched the crowd in the buffet area push away from tables, heard the noise level rise as people talked all at once.

She was good, Brooks observed. Abigail merged with the exiting crowd. As he zigzagged between her and the tailing agents, joining the people exiting, she nipped to the side and into a restroom. If he hadn't been watching for it, hadn't known the plan, he wouldn't have seen the move.

He slowed his pace a moment. 'Fire alarm,' he said into the phone. 'No, it won't hold me up. I'm heading out,' he added, as he fell in behind the agents. After he pushed the phone into his pocket, he pulled a ball cap out of his bag. Still moving, he put on sunglasses, stuffed the jacket he'd worn into

522

the buffet in the bag, pulled the strap of the bag long, then slid it crossways over his body.

They were looking for her now, Brooks noted, one of them doubling back, searching the crowd, aiming for the lobby and the main exit.

Less than two minutes after he'd pulled the alarm, she slipped out of the restroom, joined him. The long tail of her blond hair was pulled through a ball cap like his. She wore flip-flops and a pink hoodie, and had shed a good ten pounds.

They walked out together, hand in hand, then broke from the crowd and climbed into a cab.

'Dulles Airport,' Brooks told the driver, 'American Airlines.'

'Jeez, you think there's a real fire?' Abigail asked, with a hint of New York in her tone.

'Don't know, baby, but we're out of it now.'

At Dulles they got out at the American terminal, went inside, circled around, then exited to take another cab to the terminal for the private charter.

'Can't really blame the feds for wanting to tail you,' Brooks commented, once they were settled on board.

'No.'

'And you make a pretty hot blonde.'

She smiled a little, then turned her laptop toward herself. 'Cosgrove responded.'

'Already?' Brooks tilted his head.

I don't know who you are, but be aware you're attempting to blackmail a federal officer. This matter will be turned over for immediate investigation.

'Standard first-round bluff.'

'Yes,' Abigail agreed. 'I'm about to call it.' She glanced up. 'I'm a very good poker player, and it's ironic he's the one who taught me.'

Brooks watched the text come on-screen. 'The student becomes the master.'

Rudolf Yankivich was your Volkov connection on the incident. He is currently serving ten to fifteen in Joliet. I'm sure your commanding officer would be interested in this information. The payment has now increased to $75,000, and will continue to increase by $25,000 for each scoop of bullshit you serve. You now have thirty-seven hours.

'Scoop of bullshit?'

'Yes, I believe harsh language is appropriate at this time.'

'I'm so in love with you.'

The sentiment made her smile. 'I know how to say "bullshit" in several languages. I'll teach you.'

'Looking forward to it.'

She sent the e-mail, sighed.

'I can't wait to pick up Bert and go home.'

*   *   *

It could be like this—would be like this, she corrected—as she sat on the back porch with a glass of wine, the dog at her feet.

Peaceful, quiet, yes—but not solitary, not with Brooks sitting in the second chair, which he'd bought on the way home.

'Will I get used to it, do you think? Being one

person, being safe, being with you?'

'I hope you will, even to the point where you take it all for granted now and again.'

'I can't imagine that.' She reached over for his hand. 'It should happen quickly now.'

'We'll be ready.'

She sat for another moment, her hand in his, looking out over her thriving garden, the quiet woods. Just another soft evening, she thought, as spring drifted toward summer.

'I'm going to make dinner.'

'You don't have to bother. We can forage around for something.'

'I feel like cooking. Like routine. Like everyday.'

She saw understanding when he looked at her. 'Everyday sounds good.'

To her mind, no one who hadn't done without everyday could fully appreciate how precious it was.

She gathered what she needed, pleased when he came in to sit at the counter and talk to her while she worked. She chopped plum tomatoes and basil, minced some garlic, shredded some mozzarella, added some cracked pepper and poured olive oil over them to marinate. For fun she began to prepare a pretty tray of antipasti.

'I thought we could get another dog, a puppy, as company for Bert. You could name him, since I named Bert.'

'Two dogs, no waiting.' He considered. 'It'd have to be Ernie.'

'Why?'

He nipped one of the hot peppers off the tray. 'Bert and Ernie. Muppets? *Sesame Street*?'

'Oh. That's a children's program. Bert and Ernie are friends?'

525

'And possibly more, but since it's a kids' program, we'll stick with friends.'

'I named Bert for Albert Einstein.'

'I should've figured.'

'He is very smart.'

Her computer signaled.

'That's incoming mail,' she said, and stepped out of everyday.

She walked to the computer, leaned over and brought up the mail. 'It's Cosgrove.'

'He took the bait.'

Blackmail me, blackmail the Volkovs. You won't live to spend the money. Back off now, and live.

'He's tying himself to the Volkovs with this response. It's not concrete, of course, but it's a start.'

'Let me answer this one,' Brooks requested, and took a seat.

'Oh . . .' Then Abigail's uncertainty turned to a nod of approval. 'That's very good.'

Tell the Volkovs you're being blackmailed, you're a liability. They eliminate liabilities. Pay now, and live. Payment is now $100,000. You have twenty-nine hours.

'I'll route it.'

He gave her the seat, stood behind her, rubbing her shoulders, as she worked what he thought of as strange magic with the keyboard.

'Now he could call the bluff. He could let this go past the deadline, wait it out.'

'No, he won't.' Brooks leaned down, kissed the top of her head. 'He's shifted from using the law as a lever to using the Volkovs. He's sweating. His next response will demand a guarantee. How can he be sure we won't come back for more?'

'That's irrational.' Once the message was routed, she turned in the chair to look up at Brooks. 'It's all dishonest, it's extortion. Asking for a guarantee's not logical, and would cost another twenty-five thousand. He should either agree to the payment or ignore any other communications.'

'Side bet, ten bucks.'

'I'm sorry?'

'I have ten dollars that says he'll come back whining for a guarantee.'

Her brows drew together. 'You want to wager on his response? That doesn't seem appropriate.'

He grinned at her. 'Afraid to put your money where your mouth is?'

'That's a ridiculous expression, and no, I'm not. Ten dollars.'

He drew her to her feet, into his arms. Swayed into a dance.

'What are you doing?'

'Making sure we'll make a nice picture dancing at our wedding.'

'I'm a very good dancer.'

'Yes, you are.'

She laid her head on his shoulder, closed her eyes. 'It should feel strange, dancing with no music, making wagers, while we're orchestrating something so important.'

'Does it?'

'No, it really doesn't.' She opened her eyes in surprise when her computer signaled another incoming e-mail. 'So quick.'

'He's on the edge. Squeeze play.'

'I don't understand what that means.'

'Baseball. I'll explain later. Let's see what he has to say.'

How do I know you're not going to come back for more later? Let's work out a deal.

'That's a very foolish response,' Abigail complained.

'It cost you ten dollars. Keep it short. Say: "You don't. No deals. You're up to $125,000, clock ticking down."'

She studied him a moment: that slightly crooked nose, the hazel eyes—a wash of green over amber now—the shaggy black hair in need of a trim. 'I think you're very good at extortion.'

'Thanks, honey.'

'I'll put the pasta on while he considers. That's what he's doing now? Considering?'

'Sweating, pouring a drink, trying to figure out who's screwing with him.' Oh, yeah, Brooks thought, he could picture it. 'He's probably thinking about running. Not enough time to make running plans, so he'll pay, and start making them.'

At the counter, he popped an olive from the tray into his mouth, then topped off her wine. And when her back was turned, tossed a slice of pepperoni to Bert.

By the time she'd boiled the pasta, drained it, the signal came through.

Onetime payment. Come after more, I'll take my chances with the Volkovs. Spend it

528

fast, because I'm coming after you.

'Big talk.'

'You understand him very well,' Abigail noted.

'Part of the job. You have to understand bad guys to catch bad guys. Where were you figuring to have him wire the money?'

'I have an account set up. Once he's transferred the funds, I'll distribute it to a charity for children of fallen police officers.'

'That's commendable, and I don't like denying kids, but . . .'

'You have another recipient in mind?'

'Keegan. Can you transfer Cosgrove's payment to Keegan's account?'

'Oh.' Her face lit up as a woman's might when given rubies. 'Oh, that's *brilliant*.'

'I have my moments.'

'More than moments. It implicates both of them. It gives the FBI cause to bring them both in for questioning.'

'Honey, it fucks them both inside out.'

'Yes. It really does. And yes, I can do it. It'll take me a few minutes.'

'Take your time. Bert and I will go for a little walk while you work.'

He snagged a couple more slices of pepperoni on the way out—one for him, one for the dog. A nice evening for a stroll around, he thought, with time to check out the progress of the garden, think about what he might do around the place on his next day off.

'This is our place,' he said to the dog. 'She was meant to come here, and I was meant to find her here. I know what she'd say to that.' He laid a hand on Bert's head, rubbed lightly. 'But she's wrong.'

When Bert leaned against his leg, as he often did with Abigail, Brooks smiled. 'Yeah, we know what we know, don't we?'

As they circled around, he saw Abigail come to the door, smile.

'It's done. Dinner's ready.'

Look at her, he thought, standing there with a gun on her hip, a smile on her face and pasta on the table.

Oh, yeah, he knew what he knew.

'Come on, Bert. Let's go eat.'

*   *   *

Brooks spent a chunk of his morning—too big a chunk, in his opinion—meeting with the prosecutor on the Blake cases.

'The kid's crying for a deal.' Big John Simpson, slick as they came and with one eye on a political future, made himself at home in Brooks's office. Maybe a little too much at home.

'And you're giving him one?'

'Save the taxpayers' money. Let him plead guilty to assaulting an officer, resisting, the trespass. Got him locked on the vandalism at the hotel, the assaults there. All we give him is a buy on the deadly weapon. We'd never make attempted murder stick. He gets five to seven inside, with mandatory counseling.'

'And serves two and a half, maybe three.'

Big John crossed his ankles above his mirror-shined shoes. 'If he behaves himself, and meets the requirements. Can you live with that?'

'Does it matter?'

Big John lifted a shoulder, sipped at his coffee. 'I'm asking.'

No, they'd never make the attempted murder stick, Brooks admitted. A couple years inside would do one of two things, he calculated. It would either make Justin Blake into a halfway decent human being, or it would finish his ruination.

Either way, Bickford would be free of him for a couple years.

'I can live with it. What about his old man?'

'Big-city lawyers doing their big-city shuffle, but the fact is, we've got a lock there. We got the phone records proving he called Tybal Crew. Got three separate witnesses saw Crew's truck outside the house on the day in question. Got the cash money turned in, and Blake's fingerprints are on a number of the bills.'

He paused a moment, recrossed his ankles. 'He's claiming he hired Ty to do some work around the place, paid him in advance 'cause Ty needed the money.'

'*Kosseh sher.*'

'Say what?'

'Bullshit in Farsi.'

'Don't that beat all?' Big John let out a chuckle. 'Yeah, it's bullshit in any language. We can bring in a couple dozen witnesses who'd swear Blake never pays in advance, never pays cash, *always* gets a signed receipt. True enough Ty was pretty damn impaired by the end of it, but he hasn't changed his story by an inch. So.'

He shrugged, drank more coffee. 'If Lincoln Blake wants to push it to trial, it won't hurt my feelings. Make a nice splash. He's charged with solicitation of murder for hire of a police officer.

They're going to want to deal before it's done. Any way it's sliced, he'll do time.'

'I can live with that, too.'

'Good enough.' He unfolded his six-foot-six-inch frame. 'I'll make the deal with the boy's lawyer. You did good, clean work with both these arrests.'

'Good, clean work's the way it's supposed to be.'

'Supposed to and is aren't always the same. I'll be in touch.'

No, they weren't always the same, Brooks thought. But he'd like to get back to that good, clean work. Just that. He wanted the rest over and done, however intriguing parts of it were.

The everyday, Abigail called it. It surprised him how much he'd learned to value the everyday.

He stepped out of his office. There was Alma at dispatch, a pencil behind her ear, a pink tumbler of sweet tea at her elbow. Ash at his desk, brows knitted as he pecked away at the keyboard, Boyd's voice over the radio reporting a minor traffic accident off Rabbit Run at Mill's Head.

He'd take this, Brooks realized. Yeah, he'd take just this. Every day.

Abigail walked in.

He knew her, so he saw the tension, though she kept her face impassive.

Alma spotted her. 'Well, hey, there. I heard the news. I want to say best wishes to you, Abigail, as you're family now. You've got yourself a good man there.'

'Thank you. Yes, I do. A very good man. Hello, Deputy Hyderman.'

'Aw, it's Ash, ma'am. Nice to see you.'

'It's Abigail. It's Abigail now. I'm sorry to interrupt, but do you have a moment?' she asked

Brooks.

'Or two. Come on in.'

He took her hand, kept it after he closed the door to his office. 'What happened?'

'It's good, what happened.' The good made her a little breathless. 'Garrison contacted me. Her report was very brief, considering, but inclusive.'

'Abigail, spill it.'

'I'm—oh. Yes. They've picked up Cosgrove and Keegan. They're interrogating, and that may take some time. She didn't mention the blackmail, but I've followed some of the communications in-house, so to speak. Naturally, they believe Keegan blackmailed Cosgrove, and they'll use that to pressure each of them. More. More important. They've arrested Korotkii and Ilya Volkov. They've arrested Korotkii for the murders of Julie and Alexi, and Ilya as accessory after the fact.'

'Sit down, honey.'

'I can't. It's happening. It's actually happening. They've asked me to meet with the federal prosecutor and his team to prepare me for testifying.'

'When?'

'Right away. I have a plan.' She took both his hands now, held tight. 'I need you to trust me.'

'Tell me.'

*   *   *

On a bright July morning, one month and twelve years from the day she'd witnessed the murders, Elizabeth Fitch entered the courtroom. She wore a simple black suit and white shirt, and what appeared to be minimal makeup. A pair of pretty dangling

533

earrings were her only jewelry.

She took the stand, swore to tell the truth. And looked directly into Ilya Volkov's eyes.

How little he'd changed, really, she thought. A bit fuller in face and body, his hair more expertly styled. But still so handsome, so smooth.

And so cold under it all. She could see that now, what the young girl hadn't. The ice under the polish.

He smiled at her, and the years dropped away.

He thought the smile intimidating, she decided. Instead, it made her remember, and helped her forgive herself for being so dazzled that night, for kissing a man complicit in the murder of her friend.

'Please state your name.'

'My name is Elizabeth Fitch.'

She told the story she'd recounted now almost too many times to bear. She skipped no detail and, as instructed, allowed her emotions to show.

'These events happened twelve years ago,' the federal prosecutor reminded her. 'Why has it taken you so long to come forward?'

'I came forward that night. I spoke with Detectives Brenda Griffith and Sean Riley of the Chicago Police Department.'

They were in the courtroom, too. She looked at them, both of them, saw the faint nods of acknowledgment.

'I was taken to a safe house, then transferred into the protection of the U.S. Marshals Service and transferred to another location, where I remained under the protection of Marshals John Barrow, Theresa Norton, William Cosgrove and Lynda Peski for three months as there were delays in the trial. Until the evening of my seventeenth birthday.'

'What happened on that date?'

'Marshals Barrow and Norton were killed protecting me when Marshal Cosgrove, and a Marshal Keegan who had arranged to replace Marshal Peski, attempted to kill me.'

Hands tightly clenched in her lap, she sat through the objections, the jockeying.

'How do you know this?' the prosecutor demanded.

She talked, and continued to talk, of a pretty sweater and a pair of earrings, of a birthday cake. Of shouts and gunshots, of her last moments with John Barrow and his last words to her.

'He had a wife and two sons whom he loved very much. He was a good man, a kind one and a brave one. He gave his life to save mine. And when he knew he was dying, when he knew he couldn't protect me, he told me to run, because two men he trusted, two men who'd taken the same oaths he had, betrayed their oath. He couldn't know if there were others, or whom I could trust other than myself. He spent his last moments doing everything he could to keep me safe. So I ran.'

'And for twelve years you've lived under an assumed name and remained hidden from the authorities.'

'Yes, and from the Volkovs, and from those within the authorities who work with the Volkovs.'

'What changed, Ms. Fitch? Why are you testifying here and now?'

'As long as I ran, the life both John and Terry died for was safe. But as long as I ran, there could be no justice for them, or for Julie Masters. And the life they saved could only be half a life. I want people to know what was done, and I want to

535

make the life they saved worthwhile. I'm finished running.'

She didn't waver through the cross. She'd assumed it would pain her to be called a liar, a coward, to have her veracity, her motives, her actions, twisted and warped.

But it didn't. It only made her dig in deeper, speak more concisely. She kept her eyes level, her voice strong.

Testimony completed, she walked out under escort and into a conference room.

'You were perfect,' Garrison told her.

'I hope so.'

'You held tough, gave clear answers. The jury believed you. They saw you at sixteen, Liz, and at seventeen, just as they saw you now. You made them see you.'

'If they did, they'll convict. I have to believe they will.'

'Believe me, you turned the key. Are you ready for the rest?'

'I hope I am.'

Garrison took her arm a moment, spoke quietly. 'Be sure. We can get you out safe. We can protect you.'

'Thank you.' She held out a hand to Garrison. 'For everything. I'm ready to go.'

Garrison nodded, turned away to signal the go. She put the flash drive Abigail had palmed to her in her pocket, wondered what she'd find on it.

They surrounded her, hustling her through the building, toward a rear entrance where a car waited. They'd taken every precaution. Only a select team of agents knew her route, the timing of her exit.

Her knees trembled a little, and a hand took her arm when she stumbled.

'Easy now, miss. We've got you.'

She turned her head. 'Thank you. Agent Pickto, isn't it?'

'That's right.' He gave her arm a reassuring squeeze. 'We'll keep you safe.'

She stepped outside, flanked, moving quickly toward the waiting car.

Brooks, she thought.

The shot sounded like hammer on stone. Her body jerked, and blood bloomed on her white shirt. For an instant she watched the spread of it. Red over white, red over white.

She went down under Garrison's shielding body, heard the shouts, the chaos, felt herself being lifted, pressure on her chest.

She thought again, Brooks, then let it all go.

Garrison sprawled over Abigail's body in the backseat. 'Go! Go! Go!' she shouted at the driver. 'Get her out of here. I can't get a pulse, can't get a pulse. Come on, Liz. Jesus Christ!'

Brooks, she thought again. Brooks. Bert. Her pretty butterfly garden, her spot where the world opened to the hills.

Her life.

She closed her eyes and let it go.

Elizabeth Fitch was pronounced dead on arrival at three-sixteen p.m.

*　　　*　　　*

At five p.m. sharp, Abigail Lowery boarded a private jet bound for Little Rock.

'God. God.' Brooks framed her face, kissed her.

537

'There you are.'

'You keep saying that.'

Dropping his brow to hers, he held her so tightly that she couldn't get her breath. 'There you are,' he repeated. 'I may say it for the rest of my life.'

'It was a good plan. I told you it was a good plan.'

'You weren't the one pulling the trigger.'

'Who else would I trust to kill me—to kill Elizabeth?'

'Shooting a blank, and still my hand shook.'

'I barely felt the impact through the vest.'

And still the moment had shocked her. Red over white, she thought again. Even knowing the blood capsules had released on her command, that spreading stain had shocked.

'Garrison was very good, and the assistant director. He drove like a crazy person.' She laughed, a little giddily. 'Having Pickto right there, on the scene, knowing he'll report to the Volkovs Elizabeth is dead, there's no reason to doubt it.'

'And since you picked up the chatter about the bounty on your head, someone will probably take credit for it. And even if no one does, it's official. Elizabeth Fitch was shot and killed this afternoon after testifying in federal court.'

'The federal prosecutor was very kind to Elizabeth.' Now Elizabeth was gone, she thought. She'd let Elizabeth go. 'I'm sorry he doesn't know about me.'

'He'll work harder for the convictions not knowing.'

'Besides you, only Captain Anson, Garrison and the assistant director, and the FBI doctor who pronounced Elizabeth dead know how it was done. It's enough to trust. It's more than I've trusted most of my life.'

Because he needed to touch her, keep touching her, he brought her hand to his lips. 'Are you sorry she's gone?'

'No. She did what she needed to do, and could leave content with that. Now I have one last thing to do for her.'

Abigail opened her laptop. 'I passed Garrison a flash drive with copies of everything on the Volkovs. Their financials, their communications, addresses, names, operations. Now, for Elizabeth, for Julie, for Terry, for John, I'm going to take it all away from them.'

She sent the e-mail to Ilya, using his current mistress's address, with a sexy little text mirroring those Abigail had accessed from the past.

The attachment wouldn't register. That, she thought with considerable pride, was only part of its beauty.

'How long will it take to work?'

'It'll start the minute he opens the e-mail. I estimate about seventy-two hours before everything's corrupted, but that corruption will begin immediately.'

She sighed. 'Do you know what I'd like? I'd like to open a bottle of champagne when we get home. I have one, and this feels like exactly the right occasion.'

'We'll do that, and I've got something to add to it.'

'What?'

'A surprise.'

'What sort of surprise?'

'The kind that's a surprise.'

'I don't know if I like surprises. I'd rather . . . Oh,

look. He's opened the e-mail already.' Satisfied, she closed the laptop. 'A surprise, then.'

EPILOGUE

He wanted to take the champagne up to her spot overlooking the hills.

'Like a picnic? Should I pack some food?'

'Champagne's enough. Come on, Bert.'

'He listens to you, follows you. I think he likes to because you sneak him food from the table when you think I'm not looking.'

'Busted.'

She laughed and took his hand. 'I like holding your hand when we walk. I like so many things. I like being free. I'm free because of you.'

'No, not because of me.'

'You're right, that's not accurate. I'm free because of us. That's better.'

'You're still wearing a gun.'

'It may take a little time for that.'

'It may take me a while to aim one again.'

'Brooks.'

'It's done. It worked, so I can tell you, putting you in those crosshairs was the hardest thing I ever did. Even knowing the why, the how, it was like dying.'

'You did the hardest thing because you love me.'

'I do.' He brought her hand to his lips again. 'You need to know I would've loved Elizabeth or Liz or whoever you were.'

'I do know. It's the best thing I know, and I know a great deal.'

'Smartypants.'

She laughed, realized she could spend hours just laughing. 'I've been thinking.'

541

'As smartypants are inclined to do.'

'Global Network is going to close—the head of the company is going into seclusion. I want to start fresh.'

'Doing?'

'I want to go back to developing software. And games. I really enjoyed that. I don't want my whole world revolving around security and safety now.' She grinned, and this time brought his hand to her lips. 'I have you for that.'

'Damn right you do. I'm chief of police.'

'And maybe, one day, the Bickford Police Department will need or want a cyber-crimes unit. I'm very qualified, and I can forge all the necessary documents and degrees. I was kidding about the last part,' she said, when he gave her a long look.

'No more forging.'

'None.'

'Or hacking.'

Her eyes widened. 'At all? Ever? Can I qualify that? I'll want to know how the virus is working over the next couple days, and after that . . . no more hacking unless we discuss and agree.'

'We can talk about it.'

'It's compromise. Couples discuss and compromise. I want to discuss having your friends and family to dinner, and wedding plans, and learning how to . . .'

She trailed off, stopped. 'There's a bench,' she murmured. 'There's a beautiful bench exactly where I wanted one.'

'That's your surprise. Welcome home, Abigail.'

Her vision blurred as she stepped forward to run her hands over the smooth curve of the back, the arms. It looked like a log, hollowed out, polished to a satiny gleam, and on the middle of the back was a carved heart with the initials A.L. and B.G. in the center.

'Oh. Brooks.'

'Corny, I know, but—'

'No, it's not! That's a stupid word. I prefer romantic.'

'So do I.'

'It's a beautiful surprise. Thank you. Thank you.' She threw her arms around him.

'You're welcome, but I get to sit on it, too.'

She sat, pulled him down. 'Look at the hills, so green as the sun lowers, and the sky just starting to hint at reds and golds. Oh, I love this spot. Can we get married here? Right here?'

'I can't think of a better place. Since I can't'—he pulled a ring box out of his pocket—'let's make it official.'

'You got me a ring.'

'Of course I got you a ring.' He flipped the top open. 'Do you like it?'

It sparkled in the softening light, like life, she thought, like the celebration of all that was real and true. 'I like it very much.' She lifted her eyes, drenched now, to his. 'You waited until now to give it to me because you knew it would mean more. No one's ever understood me the way you do. I don't believe in fate, or in things being meant. But I believe in you.'

'I believe in fate, and in things being meant. And I believe in you.' He slipped it on her finger.

He kissed her to seal it, then opened the champagne with a quick, happy pop.

She took the glass he poured for her, waited while he poured a second plastic cup. Then frowned

543

when he added a small amount to a third, and set it on the ground for the dog.

'He can't have that. You can't give champagne to a dog.'

'Why not?'

'Because . . .' She stared at Bert as he tilted his head, watched her with his pretty hazel eyes. 'All right, but just this once.'

She tapped her cup to Brooks's.

'Soon, and for the rest of my life, I'll be Abigail Gleason.'

And while the dog happily lapped at his share of champagne, she leaned her head on Brooks's shoulder and watched the sun lower over the hills. Of home.